THE NEWCOMER

ROBYN CARR

THE NEWCOMER

HARLEQUIN® MIRA®

ISBN-13: 978-1-62490-621-3

THE NEWCOMER

One

It was a warm, sunny afternoon in early April, a rarity on the Oregon coast at this time of year. The frequent spring rainstorms meant that the beautiful wildflowers—the best in the country—were on their way. Hank Cooper sat out on the deck of Ben & Cooper's Bar in his white T-shirt and jeans, his feet propped up on the deck rail. Hamlet, Sarah's harlequin Great Dane, sat beside him, watching the sea, his ears perking up when a person, a boat or bird caught his eye. Cooper was enjoying a heavily creamed coffee and watching his lovely Sarah Dupre paddleboarding out on the bay. She wore the wet suit—short sleeves, knee-length—he'd given her for Christmas. It kept her warm even though the water hadn't warmed up yet; it was icy cold. The Pacific was always cold, except maybe down San Diego way. But Sarah was an expert; she rarely got her feet wet.

The way that wet suit hugged her body—it was like art. She had incredibly strong legs, a perfect round tush, breasts about the size of his palms. She'd been born in a coastal town and was probably as comfortable on the water as she was on the land or in the sky—diver, swimmer, surfer, helicopter pilot.

Cooper and Ham had been watching Sarah for an hour; she'd gone all the way out to the mouth of the bay and back. She was finally coming in, just ahead of the fishing boats headed home to the marina.

This life was the furthest thing from what Cooper had ever envisioned for himself. He had come to Thunder Point last October to look into the death of a good friend, Ben Bailey. To his surprise he had inherited what was Ben's falling-down bait shop and bar. For lack of a better idea he renovated the place, turning it into a first-class beach bar, and had found himself a new home. He also found a woman in Thunder Point, another surprise he hadn't been looking for. After all the women in his life, short- or long-term, Sarah was everything he'd been waiting for.

He had officially opened the beach bar—minus the bait—in late February. Now, as the proprietor, there was plenty of time to visit with folks from town, let the gentle lapping of the bay soothe him, watch his woman on her board, gently gliding across the calm water between the huge offshore boulders in the bay. Cooper had a farmer's tan, stronger shoulders from lifting and hauling bar supplies and a lot of new friends when he'd always considered himself a solitary kind of guy.

Sarah leaned her board and paddle against the dock and came up the stairs. When she reached the deck, Cooper tossed her a towel and she dried off her feet, glad of the warm sunshine.

"What have you been up to?" Sarah asked.

"Absolutely nothing. Just watching my mermaid."

She laughed. "Did Hamlet behave himself?" Hearing his name, the huge dog got up and walked over to Sarah.

Cooper nodded. "He said he'd prefer to live here, with me."

"Did he now?" she asked with a laugh, giving Ham a gentle pat. "Get your own dog."

"There isn't room for another dog around here. Come here," Cooper said, pulling her onto his lap.

She went to him, sat down, picked up his coffee and helped herself to a sip.

"Want me to make you a hot cup?" he asked. "You cold?"

She shook her head. "It's nice out there. Breeze gets a little chilly sometimes, but the sun is so wonderful. You start to crave sun around here after all the winter rains and winds."

Her cell phone rang. She'd left it on the deck with Cooper when she took her board out. She picked it up and looked at the caller ID then said, "Yes, little brother?" She listened intently and then laughed. "I'm at Cooper's. I just took my board out——the bay is beautiful. I have the Razor and the dog. Then yes, have fun and I'll see you later."

She clicked off.

"How many times a day do you talk to Landon?" Cooper asked. Sarah and sixteen-year-old Landon were a family of two and they kept pretty tight tabs on each other. And with Sarah being a Coast Guard search-and-rescue pilot who worked out of the North Bend station, sometimes it wasn't easy.

"As many as it takes. Now that he's dating Deputy Yummy Pants's daughter, I don't worry so much. Well, I worry that Mac might shoot him if he gets too frisky with Eve, but I figure that's a long shot, forgive the pun. I think we check in three or four times a day."

"At least," Cooper said. "Did I interpret that last call to mean you're now free for dinner?"

She grinned at him. "Is the chef preparing something special?"

"It won't be busy here tonight, at least after seven— it's a weeknight and by then the sunset will be over. I have some steaks in the freezer, potatoes in the cooler...."

"Do you have anything *green?*" she asked.

Cooper's bar menu was based on deli items purchased from Carrie's deli in town—simple things from pizzas to sandwiches as well as some desserts, things that could be served cold or warmed. His place was not a restaurant per se. Cooper bought himself a grill for his own use, but it was never used to prepare food for the patrons.

Cooper had also inherited a helper, Rawley Goode, a Vietnam vet who was not overly comfortable dealing with the public. While he was a good cook, he was needed for other things—maintenance, cleaning, running errands to the big box stores like Costco. Cooper had to admit that between Rawley and himself personal groceries were often in short supply.

"I bet *you* have something green," he suggested.

"I live on green things," she said.

"I know this."

"And you eat like a fourteen-year-old boy. You'd live on steak, hamburgers and home fries if it weren't for me. If I go home to shower and change and bring a salad or a vegetable back with me, will you clean your plate?"

He loved her. He was frequently shaken by the intensity of his passion for her. He'd clean his plate and then he'd tune her up for good measure. He knew his eyes glowed and knew she interpreted him correctly. When the closed sign was on the front door and the doors were locked, they'd eat steak in front of the fire and then retire to the playpen, his large bed upstairs. "Take my truck and leave the Razor."

"I have to work in the morning."

"That's okay. You can take my truck and your dog home later. Much later. Then I'll drive your Razor across the beach and trade vehicles tomorrow morning."

That night Sarah was home in bed before eleven. Not only did she have an early start the next day, but she also wanted to be home because of her brother, Landon. Landon wouldn't be either shocked or disapproving about the fact she and Cooper were sleeping together—in fact, he had met Cooper first and they were pals. If Sarah wasn't mistaken, Landon would consider it a personal favor if Sarah and Cooper somehow made a lasting commitment. That might be a possibility in the future but there were complications, not the least of which was Sarah's recent brief, disastrous marriage. She was understandably gun-shy and she had Landon to think about. He was just finishing up his junior year in high school and was headed for a fantastic senior year—his athletic prowess and academic performance would undoubtedly land him a scholarship. And they *needed* that scholarship. Sarah did all right financially but sending someone to college for four years would be a big challenge.

The next morning Sarah was finished in the bathroom and on her way out the door before Landon had even stirred for school. She left him a note and twenty dollars for gas or lunch or incidentals. She headed off to work feeling fit and fresh after her day off on the bay yesterday. A nice dinner with Cooper, followed by a couple of hours of recreation under the sheets— something Cooper had a particular talent for—helped make her feel brand-new and full of energy.

The Coast Guard station was getting ready for a big inspection in the next couple of weeks and there was plenty to do, from preparing for check rides to auditing maintenance records. They'd have to show the command they were one of the best air stations in the Coast Guard, and they'd have to get ready for this inspection while continuing to perform business as usual. Given that Sarah—Lieutenant Commander Dupre—was second in command of the flying operation at the station, her role in this prep would not be small. It was no surprise that when she turned on her computer she found a note from her immediate boss, Buzz Bachman, asking her to come to his office ASAP. She was sure, if she knew the man at all, he had a long list of things for her to do.

She made herself a cup of coffee on the way, stirring in some cream and sweetener. "Morning, boss," she said, entering his small office.

"Morning, Dupre. Shut the door, okay?"

She turned to close the door and thought, *Uh-oh, someone's in trouble.* The commander's door was seldom closed and when it was someone would generally say, "The spanking light has been lit."

"We have a busy week and an inspection team en route the end of the month."

"We'll be ready," she said, sipping her coffee.

"I want to tell you something I'm not supposed to know," Buzz said. "How's your poker face?"

She lifted an eyebrow. "When has my poker face ever let you down?"

"This could be tough. It affects you directly."

The eyebrow dropped. "Make it fast," she said. "Rip that Band-Aid off."

He took a breath. "I have a mole in HR," Buzz said. "I've been cultivating him for a long time. I want as much warning as possible for my next change of assignment. What I didn't expect was to learn that one of my 'men' was being looked at for a reassignment. An early reassignment because of compelling need. This means you, Dupre."

Sarah was stunned into silence. Her mouth hung open slightly. She forcibly closed her mouth. "I get an automatic refusal if they don't know I'm a woman. Right?"

"I wish. I shouldn't say anything. It could all go in another direction. Between now and notification, someone could put in for those air stations and this could all go away. But I wanted you to have as much time to think about this as possible—we have two retiring commanders and a compelling need with no outstanding applications for those locations and they're both…" He paused to cough lightly. "They're both on the east coast. Maine and south Florida. As you might surmise, you're probably going to be awarded a promotion to commander within the year. I suspect this makes you a better than prime candidate."

"And I'm not due for either," she said, sliding forward on her chair a little bit.

"There's no surprise here, Dupre. You're good at your job. You've had a successful Coast Guard career.

You'd make an excellent boss. You're an excellent leader now."

She looked at him earnestly, humbly. "I need another year here. Landon..."

"I know your situation and I sympathize. That's why I'm breaking protocol and leaking this. So help me, you let on and we'll have a real issue...."

"Crap, there's gotta be some wiggle room in here...."

"I just gave it to you. I think you'll be notified by June and then you will have a couple of months to make the move."

She shook her head. "This plays hell on my family... Landon is prime scholarship material, but not if I move him. That's saying nothing of the trauma of moving a kid right before his senior year in high school, moving him away from his football team, his friends, his school, his town. He's done so well here, you have no idea."

"I have every idea," Buzz said. "I know *exactly* how you feel—I've gone through two divorces, proof of how the pressures weigh down the family. At least you're not married."

But there's someone I can't bear the thought of leaving, she thought. "Damn it, I love my job. But I don't love this part of it."

"And the Coast Guard loves you, Dupre. I thought you deserved time to think of your options. Aren't you from Florida?"

"Long ago and far away. I grew up in Boca, practically on the water, but I've been north for most of my Coast Guard career. And there's no family left in Florida—it's just me and Landon. And I only have one more year with him before he goes off to college, and starts a new phase of his life."

"You always have that option we're not talking about, even if you can't retire yet."

"Resign my commission? I have no idea what I'd do outside of the Coast Guard," she muttered, looking into her coffee cup.

"And I know that feeling, too," he said.

She looked up and made eye contact with him. She gave a half smile—small wonder he'd been married twice, he was a good-looking man. Blond, expressive brown eyebrows, strong, smart and a set of choppers that would put Donny Osmond to shame. All this had earned him the nickname Buzz Lightyear. "Why do you have a mole in HR?" she asked.

"I can retire," he said. "I want plenty of notice on the next assignment, which should be coming down the pipeline in about six months. I don't want a new location or a promotion. I'd like to fly forever, I love helicopters and I love the C-130 even more. Being a captain means more desk time than flying time and I have kids in California and Alaska. I'm moving on, Dupre. In probably a year."

"But what are you going to do?"

"I'm working on that. But I've been down this road and I have done twenty years of service. My decision is made. You're the one who has decisions to make. Maybe there's some family friends around who can keep Landon in this school for one more year?"

She shook her head. "There's no one."

"Good friends?"

The only ones who came to mind were Gina and Cooper. Her friend Gina was trying to develop a new life with Mac—aka Deputy Yummy Pants—and she had a small house crowded with her mother and her sixteen-year-old daughter. And Cooper? Oh, as great a pal as he was for Landon, he wasn't in the market for instant guardianship. She couldn't ask either of them for a favor this big. "The Coast Guard has always been inconvenient," she heard herself say. "Not a lot of stability. But the job itself made up for that most of the time."

"Where does Landon stay when you sit alert overnight?"

"He's pretty much okay on his own, as long as he has his phone and my contact numbers. If I have a temporary assignment out of town, like simulator training or something, there's this guy I've been seeing...local guy, civilian. He doesn't mind Landon duty for a few days or a week, but trust me..."

"Guy?" Buzz said. "Guy? Why don't I know about this guy?"

Sarah smiled in spite of herself.

"How long has this been going on?" Buzz asked.

She gave a shrug. "Six months or so."

"You never bring him around. You protecting us from him or something?"

"I could be protecting him from you...."

"Hmm. Well bring him around sometime. Happy hour or something.

"I just wanted you to have a heads-up on the assignments," he said. "With any luck someone could request a relocation in the next couple of months—maybe just the right person will come along and take these potential east coast assignments off your hands...."

"Two of them?" she asked cynically.

"There are people who would kill for a chance like you have," he said.

"I know," she said. She could go far in the Coast

Guard; Commander was a prestigious rank in a demanding service and she'd earned it. She was only thirty-three. "I could quit, but I can't retire...." Quit and do what? There was the little matter of paying rent, buying food, making car and insurance payments... *tuition.* She stood up. "Well, thanks, boss. I guess."

"Don't panic," Buzz said. "Yet."

Sarah wasn't one to panic, unless her career was about to turn everyone she loved upside down once again. She could tell Landon, give him time to adjust to the possibility and come up with his own coping options, but she wouldn't do that—not yet, anyway. She wasn't afraid he'd balk and sulk, she was afraid he'd say, "Whatever, Sarah. Just let me know." He was that kind of kid, that kind of brother. He wasn't a typical sixteen-year-old boy, probably because of how challenging his life had been. She often worried about how much disappointment he was holding inside to spare her feelings.

Landon was only five when their parents were killed in an accident and he spent one horrifying year with their mean spinster aunt and then had spent the past ten years as her responsibility. She'd moved him five times, put him through a divorce from a man he'd grown attached to and now, just when he was happiest... No, she couldn't talk to him yet, not until she had time to think things through.

She could tell Cooper. He loved her; he was proud of her. But he'd just put all his time and energy into setting up his new local business and she couldn't put him in the position of choosing between breaking it off with her or leaving behind everything to follow her. She could tell that his new lifestyle not only suited him, but he was also very happy. Relaxed.

That afternoon she hadn't even made it home after work before Landon called her cell. "You going out to Cooper's tonight?"

"Not tonight," she said. "I have things to prepare for for our inspection."

"If Eve comes over to do homework tonight, will it bother you?" he asked.

"Nope. I'll take my paperwork to my bedroom. What are you cooking?" she asked.

He laughed at the joke. "Want me to pick up a pizza? I still have that twenty you left me."

"I'll make sloppy joes. Save the pizza money—I sit alert tomorrow night and you're on your own. And before you even ask, no, Eve cannot spend the night."

"Damn," he said, making her laugh.

She made the same excuse to Cooper, though he didn't buy it as quickly. "Can't you do your paperwork tomorrow night while you sit alert?"

"I have enough work for both nights. We're gearing up for a big inspection. I'll see you in a couple of days. I mean, we'll talk, but—"

But I have to work on my poker face.

"—I have the day off after my twenty-four at the station and I'll come out to your place. If the sun's shining, maybe I'll take out my board."

"I love to watch you on the water," he said. "The ocean is more beautiful when you're out there."

Sarah hadn't seen Cooper in a couple of days and she could've taken the Razor—the all-terrain vehicle—

across the beach with Hamlet, but they both needed some exercise. She'd just had two long nights and now she was stiff and groggy and Hamlet was restless.

Rather than getting right to their walk across the beach to Cooper's, Sarah stopped at the diner to say hello to Gina. Hamlet enjoyed that part of his walk almost as much as being on the beach. He didn't mind being hitched to the lamppost with a bowl of water and treated to pats and pets from every passerby.

Mac McCain was sitting at the counter in the diner. Gina was on the other side and they were holding hands across the counter. Sarah realized she'd been so self-involved she hadn't even remembered that almost every midmorning around this time the diner was usually empty and Mac took his coffee break with Gina. They were so focused on each other, Sarah was impressed that they looked up and smiled at her. "Hey," she said.

"Hey, yourself. I hear you've been putting in a lot of hours," Gina said.

"A lot of hours, but I'm off today."

Gina and Mac might be the cutest couple in Thunder Point. They'd been best friends for years. Both single parents, their sixteen-year-old daughters were also best friends. Just a couple of months ago, they came out as a couple. A real couple, not just a couple of good friends, and ever since that had happened, they'd been staring soulfully into each other's eyes when they weren't stealing the occasional kiss. For a brief moment Sarah turned cynical and almost said, *"Look out—when you think you're staring happily ever after in the face is when the fates get jealous and pounce."*

"On your way to Cooper's?" Mac asked.

"Yep. I think I'm going to take my board out for a

while. There's sun today and I could use some exercise." *And alone time, think time.* Not that she hadn't had enough of that over the past day or two. "And Cooper always needs quality time with Ham." She laughed. "If we ever break up, I'll have to share custody."

"You'll never break up," Gina said. "You're down for the count."

No, she thought. Just down…

Two

Mac and Gina might be enjoying new love, but that didn't keep them from spending plenty of time talking about their families. While Gina only had one child, sixteen-year-old Ashley, Mac had three kids. His oldest, Eve, also sixteen, his son, Ryan, was twelve and another daughter, Dee Dee, was ten. Recently, their sixteen-year-old daughters seemed to take up most of their conversations about kids—Eve was a little too in love with Landon, sometimes worrying Mac, and while Ash had had a steady boyfriend for the past year, she had seemed a little out of sorts lately. Ashley was sulky and down in the dumps.

"Things haven't been what you'd call hearts and flowers between Ashley and Downy lately," Gina said, wiping down the counter. "All Ashley will say about it is that Downy seems to be too busy to take her calls or return them, something that hasn't happened before now."

"And I've got nothing but hearts and flowers between Eve and Landon," Mac said. "Doesn't help me sleep at night, either."

Since teenage girls can fluctuate between true love

and moodiness with regularity, Gina didn't worry overmuch about Ashley's sulk.

After work, Gina walked home to find a message from the high school on her answering machine. The school had resorted to leaving recorded messages that informed parents if their child had been absent. Ashley had missed her last two classes. Since she'd borrowed Gina's Jeep for cheerleading practice after school, Gina wondered what was going on. She immediately called her daughter, but Ashley didn't answer her cell phone. Gina then called Eve, who answered right away. "She skipped practice," Eve said. "I don't know why—she didn't say anything to me."

"Do you have any idea where she could be? She's not answering her phone."

"I have no idea," Eve said. "If she calls or shows up, I'll be sure she calls you."

Gina's mom, Carrie, had just returned home herself, and hearing Gina's story she said, "You know how these girls can get distracted. You left her a message, right?"

Of course she had. And Gina was not typically a worrier, but Ashley had been in a real funk for the past week, complaining that Downy was acting weird, as if he couldn't be bothered with her. After a year-long, intense romance, one in which the phone calls and texting seemed annoyingly constant, even Gina wondered what was up. But Downy was a college freshman now and baseball was in full swing. He was attending Oregon State on an athletic scholarship; he was a baseball star. Maybe he just had a lot going on.

A couple of hours later, just as the sun was going down, Gina called Downy's cell phone. He didn't answer, either, and she left yet another message. "Downy, it's Gina. I don't know where Ashley is and I'm really worried. Have you heard from her? Call me please."

A half hour later Carrie said, "You're pacing, Gina. Call Mac. Maybe he'll have some advice."

Gina sat at the kitchen table and punched in his numbers. "Mac, I have a problem. As far as I know, no one has seen or heard from Ashley since about one o'clock this afternoon. She skipped her last two classes, didn't go to cheer practice, isn't taking or returning calls. Eve hasn't seen or heard from her and Downy isn't picking up." She felt her voice go all warbly. "I'm worried. I don't know what to do. I'd go look for her, but I don't know where to look. Could Downy be playing ball? Maybe that's why he isn't picking up?"

"Stand by, let me check," Mac said. A moment later he said, "No game today. The next game is in three days and it's a home game."

"My God, where could she be?"

"Leave another message for Downy. Maybe call some of her other girlfriends?" Mac suggested.

"Okay, I'll see what I can find out." Gina disconnected and placed another call to Downy. This time she used her mother voice. "Crawford Downy, I can't find my daughter. If I don't hear from you in five minutes, I'm going to call the police." Then she clicked off.

"You *did* call the police," her mother said, placing a glass of wine in front of Gina. "Calm down. What are you so afraid of?"

She looked at Carrie imploringly. "That she's in some kind of trouble. That she's missing. That she ran off with Downy or something…I don't know. This really isn't like…" Her phone twittered. "Downy," she said to her mother. She picked up the call immediately. "Where's Ashley!" she demanded.

"Easy, Gina," Downy said smoothly. He'd grown up in Thunder Point, just like Ashley had. He'd known Gina and her mother since he was a little kid. "She's on her way home. She's fine."

"On her way home from *where?*" she demanded.

"She came here, to State, to Corvallis." He took a breath. "She wanted to talk about our...ah...situation. I was going to talk to her in person after our weekend game—I was coming home mostly to talk to Ash. But she couldn't wait and drove up here."

Gina sank weakly onto a kitchen chair.

"She'll be home in a couple of hours or less," he said.

"She drove all the way to Corvallis to ask you why you don't pick up or return her calls and you say she's *fine?* Downy, what the hell is going on?"

"Can you just ask Ash about that, okay? Because it's—"

"Is my daughter pregnant?"

She felt rather than saw her mother sit straighter, even more alert. Gina had been an unmarried teenage mother.

"No! God, no!" Downy nearly yelled into the phone. "Listen, really, if you'd just talk to Ashley about this when she gets home..."

"Tell me right this second, Crawford Downy! My daughter has been upset about your relationship and she lied to me to take my car, drove three hours to Corvallis to talk to you and she's just now on her way home? Tell me right now or I'll call your mother!"

The young man took a deep breath. "I don't want to tell you this, Gina. It's really between us, but...I felt like we might be getting too serious. I thought we should take a breather, maybe date around a little, you know."

Gina felt her stomach tie itself in a tight knot. Oh, God, her poor girl. No one could know better than Gina how something like that felt.

"Let me guess, there's someone at State you've started dating *a little?*" she asked acidly.

"Come on, hey. I'm all the way up here, only see Ash a couple of weekends a month at the most. It got kind of old, sitting around my room alone twenty-six days of the month. She should be getting out more, too. It's not that big a deal. We just need to lighten up a little, y'know?"

"Why didn't you tell her this before she drove all the way to Corvallis to find out what's going on?"

"I didn't want to say it over the phone! I wanted to be decent about it!"

And he hung up on her.

It was just as well. She was going to have to kill him, anyway. Downy was eighteen. His behavior was hardly odd for a boy his age. Still...

Gina looked at her mother. "I would not have let her drive all the way to Corvallis alone. Driving home alone. At night."

"I know. But she'll be okay," Carrie said. "She's a bright girl. There's no rain tonight. She knows the way as well as you do."

"God, I hope she's okay," Gina said.

There was a knock at the door. "Mac!"

Carrie got up from the table and let him in. "Hey, Mac," she said.

"Hey, Carrie. What do we know?"

Carrie just inclined her head toward Gina.

"She drove to Corvallis to talk to Downy, who, I gather, dumped her and sent her back home."

Mac lowered his gaze and shook his head.

"She'll be home in a couple of hours," Gina said. "But what if she's so upset she's not safe and something happens?"

Mac walked into the kitchen, slipped a strong arm around Gina's waist and pulled her against him just briefly. He put a finger under her chin and looked into her eyes. "Never a good idea to drive when upset, but try to be realistic—if teenagers who just had a breakup had accidents, the accident rate would be too shocking to imagine. The road is good, the weather is good, she'll get here. And she'll need some comforting, I imagine." He lifted one of her hands, which was trembling. "I think the wine is a good idea. Just calm down and be ready to be wise and understanding."

"What if I have to go get her or something?"

"I'll do it. Or Carrie will. Gina, honey, stuff like this happens. It's not deadly."

"It sure feels that way," she said in a small voice.

Gina and her mom sat at the kitchen table together talking quietly, waiting for Ashley to arrive, while Gina sipped on a glass of wine. They were two women who knew how deeply a girl of sixteen would feel the trauma of a breakup. Leaving the two of them to talk, Mac stepped away, into the living room, where he used his phone.

When Ashley started dating Downy, Gina was brutally honest with her about the possible consequences of too much love too fast. She tried to discourage the dating, but there was little she could do—they saw each other at school every day and it was a match made in heaven. Gina had worried about what would happen when Downy moved on to college, leaving Ashley—who was two years younger—behind. But they had managed to make it work. Downy was back in Thunder Point most weekends, especially during football season and for holidays, and they talked and texted every day, many times a day.

And then, in the peak of spring, with love all around, suddenly and without warning, Ashley said, "Something is wrong. Downy sends me right to voice mail and he doesn't call me back. Mom, something is *wrong*."

Gina had said, "He's probably overwhelmed. He's got baseball and, academically, he sometimes struggles. Try to be patient." Downy was a jock, but not a strong student, which presented problems for some college athletes.

"It never happened like this before," Ashley wailed. "He's said about ten words to me in a week. He's busy, he says. He's studying, he says. He doesn't call me back because he doesn't have time. He doesn't answer my texts. He always texted more than me—right during class. I think he might be with someone new."

"Did you ask him?"

"Of course! He said no! But he's lying. I can tell he's lying. And he's never lied to me before!"

"Ash, he's only eighteen. You're only sixteen. Let's try not to go crazy here. Maybe this is a little adjustment of some—"

"He said he loved me! What am I going to do?"

The poor darling, Gina thought. Shattered and helpless. She took another sip of wine. Glancing at her glass she said to her mom, "Good suggestion."

"It's always more dramatic when it's your daughter. It cuts deeper," Carrie said.

"I don't want her to ever hurt." Gina whispered.

"I know," Carrie said. "Believe me, I know."

Gina hadn't taken Ashley's pout over Downy too seriously. After all, he was the scholarship kid with the atomic arm, gone to State to play ball and it was spring—baseball was the game of the day and Downy, a freshman, was starting pitcher. He was busy with practices and games, maybe too busy now to text and call Ashley all day. But Gina's attention was definitely snagged by Ashley's flight to Corvallis and Downy's explanation that, stated simply, he was done with her. There was not a woman on the planet who didn't know how much getting dumped could hurt. And as for mothers? It hurt more when your little girl suffered than when you suffered yourself.

Mac came into the kitchen, poured himself a cup of coffee and sat down with Gina and Carrie. "I called my aunt Lou and told her what was going on and that I'd be staying with you until we knew a little more. Lou will manage the family while I'm here. And I talked to Eve. She knew Ashley was all sideways about Downy and she was worried about her, but she didn't know she'd driven to Corvallis. I find that strange—they usually know everything the other is doing. Eve thought Ashley just skipped out on practice. So I'll stay with you until she's home."

"You need to get home to your own family, Mac," Gina said, but inside she thought if he left her now, she'd collapse. "It's just a broken heart."

"There's no such thing as *just* a broken heart," he said.

And he should know, Gina thought. His young wife left him with three little kids when he was twenty-six years old and even though Gina hadn't known him then, she knew him now and knew he hadn't been with a woman in the ten years since. Until Gina. They were two single parents who had waited a long time to find each other.

Mac muttered something about how, given a choice, he would never want to go back to those youthful days—those young years are so serious and painful. Gina said even more painful was when your kids hurt.

"I'll never forget when Ash wasn't invited to the very first boy-girl party ever because the mother of the little girl throwing the party didn't approve of me, a never-married single mother. Ash didn't understand that, but she was devastated by being excluded and I had at least six months of guilt and pain."

"When Eve was six," Mac said, "after Cee Jay left us, she didn't want to go to school. She was afraid her mother might come home during the day and Eve didn't want to miss her."

"When I was a young mother," Gina said, "there were very few other young mothers with small children who were friendly toward me. Certainly none who were sixteen…"

"Small towns are brutal," Mac said. "The best thing about Thunder Point was leaving Coquille, where I made all my mistakes. Of course, they followed me— my kids were soon known as the kids of the deputy and the woman who abandoned them."

"Is there any way to keep them from paying for our mistakes?"

"Yeah. They'll eventually make enough of their own

to take the heat off. Meanwhile, we just have to stay strong and know we are doing the best we can."

Carrie got up from the table and started rummaging around in the refrigerator. Being the owner of a deli and catering service, she always had special meals on hand. She did a little slicing and scooping, microwaved a couple of plates—tri-tip, red potatoes, Broccolini spears, a little dark au jus. She made a large helping for Mac, smaller ones for Gina and herself and the three of them ate, though not with big appetites. Everyone at the small kitchen table had personal experience with this kind of heartache. Then Carrie cleaned up and put a pan of her healing chicken soup on the stove. "She might not want anything to eat, but if she does at least it'll be something soothing," Carrie said.

It was eight-thirty when they heard the car. Everyone stood expectantly, fearful of what they would see walking in the door. And then Ashley came into the kitchen through the back door.

She was messy; there was evidence of crying in her puffy eyes and pink cheeks. Her beautiful red hair was flat and slack and her clothes wrinkled, but otherwise she looked normal. Except for the expression on her face, which was one of pure agony.

"I had to do it, I had to go to State," she said. "I sent him two hundred texts and voice mails that he ignored, so I went to face him. I'm sorry I lied and took your Jeep. I promise, I'll never do it again."

Carrie took a step toward her. "I made you some soup, honey."

"Thanks, Gram, but I don't want any...."

"I'll be going. Now that you're home safe," Mac said.

"You don't have to go, Mac," Ashley said. "I'm going to bed."

"We need to talk, Ashley," Gina said.

"There's nothing to say," she said, walking through the house toward her room, her head down, dragging her backpack behind her.

"Ashley," Gina said, following her. "Ash, I really want to talk to you. Please."

She turned sharply to face Gina. "He doesn't want me anymore," she said coldly, tears gathering in her eyes. "I gave him everything he wanted and now he's done with me. The guy I saw today? I don't even know that guy. That was not my Downy." Then she went into her room and closed the door.

Gina turned back to face Mac and her mother. "Oh, God," she said. And then the only thing she could think of. "Thank God there were no cell phones when my heart was being ripped out."

Ashley laid down on her bed in her clothes. In fact, she laid there for a while before sitting up and throwing off her jacket.

She was probably about six years old when she first noticed Crawford Downy Junior. Everyone had always called him Downy; only his mother called him Crawford. Ashley went to school with his younger brother Frank. There was a third brother two years younger than Frank—Lee.

That was back when Ashley's mother or grandmother wrestled her naturally curly red hair into braids in the morning. Downy called her twerp or carrot top or pesky pants. She alternately crushed on him or thought he was a giant turd. She liked him when he said things like,

"Good catch, CT," instead of carrot top. She hated him when he said, "Stand back, she's going to let down her hair!" and put out his arms as if her curly mane would be bigger than the Goodyear Blimp. Right up to junior high she had those ridiculous red ringlets *and* thick glasses. Frank had thick glasses, too, so Downy never teased her about the glasses. Then when she'd barely figured out how to control her wild hair, she had braces. "When you getting the tin out of your mouth, CT?" he'd ask her.

Ashley and Eve McCain met in seventh grade and spent the next two years studying teen magazines for trending clothes, makeup and hairstyles. Eve was always naturally beautiful with thick dark hair, bright blue eyes, but she also had braces. It was one of the first things that had bonded them. That and the fact that they had single parents and neither had much money to spend on clothes—so they improvised and shared.

Sometime in ninth grade, Ashley made peace with her hair. She discovered the magic of detangler, the circular brush, a blow dryer. Her thick crazy hair became soft waves. Some of the orange of her youth was replaced by a darker, copper-red. The braces came off, she got contacts and she made the junior varsity cheerleading squad. And one day in the spring of her sophomore year, when she was wearing her short, pleated cheerleader skirt, Downy said, "Hey, Ashley." He actually used her name!

And she said, "Hey, Downy."

He was a senior then and the toast of Thunder Point athletics. He played football, hockey and baseball. Frank was more academic and Lee was still too young to be taken seriously.

And Downy said to her, "We should go out some-time."

"Out?" she asked.

He laughed and said, "You know. On a date."

"Oh."

"Oh?" he repeated. "Is that a yes or a no?"

She nearly died. But before she died she said yes. But she was fifteen and Gina would only let her go if they double-dated. He took her to a movie in Bandon along with two other couples. But the other couples went in one car and she was alone with Downy so all the way there they talked and laughed. After the movie they went to a pizza place. She was the only sophomore— the rest of them were all seniors. After pizza they went to a pretty secluded outlook facing the ocean and made out. Downy kept trying to get under her shirt and she kept slapping his hand away. At some point he said, "I knew I shouldn't be messing with a fifteen-year-old. You're just too young."

She said, "Fine. We won't go out again. But don't think you're all that and I'm going to just give it up be-cause you're good at sports and kinda cute."

He grinned and said, "You think I'm cute?"

"Not *that* cute," she said.

But he walked her to every class, held her hand, leaned into her at her locker to kiss her, asked her re-peatedly if she'd be at his game. They talked on the phone every night when they weren't together, texted all day until Downy had his phone confiscated by a teacher for two weeks. Then, at assembly, his full ride scholarship to State was announced. At the end of sum-mer, he'd be gone to football camp and then to school, three hours away. "I suppose you'll just break up with me now," she said.

With a look of serious misery he said, "I'm trying to figure out how to take you with me. I think I love you."

So she let him touch her breasts. And said, "I think I love you, too."

Before summer was very old, Ashley was on the pill. Surprisingly, college had not seemed to be the barrier Ashley had feared. They talked and texted constantly, Downy came home to Thunder Point as often as possible if he didn't have a football game or practice and since he was a freshman, he wasn't first string, so he had a little freedom, though he practiced hard all week. "And by the time I'm playing a lot, you'll be at State and we'll be together," he told her.

And then in one week in March, almost exactly a year since they started dating, it all fell apart without warning. The calls dwindled to nothing; the texts weren't answered. He didn't come home on the weekend and knowing—*knowing*—something was terribly wrong, she drove to Corvallis. She went to his frat house. He was sitting on the porch with a girl, his arm around her shoulders, leaning close to her like he was finished kissing her or just about to start.

"Downy!" she shouted.

"Ash!" he shouted back, backing off the girl like she was on fire.

"Who is *that?*" the girl with him asked.

He stumbled and blubbered for a moment before he said, "The girl I dated back home."

"Well, take care of the child and call me later," she said, getting up and walking away. Gliding away, full of confidence, not the least bit intimidated by Ashley.

To Ashley, the girl looked like a sophisticated runway model, full of poise and beauty and maturity, all the things she didn't feel she had.

The next two hours were a blur. He wouldn't talk to her at his frat house within hearing of his fraternity brothers. They went to Gina's Jeep, sat in it and Ashley sobbed and fought and yelled while Downy just shrugged and shook his head. He said he worried they'd been getting too serious, needed a little space, a little freedom, a little dating experience. "Have you *slept* with her?" Ashley demanded. "Are you *doing* her, Downy?"

"It's different in college, Ash. People don't make such a big deal about sex in college."

So *of course* he had.

He finally insisted she go home. She wasn't done with him but he was clearly done with her. "I care about you, Ash," he said. "But we need to cool things down a little right now. I can't get home every weekend during baseball—I'm playing every game. It's not like football where I'm the junior player and mostly warm the bench. I'm starting. In fact, the baseball coach will probably make me quit football—we can't start the season with injuries. We should use this time to…you know…branch out. Date around, maybe."

"And summer? What about summer?" she asked. "You just plan to get back together again in summer?"

"I don't know. I'm thinking about staying up here. Taking some classes, getting a job…I'll play ball all summer if we make finals and it's too far to commute. Then football camp is in August. If I'm still playing football then."

She sobbed so hard all the way back to Thunder Point she could hardly breathe. She had to pull over once because her chest started hurting. She knew her mother was going to be furious that she'd taken the Jeep but she didn't care. There were moments on the drive home that she wondered if life wouldn't be easier if she just went off the road at one of the high-cliff curves, but something kept her going.

When she was alone in her room, she called Eve's cell phone. She could barely tell her story, the sobs came so hard. And Eve was outraged. "Want me to call him, Ash? Give him a piece of my mind?"

"It won't matter—it wouldn't help. He dumped me for a college girl. And she's beautiful, Eve. She *owns* him. You could tell in one second!"

"He's slime. He's scum. I will never forgive him for this!"

"But...what do I do without him?" Ashley had cried.

After they hung up, Ashley just cried for another hour. There was a light knocking on her door and she knew it was her mother. She didn't answer or say "come in." She laid there, her head on her pillow, leaking tears, gripping her cell phone in case Downy called her to say he'd made a terrible mistake.

Gina came into the room and sat on the edge of the bed. "I brought you some tea," she said, her hand on Ashley's back.

"No, thank you," Ashley said thickly.

"Ash, I'm sorry this happened."

"Really, I can't talk about it anymore."

"Just a little, please? So I can understand where you are right now? Emotionally."

Ash rolled onto her back, her wet eyes red and swollen. "He has another girl. A beautiful, snotty college girl who he's screwing because he says it's not that big a deal. And right now I just don't want to even live."

"Ashley, please, don't say that. Don't ever say that."

"I'm not going to school tomorrow. Maybe not the next day, either. Maybe never."

Three

Cooper noticed Sarah had been preoccupied over the past couple of days. Quiet and maybe a bit sullen. She said the inspection was going to be hell and while she might not be worried about her team, a strong leader always worried about the inspectors. They had to be ready for anything.

All Cooper could do was be available, support her in any way he could. He found himself fighting the worry that Sarah had changed her mind, that something had caused her to reconsider those three little words. *I love you.* Yet when he possessed her, when she was joined to him, her passion for him drove worry from his mind. During those times she was one hundred percent his and he was completely hers.

In the meantime, he had a business to learn. This beach bar was unlike anything he had ever done before. Ben's old helper, Rawley Goode, *old* being the operative word, might be a little on the strange side, but he had turned out to be a damned good assistant. Rawley was somewhere in his sixties and he'd been ridden hard. Rawley told Cooper that Ben used to only be open in the mornings and evenings. Ben had put in his longest days during summer, and he bumped up the schedule with the help of part-time teenage help. Rawley said, "I clean and get supplies. I can work in the kitchen or behind the bar, but I ain't social. You give me a list and cash. I go to Costco and other stores. But in summer, you have to stay open late. The sunset over the bay is better 'n football on HD."

During his first week of operation Cooper noticed that the bulk of his traffic was between seven and ten in the morning and four and seven in the afternoon. There were stragglers here and there at other times. Those patrons were almost exclusively Thunder Point residents. But on the weekends, particularly in good weather, there was heavy traffic all day and into the evening—bikers, cyclists, pleasure boaters, sport fishermen, folks traveling on Highway 101 in want of a meal. He did an impressive business on bottled water alone, not to mention the other things he was able to offer. When he inherited this place, it had been a run-down shack with a home-made sign on the road that said *Cheap Drinks*. Now it was upgraded and classy and he was damn proud of it. Cooper put a decent sign on his property at the turnoff from highway 101. *Ben & Cooper's*. And beneath that, *Food and Drink*. He stocked liquor and non-alcoholic beverages and had a contract with Carrie James, owner of the town's deli, for prepared and wrapped food items. The reopening of the bar benefited both of them.

A lot of his first patrons from out of town wanted to know what had happened to Ben. Well, it was a sad story and he didn't like to dwell on it, but the fact was that Ben had been found at the bottom of the cellar stairs and at first it was thought to be an accident. But, since then, there had been evidence to suggest he'd been killed by a blow to the head that caused the fall. The suspect—a seventeen-year-old kid from town—was out on bail awaiting trial. That still blew Cooper's mind—a seventeen-year-old kid. The kid, Jag Morrison, had been trying to convince Ben to sell the beach and adjacent property to his father, a local developer.

Cooper had been just going through the motions— renovating and opening for business. He didn't think he was a shopkeeper or bar-owner kind of guy. He had been a pilot for fifteen years—helicopters. But the more he got to know the town, the people and the many moods of the Pacific Ocean, the more the place grew on him. After just a short period of time instead of moving on, he was considering making even more improvements to the property. After watching Sarah on the water, he thought renting kayaks and paddleboards would be an excellent idea.

None of it came naturally, however. Cooper bought himself a new laptop with a decent accounting spread-sheet program and was still figuring it out. Rawley wasn't able to help him out with this part of the busi-ness. It was during his weekday midmorning downtime that he sat at his own bar and was plugging numbers from bills and receipts into his spreadsheet that the door opened and Mac McCain walked in. With relief, he closed the laptop. "Hey," he said. "Aren't you usu-ally at the diner about now?"

"Usually," Mac said. "Gina's daughter stayed home from school. She went home to check on her and I didn't feel like having coffee with the cook. Stu just isn't as pretty no matter which way you cut it."

"I noticed that. How's everything else?"

"Same," he said. Mac went right behind the bar and helped himself to a cup of coffee. "You? Business shaping up?"

"Aw, I don't know. I mean, business is good. There are people in here all the time. But I'm not real clear on the accounting and that sort of thing. Kind of makes me wonder how Ben managed. He was a genius with a wrench but he didn't seem to take to paperwork and numbers."

"Everyone wondered that same thing," Mac said, sipping his coffee.

"It's tedious, that's for sure. Say, something's been weighing on my mind a little bit. Been a long time since I had a girlfriend, you know? You ever wonder what the hell's going on in Gina's head?"

Mac broke into a huge grin. "You're kidding me, right?"

"So that's a no? Because Sarah—she's got a lot on her mind, I know that. But man, she's on another planet sometimes. Makes me wonder if anything is wrong. But then she's back and I wonder why I wondered...."

"Coop, you remember how many women I live with, right? There's Lou, Eve and Dee Dee at home, but then there's Gina and all her women—her mother and her daughter, who at the moment is a mess over some boyfriend issue. Half the time I don't have any idea what's going on in any of their heads!"

"Oh," he said. "That's a no?"

"That's a no."

"How do you handle that?"

"Do you see me handling anything? I pretty much just duck."

"Oh, you're a big help...."

"Sorry, man. I just do as I'm told most of the time," Mac said.

Cooper just stared at him. "Why aren't you completely bald?"

"It's a wonder, isn't it? Lou says there's something in the male hormone that prevents me from getting it. She's probably right."

Gina went home during the midmorning slow time at the diner to check on Ashley, as she'd done the two previous days. This was her third day of grieving and Ashley just lay in her bed, clutching her phone. Gina had tried prying it out of her fingers once but her daughter tearfully whimpered, "But what if he calls me?"

"It would probably be best if you just turned the phone off," Gina said. "If he calls you, let him find you're over him!"

"I'm so not over him," she said.

"This can't go on, Ash," she said. "You have to get a grip. You have to get up, get cleaned up, go to school."

"You have no idea what you're saying," she cried.

"Don't I? Ashley, my boyfriend left me pregnant at fifteen. When I told him, he ran far and fast and never looked back! Ashley, I know how this hurts, believe me."

She rolled over, her red hair everywhere, and tearfully said, "I wouldn't mind that, you know. At least you still had a part of him to live for. What do I have?"

Gina wanted to shake her. "Your dignity! He cheated on you—you should kick him to the curb, not suffer in rejection. Get mad! I hope the sorry bastard gets a disease!"

"Mama," she cried, fresh tears spilling all over her

face. "Don't say that, Mama. You love Downy. And my heart hurts...."

She didn't love Downy anymore. How could he take her little girl's innocence and then dismiss her so cruelly? Describe her as "the girl I dated back home" like she was history? He should be brutally punished. *How could he?*

Because he's an eighteen-year-old boy, her wiser self said. He did what most eighteen-year-old boys do. And Ash is just a sixteen-year-old girl, doing what comes naturally—grieving her loss. It could just as easily have gone the other way—Ashley could have become bored with her absent boyfriend and found someone new at school, some current popular jock who had time to date, to take her to the dances and games. This could be Downy wallowing in depression because his girlfriend had dumped him.

Why couldn't it be that way, huh? she asked herself. She didn't want her daughter to be mean and insensitive, but she also didn't want this—this sobbing, broken mess who wouldn't get out of bed.

"I'm going back to work," she said. "When I get home later I want you up. I want you showered, doing your best to get on with life because you can't fix this, Ashley. I'm not going to let you shrivel up and waste away just because Downy was an unfaithful ass. Do you hear me? Tomorrow you go to school, no excuses."

She rolled over and looked at her through wet eyes. "I loved him," she whispered. "I loved him so much."

"But you can't make a person love you back," Gina whispered.

"Are you sure? Because somehow I made him love me once."

Gina smoothed her crazy red hair back off her brow. "I know, baby. Someday you're going to understand that you dodged a bullet here. You don't want a boyfriend who can't be faithful, who can't keep his promises. Believe me."

Ashley just shook her head. She rolled over and, gripping her phone, as she had been for days, she gently wept.

Gina got away from the house. She walked down the hill to the diner before pulling out her own phone. She stared at it for a moment. She sat down on one of the benches outside the diner's front door and clicked on Marjorie Downy's number. When the woman answered she said, "Marjorie, hi. It's Gina James."

"Hi there, Gina."

"I wonder if you know—Downy and Ashley broke up."

There was a heavy sigh from Marjorie. "I did hear that. I can't say I'm surprised. I thought that when they were apart for a while, at different schools, it might end up like this. That's too bad for Ashley, Gina."

"She's devastated. She said Downy has a new girlfriend."

Marjorie sighed again. "Well, look, Crawford is in a new place now, a different place. Their worlds...you know what I mean. Their worlds are now orbiting different suns. There's college and there's high school."

"He promised to take her to her prom," Gina said because she just couldn't help it, though she didn't have any intention of Marjorie helping with that problem.

"I know. I have to be honest with you, Gina—I never approved of that idea. Crawford should be spending what little money he has for dating on college events, fraternity events, not on high school dances."

Gina stiffened. "Well, then, perhaps he shouldn't have promised," she said. "Poor Ashley."

"Oh, Gina, I do feel sorry for Ashley, I do. I'm sure she'll be all right."

"She's not all right at the moment. She's shattered. Heartbroken. Downy wasn't very nice to her."

"Poor thing. But I worried about this from the start. Crawford is quite the catch at State—handsome, athletic, fun, smart. I knew it was only a matter of time before some pretty college girl caused him to forget the girl back home. Ashley really shouldn't have pinned her hopes on him."

Gina felt her heart squeeze. "Maybe not," she said weakly. For a moment she felt as though she should have found a way to prevent this romance, a way to keep Ashley from being hurt.

"Despite what Crawford and Ashley might've thought, I knew this wasn't a lasting thing. The age difference..."

"But Downy told me you knew they were sexually active. Involved. Committed."

"I found packages of condoms. It broke my heart. I was extremely disappointed by that. In my day young ladies were much more cautious with their bodies, with their virtue."

Gina's eyes grew round and her neck nearly snapped from straightening so fast. She was instantly on her feet. "And in your day, were young men also cautious?"

Marjorie actually laughed. "I wish I could say they were. You'd understand if you were the mother of sons. Boys—a different animal entirely. Which is why it's important to raise young ladies with strict standards. You know what I mean, Gina."

She hoped she wouldn't break a molar, clenching her teeth so hard. "I'm sure I have no idea what you mean."

"I mean that invariably it's up to the girl."

Gina was speechless. "You're not serious," she finally said.

"I couldn't be more serious!" Marjorie insisted. "Men are men—they're single-minded and a little crazy. But my boys were raised proper—if the girl says no, the answer is no. They're not villains, they're just men."

"You really can't believe this," Gina said.

"Gina, perhaps Ashley thought there wouldn't be any consequences for having sexual relations at the tender age of sixteen. And as you can see from your poor darling's broken heart, having a baby out of wedlock isn't the only consequence."

Gina felt her face burn. "You didn't just say that to me," she said. "You didn't."

"Oh, Gina, please! I meant no offense, it's just that—"

"Is that what you teach your sons, Marjorie? That if they can pressure a girl into giving it up, all's fair? It's not the boy's fault or responsibility?"

"No! Oh, God, no!" Then she was quiet for a second before she muttered, "I wouldn't teach them such a thing. I'm not surprised that they think that way, however. I live in a house full of males. For all I know, my husband could have conveyed the message."

"If he did, he should be hung up by his balls!" Gina snapped, disconnecting the call. She sank to the bench once more. She leaned over, elbows on her knees, her head resting in her hands. She couldn't believe comments like that could still be so painful. And she knew that wasn't how she was commonly regarded in this town—the unwed mother. She knew she and her mother were both respected citizens here. Ashley, a lovely girl and good student, was thought of highly.

But there were still a few, like Marjorie, who put it all on the woman. As if a girl gets pregnant all alone.

For a moment, she felt hot and damp at the same time. Mortified. Humiliated, as if it had been yesterday that she'd said to Carrie, *Oh, Mama, I'm pregnant! And I don't know what to do!*

"Hey," a familiar deep male voice said.

She looked up to see Mac standing in front of her. Looking down at her.

"You okay?"

She let out a breath and stood. "I called Marjorie Downy. Stupid thing to do."

"What happened?"

"From her perspective, Ashley held him down and forced herself on him and he is completely blameless in this situation. Kind of a boys-will-be-boys attitude. And she couldn't convey that without a dig or two at me for bearing a child out of wedlock."

"Did she actually say that?"

"Pretty much. In her day girls were held to a higher standard and her boys were raised to understand that if a girl says no, it's no. And having a child out of wedlock isn't the only consequence of being sexually involved. In other words—"

"Jesus," he said. "She's as stupid as she is ugly."

That almost made Gina smile. "I should never have called her. I knew Marjorie and I weren't on the same wavelength. I always liked Downy, even before he started dating Ash. I think he's basically a good kid. I want to think this just went the predictable course—he grew away from her when he went to college and they broke up. And yes, it hurts her terribly, but she'll have more than one boyfriend before all is said and done."

"Downy's not a bad kid. But his mother is as dumb as a box full of hammers."

"Yeah, Downy's all right, even if he did upset my girl. And I bet in a few weeks I'll stop hoping he gets a disease and his dick falls off."

Mac smiled at her. "I need to take you somewhere. Dinner, maybe. Or just out of town for a few hours. Or maybe to some sleazy motel with mirrors on the ceiling—but if you say no, hey, nothing will ever happen...."

She put a grateful hand on his arm. "I gotta get my girl out of bed first, Mac. She's a mess. Then I'll be ready for a dinner out of town and some time alone with you."

"You know all you have to do is snap your fingers."

Lou McCain had raised her nephew since his parents—her brother and sister-in-law—were killed in an accident. He had been only ten years old at the time and lived with her until he married. And for about the past ten years she had lived with him to help him raise his three children. They had moved to Thunder Point from Coquille four years ago when Mac had been given the Thunder Point substation to manage for the Sheriff's Department. When they first discussed the possible move, Lou hadn't been very keen on it—she'd lived in Coquille her whole life. She had a good teaching job and friends there. She suggested he commute to Thunder Point instead of moving there, which is what other deputies tended to do.

But the move had turned out to be a good idea on many levels. Lou was able to get a teaching job at the middle school right away—eighth grade English. She liked the town and the people. Eve's instant friendship with Ashley had resulted in Lou's friendship with Carrie and Gina, two women she'd grown very close to. And of course, there was the simple fact that in a little town like Thunder Point, a place with only a small fishing industry, she and Mac could pool their resources and afford a home large enough for himself, three kids, two dogs and an aunt.

Lou knew a lot about kids. She was working on raising a second generation of them, for one thing. She was a very intuitive teacher, for another. Mac's kids, her nieces and nephew, hadn't presented too many challenges yet. But they were definitely getting there. Eve was pretty serious about Landon Dupre. There hadn't been too much drama yet, but as Lou knew only too well, that was probably coming—teenage love could be complicated. In fact, Eve's best friend was going through it right now; Ashley was devastated by her breakup and was acting out in bizarre and frightening ways. Ashley needed an intervention.

To that end, Lou grabbed ten-year-old Dee Dee and twelve-year-old Ryan after school and took them with her to the diner. This wasn't exactly rare for Lou—she enjoyed stopping off there for a cup of coffee on the way home from school at least once a week on days the kids didn't have lessons or practices of some sort.

Ryan and Dee Dee ran straight to their favorite

booth. "Can you get those hellions a couple of colas and an order of fries?" she asked Gina.

"Coming right up," she said with a smile.

Gina went to the kitchen herself to serve up a plate of fries. She made two trips with the sodas and fries and then, back behind the counter, poured coffee for herself and Lou.

"How's school?" Gina asked.

"Some days you're the bug and some days you're the windshield," Lou said. "Gina, do you know where Ashley is?"

Gina instantly got a frightened look in her eyes. "School?"

Lou shook her head. "Eve, Landon and Ashley cut out of school. Just the last class. Landon drove them to Corvallis to watch a baseball game. Ashley promised to tell you, but I knew she wouldn't. Listen, the girl could use some help."

"Oh, God," Gina said weakly, looking down. "You knew they were going? Doing that?"

Lou nodded. "Ashley wanted Landon to take her because she promised you she wouldn't take your Jeep again, like she did before. Eve insisted on going along, I suspect to keep Ashley from throwing herself at Downy. I think it's good that Eve went. Landon, God love him, would be like a deer caught in the headlights if Ashley had a meltdown."

Gina took a breath. "What did Mac say about this excursion?"

"I'm going to tell him at dinner. I made a management decision. It's not as if we haven't gone to Oregon State for a ball game or two—it wasn't a ridiculous request. Kids from Thunder Point go to State all the time to watch their old classmates play college ball. But I don't want either of our girls wandering around alone up there. Landon might not be much good in a romantic crisis, but I trust he'd never let anyone give our girls trouble."

"True," Gina said.

"After not seeing her for a couple of weeks, she finally came to dinner at our house last night. I suspect she came because she had a special request—a trip to Corvallis. She doesn't look good, Gina."

"I know," Gina said in a whisper.

"She's lost weight, I can tell she's not eating or sleeping," Lou said. "I'm used to the girls never shutting their mouths at the dinner table, and now... She's really despondent."

"How do you make a person eat and sleep? Or stop crying every night, for that matter? I can hear her and if I go to her room, she doesn't want to talk to me."

Lou opened her purse and took out a slip of paper. "This is the name of a counselor. Her practice is in Bandon, so it's a ride. I'm told she has a sliding scale if your income isn't high. Or maybe your benefits cover counseling—you're the one to know. A friend of mine—a teacher—recommended her."

"There's a counselor at the high school...."

"Garvey," Lou said sourly. "He's a horse's ass. Based on some of his comments, he thinks girls are stupid ninnies—a running bone of contention between us. One of my girls from eighth grade English had him as a guidance counselor her junior year and he told her *and* her parents that she wasn't college material. She's one of the smartest girls I've taught. I've seen him at school board and PTA meetings. I think he has seaweed between his ears. I think Cliff gives better advice at the Cliffhanger's bar than Garvey does."

Gina just kept staring at the slip of paper. "You think she needs counseling?"

"I think it would be a mistake to take a chance. Gina, I know we all want to say it's just a teen romance, but teenagers feel things so deeply, so intensely. They're years away from realizing how minor this is in the grand scheme of things, how much more manageable life will be when they're just a little more mature. They can get very sick, make some very stupid mistakes, do crazy things that can't be undone. They sometimes have suicidal thoughts."

Gina gasped.

"Yes, they do. Sometimes it's self-image problems, sometimes their home life is totally horrible or they're relentlessly picked on at school, sometimes it's depression, which can present in adolescence. And sometimes it's love gone sour. Sometimes, sweetheart, it's a desperate, emotional act that can't be reversed. Take her to this woman," Lou said, pointing at the paper. "This Simone Ross."

"What if she doesn't want to go?" Gina said softly.

"Don't ask," Lou said. "Take her."

And then Gina's eyes misted over. "I think this has been as hard on me as it's been on her. My heart aches for her. I think it's harder when your kids hurt than when you do."

"I agree, it's harder when it's your kids. When Cee Jay walked out on Mac and the kids, he really took a dive. And being a man, expressing his feelings was like torture, so he sulked and got angry a lot. But I know him, I knew he was in terrible pain. I've been dumped a time or two, I've done the dumping a time or two, but watching my family go through it was worse than anything I've ever experienced. He was too old to take to a counselor but he took my advice and got Eve in counseling when Cee Jay left and he did go with her. Thank God we got through it."

"I wonder if her office is still open," Gina said. "Three weeks ago, when she realized Downy was with another girl, she said she didn't want to live."

Lou leaned forward, nearly glaring at Gina. "Tell them this could be urgent. Tell the counselor's office that your daughter has made suicidal statements."

"Couldn't that be an exaggeration? I'm not sure she really—"

"Gina James, would you rather be guilty of overdramatizing or lack of action? Jesus. Do as I say."

"Yes, you're right," Gina said. "Why do we do that? Fear being an inconvenience? I'm stronger than that!" She pulled her cell phone out of her pocket and punched in the numbers.

It was the only thing Ashley could think of to do— go to one of Downy's games. When they were in high school together, that was the most important thing to him. He believed he couldn't play well if she wasn't there. Even though Eve thought it was a terrible idea when Ashley said she'd take her mother's car again, she finally relented and said they could all go together. And Ashley hoped, hoped so much, that Downy would know she was there, know how much she loved him, and this whole nightmare would be turned around.

Landon, Eve and Ashley got to the game in the fourth inning. Downy was playing first base, a change from his usual position as pitcher but just as natural for him. He played four more innings and was up to bat four times—two base hits, a double and a home run just while the Thunder Point contingent was there. He was magnificent; he had the stadium on their feet. Then the game ended and Oregon State had shut out Arizona. Ashley was on her feet, screaming herself hoarse for Downy and the team at every play. The stands were full and the sun was setting, the stadium lights coming on before all was said and done.

People were streaming out of the stadium when Ashley said, "I want to see him."

Eve stopped short. "What for? Ashley, what for?"

"I just want to tell him, good game. That's all."

"No, Ash. I don't think you should," Eve said.

"What can it hurt? Landon? What can it hurt?"

Eve shook her head. "He hasn't called you," she said. "It's going to hurt."

"Maybe. Maybe not," Ashley said, stalking off toward the exit. But rather than heading for Landon's car in the parking lot, she walked around the stadium. She looked over her shoulder at Landon and Eve. "I know where the locker room and exit is—back here," she said. She put a little skip in her step as she headed down the walk toward the back.

She had good instincts—she found what she was looking for. It wasn't exactly an original idea. There were quite a few students waiting back there. Also, a player's bus was parked off to the side—probably for the Arizona team, taking them either to a hotel or the airport, or perhaps even home.

People were loitering, standing around and leaning against cars, waiting for the players to come out.

The first couple of guys came out and were greeted by friends and girlfriends with whoops, cheers, high fives and kisses. A few more emerged and got into the Arizona bus. Ashley stood back, waiting. She couldn't help it, she twisted her hands a little bit. All she wanted in life was for Downy to see her and be as thrilled as he had been in the old days.

More players came out—a big rush of them, duffels in hand, shoes dangling by the laces—all of them still pumped from the game.

"Dupre?" Downy shouted, noticing Landon and rushing over to him, hand outstretched. "What are you doing here, buddy?"

Landon took the hand. "We came up to see you play. Great game." Then he inclined his head toward Ashley.

And Downy frowned. "Oh, man. This isn't good."

"She wanted to see you play," Landon said.

"Hey, Ash."

She stepped forward, smiling, still holding her hands together, trying to keep them still, praying. A few weeks ago she would have thrown herself into his arms and he would have lifted her and kissed her silly. "Downy," she said smiling tremulously. "Good game."

"Thanks," he said. "You shouldn't be here."

"Why? You used to love it when I came to your games."

He dropped his duffel and looked at her harshly and she felt her lips quiver. "I'm sorry things didn't work out. You have to stop now. Stop calling and texting all the time. Don't come to the games."

"Can't we be friends?" she asked, her eyes tearing. "We've known each other since we were about five."

He pulled his phone out of his pocket, clicked a little

and held it toward her so she could see the million texts and pictures she'd sent him. "This is not friendly. This is just about harassment."

"Well, forgive me for living," she snapped. "I thought you might appreciate some friends coming to your—"

"Downy!" a female yelled. *"Baby!"* And the tall, slim, dark-haired girl from the frat house threw herself on him, wrapping her legs around his waist and hugging his neck. "You are such a *stud!*" she yelled against his shoulder.

Her, Ashley thought. It's still her.

"Selena," he said, gently putting her on her feet. She looked a little confused when he put her down. "Some of my friends from home," he said. "Landon, Eve and Ashley."

At first Selena smiled, but then she glowered. She turned her attention toward Downy. "Is this the little psycho who keeps calling you and sexting you, day and night?"

Ashley felt the growl come out of her before she realized what was happening. Little psycho? She put up her hands in the shape of claws, nails bared, and took two giant steps toward the girl named Selena. She was going to claw her face and rip her hair out. But as fast as a lightning bolt, Downy put Selena behind him and Landon jumped between them. He grabbed Ashley's wrists.

"Hey, hey, hey," Landon said.

And Downy yelled, "What the *hell,* Ashley! Are you *crazy?*"

"Okay, we're outta here," Landon said. "Good seeing you, Downy." He looped his hand through Ashley's arm and gripped her tightly. She pulled against him and snarled, but he held on. "Don't even think about it or

I'll throw you over my shoulder," he muttered. "Come on, Eve. Come on."

Landon made pretty fast tracks around the building to the parking lot. Eve was scrambling to keep up behind them while he was dragging Ashley.

"Let go," Ashley said.

"Not a chance. I don't want to have to tackle you." Then he laughed without humor. "Seriously? A cat fight? Have you totally lost it?"

"He *hurt* me," she said fiercely.

"And so you were going to scratch her eyes out?" he asked, marching her along.

"She called me a little psycho!"

"So you were going to prove it?"

She groaned and kept up with him somehow. But by the time they got to the SUV, Ashley was softly crying. "You just don't get it," she said softly, pitifully. "He said he loved me, that he'd love me forever...."

"I get it," Landon said. He turned her toward him and gripped her upper arms. Eve caught up to them. "I get it. You were serious. You were a couple. And you broke up. I'm sorry, Ash. You think you're going to get him back by acting like a psycho and beating up his new girlfriend?"

She stared at him, knowing the truth and wisdom in what he was saying, but it somehow didn't help her at all. She could feel her face contort, then crumble as a fresh flood of tears ran down her checks. "It can't be over," she whispered, sobbing and gasping softly. "It can't. It can't. It can't."

Gina made the appointment for Ashley. No discussion. She tried to channel Aunt Lou and merely announced to Ashley that she was going, then drove her to Bandon. "I'm *not* crazy!" Ashley railed at Gina.

"Of course you're not—you're upset, that's what you are. And you have good reason to be upset and broken-hearted and angry. Counselors have helped people get through all kinds of emotional situations and crises. Just talk with her. It certainly can't hurt."

"I'm not telling her my personal business!"

"And I'm sure she's been through plenty of that before, too," Gina muttered.

The ride to Bandon to the counselor's office was quiet and sulky. Every now and then Ashley muttered, "I don't want to go" and "I'm not telling her anything."

The office of Simone Ross was small, nondescriptly furnished in what resembled cheap, old apartment furniture, maybe dating back to the *I Love Lucy* show. There was no one in the waiting room, however there was a desk with a clipboard, piece of paper, pen and at the top of the page it said, *Please Sign In.* There was a door, presumably to an interior office. After sitting in the waiting room for ten minutes, the interior door opened and a grandmotherly woman with an ample bosom, pink cheeks, short silver hair and wide hips smiled. "Ashley?"

Ashley nodded nervously and stood.

"Hello. I'm Simone. Why don't you go inside." Then she turned to Gina. "Ms. James? We'll be about forty minutes. You can wait here or step out for a while."

"I'll...ah...wait."

Simone gave a nod and immediately closed herself in with Ashley.

Gina sat on one of the uncomfortable chairs, alone in the reception area, listening. She didn't hear a mur-

mur from that inner office and she was aching to know what was happening in there.

Support like this was relatively new and many people relied on the right insurance coverage. When Ashley was born, Gina's mom had been working at the diner for Stu. It was that event, the cost of the birth, that caused Stu to amp up his coverage for his full-time employees, of which there were two besides himself and his wife. It had been enormously expensive. It hadn't gotten any less so, but Stu had gotten used to it. The coverage included some counseling.

This was what Gina would like to do one day, once she completed her master's degree in counseling—help people through crises just like this. She had two reasons for this pursuit—she knew that things like this didn't kill you and with the right kind of support, you grew stronger and wiser. Truthfully, since the moment Ashley and Downy started dating, Gina had feared the extremes—that they would marry young before ever experiencing life or finishing their educations, or that it might end disastrously, leaving her beautiful girl brokenhearted.

Ashley so needed this objective assistance. Gina would remember to thank Lou for insisting on something Gina should have thought of herself.

She leaned back and closed her eyes. Wasn't this just the rule rather than the exception...? Just when you thought things had fallen so sweetly into place— Carrie's business was good, Ashley had been happy, Gina had finally come together with Mac—some life event shook everything up. Right now all Carrie and Gina could think about was Ashley, suffering in sadness and depression, losing weight just as efficiently as any divorce diet, weeping into her pillow at night.

It was a long forty minutes before Simone opened the door to the reception room and Gina shot to her feet, betraying her anxiety.

"Will you join us for a few minutes, Ms. James?"

"Gina," she said. "Please, just call me Gina." And then she followed the older woman into the office.

Ashley held a wadded-up tissue in her grip and it was obvious—she'd done a little crying for the counselor. This suggested she had shared her personal business. Gina tried not to smile. The counselor indicated a chair and Gina took it expectantly.

"Ashley and I have talked about things and I've asked her to come back in two weeks for another talk. But in the meantime I'd like her to try a teen group that meets here, in this office. Their issues run the gamut—a little of everything—but they seem to be very helpful to each other. That group meets Tuesdays and Thursdays here—my associate moderates the group and he's terrific. Ashley is willing to give that a try."

"Okay," Gina said. Why did she think this one counseling session would provide a cure? She knew better. And why did she fear group therapy? Ashley had a broken heart—almost a rite of passage. She feared hooking her up with a bunch of troubled teens, some possibly there by court order. "You're good with that idea, Ash?" she asked.

"My first choice is to go home and just sit in the closet for a year," Ashley said.

"Thus the counseling, group and individual," Simone said. "The closet is not a good idea. Not designed for recovery. You move at your own speed in group," she went on. "They're not going to hold you down and make you talk—that's entirely up to you. And if it's not right for you, well, we'll just try something else. In the meantime, please call me if you're having a hard time." She looked at Gina. "Ashley has my cell number and I'll take her call if I'm not in session. If I'm in session, I'll return the call as soon as I can."

Four

Cooper had driven to North Bend a few times to meet Sarah, twice for lunch and twice for dinner when she was sitting alert and stuck at the air station. But she'd never invited him inside to pet the helicopters or meet her colleagues or crews. When she invited him to join her at the end of inspection blowout at a local pub, his face lit up like a beacon. They were even arriving and leaving together.

As they were driving from Thunder Point to North Bend he said, "You're bringing me out of the closet," he teased, obviously incredibly pleased.

"I try to keep my professional life and my personal life separate," she said.

"You're letting the guys know you have a boyfriend," he said, laughter in his voice.

"How do you know I don't just need a designated driver?"

"It wouldn't surprise me at all if you planned to get wasted," he said. "You've been really stressed out over this inspection. Maybe now you can relax a little bit."

But it was not the inspection, Sarah thought. The inspection was a lot of work, but her team was outstanding and she never worried for a second—she knew they'd come out smelling like roses. It was that other matter— facing a potential reassignment in the near future and having no idea which way to turn.

Note to self, she thought, *I need a better cover! I can't let it show! Not until I'm ready to talk about it and I can't talk about it until I know what the hell to do!*

When she told Buzz she was bringing a date, she emphasized, "No one knows about your little HR bombshell so don't breathe a word at the party."

"Since I swore you to secrecy, no one better know," he said.

"I mean, not even Cooper. *Especially not Cooper.* So don't take him out by the keg for a private little chat."

And then Buzz had lifted his blond eyebrows and said, "You know, when stuff like this came up, even if it's secret stuff, if it affects the family, I would always talk to my wife," he said.

And she said, "And now? Twice divorced? Who do you talk to now?"

"Okay," he said. "Got me there. I wouldn't talk to a girlfriend. If I had one."

"Exactly," she had said.

And to Cooper she said, "Listen, do me a favor. Don't mention to anyone at this party that I've been stressed out. I wouldn't want them to think I'm anything but cool and calm. When women get command positions and act like nervous girls, it really plays hell on the leadership role. Got that?"

He just grinned at her.

"I'm not going to get wasted and you better not, either."

He grinned bigger.

"If they start to get a little nuts or start doing shots, walk away," she ordered.

"And if I don't?" he teased.

She reached across the cab of his truck and squeezed his thigh. "If you ever want to have sex again, you'll behave."

He laughed and said, "Now you're speaking my language. And boy, am I glad you've got this inspection behind you!"

I need another kind of inspection, she thought. *Something to keep his mind off my mood.*

Most things about the party were entirely predictable—like the fact that everyone was loose and happy and got the biggest kick out of Sarah bringing a man, as if she were a nun or the resident lesbian. The fact that he was a helicopter pilot really charged them up and there were lots of questions about his civilian jobs. Cooper had worked for private contractors who provided the military with services from flying Blackhawks in foreign countries, to years working for oil companies in the Gulf of Mexico. There were many toasts to the XO and CO for the winning performance in the inspection and before long there were toasts for just about anything— for taking a breath, for standing after a couple of hours of steady drinking. And when the captain and XO left the party, they got louder and started doing shots.

Cooper was having a good time and, as ordered, did not do shots. But Sarah got pulled into the fray and threw back at least a couple, and she didn't miss the twinkle in Cooper's highly entertained eyes. She received many slaps on the back, many high fives, and it was confirmed that she was a lot more fun when she had a boyfriend. But when her face became flushed, Cooper said, "Okay, missy, that should do it for you. Let's take off."

"Please," she said. "Oh, please..."

"I don't need a bucket for the truck, do I?"

"Don't be silly," she said, eyes at half mast. "I can hold my liquor!"

"Oh, you're doing great," Cooper said. "It's ten o'clock." Sarah wasn't sure they had cleared the parking lot before she was asleep. She had vague memories of being half carried, half dragged into the house.

In what seemed like three seconds later she groaned and muttered, "Turn off the light."

"I don't have enough cosmic power to turn off the light," Cooper replied. "It's morning."

She sat up as though a cattle prod had assisted her. The second she was upright, she groaned and grabbed her head. Slowly, very slowly, she opened one eye and looked at him. He was lying beside her on her bed in his jeans and stocking feet. "What are you doing here?"

He put his hands behind his head. "Well, by the time I put you to bed, let out the dog and filled his water dish, Landon still wasn't home. So—I turned on the TV, laid back down and fell asleep."

She gingerly lifted the covers. She was wearing her shirt and panties. "Great," she said. "My brother knows you undressed me."

"More important than that, he knows you were toasted. By the way, you sure talk a lot in your sleep when you're drunk."

"I wasn't drunk, I was just..." He was smiling at her. "Okay, I was drunk. Remind me that tequila shots on top of beer is not recommended. Why did you stay the night?"

"I was tired," he said. "Believe me, Landon knows there was no nookie. Are you going to live?"

"It's questionable."

He lifted one eyebrow. "Little hair of the dog?" he asked.

"Don't talk like that. It could get messy."

"You're a lightweight, Dupre." He sat up. "I should get out to the bar before Rawley shows up and reports me missing. You coming out later?"

"Maybe after I get a new head."

Cooper suspected Sarah had gone back to sleep. It was nearly noon by the time she showed up with Ham— they'd walked across the beach. And she looked both rested and recovered. "I was afraid to call you. Afraid you might be sleeping it off."

Right at that moment, her cell chirped. "Landon has felt no such restraint," she said. "He made as much noise as possible getting ready for school and he thinks it's extremely funny that I'm hungover." Then into the phone she said, "What?"

A few moments later Cooper said, "That can't be the first time he's seen you a little tiddly."

"Cooper, I was not tiddly. I was wasted. And yes, that probably was the first time he's seen that. You're right, I'm a lightweight."

"And he's punishing you with phone calls?"

"He's between classes, calling from the men's room—I heard flushing. They're not supposed to make calls during school hours. So, he wants to go over to Eve's house. And I'll be more than happy if he does."

"Sounds fine to me. Jeez, I have to get a better system around here. I'd buy Rawley a cell phone, but he probably wouldn't use it."

"What's the matter with Rawley?"

"He doesn't talk to me unless he has to. He didn't show up today. He pretty much makes his own hours, which is fine. Everything we have to do gets done. But if he's not coming at all, he should let me know. That way when he doesn't let me know, like today, I know he's all right."

"Do you think he's not all right?" she asked.

"No telling. I've been thinking about driving over to Elmore to check on him, but there's no one to watch the store."

"Cooper, I'll keep an eye on things. How long could it take?"

He shrugged. "Almost a half hour each way, then seeing if he's around. He takes care of his father, who is an invalid. When Rawley works, a neighbor lady who's a nurse's aid in a nursing home looks in on him. If I can't find Rawley anywhere, I'll need to call hospitals or something. Rawley is strange, but he's pretty reliable."

"Then just go. Will you make me dinner for me tonight?"

"Sure," he said, pulling her in for a kiss. "I'd rather lock the doors and take you upstairs for a while. You were less than romantic last night." He kissed her again. "But I should make sure Rawley is okay. I don't know how old he is, but older than dirt, I suspect."

"Just go. Ease your mind. Then if there aren't a lot of people around later, we can make out awhile."

"Can we make out naked?"

"No," she said with a laugh. "What if my brother popped in for some reason?"

"Your brother. You know, I like Landon, but is it too late to put him up for adoption? We could get visitation a couple of days a week...."

"And the rest of the week?"

He nuzzled her neck. "I think you know...."

"Go," she said. "I'll check out the freezer and decide what I want for dinner."

Cooper found Rawley's red truck in the driveway at his house, indicating he was at home, but there was a for sale sign in the back window of the truck. Maybe he'd decided to work on restoring Ben's old truck and drive it at the same time. When Cooper found all the stuff in Ben's old storage shed—truck, Razor, tools, etc.—he'd given Ben's truck to Rawley and invited him to use any tools he needed to work on it. He gave the Razor to Sarah and Landon since he had a Rhino for himself.

Cooper parked on the street, walked up the brick steps and knocked on the door. He knocked again before Rawley opened the door. Rawley was wearing a white dress shirt with his jeans—a new look for him. There was no bandana tied around his head, either. And his hair—extremely thin on top and usually long—had been trimmed.

"What's up, Rawley?" Cooper asked. And Rawley just held open the door so Cooper could step inside. "You're selling the truck?" he asked as he entered. And then he saw the empty wheelchair sitting in front of the fireplace. "Rawley..."

"He passed real quiet," Rawley said. "In his sleep. I found him this morning."

"Aw, Rawley. I'm sorry, man. You should have called me."

Rawley just shook his head. "I knew what to do."

Cooper reached out and put a strong hand on his shoulder. "I could've helped."

"You got a business to run."

"I also have commitments to friends," he said. "I would've put the big thermos on the porch, some dough-nuts on a plate under the glass so the birds wouldn't get in 'em. There's just the two of us out there on the beach. There's gonna be times we have to be somewhere else."

Rawley, so unexpressive, looked surprised by that. "Just figured I'd get 'er done."

"You're selling the truck?"

He shrugged. "My dad, he had himself a plot, paid for, but that's about it. It's either sell the house or the truck."

"To pay for the funeral?"

"Won't be no funeral, there's just us. But he needs a box."

Cooper stood uncertainly for a moment. "Could we sit down in the kitchen and have a cup of coffee?"

Without answering, Rawley turned and headed to-ward the kitchen. Once there he brought a fresh cup out of the cupboard and filled it for Cooper. Then he filled his own cup. Then, to Cooper's surprise, he put cream and sugar on the table, along with a spoon. And he sat down.

Cooper didn't really know where to begin. "Mac said you've been hanging around the bait shop for a few years now."

Rawley nodded.

"Where did you work before that, if you don't mind me asking?"

"Odd jobs. Here and there."

"And lived here with your dad?"

He shook his head. "I just got reconnected with my dad four years ago. Ben forced that issue," he said, naming their late friend.

"Where were you living before that?" Cooper asked.

"Here and there." Cooper decided to wait him out. He sipped his coffee, excellent coffee, and just didn't speak for a couple of the longest minutes of his life. "I didn't get on with people so much after the war," Rawley said. "It wasn't like now—folks didn't celebrate Vietnam soldiers too much. Made a person want to disappear. That, and bombs going off while you sleep—makes a man just want to be alone."

PTSD issues, Mac had said. "Understandable," Cooper said.

"I stopped by to see my dad sometimes. Just for a day or so, every few years or so, but not for long. I had burdens. You know."

"I know," Cooper said. And he thought, there are so many of us. Men without strong attachments who just wander. Cooper didn't have PTSD issues that he was aware of, but he still felt like a loner often enough. And, like Rawley, after leaving the service he hadn't gone home to his family. He'd kept moving.

"My dad used to fish off Ben's dock," Rawley said. "He'd have a shot of Wild Turkey sometimes before heading home. Ben found me. I hung out with a couple of vets around Eureka, not too far from the VA. Sometimes if we needed something, like food or money to eat, the VA was as good a place as any. Used clothes, too. Then Ben said my dad was doing poorly. He hadn't been fishing in so long, Ben checked on him and my dad couldn't get himself upstairs to go to bed most nights so he slept in the chair. Ben said my dad needed help. He said he'd give me a part-time job if it could be worked out."

"So you came home to help your dad," Cooper said.

"It's different coming home because you're needed than coming home because you're needy," Rawley said.

Cooper lifted his coffee cup to his lips. "Exactly right," he agreed.

They drank their coffee in silence for a while.

"So, you have a house here," Cooper said. "Place to live and a job. I guess that means you'll be staying."

"It's almost habit now," Rawley said.

"You keep this place real nice, Rawley," Cooper said. "It must have made your dad real proud to leave it to you."

"Like I said, it's just us. Buried my mother some thirty-eight years ago. The Red Cross brought me home from Vietnam. Since I was an only son."

"And then you went back?"

"Yeah. But that was okay at the time. I knew how to act over there. I wasn't real sure over here. Times were different. Soldiers weren't heroes back in those days. It was hard times here."

"I'm glad you told me this, Rawley," Cooper said.

"Why?"

"It's not easy to work side by side with a man you don't know anything about," Cooper said. "I realize sometimes a man's private."

"I ain't all that private," he said. "Sometimes you get to know a person and you're sorry."

Cooper laughed. "I guess that's true, too." He drained his cup and stood up. "You order a box for your old man yet?"

"Yup," Rawley said, standing.

"No funeral, huh?"

"A graveside prayer. A prayer for soldiers, that's all he wanted. He was real specific. He was in the Army, too. But I think he ordered it up more for me. He was that kind of man."

"Where is the service?" Cooper asked.

"Why?"

"I thought I'd come."

"Why?"

"You're my friend." Cooper remembered the day Rawley handed him the envelope with Ben's will and a key without a word and then just high-tailed it out of there. "In fact, one of my first friends since I've been here, even if you did leave me to deal with that shithole of a befouled bait shop alone."

And at that, Rawley grinned. He had a good pair of dentures. "Stank up real bad, didn't she?"

"Real bad," Cooper agreed. "But that's rotten septic over the dam. Now, I'd like to take care of that casket for you, Rawley. I think if Ben were alive, he'd want to do that."

"Charity don't sit well with me," he said.

"Sure it does. You took all Ben's old clothes and stuff to the VA. The washers and dryers, dishes, glassware and flatware went to some church group you knew about. You could've kept it and had a garage sale, but you didn't. I have no doubt you'd give the shirt off your back if someone needed it. Now take the sign out of your truck, tell me what funeral parlor is taking care of the box, what time to be at the cemetery and where. Let's not argue. I wouldn't offer if I didn't want to."

So Rawley told him where to be at 10:00 a.m. on Thursday.

"You have a suit?" Cooper asked.

"I don't need a suit. My dad might not even recognize me in a suit."

Cooper laughed. "My brother-in-law is some big-shot executive, but he got fat. My sister sent me a few of his suits. I'll be here at eight on Thursday morning with one of my hand-me-down suits that I never wear, anyway. If you don't drown in it, it's yours. With any luck, you'll wear it exactly once. Unless you get married or something."

"Coop," he said, using a name on him for maybe the first time. "Ben was right about you. You're a kick in the ass."

"Yeah, that's me. Flattery will get you nowhere."

Rawley filled out the suit pretty well. There was more to him than met the eye. In his old worn-out jeans and shirts, with his thin hair and drawn face, he looked scrawny, like a skinny old guy, but in fact he was sixty-three, long-legged and had some strong arms on him. Cooper should've guessed; Rawley worked pretty hard at the bar, especially buying and delivering large boxes of supplies. And now that he thought about it, there had been no wheelchair lift in their house. Rawley had probably been carrying his father to bed. If he had a run-down look about him it probably had more to do with living an unstable life for forty years or so.

He had shaved, something Rawley didn't do every day. His hair was slicked back, his nails clipped, his best shoes cleaned and polished. And he was very somber.

"I'll drive," Cooper said. "This is a tough day for you."

"He's resting now. The last few years were hard on the old man."

"I'm sure. At least he had his son with him."

"You ever had a son, Cooper?" Rawley asked.

Cooper shook his head. "No son, no wife. We're a lot alike, Rawley. Couple of guys just moving where the wind blows us. Drifters."

"Maybe that's set to change," Rawley said.

"Let's get to the cemetery and say a last goodbye."

There was no more talking until Cooper had driven them almost to the cemetery gates. Then Rawley said, "He was a real good father when I was a kid. When I was growing up. He was a better father than I was a son."

After a moment of respectful silence Cooper said, "I think maybe a lot of us feel that way about our dads, Rawley."

The cemetery appeared to be crowded for a Thursday morning—plenty of cars parked along the winding roadway. And then Cooper saw the Sheriff's Department SUV and Gina's old Jeep. And there sat the van from Carrie's Deli. But Rawley was the one to speak first.

"What the hell," he said. "What did you do, Coop?"

Cooper shook his head and looked for a place to park.

"I didn't say anything. I only told Sarah and Mac, that's all. And I only told them so they'd know why I wasn't going to be around this morning."

"Well, Jesus," Rawley said. "Lookit those people. Must be twenty or thirty of 'em. They didn't know my dad."

Cooper pulled along the side of the road and killed the engine. "They're here for you, Rawley."

"They don't know me, neither."

"Sure they do, Rawley. Maybe you don't chew the fat a lot, but most of those folks see you all the time. You're one of them. By the way, was there anyone you talked to regularly?"

Rawley shrugged and made to get out of the big truck. "Ben. Just Ben. Till you came around. Am I gonna have to make conversation with all of them now?"

"I don't think they expect that," Cooper said with a laugh. "If the spirit moves you, you might thank them for the effort." They walked toward the casket. "It must be a comfort to know Ben will be holding the door open for your dad."

The casket was covered with an elaborate spray of white flowers.

"I didn't buy no flowers," Rawley said.

Cooper said, "I just took care of that one bouquet at the end there. It'll sit on the grave site after we're gone."

Rawley and Cooper stood on one side of the casket opposite the minister, who could only be identified by the fact that he held a bible. Mac and Gina and the others stood respectfully around the grave and waited for the minister to start the service.

"Shall we begin? Just a few words before we lay

our friend William Goode to his final resting place—
William was a kind and patient man. It was about a year
ago when he told me he was tired, that he was ready to
go, that he had no regrets about his life and hoped that
when he met his maker it would be a joyful reunion.
His wife departed long ago and he had missed her every
day but was confident he'd see her again. And I thought
to myself—I hope I face my final days with that peace
and tranquility. Bill, as he liked to be called, was difficult to understand since his stroke a year ago, but I
asked him if he'd made his peace with God and he nodded and said, 'My staying any longer is a waste of time
and medicine. This is enough.'

"He wanted one prayer. He wanted to honor our military and chose the veteran's prayer. He was very clear—
no elaborate fuss—just a prayer to 'launch him' as he
put it. He said a toast now and again wouldn't offend
him. William Goode is right with God and on his way
home. Here's to you, William Goode.

"And William wanted a poem written by a soldier to
be read at his burial. This poem—'Final Inspection'—
was written by Sergeant Joshua Helterbran.

The soldier stood and faced God
Which must always come to pass
He hoped his shoes were shining
Just as brightly as his brass.
Step forward now, you soldier,
How shall I deal with you?
Have you always turned the other cheek?
To My Church have you been true?
The soldier squared his shoulders and said,
No, Lord, I guess I ain't

Because those of us who carry guns
Can't always be a saint.
I've had to work most Sundays
And at times my talk was tough,
And sometimes I've been violent,
Because the world is awfully rough.
But, I never took a penny
That wasn't mine to keep...
Though I worked a lot of overtime
When the bills got just too steep,
And I never passed a cry for help,
Though at times I shook with fear,
And sometimes, God forgive me,
I've wept unmanly tears.
I know I don't deserve a place
Among the people here,
They never wanted me around
Except to calm their fears.
If you've a place for me here, Lord,
It needn't be so grand,
I never expected or had too much,
But if you don't, I'll understand.
There was a silence all around the throne
Where the saints had often trod
As the soldier waited quietly,
For the judgment of his God,
Step forward now, you soldier,
You've borne your burdens well,
Walk peacefully on Heaven's streets,
You've done your time in Hell.

After a brief prayer, the crowd began to disperse.
Carrie James approached Rawley. "My condolences,

Rawley. I have a couple of platters and a casserole for you. I could bring them by your house or you could take them now. I have them in the van."

He lifted his brows. "You know I did all the meals for my dad, right? He was infirm."

"I know. But you might not feel like it right now. And it's important you eat."

Cooper could tell he was speechless. It took a while but finally Rawley said, "I could make coffee."

Carrie smiled and said, "That would be nice, Rawley. We'll follow you home."

It was a very brief open house at Rawley's place— the folks had to return to work. But there were twenty of them including Cliff from Cliffhanger's and his wife, Aunt Lou, Ray Anne, Stu from the diner and his wife, Belinda. Landon got a pass from school to represent Sarah, who had to work. A few of Rawley's neighbors showed up. Carrie and Gina brought a couple of big trays of cold cuts, cheeses, olives, pickles, sliced tomatoes, lettuce and red onion. Some of Carrie's small sandwich loaves and condiments were placed on the table. There were seven covered dishes that could be frozen—each one bearing the name of the contributor so the dishes could be returned. "If you just bring them by the diner whenever it's convenient, Gina will see they get back where they belong," Carrie suggested.

Rawley showed up at the beach bar first thing the next morning and his whole face looked different. He had not expected this kind of outpouring from folks he felt he knew only in passing. "Ain't this place something?" he asked Cooper.

Cooper shook his head in wonder. "It really is something," he agreed. "You okay on your own for a while? Like a few hours?"

"Take a day off if you want," Rawley said. "I got things covered."

Five

Another April day had dawned bright and clear. Four days after the funeral, Sarah finally had a day off. Leaving Rawley in charge, Cooper got out the Harley and took it to Highway 101 and drove the five miles to the exit to Thunder Point and to Sarah's house. When she opened the door, she was just drying her hair, fresh out of the shower. She wore jeans and a T-shirt and her feet were bare—she was barely dressed and that made him smile.

"Well, Mr. Cooper, this is a surprise," she said. "I don't usually see you this early unless I walk across the beach with Hamlet."

"I thought I'd take you into the hills to see the wildflowers—all that rain was good for something. I thought we'd just get out of town. But, seeing you, I'm having some second thoughts...."

"Are you now?" she asked with a laugh.

Cooper stepped inside, slipped his hand around to the back of her neck and pulled her lips onto his. She parted her lips for him, embraced him and he gave the inside of her mouth a healthy taste. "We haven't made love in a while," he pointed out to her.

"It's been a few days," she admitted. "But I want to see the flowers."

"You will. You will. But first I want to strip you naked, kiss every inch of your body, turn you on, stir you up, make you scream my name…at least twice."

"Only twice?" she whispered, breathless already.

"Then I'm going to put you on the back of that Harley and take you to see the flowers on the hillsides. And vibrate all your tender lady parts so you'll want me again."

She laughed at him. "Cooper, you are such a sweet talker."

"Let's not talk right now," he said. "Let's talk after."

She took his hand to lead him to her bedroom. The bed hadn't even been made yet. She stood beside the bed and said, "If you're going to seduce me, you have to undress me." Then she slid a hand over the crotch of his jeans and said, "Quickly."

"Maybe we don't have to be quick today," he said. "Maybe we can be slow and easy and—"

And she laughed. He loved the sound of her laughter and hadn't heard enough of it lately. "We've tried that," she said. He lifted the T-shirt over her head and her hands went to the snap on his jeans. "It takes about three minutes for me to start begging and you to start delivering."

"I have to admit, I do like that part."

Lately he'd been concerned; Sarah had been quiet. Too many times he'd looked at her and found her staring off at nothing, distracted by some deep thought. Or he might say something and she'd miss it, her mind wandering. He knew something had been bothering

her and now he knew it was not the inspection at the
Coast Guard station.

And yet, when they were like this, falling into each
other, she was entirely his, there was no question about
it. You don't fake this. Her body responded and her
thoughts only wandered to him.

She shoved down her jeans, kicked them off, flopped
back on the bed and waited for him to dispense with
boots, socks, jeans, shirt. And then he just looked at
her because, God, she was so beautiful to him. "You're
staring, Cooper," she said.

He knelt gently beside her, laid down next to her,
pulled her into his arms and while one hand cradled her
jaw for a deep kiss, the other went roaming, immediately sliding into her most erogenous parts. She moaned
and he smiled against her lips. He had been with too
many women and yet, had never had a woman like this,
a woman who wanted him as much as he wanted her.
She wanted him as quickly, as powerfully, as completely
as he wanted her.

He spent a few minutes kissing her neck, ear lobes,
breasts, nipples, and then he was sliding into her. "Have
I thanked you for coming into my life?"

"Over and over," she said a bit breathlessly. Then she
moved his fingers back to that special place, the place
that brought it all together.

"I love it like this—skin on skin. When you come..."

"You do," she finished for him.

"I do," he said. But he didn't move. He held her
still, savoring the connection. "When I'm in this place,
Sarah, I feel like I'm completely yours and you're completely mine. I love you, Sarah."

"Cooper, let's say we love each other after..."

"You in a hurry, sweetheart?"

"I didn't think I was, but I guess—yes. Do what you do so well." She opened her legs wider, grabbed him with her legs to pull him deeper. "Ohhh, Cooper…." And he could feel her building to it. He took turns on her mouth, her nipple, moving in and out of her, massaging her, listening to the tempo of her sounds rising, increasing, and these were the sounds he loved. And when that great sound came…*Cooper!* He held her still and deep, his hands on her head holding her for his kiss. He felt her close around him, pulsing, and he really had no choice. He let it go with a loud hum, a long and low groan, a few moments later followed by many small, loving kisses and murmurs about how amazing she was, how beautiful, how erotic.

"Sarah, what you do to me…" he said. And then slowly, without letting go of her, he rolled onto his side, pulling her near, and just held her.

"So much for slow…." she whispered.

He chuckled and squeezed her. "We get the job done."

"Yes, we do," she replied, curling up next to him. "Am I going to see the flowers today?"

"Uh-huh. When I can let go of you. I can't yet," he said. "God, what you do to me…"

"You said that already."

He ran a hand down her body, over a plump breast and down to the apex of her thighs. "I told my parents and sisters I was dating a helicopter pilot and my youngest sister asked me if I was gay."

"Do you need a letter of affirmation for the family? Because that's one thing you are not."

He chuckled. "I just need you to be my girl, that's all."

"Does it make you nervous to love a commitment-phobe?"

Was that what was bothering her? Her avowed fear of commitment after a disastrous, brief marriage? "Nope," he said. "I'm patient. And as long as you love me, I'm happy."

"You're not afraid I'm going to get scared any second and run?"

"Nope."

She propped up on one elbow so she could look into his eyes. "I hope I don't disappoint you, Cooper."

"You haven't yet," he said. Then he grabbed her, rolled with her and looked down into her eyes. "You're everything I want, Sarah. When I said I loved you, it wasn't conditional. And it wasn't temporary. And it's not something you have to live up to or down to—it just is. If you think I'm going to quit early, you're crazy. See, the truth is, I could disappoint you. I might not be enough for you to stick it out. But I'm going to die trying. Now do you want to see those flowers?"

"I thought you wanted me to scream your name at least twice...."

"The day's not over yet, Sarah." And then he kissed her as convincingly as he could.

While she showered a second time, Cooper let out the dog and refilled his water bowl.

Women, he thought. They always had some mysterious list of requirements. They were famous for accusing men of not being committed enough or intimate enough but the evidence was in, sometimes there was no such thing as *enough*. And Cooper had been around the block—he was only capable of feeling his feelings. He wasn't the best at expressing them, but he had gotten damn good at feeling them since he found Sarah. He felt them down to his toes. He wanted her forever. He'd love it if she wanted him right back, also forever, but the ball was in her court now. She had issues and he had plenty of time. He would concentrate on making her happy. For as long as it took. He was confident he could outlast her.

The flowers were just getting started in the foothills, but the ride was still fantastic for Sarah. Cooper took her into the foothills south of Thunder Point, getting off Highway 101 at Port Orford and traveling east into the Pacific Coast Ranges. They traveled down a couple of unmarked roads back into the wilderness and it seemed as though every ten minutes they were crossing a river. He drove them up mountain roads, then down again. It was fairly deserted out there, just the occasional house or vehicle, and the air was cool. They passed a sign for Wild Rogue Wilderness and Sarah thought that name suited Cooper perfectly. Along the side of the road the new spring growth bloomed in orange, white, purple and yellow. There were big orange flowers that looked like small sunflowers or large daisies, some that looked like pansies in pastels, little purple puffs and large white blossoms mixed with the green. Spattered among the pine were trees laden with new buds. They drove through a myrtle grove and up along a ridge where they could stop and look down a couple thousand feet to a rushing river that had a few fishermen along the banks.

They found a good spot to stop and Cooper helped

her off the Harley. He found a big rock that overlooked the river and sat on it and she came to him, ruffling her hair to get rid of the helmet head. She pushed his knees apart and sat between them and his arms went around her, holding her.

"Lot's more than just flowers out here," she said. "This is beautiful."

"I've never been here. It just looked like an interesting road."

She sighed deeply. "I stay too busy with work, chores and Landon. I haven't been exploring enough around here. I'm glad we did this today."

"Well, there was that divorce last year," he reminded her. "That probably took up some free time."

"Tell me about it," she said with a rueful laugh. "The lawyers were very efficient. Most of my time was spent licking my wounds, then looking for a place to settle with Landon. I couldn't stay in that house and I couldn't afford it, either."

"No support?" he asked.

"Are you kidding? I make a little more than Derek, my ex. I have more time in the Coast Guard. And Landon was my responsibility, not his and mine. I never would have accepted support payments, but I would have liked it if Derek had called Landon, acted like there was some loss there, even if it was only a phone call."

"I want to ask you something about that," Cooper said. "You know, the divorce and stuff?"

"What stuff?" she said, caressing the arms around her waist.

"That's over, right? Not just on paper, but in your head?"

She turned slightly to look at him over her shoulder. "Of course it's over. What are you asking?"

"You've been in a real mood lately," he said, and she turned back, looking down at the river. "Don't bother denying it, we both know you're not that great at hiding it. You're in a real mood, running hot and cold, real distracted. And—"

"Cooper, I'm sorry about that. Just give me a little time, okay?"

"But that's it—time for what? Is your ex giving you trouble? Pressuring you? Telling you he has regrets? Making you have second thoughts about the divorce? About us?"

"What?" she asked with a laugh, turning again. "Really? Oh, Cooper, I am so over Derek. I thank you for that, by the way. I was not interested in getting involved with a man, but you're relentless. If there was anything left for Derek, it's been long gone since the day you first kissed me."

"Then what is it, Sarah? Is it just me? Do the other pilots and crews notice? You're not acting like yourself."

"No one has noticed anything because they're almost all men and they think women have two behaviors— having a period or not having one." She smiled at him. "Cooper, it's a work-related issue that I have to handle on my own. Not only is it confidential, you can't help with this. I need a few more weeks to figure it out. It's got to do with my Coast Guard career path. I've been lucky, I've been on the fast track."

He tightened his arms around her. "I doubt luck had much to do with it."

"Gender might have played a role. I don't mean that they'd throw me promotions for being female, but the boys upstairs might get a little excited to come across a woman who can pull her weight since there aren't enough of us—know what I'm saying?"

"You're saying you've been offered something...."

"No, Cooper. I'm saying I'll be at a crossroad soon and I'll have to be ready to decide if I want to make a change in direction."

"And you don't think it would help to talk it out?" he asked.

And how would that sound? she asked herself. She was a woman with no good options—getting out without means of support or staying in and going to the other coast. Leaving her brother behind or wrenching him out of an ideal situation in Oregon. Would opening up to Cooper sound like, "Please offer to marry me and support me?" Would it sound like, "Help me say goodbye, help me to give you up?"

"There will be time for talking it out," she said. "Right now I have to try to think about the situation without any influence from any quarter. And that's hard. But it's what I should do, for now."

He rubbed a knuckle along her cheek. "No tempting ex, huh?"

She gave a little laugh. "He's long gone. Rumor has it he's already found someone to date and cheat on in Alaska."

A week later Gina was wiping down counters after the morning rush at the diner, feeling a little better about things. Ashley wasn't exactly markedly improved after one individual counseling session and one group session, but she seemed slightly better. She loved Simone Ross and said of the group, "It's nice to know they're way more screwed up and miserable than I am, and I can't tell you a single other thing about them. I swore." And Gina didn't hear her crying at night as often or for as long.

Ashley's thinness wore on Gina. Ashley didn't look starved, but her weight loss was so obvious. She normally had such lovely, delicious curves and over the past few weeks she'd probably lost a good ten pounds. Young girls seemed to relish that pencil-thin figure, but a mother looking at her daughter wasn't thrilled by it. Ashley had never wanted to be supermodel thin, but her clothes were hanging on her.

"Eve said she's thinking of breaking up with Landon just long enough to lose five pounds," Ashley said.

But all Gina wanted was for her little girl to get her appetite back. And Carrie was working just as hard to help achieve that, preparing all of Ashley's favorite and most desired meals every evening. Ashley was still slim as a straw, but Gina and Carrie had each put on a few pounds on her behalf.

Gina filled the scrub bucket and pulled on her rubber gloves. It was her curse that when she had a lot on her mind, she cleaned. She was just about to get on her hands and knees behind the counter to give the floor a good scouring when the door to the diner opened. She looked up to see a woman come in. In fact, the woman nearly took her breath away, she was so stunning. She had thick raven hair that fell to her shoulders in those soft Hollywood curls, shining blue eyes, ivory skin, pink cheeks and luscious lips. She looked familiar and Gina wondered if she'd seen her in a movie. She wore very expensive clothes as only a woman like herself, who bought discount whenever possible, would know.

Designer slacks, shiny pumps with very high heels, a leather blazer with a designer logo on the breast pocket. And her purse was worth at least a week of Gina's tips—a Dooney & Bourke.

Gina pulled off her gloves and smiled. "Hi," she said.

"Hi," the woman said, smiling with straight, white teeth. "I wonder if you know—will the Sheriff's office across the street be closed all day, since it's Saturday?"

"No, but since they usually have only one of the deputies in on the weekends, he's in and out. Do you need the police?"

"No," she said with a laugh. "I just wanted to see Deputy McCain. I wonder if he's going to be around today?"

"Well, you might just have stumbled into the right place." Gina looked at her watch. "He's working today and in about an hour, he'll probably be stopping by for his morning coffee. Unless he's tied up somewhere."

"That's good. If you don't mind, I'll stick around. See if he comes in."

"I can call him for you, if you'd like."

"You know him?"

Gina laughed. "Everyone knows everyone here. Plus, their office being across the street from the diner means we see each other almost every day. I'll check and make sure he's coming by this morning."

"Thanks," she said, digging into her expensive purse for her cell phone. "I should return a couple of calls while I wait."

"Perfect. Can I get you a cup of coffee? Anything?"

"Coffee would be great. And how about a slice of that pie?"

"Coming up. I'll get that for you before I call him."

While the woman went to a booth in the rear of the diner, presumably so that Gina wouldn't overhear her talking to her good friend George Clooney, Gina served up a cup of coffee and slice of pie. She took it back to the incognito movie star. Since she wasn't talking on the phone yet, Gina asked, "Can I tell him who's waiting for him?"

"Well, I wanted to surprise him, but go ahead. Tell him it's his wife. I'm Cee Jay McCain." And she flashed that glorious smile.

Gina was frozen. Stunned. The coffee and pie were suspended in midair. "Wife?" she asked weakly. "I thought Mac was divorced."

"Right. Ex-wife," she amended. "We've been out of touch and I'm looking forward to seeing him."

Gina put down the pie and coffee. "Let me make that call," she said, scooting back behind the counter.

Gina's hands actually trembled as she fished her phone out of her pocket. She had a lot of bizarre and random thoughts as she punched in Mac's number. *I should get my teeth whitened,* she thought. *Underwire, I need more underwire....*

Glancing over, she could see that Cee Jay was chatting and laughing into her phone. Gina turned away so that her back was facing Cee Jay.

"McCain," he answered.

"Mac, I think you'd better come to the diner if you can. There's someone here to see you."

"Gina? You all right?"

She cleared her throat. "Mmm. Yeah, fine. Are you coming?"

"Who's there?"

"Mac, you're not driving, are you?"

"Why?"

"I don't want you to drive up a pole...."

"I'm pulled over. What's going on?"

"It's Cee Jay, Mac. She's here. To see you."

Dead silence answered her. And it stretched out.

"Mac?" she asked.

"Good thing I was pulled over. Listen, try to keep this quiet. I have to know what she wants and I don't want the whole town to know before I have a chance to talk to my kids. And to Lou."

"Not a problem," Gina said.

"I'm there in five."

"Sure. Fine. Drive carefully."

Gina disconnected. She looked down at herself. Cheap black pants that were no longer as black as they had once been, checkered blouse, name tag.... Why did she always wear that stupid name tag? There had been about four people she didn't know in the diner in the past month. God, the woman was so beautiful. And no wonder she seemed familiar—Eve was a younger version of her mother.

Gina felt a devastation come over her. Grief. After four years of devoted friendship she and Mac had finally become lovers. They tried to be discreet since their sixteen-year-old daughters were best friends, but at long last they could hold hands, embrace, even a chaste kiss was appropriate. Privately, there was more, so much more. Passion so rich, her whole life had been changed by it. They loved each other, they'd said so.

But now? What would he do after seeing Cee Jay? Would everything change? Even if Cee Jay hadn't come back to reclaim her ex-husband, would Mac take one look at her and fall in love all over again? How could he not?

Gina poured herself a cup of coffee. She wasn't much of a drinker but she sure wished she had a shot of something to jack up that coffee. Her hands trembled as she lifted the cup to her lips. And while Cee Jay laughed and chatted into the phone, taking petite bites of her apple pie, she appeared so carefree. So animated. How do you leave your three children, not see them for ten years, then stroll back into their lives all happy-go-lucky? How do you do that?

Gina had the sense that the world she knew was changing, and she had no idea what the outcome might be, but she was suddenly afraid.

The Sheriff's Department SUV rolled down the street, parked in front of the deputy's office and Mac strode purposefully across the street, hitching up his heavy gun belt as he walked. He came into the diner, gave a nod to Gina, walked right past her and stood at the booth, looking down at his ex-wife.

Cee Jay looked up at him, smiling. She disconnected from her call and stood from the booth. Gina could see the happy expression on her face, and then it fell into a serious look as she listened to Mac.

And then they walked out of the diner, Mac striding in front of his ex-wife and leaving her to follow. He walked across the street to his department vehicle while Cee Jay momentarily disappeared. And then Gina saw her drive by, following Mac in a shiny sports car convertible. Her car wasn't white, it wasn't beige or soft gold. It was *pearl*.

Then Gina had to sit down. Her legs would no longer hold her up.

Six

Mac called Deputy Steve Pritkus at home. "Steve, can you cover the town for a few hours? I have a family emergency."

"Everything all right, Mac?"

Far from all right. *Far!* "No injuries, Steve. Just a situation that has to be dealt with immediately. I can explain more later. It's sensitive. Should I call Charlie?"

"Nope, I got it. I'll be parked in front of the office in ten."

"Thanks, I owe you one."

Mac then drove to a Denny's restaurant on the outskirts of Bandon, parked and went inside. Cee Jay pulled up right beside him but he didn't wait for her; he just walked straight into the restaurant. When he faced the hostess holding her menus, he pointed to the booth he wanted, far to the rear of the restaurant. "Just two coffees," he said. "No menus today."

"Whatever you want, Officer," she said with a smile.

Mac took a seat in the booth with his back to the wall, facing the restaurant. Cops never sat with their back to the crowd. A few moments later Cee Jay came in and, seeing her, he scowled. Well, she'd done all right for herself. She probably thought herself tempting, looking so fetching and sophisticated. Well, hell, Cee Jay had always been pretty. But now she looked elegant, as well, and it pissed him off. Here he'd been scrimping, saving, trying to inch by on a deputy's paycheck with three kids and she was driving a brand-new Lexus coup convertible. He hated her.

She slid into the booth. Her smile was a little subdued. The waitress was immediately there with two coffees, then departed just as quickly.

"What do you want, Cecilia Jayne?"

She was a bit taken aback by the formal use of her name. "It's been a very long time. I wanted to see how you were."

"Just fine. That it?"

"I thought we could talk. How are the kids?"

"Just fine. And I don't want to talk."

"Mac, look, I know what I did was wrong. I'm sorry. It took a lot of time to work up the courage to come here, and to apologize. I know there's no way I can make it up to you. I was a screwed-up abused foster kid and shouldn't have gotten married at the age of sixteen. I shouldn't have—"

"You had a nice family," he said through gritted teeth.

"Shows what you know," she said, her eyes narrowing. "They weren't my family, they were about the eighth one and they were only nice in public. It was awful. I suffered. I was messed up and was trying to escape."

Mac's eyes narrowed, as well. Being in law enforcement, he wasn't easily duped by how people appeared on the outside. Just a couple of months ago he'd arrested a seventeen-year-old for battery, for beating up his elderly father, and he came from the richest, snootiest family in town. The kid had everything, and it still wasn't enough.

He was trying to remember Cee Jay at sixteen—she was a cheerleader, in lots of school clubs, always looked well-heeled, had a curfew that was too liberal and could borrow the family car often. They let her talk on the phone till all hours. He'd been to her house many times. There were a lot of kids in that house, but he'd grown up with Aunt Lou. Hell, Lou did more yelling and disciplining than Mac had ever seen at Cee Jay's foster home.

He had been silent too long. Since she'd said *"I... was trying to escape."*

"And so you did," he said. "Are we done here?"

"Mac, I want to see my kids."

"You signed away custodial guardianship and visitation, Cee Jay. I'd appreciate it if you'd just leave now. Leave town, leave the area, like you did before."

"Will you please *listen* to me? Mac, I made a terrible mistake, but I was twenty-three and had three kids. I was half-nuts. I just about had my life together, my mental health straightened out, when you sent the divorce and custody papers. It was very clear—you were done waiting around for me and you didn't want me near our kids. I was devastated, but I was also feeling terribly guilty. I couldn't blame you—so I just signed. That was almost five years ago and I regretted it almost immediately. I want a second chance. I'm begging you."

He rested one forearm on the table. "Do you have *any* idea what you did to our children? The babies cried day and night. Ryan wandered aimlessly around the house calling out for you. Dee Dee was so screwed up—she stopped sleeping, napping, just couldn't get comfortable, couldn't be soothed. But that's nothing to what it did to Eve! We could hardly get her to go to school, she was so afraid you'd come home and she wouldn't be there. She wet the bed, threw up, cried herself to sleep, wouldn't socialize with the kids at school. I had at least two kids in my bed every night for a year, usually three. Cee Jay! You fucked up the whole family because *you* couldn't take it! Because getting laid by some golf pro looked better to you than bottles and diapers! No, you are not coming back into their lives now! Keep me posted on your location and when they're over eighteen, I'll tell them where they can find you if they want to see you or talk to you."

Her lips thinned, her nose grew pink and a couple of fat tears rolled down her cheeks. Her voice was a whisper. "I want to make amends."

"Not this year, Cee Jay. Is this part of some program? Because the rule is—make amends where it doesn't cause any harm. This—this would cause harm."

"But no, I don't want to cause any pain. I just want to know them."

"We. Can't. Trust. You."

"I give you my word!"

"Your word isn't worth shit around here."

"I can't believe how unforgiving you are," she murmured, wiping her eyes. "You were never like this before."

"I've been burned real good," he said. "I'm a big boy, I can take it. But my kids are vulnerable. You mess

with my kids and you're going to see how unforgiving
I can be."

"Mac, they're not just yours...."

"Yes, they are. Because their mother abandoned them
and then signed them away. Don't you dare screw them
up and hurt them now. Don't you dare."

She straightened. "I'm going to file to amend the custody agreement. You'll hear from my lawyer."

"Fine," he said smoothly. He pulled a notepad out of
his pocket. "You can have your lawyer call my lawyer."
He scribbled down a name and city—he hadn't talked
to Sidney Mikowski in almost five years. "Until you
get a ruling from a judge, stay out of Thunder Point."

"You can't tell me where I can be."

"Yes. I can. I'll have a restraining order before close
of business today and it will be my absolute pleasure
to arrest you. And, if you sue for custody I think you'll
find that I'll be suing for back support. That car out
there—the price tag on that should help with tuitions
and braces."

"God, you're so hostile! I never expected this rage
from you!"

He leaned toward her. "Do you have any idea how
long I hoped you'd think of your children, even if you
didn't think about what you'd done to me? Do you have
any idea? I prayed for a phone call! For years I waited,
hoping you'd send one of them a fucking birthday card,
but there was nothing! I even decided that for the sake of
the kids I wouldn't make you grovel too much, if you'd
just promise not to stray again." He sat back. "Cecilia
Jayne, I'm afraid I got over that little fantasy quite a
while ago. You can't just stroll into town and pick up

where you left off. It's over. There are consequences—
you'll just have to live with that."

"I *am* living with it!"

"Leave, Cee Jay. Leave and don't look back. This
meeting is over." Mac stood and fished out his wallet,
throwing a ten on the table for the coffee, extreme over-
payment. Her clothing, jewelry and car made him act as
if he was a rich man when in fact he'd struggled with
money every day for the past ten years. He was going
to struggle for the next ten. Probably twenty.

"Who are you with now, Mac? I know you're not
remarried—I checked. Gotta love that internet. So, who
is it?"

"We're done talking," he said.

"Not that washed-out little blonde at the diner, is
it?" A fierce look must have come into his eyes because she laughed.

Ah, there was the true Cee Jay. One minute crying,
the next laughing, always manipulating. "What are you
really after?" he asked. "Tell me now because I'm going
to find out. Are you looking for money? Because I don't
have any. If I did, I'd give it to you to make you go away,
but it's been a real challenge holding it together. What
do you really want? You're not exactly dressed for Little
League or soccer practices."

"I want a chance to reconnect," she said.

He stared down at her. "Not gonna happen. Drive
carefully." And he walked out of the restaurant.

Mac sat in the Denny's parking lot. No judge would
give him a restraining order, not even a judge who was
his biggest fan. Cee Jay hadn't threatened any of them.
That was just all talk and, by now, if Cee Jay had called

her lawyer, she probably knew that. He dialed Lou's cell phone. "Where are you?" he asked her.

"Grocery store. You have some special request?"

"And the kids?"

"Dee Dee's at gymnastics, Ryan is at soccer, Eve is at cheer practice. Or maybe that's over and she's with Ashley—Ashley drove today and gave Eve a ride. Why?"

God, he thought. Did Cee Jay have any idea what these lessons, teams and activities cost? Just the sign-ups alone without factoring in uniforms, gear and associated costs were a strain. Twenty dollars for this gymnastics meet, twenty bucks for the bus for that soccer tournament out of town. Just to get your kid in the parks-and-rec soccer league was over fifty bucks. Then there were uniforms, shoes, your turn supplying sports drinks and bottled water and snacks, then there were regular pizza parties and barbeques to celebrate wins and season close. Piano, gymnastics, dance and cheerleading—those were expensive teams, lessons and uniforms. It never stopped. More than the money, which was always tight, the emotional and time investment could be exhausting. It took more than bread and water to raise a family. If he hadn't had Lou the past ten years, he'd have been completely lost.

"I need a couple of things, Lou. I need you to gather up the kids and get them all home. And I need you to stay cool."

"Why? Are we under nuclear attack?"

"Cee Jay's in town. She wants to see them."

"What!" Lou shrieked.

"I have to talk to the kids before they hear from some other source that their mother is around. And, Lou, Cee

Jay rules apply. Do not lose your cool. Do not. I already lost mine a little…."

"Did you strangle her?" Lou asked with a shaky voice.

"No, but I wanted to."

"You're an underachiever. Oh, God," she said. "Oh, dear God."

Cee Jay rules actually had been Lou's suggestion, but in the end it was harder for Lou than it was for Mac. They *never* said nasty things about Cee Jay in front of the kids—it simply wouldn't serve any purpose to trash their mother. Wasn't it hard enough on them to know she left them?

"Lou?"

"You're right. You're right. We'll hold it together. Where is she?"

"Now? I met her for a cup of coffee at Denny's just off the highway in Bandon and I asked her to leave. I told her she couldn't see the kids and that I wanted her to go away and leave us alone. And she said I'd hear from her lawyer. We have to be ready, Lou."

"She can't do anything, can she, Mac?"

"I don't know. One thing at a time. I'll see you at home."

He signed off and then just sat in the Sheriff's Department vehicle. He could barely remember when he was eighteen, nineteen. He was a freshman at Oregon State, boinking his high school girlfriend wherever they could find a time and place to be alone. She was on the pill; they were supposed to be safe. Now he wondered, of course, if she hadn't maneuvered that like everything else. For his part, he had such passion for her he could hardly think straight. So when the pregnancy came, they got married immediately, running off to Idaho to a justice of the peace and spending one night in a cheap roadside motel.

He had believed he loved her. He held back her hair while she was sick during her pregnancy; he rubbed her back, worked two jobs, did everything he could think of to make her happy. And after Eve was born, Cee Jay organized a big fancy white wedding and reception they couldn't afford, just so all her friends could fuss over her and party with her.

Lou had been appalled. But she'd been there, holding Eve most of the time so Cee Jay could party.

After that, Mac couldn't remember them ever being happy. Maybe he'd just been too goddamned tired.

Before leaving the Denny's parking lot, Mac drove by the side of the restaurant to look at the booth where he had just been sitting. He could see Cee Jay sitting in the same booth, laughing animatedly into her cell phone. How could she do that—laugh and joke after a meeting like that with her ex? After tears and begging and anger, how could she switch it all off?

Lou felt as if her face was on fire. Her heart was pounding and she put a hand to her solar plexus. She realized she was standing in the frozen food section, nearly yelling into the phone. A couple of people were looking at her—thankfully not people she knew. A man in his seventies dipped his chin and said, "You okay, miss?"

Miss? Lou was sixty! "Fine. Thanks, I'm fine."

And then she wondered if she should leave her cart and run. Instead, she shoved her list in her pocket, ignoring what was left on it, and made a mad run through the frozen foods, throwing pizzas, casseroles, burritos, fried chicken and various other frozen meals in her cart. In went French fries, Tater Tots, garlic toast, peas, beans, cheesecake, cookie dough. She rushed to the dairy aisle and grabbed milk, cheese, cold cuts, sour cream, yogurt. She found the spaghetti sauce and pasta and loaded up. On her way to the checkout, her cart heaped with a mountain of food, she grabbed bread, chips and pretzels, two bottles of wine and a two six-packs each of soda and beer. It was like stocking for a hurricane. Yes. Hurricane Cee Jay.

"Whoa, Lou," the cashier said. "Having a party?"

She was stunned by her mania. "Ah…just some friends."

She wanted to take the kids home and bar the door. She had enough food to keep them going for more than a week. Maybe during that time they could figure out what to do about Cee Jay. *Oh, God, she's going to take them away from me,* Lou thought in near despair.

She had to have help to load the groceries in the minivan and she rushed to get the kids.

"Why did you take me out of practice?" Ryan asked.

"Your dad asked me to round up you kids and bring you home. He wants to tell you something."

"What?" Ryan asked, pulling off his shoes in the backseat.

"Well, I'm not completely sure," she said, because she wasn't. What was Mac going to say to them? Your mother is back—be nice to her?

While she was waiting for Dee Dee to load up her backpack from gymnastics, she dialed Eve's cell phone. Eve was just leaving cheer practice and was going to go to Ashley's house for a while. "I need you home—

I have something I need help with. Stay at school, I'll pick you up in about five minutes."

"What's going on?" Eve asked when she got in the front seat next to Lou.

The whole car smelled gamey, filled with the wild scent of sweaty kids. Lou had been doing this since before Dee Dee was walking—shuffling them to school, games, lessons, everything. The weekends were jam-packed, as well, they had so many things to attend to—housecleaning, laundry and general chores. They had a list—assignments for everyone. Seven days a week, twenty-four hours a day, Mac and Lou operated a split shift, making sure that everyone was covered and that everyone felt they were getting an equal amount of adult time and love.

Oh, God, she's going to take them away from us and hurt them!

"Aunt Lou? What's going on?" Eve asked.

"Your dad just asked me to round you up and bring you home—family meeting I guess. But hey—I bought a ton of food that's extremely bad for you, so before we give him the podium, I'm going to need every hand to get this stuff in the refrigerator and freezer. Pizzas, lasagna, Stouffer's mac and cheese, the really good stuff. And I didn't even buy lettuce—we can work on our cholesterol later. We all on board here? Let's get this stuff put away before we hunker down with your dad."

"I thought he was working today?" Eve said.

"He is. I'm sure he allotted fifteen minutes for this family meeting. Try not to insult him with boredom."

But Lou was secretly terrified and Lou was strong— it took a lot to terrify her. When she pulled in to the garage, she yelled, "Everyone, grab at least two bags!"

When they all walked in, heavily laden, Mac was standing in the kitchen waiting for them. He looked at them. "There are a few more in the car," she said.

"Jesus, Lou. Was there a sale or something?"

"Or something," she said, beginning to shove things into the freezer, her head down. "Let's not let it spoil."

"Let's do it," Mac ordered. "Let's put all this stuff away. Then we're going to sit down for a talk."

"Who's in trouble?" Ryan asked.

"Me," Mac said.

They sat at the dining room table. "There's no way to sneak up on this, kids. I had the shock of my life today. I saw your mother."

He was faced with three astonished faces. Big eyes. Open mouths. It was Eve who asked, "You just *saw* her?"

He shook his head. "She came to town looking for me. We had a cup of coffee together. We talked." He took a breath. "It seems she realizes it was a mistake, leaving our family as she did."

A bark of laughter came out of Eve and the look on her face was downright evil. "A *mistake?*"

He took a breath and noticed that Lou had her hands folded on the table and was staring down at them. Probably trying to keep herself from screaming. "I think it's pretty normal to be angry about that," he said evenly. "I was very angry for a long time, but at some point I decided it wasn't good for us. It wasn't good for me or for you. And at the time we got married, at the time your mom left, she was too young to make good decisions. She was only sixteen when we got married. I know every sixteen-year-old thinks they're brilliant and wise and capable of making big life-altering decisions, but I've got news for you—in fact, when your mom left, she was still very young. She'd been thrust into adulthood, had never really lived, was so overwhelmed by responsibility..."

Eve leaned toward him. "It didn't overwhelm *you!*"

"Yes, it did, Eve. I couldn't manage. I had to ask Aunt Lou for help. And believe me, I was too young, too. So I did everything your Aunt Lou told me to do."

Lou lifted her eyes. A very small half smile played on her lips and she gave a slight nod. Because, yes, he had. He was drowning and terrified and so angry. Lou, a savvy woman, mature with a lot of experience, talked him through it and helped take care of the kids.

"Eve, we've talked about this before and you've talked with your aunt Lou about this—this is the kind of hardship young families run into when they're not grown up enough, not really ready to take on the world before they have the experience. That's why I hope you graduate from college and have a handle on what you want out of life before you make the kind of promises and commitments your mother and I made. Promises and commitments we weren't prepared for and didn't know how to keep. I'm sorry, Eve. It's as much my fault as anyone's."

"It's not! You didn't leave us!"

I got her pregnant, he thought. "Everyone has their own way of handling stress."

"Aren't you pissed?" Eve fired back.

"Yes," he said. "But I'm not going to let that run my life. I don't have to let anger control me and I won't."

"Dad, she left you! She signed us away!"

He so could use a drink right now. Not a beer, but

a shot of something strong. "There are times I regret being so honest with you. Maybe it's the cop in me—I always start with the truth. I just can't keep track of a lot of lies. Listen, when I sent your mother those divorce and custody papers, I had absolutely no idea what her life was like. She could've been living in her car for all I know. I had to locate her and all I got was an address."

"So?"

"So maybe she signed the papers as a favor to you. To me. To get it over with so she wasn't a burden on anyone, I don't know. And maybe she came back to say she was sorry because it's taken her this long to get her life together—I honestly don't know. All I know is— it's not our problem. We have a pretty solid family and we're going to keep our family solid. We're strong, Eve. We can afford to be calm and kind."

"Well, I might be solid, but I'm still pissed," she said, giving the table a thump with her fist.

"I think that's normal. Your life has been tough enough with only a dad and aunt—try not to let this event and your anger make your life any tougher."

"Where is she?"

"I don't know," he said. "I was so surprised to see her, I forgot to ask. But I'm sure she'll contact me again."

"Are you letting her back with us?" Eve asked. "Are you?"

Mac was shocked by the question. He shook his head and frowned. "No," he said, confused. "Eve, my marriage with your mother ended ten years ago, years before our divorce was final. I haven't said this to you kids, but I know you realize it—I love Gina. We've been best friends for years and I trust her and care about her.

And I love her. That doesn't mean we're getting married or moving in together or changing our families right now—but it's a fact. And no other woman, not even my ex-wife, is going to change that." He shook his head. "She will always be your mother, but she hasn't been my wife in a very long time—so no, I am not inviting her to come home to us."

"When she calls you again, tell her I want to see her," Eve said angrily.

Everyone turned shocked faces toward her.

"That's all. I want to see her. That's all." And then Eve got up from the table and left the kitchen. Momentarily her bedroom door slammed. There was silence around the table.

"Is she pretty?" Dee Dee finally asked, her voice a little smaller than usual.

They had pictures. There weren't any pictures of Cee Jay displayed in their house, but the kids each had an album of photos taken during early childhood, pictures they could look at if they wanted to. That was Lou's doing. Remarkable, given Lou was probably even more angry at Cee Jay than Mac was, if that was possible. But no one could make Cee Jay disappear and the kids were curious, naturally. For years Eve was obsessed with why her mother had left her but the younger kids just wanted to know who she was.

"She's very pretty," Mac said. "That's probably where you kids got your good looks. She looks like the pictures you have. Hasn't changed a day."

"I want to see her, too," Dee Dee said.

"So do I," Ryan said. "Think she'd maybe come to a soccer game?"

"I don't know, son. I guess anything is possible. But

I think it's pretty likely she's just visiting around here. I wouldn't count on her staying long. To be honest, I don't know what her plans are. I've never known. I think she'll get in touch with me again, but I don't know for sure."

"Were we too much? Is that why she went away?" Ryan asked.

They'd been over this a hundred times. That question always came out of the blue at odd times. The answer was always the same. "Everything was too much, son. I worked all the time, there wasn't enough money, the house was falling apart, your mom was so young and lonely and felt cheated by life. We argued too much. It was just too hard for her, I guess. And I've asked myself a thousand times what I could have done to make it better. Easier. And I don't know."

"I wish't I could just see what she looks like for real," Dee Dee said.

Mac reached across the table and squeezed his baby girl's hand. "I hope she calls, punkin. I'll sure tell her you want to see her."

Dee Dee grinned. "I'm going to practice piano," she said, scraping back her chair and heading for the basement stairs.

"Can I get on the computer?" Ryan wanted to know.

"I'll be checking your Facebook stuff, so no funny business," Lou said.

"Yeah, yeah, yeah," he replied, following his younger sister to the basement. All the kid stuff was down there.

And then they were alone, Lou and Mac.

"Eve's pissed," Mac said. "I should go talk to her...."

"No," Lou said, shaking her head. "Not so fast. Let her simmer, I'll talk to her in an hour or two. And the younger ones? They took in your shocking news, blew it off after a minute and headed for their favorite toys." She shook her head and laughed. "To them, Cee Jay is a myth. Kids. Don't try to guess what they'll do next—it's exhausting. Are you going back to work?"

"For at least a couple of hours. I'll try to come home early."

"I'll handle Eve. This is a huge event in her young life," Lou said. "I'm sure Eve didn't think she'd ever see her mother again."

"Right," he said. "And we'd better hide all the sharp objects."

"It's very selfish of me, but I'm glad she's angry," Lou said. "I think I had a panic attack at the grocery store, afraid Cee Jay would take the kids away from us. I bought everything I could fit in a cart in about three minutes."

"She's not going to take the kids away from us," Mac said. "Worst case, she'll see them. No, that's not the worst case—worst case is she'll hurt them emotionally. Build up their hopes, let them down, reject them all over again. I'm going to try to head that off if I can."

"How?" Lou asked.

"Hell if I know."

Seven

Gina was beginning to relate to Ashley—she had been gripping her phone ever since Mac walked out of the diner that morning, followed by Cee Jay. In her most rational musings she saw him dealing with the many questions his kids must have had about their mother. Ryan and Dee Dee couldn't even remember her, but Mac had told her how traumatized Eve had been, still was on some days. In her most irrational fantasies, Cee Jay was moving her beautiful wardrobe into Mac's house, into his closet, curling up with him while the children welcomed her with tears of joy.

When there was a soft knock at the door at 9:00 p.m. she jerked it open. There he stood, holding two bottles of beer by their necks. "What a day," he said.

She let out such a sigh of relief she almost collapsed. "You might've called."

"Honey, there was no time. Well, I could have sent you a text, but I really wanted to see you, to tell you about it. I couldn't figure out a text or voice mail short enough to send that would also explain everything. Grab a sweater or shawl—come out on the porch with me."

She grabbed Carrie's wrap off the hook by the front door. Her house was quiet. Carrie had gone to bed, exhausted from the hard day of running a deli and Ashley had retreated to the solitude of her room. She sat down with Mac on the porch step.

"Expecting a call?" he asked with a slight smile, glancing at her cell phone.

"I think it's attached itself to the palm of my hand...."

He chuckled and opened a beer for her. She finally let go of the cell, laying it on the porch, wiping her sweating palm on her pant leg.

"My kids are doing better than I dared hope. Well, Eve's acting out—completely expected. She wants to see her mother, but I suspect it's not to welcome her home. She's outraged, which she's entitled to be. But Lou? She's over-the-top—I left her with a bottle of wine that was slowly disappearing."

Gina laughed. "Taking it hard, is she?"

"She's afraid Cee Jay is back to wrestle the kids away from her. That's not going to happen, but Lou's what I would call overwrought."

"Has Lou seen her yet? Cee Jay?"

He shook his head. "I believe you alone have had the honor."

"You might've mentioned that this illusive ex of yours is drop-dead gorgeous."

"Hell, she's always been pretty. Now she appears to be pretty and rich. I'm going to have to do some digging, see what she's been up to. See if I can figure out what she wants. I find it hard to believe that after ten years she wants her family back."

"Mac, she's not pretty. She's probably the most beautiful woman I've ever seen. She literally took my breath away. Before I knew who she was, I thought a famous actress whose name I couldn't remember had stopped into the diner."

"Come on," he said doubtfully.

"Seriously. I've been having really awful wide-awake nightmares all day. There's this one very bad scenario I've been playing over and over where you take one look at her and start peeling her clothes off and begging her to come back to you."

He lifted a brow, then took a slug of his beer. "Well, you were there when I took my first look at her. Is that what you saw?"

"Actually, you looked very pissed."

"To put it mildly. What nerve. She's been gone since Dee Dee was nine months old—ten years ago now. She hasn't called or sent a birthday card or Christmas present in ten years and then, without any warning, she sashays into town in a sixty-thousand-dollar car, looking as if she just stepped out of a fashion magazine. And she wants to know her kids? Maybe she'd like to start by getting to know their orthodontist bills."

"What did she say, Mac?"

He took a deep breath and told her parts of their conversation. "I told her to just leave town. I threatened her with a restraining order—a completely empty threat—and she said she was going to legally challenge the custody agreement. I told her to have her lawyer call my lawyer. I haven't talked to my lawyer since he gave me a very nice discount to file the divorce and custody papers for me five years ago. Papers she signed without a question, a call or a visit, by the way."

"Did you tell the kids this?" Gina asked.

"I'm real careful about what I tell them. I try to tell

them the truth without telling them that their mother, half of their gene pool, is a selfish unfaithful bitch who left them as babies without looking back. It's not easy. But she's done enough to them. I don't need their self-esteems attached to her irresponsible and cruel choices. They're innocent, after all." He put an arm around her, pulling her closer. "Besides, who's the genius that knocked up a sixteen-year-old? I have to own my part in all this."

"I know. I do know how you feel," she said.

"I suppose you have similar issues with Ashley's father," he said.

"Not so much, no. He was the new kid in town for a year or so, dropped out of high school but we hung around the football games and beach parties, and when I told him I was pregnant, he ran for his life. I don't know if he was running from the responsibility or the fact that I was fifteen and he was eighteen—it could've been that. But I was thinking of my own father. He left us when I was five. They never got divorced, but five years later he died and guess what? He had a new family—and a will. He didn't leave us any of his insurance money or pension—signed it all over to his new family even though my mom was the official widow. Now, how do you get past that? Maybe that had something to do with my own teenage issues, huh? Maybe I had abandonment issues?"

"See, that's what scares me more than anything— Eve being like her mother. Ryan being as stupid as his father...."

"It was a hard day for you today," she said. "Revisiting the past is always so scary."

"I'll tell you something, Gina," Mac said, pulling

her closer. "It would have been a lot worse if I didn't have you. Here I was, so freaking scared to get involved again because of what happened in the past, yet today I found out what it means to have a solid relationship when the shit hits the fan. I told them today. I told the family. I told them about us. Eve was a little panicked, asked if I was going to let her mother come back and it just came out—I said their mother left our marriage a very long time ago and I love Gina. There's no coming back, there's only moving forward."

She leaned against him. "God," she whispered. "Being in love with you can be stressful."

"Not being in love with you can be more stressful. If we ever get our families under control, we're going away. Just for a weekend, maybe, but away."

"They'll all know we're having sex," she said.

"Well, what the hell! They've all been having sex!"

"Not all of them," she said with a laugh. "In fact, I think Lou's the only one in that boat at the moment."

"I don't think Eve is there yet—Lou promised me she's got that covered. Eve's more comfortable talking to her about that part of her life. And Ashley's in a bad place right now, but she'll recover and move on and...I don't care, Gina—I don't know how we can blend these two crazy families into one circus yet, but we deserve a little break. Don't you think?"

She kissed his cheek. "Yes, I think so. Maybe when Ash is better and the most beautiful woman in the world has left town."

"The most stupid woman in the world is more like it," he said. "She doesn't seem to understand how much advantage she would have if she took things slow. A few cards, phone calls, maybe a lunch or trip to a pizza parlor before she sics the lawyer on us." He shook his head. "She might come up against their anger and find out she's not snuggling up to some precious little babies who long for her. She's facing off with some kids who were dumped on a very hurt, very angry father—and they're not willing to suffer fools gladly. They might rip her apart. A part of me hopes they would."

He put down his beer and pulled her into his arms, covering her mouth in a deep kiss. "Never be afraid again, Gina. Don't be afraid of some mean woman just because she has a good haircut and fancy clothes."

"Okay," she whispered. "We've had such a hard time getting this romance off the ground...."

"Patience," he said.

Just then Gina's cell phone rang. She picked it up and saw that it was Ashley calling from inside the house. "Hi, Ash," she said.

"Where *are* you?" her daughter asked through tears.

"I'm on the front porch, having a beer with Mac. Is something wrong?"

"I need you! Now!"

"Hmm," Gina said to her lover. "My daughter, calling from her bedroom, having another meltdown."

"This happen a lot?" he asked.

"Lately? Regularly. Want to wait for me?"

"I do want to wait, but I should go home, scrape poor old Lou off the floor and pour her into bed. Her worst nightmare came to town today—by now she's probably drunk. I'll call you in the morning."

"I'd like that. And listen, thank you."

"For?"

"Two bottles of beer and a little reinforcement. I love you, too."

He kissed her again. "We got the shaft," he said. "We got together when our baggage was so heavy. I'm going to make this up to you somehow."

"No, don't worry. This is good. I like you this way. Once I got over the first guy, I got really hot for responsible men."

"Are you sure that's sexy?" he asked with a smile.

"I am so sure."

Gina went into Ashley's room and saw her sitting cross-legged on the bed, her laptop perched on her knees, her phone clutched in her hand, tears streaming down her red face. "Mom!" she shrieked, holding the phone toward her.

Gina looked at the text message including photo and there was her daughter, eyes seductive slits, mouth open in a very sexy pose, breasts bared. For a moment she was completely confused. The message read, *Say hi to Downy's ex psycho slut.*

Huh?

"Her! It's her! Downy's new girlfriend! She sent it out to everyone in Downy's phone directory! Oh, my God!"

"Ashley?" Gina asked, still not believing.

"It's fake, Mom," she sobbed. "I would never let anyone take a picture of my boobs! Those aren't my boobs! Oh, God."

Gina felt her knees go weak. She sank onto the bed, staring at the grotesque photo on the phone.

"And on Facebook! She put it on Facebook! I saw it because she's Downy's friend and Downy's my friend! Oh, God, people are going to think it's me—that I posed for that picture and sent it to Downy or something. Oh Mom, I've never been so...*embarrassed!*"

"Why is she doing this?" Gina asked. "Ashley, have you been calling and texting Downy a lot?"

"No," she said, shaking her head. "Not in a long time. Not since I started counseling and group. I agreed to stop reaching out to him. Why is she doing this to me?"

"Listen, I'm not up on this internet stuff like I should be—but isn't this against the law? Isn't it harassment or something?"

She shook her head. "I don't think anyone ever gets caught. Not really."

"Have you called Downy? Could he have done this?"

"And called me 'Downy's ex psycho slut'? Wouldn't he have said '*My* ex psycho'?"

"Ashley, this is almost the nastiest, meanest thing I've ever seen. Can Downy really be okay with this? Have you called him?"

"He won't take my calls. I called Landon. He'd already seen it—that's how fast this stuff moves. It came over his texts. He said he's going to call Downy and tell him to shut it down. But Mom, it's too *late!*"

"Listen, listen. You just laugh if you can and say, no one in their right mind would ever believe that's me. Like those are my boobs? Gimme a break! His new girlfriend is obviously very threatened and has gone to a lot of trouble to try to make me look bad! Can you do that, Ash? Because it's not you! It's not! It's her!"

Ashley looked straight at Gina, tears pouring down her cheeks. "If you think I'm *ever* going to school again, you're *crazy*," she said in a whisper.

* * *

Landon called Downy the minute he hung up from talking to Eve. Downy answered, "Dupre! 'Sup, man?"

"You really have to ask, Downy?" Landon countered. "Ashley's pretty much destroyed! What the hell, Downy?"

"Aw, I didn't do that. That was Selena, just screwing around, that's all."

"That's all? She sent it to everyone! Everyone on your phone directory and posted it on Facebook! A picture of Ashley looking like she just had the sex of her life, her naked boobs hanging out!"

"Yeah, my mother got that," Downy said. "I had to tell her it was a practical joke—that someone on the team did it. I texted everyone and said it was just a bad joke and I didn't do it."

"Right. And before anyone got that text, I'm sure they forwarded the picture to everyone they knew...."

"But man, it wasn't me! And Selena said she's sorry. So tell Ash, we're sorry."

"*We're* sorry?"

"Yeah, see, we had a little fight. She wanted me to get all my old pictures of Ash off my phone and I just didn't do it fast enough and it pissed her off and... Listen, it's no big deal. Everyone knows it's just a crank, it's not real...."

"Are you brain-dead?" Landon said. "Jesus, Downy, you're killing the girl! As it is, Deputy McCain saw it when Eve asked him if it was against the law, if it was something you could be sued for! I think he's gonna call your dean, your coach!"

"Aw, man, why'd you do that? Why'd you show him that?"

"Because if you'd done that to Eve, I'd be on my way up there to beat the shit outta you, you stupid asshole!"

"Why would I do that to Eve?" Downy asked. "I didn't even do it to Ashley! But come on, I told her we broke up and she wouldn't let it go and Selena—she doesn't like seeing another girl on my phone, you know? But she's over it and she said she won't do it again."

Landon was stunned quiet. "Let me see if I have this right," he finally said. "You asked Ash to go with you, right? To be your steady girl. To take off her clothes for you, to do private things with you, and you promised to respect her. Promised to take her to her prom, promised to be faithful, said you loved her, and now because you fucked some girl at State, now you want her to just go away quietly?"

"I wouldn't've put it exactly like that, but I guess that's sort of right. Look, we grew apart.…"

"Grew apart? One week you spend nine hours on the phone with her and the next week you grew apart?"

"Dupre! Back off. It didn't work, okay? And it's not that big a deal—everyone knows that picture was doctored! Everyone knows it's not real! Lighten the fuck up!"

Landon just shook his head. "I don't believe you," he said. "You know what you are, Downy? You're a prick, that's what you are. A *stupid* prick with his brain in his dick. I hope Selena dumps your sorry ass!"

Landon hung up. Then he called Eve. He could hear the tears in her voice when she answered, but this was not just about Ashley. She was having her own terrible day—her long-lost mother had suddenly reappeared and she was struggling with that.

"Hey, babe," he said. "Look, I know you're not in

good shape right now, but would you do something for me? Would you show your dad that picture, tell him Downy admits it's faked and ask him if there's anything he can do? Like, I don't know...I suppose life in prison is a little harsh... Could he call the dean or the coach or something...? Because Downy's girlfriend got her hands on his phone and did that. And that is just *wrong*."

"You talked to Downy?" she asked.

"Yeah," he said, his voice full of disgust. "He said it was no big deal and Selena did it, but she said she wouldn't do that again."

"Oh, that's comforting," Eve said. "I've been calling Ashley. She won't even answer my call," Eve said. "Oh, Landon, I think everything is falling apart all over the place."

"Just ask your dad, okay? That's all. He's probably going to say it's just one of those ugly things, but ask, anyway, okay?"

"I'll ask. But don't get your hopes up. I've seen this stuff happen before. Really mean stuff. And no one ever does anything."

"I know," he said. Because Landon had seen it before, too. If he'd done something like that and the school called his sister, she'd tie him up and work him over with a baseball bat. Sarah didn't stand for that kind of nasty stuff. "You doing okay, baby?"

"Oh, you know. I'm a little shook up, can't decide if I'm going to throw things at my mother or hug her."

"What's in between?" he asked her.

"That's what I'm trying to figure out. A little coffee talk? 'So, how've you been? What kind of interesting things have you been up to for ten years while I was growing up?'"

He laughed in spite of himself. "Have I told you lately how awesome you are?"

"You can tell me again if you want," she said. "Listen, would you do something for me? I'm kind of caught up in the mother drama here—everyone in the family is all upside down. Will you help me try to take care of Ash? Because this has got to be like the worst thing that's ever happened to her and I don't know what to do."

"I'll check on her," he said. "She asked me to call Downy so maybe she'll take my call. I just don't want to tell her what he said. I'll tell her about your mom, tell her you're worried about her."

"Thanks. Landon, you're awesome, too. And I always loved Downy...I never would've believed he'd let something like this happen."

"Me, either. I don't know what he's smokin'."

Gina thought it was reasonable to allow Ashley to stay home from school the day after the sexting incident, but it was difficult to bear. It was as if they were back at square one, if not worse. She'd slept or sobbed on and off all day. Gina went home from the diner several times during the day to check on her and found no improvement.

So Gina took Ashley's phone, turned it off and slipped it into her apron pocket. This was a very bad time for her daughter to be making or taking calls. She could hardly blame her—it was tempting even to Gina to check the phone for inbound calls. But she resisted.

She had not confiscated the laptop. When she got home from work that day she asked Ashley if the Facebook debacle had been dealt with.

"The picture was taken down," she said morosely. "But there's lots of talk—people arguing back and forth about whether it was faked by a mean girl or the real deal...my desperate attempt to lure Downy back. I threw up four times today."

Gina sat down on the edge of the bed. "We have to pull it together, Ash. The sooner you face it, the sooner it will fade away."

"You're kidding, right? I'm never facing this. Never! It's just too cruel!"

Gina gave her a second day to sulk and work it like a hangnail because the following day was her group therapy. Gina had high hopes for that group. Before leaving Ashley in bed, she returned the phone. When she got home to check on her, she found the phone on the kitchen table, shattered to bits. Beside the wreckage was a hammer.

In a panic, Gina ran to Ashley's bedroom. "What happened?" she asked. With a hand on her shoulder, she rolled her daughter onto her back. "Ashley, what happened?"

"I turned it on," she said on a sob. "There were so many messages, the mailbox was full. I listened to about four and they were mean. 'You're a slut, Ashley! You'll never get him back, Ashley—not even with your pathetic tits!' There was even a guy—I don't know who— who called me a whore." She rolled back and sobbed.

"All right, you have to get up," Gina said. "You'll share this in your group, get some advice. Kids go through terrible bullying ordeals and survive. Not just survive but get stronger. Look what happened to Landon last fall, getting beat up by the likes of Jag Morrison! You have to stand up to this, Ash!"

Ashley rolled back. Her eyes were so red they were nearly crusty. Her whole face was swollen. "If you think I'm ever going anywhere, you're crazy. I just want to die!"

"No, Ash. You have to fight back!"

"No! There are too many of them!"

"You have Eve, Landon and your friends!"

"I can't even see them in the crowd!" Ashley whimpered. And then she pulled the covers over her head.

Gina left Ashley's bedroom because she was beginning to shake. She didn't know how to pull her girl out of this. She went to the kitchen and wondered who to call. Carrie? The useless Mrs. Downy? Finally, desperate, she got out her phone and dialed up the counselor, where she was forced to leave a message, which she left in low tones. "Mrs. Ross, it's Gina James and I have a crisis—Ashley has been dealt another terrible blow. Her ex-boyfriend's new girlfriend used Photoshop to create a naked picture of Ashley and texted it to the boy's entire directory and launched it on Facebook. Ashley has been sobbing for over two days, refuses to get out of bed and I found she smashed her phone with a hammer. She says she wants to die. I don't know what to do. Please help." And she left her number, which Simone Ross undoubtedly already had.

Then she sat at the table, where she was determined to wait for a return call, no matter how long it took.

Tears ran down her cheeks. She'd read about teen suicide and wondered if those kids had said to their parents, "I just want to die!" Young girls harassed on social media sites or in chat rooms, escaping the pain through self-destruction? Young boys picked on so re-

lentlessly they felt they couldn't go on? Who put a stop
to it all? Who intervened before it was too late?

The phone finally rang and she saw it was Simone
Ross.

"I want you to bring her in," Simone said. "I'll see
her in my office in one hour."

"What if she doesn't want to?" Gina asked.

"Bring her. Get help if you need help, but bring her.
Let's not play around with this. She's had a bad experience, is experiencing feelings of hopelessness and
worthlessness and I don't want it to escalate."

And so that's what Gina did. She told Ashley she
was taking her to the counselor and when Ashley re-
fused, Gina threatened to call Mac to help get her in
the car. And Gina reluctantly watched as Ashley threw
on a wrinkled and smelly sweat suit from the bottom
of the laundry pile. She just wanted her in the car; she
wasn't going to fuss about her wild hair, her sloppy appearance, nothing.

Once they were underway, Ashley said, "I don't
know why we bother. She can't fix this."

"We bother because you could use the support," Gina
said. "It's hard to get through stuff like this alone. You
need a team."

"I just need to go away...."

This was their first trip to Simone Ross's office during regular business hours and there was actually a re-
ceptionist behind the desk, a young woman with green
hair and eyebrow and lip piercings. She didn't even ask
who they were—she used the intercom to buzz Simone,
who came out immediately.

It wasn't until Simone and Ashley were behind
closed doors that Gina realized she hadn't called Stu!

Her boss had no idea she wasn't coming back to work
and by now the lunch crowd was beginning to arrive.
When he answered she said, "Stu, I'm so sorry!" And
then she burst into tears.

Eight

"Do you feel like telling me what's going on?" Simone asked Ashley.

Looking down into her lap, Ashley said, "Didn't my mom tell you?"

"Bits and pieces, but I'm interested in your version. Your mother is afraid, Ashley. She cares about you so much. Seems you're getting picked on. Exploited. Or something."

She lifted her eyes. "Picked on?" she asked, her eyes nothing more than swollen slits. She told her about the picture. "Downy's girlfriend sent it to everyone in the world! Including all the kids at school and half the adults in town including the football coach. She put it up on Facebook. It was taken down, but not before the whole world saw it and shared it."

"What about this is bothering you the most?" Simone asked.

"All of it," she said.

"Help me out with some feelings here," Simone entreated. "Hurt? Embarrassed? Angry? Sad?"

"All that," she said. "Totally humiliated. And they believe it. People believe it."

"So—your response to that is to do what?"

She thought for a moment that stretched out. "I called Downy to tell him how mean that was, but he didn't pick up. He won't answer my calls or texts. Not for any reason."

"And what did you do next?"

She shrugged. "Cried. Fell asleep. Woke up and cried."

"Have you gone to school? Talked to friends?"

Ashley shook her head. "I can't." Her voice was so small.

"Has it occurred to you that you're grieving?"

"You said I was, so yes. I guess."

"Have you been angry?" Simone asked. "Have you felt like this can't be true?"

She just shook her head. "When you see it, you know it's true. If I hadn't smashed my phone, I could show you. It's horrible. I know Downy wants to break up, I get it. But why would he let someone do this to me? Even if he hates me?"

"Tell me something, Ashley. Are you going to lay in bed forever? Are you going to get up at some point? Put on clean clothes? Call your friends? Go to school? Maybe go to a party or dance, like you used to?"

She shook her head dismally. "None of that stuff matters anymore...."

"Hold out your arm, like this," Simone said, demonstrating. "I'm going to pinch you a little bit—just to look at the elasticity of your skin."

"Why?" Ashley asked even as she held up her arm.

"Just to check something. I can see from your eyes

that your face is swollen and… Ah, you've been crying so much and refusing food and drink so much that you're dehydrated. I'm going to get you a bottled water."

"I don't really want anything," Ashley said. "My stomach has been upset."

"I know," Simone said, but she got up, anyway. She went to the cupboard behind her desk and brought Ashley some water. "Try a few sips, please. I need to talk to your mother for just a minute. You'll be all right here for a few minutes, won't you?"

Ashley shrugged before she nodded. "What for?"

"I'll explain. Just give me a second and try to get some of that water down. Okay?"

"What if I just throw up again?"

"Trash can, darling. It's right there. I'll be right back."

Simone went into the outer office and Gina was immediately on her feet. "Sit down, Gina." Simone took the chair beside her. "Ashley is showing symptoms of depression and I think she needs medication. If she were older, I'd just get her a script, but given her age and the severity of her symptoms, I want to admit her under the care of a psychiatrist. She's dehydrated and despondent. I gave her a bottle of water, but she's uncertain she can keep it down. She might need an IV, which I can't administer."

"Depression? How bad do you think it is?"

"She's isolating, not eating, sleeping all the time. She hasn't bathed. She's dirty and doesn't care. This isn't like her, is it?"

Gina shook her head. Her lips quivered. "That damn Downy," she whispered.

"The reason I want to admit her, Gina—this could

be an emotional reaction to a bad breakup or it could be classic depression, which usually presents between the ages of fifteen and thirty. Is there depression in your family? In the extended family?"

Gina looked down. "I'm not sure. I'll ask my mother, but we've been a family of women. My dad left when I was just five. I was pregnant at fifteen, delivered Ashley at sixteen and my boyfriend..." Tears came to her eyes for the first time in so many years. "Long gone," she said weakly.

"It does run in families sometimes. I'm not saying she's suffering from clinical depression but it's entirely possible. If you can check with your mother and even Ashley's paternal biological family, it would give us more information. Meanwhile, I want to take her to city hospital in North Bend. We can take her together, check her in. She'll be safe there." Simone reached for Gina's hand. "I don't want to take any risks here. She could be a danger to herself."

"You think she'd kill herself?" Gina asked.

"I don't know. I worry that she might let herself die if there's not an intervention. There's really no point in risking this. Come with me to explain all this to Ashley. Then I should make a couple of calls."

And Simone went back to Ashley without another word.

Gina followed. She listened numbly while Simone explained to Ashley—depression, dehydration, isolation, risk. Ashley merely nodded.

"I want you to stay at least overnight in the hospital, Ashley, so we can give you an antidepressant and monitor the way you respond. It might be for a few days, but I'm fairly sure it won't be long-term."

"Long-term?" Ash asked.

"Some patients are critical and really need hospitalization for a couple of weeks, maybe a month. I don't think that's the case, but you need medical intervention—you're sick to your stomach, dehydrated, can't get out of bed. Let's take care of this."

She nodded weakly. "No matter what you do, I'm not going back to school."

"I understand," Simone said.

And Gina thought, *Please God, let me be as sharp as she is when I finally achieve my degree.*

Tears were wetting Gina's cheeks. She'd sacrificed everything to keep this girl healthy, safe and well-adjusted, yet one eighteen-year-old boy had just about ruined them all!

"Thanks," she heard Simone say into her cell phone. "Yes, her mother will handle the forms and we'll be there within the hour. I'd rather not go through admitting. Oh, thank you—we'll meet you on the third floor."

She disconnected and stood from her chair. "Let's go get this difficulty taken care of."

Mac was surprised to see an Oregon State Police Trooper vehicle pull into town. Mac had been standing outside his office, chatting with old Sam Connie about the weather when Joe Metcalf parked and got out. He was more than just another officer to Mac. He was the man his aunt Lou had been seeing for the past year and a half, though she'd done her level best to keep him secret until six months ago.

Joe gave a nod to Sam then shook Mac's hand.

"Looks mighty official," Sam said. "I'll leave you to it." And off he wandered, using a cane as leverage.

"What's up?" Mac asked.

"I should probably ask you," Joe responded. "Lou says the place is falling apart."

"Not the town, thank God. Just a few people in it. But they're all real important to me." Then Mac held open the door to the office so they could go inside. "I guess Lou told you about Cee Jay coming to town?"

"Yeah, she's pretty sideways about that. And now I hear Gina's daughter is in the hospital?"

"Did she tell you about it?" Mac asked. "That sexting business?"

He nodded. "And the amount of bullying on social networks is out of control—everyone from vulnerable young teens to rich and famous stars... Too many victims. Lou said there's some question about Ashley's stability...."

"She's been in the hospital for three days, but it appears she's going to be all right. She's a lot better in three days. Lots. She's depressed, but not clinically depressed. I have to admit, if someone sent a naked picture of me to all my friends, I might get a little whacked out of joint. I worry about Gina. Her only child. I wish I could get her away from all that, but I worry about leaving Lou and the kids. The second I leave the house, Cee Jay could decide on a surprise visit."

Joe tilted his head and smiled slyly. "I might be able to help out with this situation," he said.

Gina went to visit Ashley in the hospital. Many of the patients in her ward at the hospital were being evaluated for long-term care. Some were there by court order and some were either drugged and hazy and others looked, on the surface at least, like perfectly normal young people between the ages of fourteen and twenty-five, their issues secret from Gina. Not all of them were allowed visitors.

Ashley embraced Gina. "I'm better," she said. "I really am."

"How do you know?" Gina asked.

"I've talked about it a lot—the whole thing, from breaking up to the mean sexting. Did you know that's what it's called and it happens a lot? I can't think of one time that's happened at my school. I mean, there were mean rumor things, but nothing like this."

"I guess I didn't think it ever would," Gina said. She looked around. "There seem to be just a few young people here. Lots of older people."

"All ages," Ashley said. "There are a couple of old people who hurt themselves by accident and they're going to go to a home where they'll be safe and cared for—they're sometimes completely normal and sometimes in some time warp." And she smiled.

"Do you feel safe here, Ash?" Gina asked.

She nodded. "The only thing I don't like is that they lock the ward doors at night—that bothers me a lot. Like what if I need to get out for some reason, like a fire or something? But there's a button to push—a bell and a light. Besides that, I feel okay."

A young girl in a hospital gown over scrubs walked past them and lifted a hand to Ashley. Her wrists were bandaged. Ashley looked at Gina. "That is what you think it is. Not the first try, either. Look, I know I was pretty bad, but no matter how bad I looked, I wasn't that bad. I wanted to disappear, I didn't want to *do* anything to myself."

"Oh, Ash," she said, hugging her again. "What turned you around? You're so much more like yourself!"

"Seeing how far down the hill you can roll, for one thing. But the nurse in charge keeps reminding me that sometimes what a person needs most is medicine. I had an IV for a whole day—that made me feel a lot better. And this medicine? It's not supposed to really kick in for a few weeks, so I doubt it's really the medicine, but if Simone insists I try it, I guess I will. Do you think it's normal that I still want to kill Downy?"

Gina couldn't help but smile. In fact, she liked the sound of that so much better than "I just don't want to live." But she did know Ashley would never hurt anyone. She was kind to the core of her being.

"Is Gram okay?" Ashley asked. "She's not all worked up about this, is she?"

"She was very worried. She's relieved you're under a doctor's care. When I tell her how great you look and sound, she'll be more relieved."

"Doctor, phhhhttt. I saw the doctor for three minutes. The nurse is running this show. Her name is Judy. She has zero patience, but I can see where some of the patients would push her around if she gave them an inch. I stay out of her way. She doesn't like anyone. I told Simone she was mean as a snake and hated everyone and Simone smiled so big I thought her ears would fall off. Think that means Simone isn't crazy about the nurse?"

Gina felt her eyes well with tears and she squeezed Ashley's hands.

"What's the matter, Mom? Why are you crying?"

She just shook her head. "I was afraid you'd never be a smart-ass again, never make me laugh again...."

"Have you talked to Simone today?"

"Not today. Why?" Gina answered.

"She asked if I'd stay three more days. She said it's up to me. I said I didn't want to and she said I've gotten so much better in just a couple of days, she'd really like me to stay a little longer. I said okay. But not any more than that."

"I'll pick you up the first second you can leave," Gina said. "You sure about this decision?"

She nodded.

"And when I bring you home, you're going back to school?"

"I guess," she said with a shrug. "I can't exactly quit school. It'll be awful, though."

"Maybe not, Ash. You have good friends there."

"I also have some jerks there."

"As it is in the world," Gina said. "Good people and jerks and millions you haven't met yet. I'm so relieved you're stronger."

"I'm sorry I scared you," she said. "I'm sorry I gave up and hit the bottom."

"I'm just so glad we found the right support," Gina said. "Because I love you so much. You're my life, you know."

Mac had convinced Gina they had earned a night away from Thunder Point and with Ashley in safe hands, they should take their chance. Once Ashley came home, he knew Gina would want to be on hand. But, with Carrie's approval, they packed overnight bags and left town around two that afternoon.

"Exactly where are we going?" Gina asked Mac. "I really don't like being away from my phone. Just in case

Ashley needs me. She was fine yesterday. In fact, she was better than she's been in a month, but you know…"

"Don't worry," he said, reaching for her hand, giving it a squeeze. "Carrie promises to keep your phone close all night in case anyone calls about Ashley and she has my cell number. I had a break today—I was talking to Joe, telling him how ripped up our families are, how much you and I needed a little break, but neither of us felt like we dared get away. And he said he had this little one room fishing cabin on Lawrence Lake—close by but not too close. When I told him I'd love to borrow it but didn't want to leave the family with Cee Jay lurking, he offered to spend the night at my house. If Lou needs anything or anyone, he's right there. He's savvy—he wouldn't let Cee Jay get by him."

"Wow," she said. "Why didn't you just tell me?"

"I did just tell you," he said, smiling at her. His cell phone chirped and he glanced at the caller ID. "It's Carrie," he said, passing it to her.

She grabbed it. "Hello?" she answered urgently. Then she visibly relaxed, listening. "Really?" she said. "Oh, God, Mom, that's such good news." She thanked Carrie for calling her and ended the call. She looked at Mac. "Ashley called my phone—she had a nice talk with my mom. She's feeling good, looking forward to coming home in a couple of days and asked my mom to call Eve, tell Eve she'll talk to her as soon as she gets home. Just that little thing makes me feel so much better. Now maybe I can feel a little less guilty about escaping for a night."

"I'm going to heat up a casserole and some of your mom's fresh bread I found in our freezer, we're going to build a fire and drink a couple of glasses of wine, get naked if you want to or we can talk—unload some of that worry you've had the past few weeks...."

"What about your worry?" she asked.

"What I really want to do is just hold you. God, Gina, there have been times I've wondered if we'd ever catch a break."

Gina seemed to sink into the passenger seat of his truck. She leaned her head back and sighed. Then she slowly lifted his hand to her lips, kissing his palm, then each of his fingertips. "How far?" she asked.

He smiled. "I might have to pull over," he said, his voice husky.

The late-April sun was going down later each day so they had some daylight left by the time the reached the cabin. The afternoon sun was casting long shadows from the pines surrounding the lake. It wasn't quite four when Mac pulled up to the cabin. There was a long lawn down to a dock, a bass boat lying facedown on the grass. "Here we are," he said.

He pulled a cooler and a canvas bag out of the truck bed, carrying it to the cabin. He unlocked the door and let Gina step inside. He followed her and they both just stood inside the door, taking it in.

Mac wished he had asked Joe how long he'd had this place because it wasn't what he expected at all. It was much too nice to be a bachelor's fishing cabin. On one wall there was an efficiency kitchen with a small stovetop and oven, a few cupboards but a full-size refrigerator/freezer. A small table for four sat in the corner. Along another wall were a sofa and recliner along with a couple of accent tables. On the third wall, a bed and small chest of drawers and on the fourth, a fireplace and set of double French–style doors on one side of the hearth and a single door on the other. The single door stood ajar and inside appeared to be a very upscale and large bathroom. Now that had to be a woman's touch; bathrooms are very important to women. For men, not so much. He briefly wondered what history Lou had with this place, then put that thought from his mind.

Mac put down the cooler and bag and opened the doors to a small covered porch that looked out onto the lake. There were two chairs facing the lake and a small table—a nice summer retreat, but not exactly for a solitary man. The chairs and table were covered with weather-proof drapes.

While he was checking out the deck and lake, Gina had taken the cooler and canvas bag to the kitchen. He wondered if this place would be available to borrow in summer; he wouldn't mind getting her out there in that bass boat, rocking with the waves.

"Hey," she called. "Look what I found."

"Let me start this fire first," he said, closing the doors and checking out the fireplace. He should've known—there was a switch. It was gas. Up here in the forest, logs and floating ash were a risk. Wildfire wasn't out of the question. Joe was a practical man. And as the shadows lengthened, the late afternoon grew cool and the night would be wonderfully cold, just right for holding someone close.

When he joined her in the small galley kitchen, she was holding a container of vanilla ice cream, spoon in hand. She scooped some out and held it toward his lips.

"This isn't old, is it?"

"I'm the daughter of a cook, Mac. I know how to read the expiration date." She spooned it into his mouth and he took it in.

And his eyes, locked on hers, heated. Bright blue turned to hot, dark blue. He leaned toward her and touched her lips with his. His hand found her waist and he leaned into her, parting her lips with an icy tongue, kissing her, sharing the ice cream, causing her to moan and lick his mouth. The moan turned into a groan and she tipped back her head, letting him take her mouth. His hand was in her soft golden hair, cradling the back of her head, keeping her mouth under his. He pulled her against him and he was instantly hard. It was a long moment before the ice cream matched the temperature of their mouths. Their lips were sticky and she stood on her toes to lick them.

"Cold," she whispered against his mouth.

"Hot," he said. "Real hot."

She put the container on the table and fed him another spoonful, immediately offering her mouth, which he took, letting her lick the ice cream from him.

And he got harder.

"I thought we'd make it till sunset," he said. "I don't think we will…"

"Dessert first?" she asked.

"Dessert all night, maybe. Want to play a little ice cream game?"

"I do," she said. "I've never done anything like this before."

"Me, either. I bet we get the hang of it right away."

"I've never been this alone with you before," she reminded him. It was always catch as catch can at either her house or his, always the possibility someone might come home unexpectedly, a reality that made them far too quick about their lovemaking. But they were alone in the woods, on a lake, doors locked, a carton of ice cream handy. "Oh, God," she said, rubbing up against him.

He led her the short distance to the bed. The fire was blazing, the room was dim and pleasant, and he put the carton down. He slowly undressed her, intermittently sharing a bite of ice cream with her. When she was naked, he got rid of his clothes as quickly as possible, joining her on the bed. Her hand went to his raging hard-on and he groaned.

"I better cool you down," he said hoarsely. He grabbed himself a mouthful of ice cream and kissed her, but before he'd let her scoop it out of his mouth, he covered her erect nipple with the sweet ice cream and she arched against him. Her nipple got harder and he moved to the other one, licking and sucking.

"Oh, my God," she whispered. He moved back to her mouth, kissing her deeply. She smiled against his lips. "Who knew?"

"Turn you on, baby?"

"See for yourself," she challenged.

He slid his hand over her flat tummy and with curious fingers, found her ready for him. But he wasn't done with her.

He trailed another mouthful of ice cream over her belly button, then down to the apex of her legs, pushing them apart, putting his cold mouth on her soft moist folds, licking her hard. She squirmed under him, pushing herself against his mouth, the sweet noises that came from her making him pleasure her even more. He took another mouthful, just enough to make his tongue cold, then went after her again, holding her hips down while he lapped at her. Her fingers threaded through his hair and wouldn't release him until he lifted his head, only long enough to grab a little more ice cream, torturing her in the best possible way.

He went back to her mouth, whispering against her lips. "I have to get in you," he said. "I can't wait another second."

"Want me to cool *you* down?" she offered.

"No. I want you to come." And with that he entered, drove deep and hard, one hand on her butt, the other on the back of her head, holding her mouth against his. He growled with the effort it took to hold back long enough for her to make her moment. Thankfully it didn't take long. He moved a little, deep in her, and she clenched, bit his lip, whimpered, and he felt her wonderful spasms. She held him tight, wrapped her legs around him to hold him and went a little wild with her climax. There was nothing more for him to do but join her and it was shattering. His eyes watered with the intensity and he flew. For a few seconds there he was in another solar system.

And then, panting, they slowly came back to earth. He lifted his head enough to look down into her eyes. "When I'm in you like this, I feel like I could lift the world."

She smiled sleepily. "We're all sticky."

"I'll shower you," he promised. "But I might make you sticky all over again. You make me wild." He kissed her lightly. "I have to admit, I never looked forward to a shower so much. Or to ice cream. In fact, I don't think I ever liked ice cream this much before."

She laughed softly.

"What?"

"I don't think I'll ever look at a pint of vanilla the same way again."

"Good." He stroked the hair back from her brow. "Gina, I want you to know something. Even though I was married, I never had anything like this. You're brand-new. And I love you more than you can imagine."

She put a palm against his cheek. "I know, Mac. Somehow I know. And I've never spent the night with a man before...."

He pulled back in surprise, holding himself up with his arms. "Seriously?"

"I dated, I had a relationship with one guy that included sex, but I had Ashley. I didn't stay away from her overnight. Besides, I never felt like this before."

He was quiet for a minute, just looking down at her. "You know what this means, don't you?"

"Hmm?"

"We really have to find a way to get married...."

"Mac, our lives are a complete disaster...."

"I know," he said. "But we'll get them straightened out somehow. We have to figure out how we're going to sleep in the same bed every night. There are lots of things to work out—and we'll work them out somehow." Then he frowned. "You will say yes, won't you?"

She laughed at him. "If we ever figure it out and get our families on track, I'll say yes," she promised. "But right now I'm hungry...."

"I can warm up that casserole...."

"I think I can make do on ice cream."

Nine

Cooper liked the tempo of his life, and this was a first
for him. It was almost the end of April, and virtually
every other day was sunny. Sometimes they enjoyed the
sun all day long. He had something of a schedule going.
He liked schedules. He had been in Thunder Point for
six months and felt more settled than he had in places
he'd lived for much longer. After making sure there
was coffee and sweets left for the beachcombers out
on the deck, he often went out on the bay on his Jet Ski
or paddleboard. Sometimes Sarah came out very early,
tying Hamlet up at the dock and going out on the bay
with him. He had many chores during the day—fixing
things, cleaning things, buying things, taking delivery
on things so the bar/deli could run smoothly. Evenings
he served drinks and food—deli food—because the
sunset was astonishing in its beauty and drew people
to the beach and to his deck. And many evenings Sarah
was with him, like this evening.

They'd locked up the bar at about nine, gone upstairs to his room, shared a meal prepared by Carrie,
made excellent love and cuddled in front of the fire—

a second-floor extension of the hearth he'd had built in the bar—and watched TV.

The principal people in his life had their issues— Mac's ex had been around, disrupting his family life, and Gina's daughter had suffered some sort of emotional problems. Sarah was still troubled on and off about her future with the Coast Guard, except when he was holding her—then she seemed to have no worries. But his little beach bar made a surprising amount of money and he loved it. All things considered, from Cooper's stand point, life was pretty stable.

And then the phone rang.

He looked first at the caller ID—his parents were calling. Then he glanced at his watch—it was 11:00 p.m., 1:00 a.m. in New Mexico. Trying to mask worry he felt given the time of night he answered the phone. "Hello?"

"Coop," his father said. "Sorry about the time, son."

"I'm up, but it's the middle of the night there. What's going on, Dad?"

"I just got a call from a man named Spencer Lawson, Coop. He's married to Bridget."

"I know who he is," Cooper said. At one time Cooper had been engaged to Bridget. They parted over ten years ago. First they broke off their engagement because they just weren't on the same page with all that meant. Then they ended it completely when Bridget stopped seeing him because she'd met someone else, someone she ultimately married. "What did he want?"

"He left a number, said it was urgent that he get in touch with you. I told him I'd call you, but I wouldn't give him your number."

For a moment, Cooper had a sinking feeling in his gut. "Is she okay?"

"No, Cooper. Apparently she's sick or something. I tried to get the details out of him but he said he'd only discuss it with you. I'm sorry, that's the best I could do."

"I'll take care of it," he said. "Give me his number."

After Hank Senior reeled off the digits, he added, "He said to call any time of day, don't worry if it's late or early—he'd be there. And, Coop? Let me know what this is all about, will you?"

He let go a dry laugh. "If it's not too embarrassing," Cooper said.

He hung up and stared at the number. Then he went to his sofa to sit beside Sarah. "Very strange," he said.

"What is it?"

"I told you I was engaged twice," he said. "The first time was to Bridget Cunningham. We dated for about six months, got engaged, couldn't agree on anything, broke up pretty soon after. I was doing contract flying for a security company that was outsourced by the Army—I was away a lot. Out of the country most of the time. After breaking up, we were on and off for a while. We were young—we knew pretty quick it wasn't going to work."

"What went wrong, Cooper?" she asked softly.

"I'm not sure," he said. "We didn't seem to want the same things. She expected me to find a more stable job, for one thing, so I'd be around all the time and stability was not exactly my middle name. It wasn't too long before she told me there was someone else, but you know me—I mean the younger me. I didn't take her too seriously. I hadn't talked to her for a long time—months—and called her when I was back in the States. She told me she was married. To this guy," he said, showing her the phone number.

She ran a finger around his ear. "Did she break your heart?"

"A little bit," he said. "I got over that pretty quick. I haven't even thought about her in a long time. Now her husband needs me to call him—says it's urgent."

"Call him," she said.

"It's late, and I see by the area code, they're still in Texas. He did tell my dad not to worry about the time. Maybe tomorrow..."

She laughed at him. "Men and women are so different. Aren't you curious?"

"I can be curious until tomorrow," he said.

"Listen, if you don't want to call him while I'm here, I was planning to go home, anyway," she said.

He grinned at her. "Well, I never thought I'd say this, especially to a woman, but I don't have any secrets from you." He punched in the numbers. The call was answered on the first ring.

"Stand by," Spencer said rather than "hello." Cooper could hear some moving around; he heard a door close. Then came the hello in a stronger voice.

"Spencer Lawson?" Cooper asked.

"Yes. Cooper?"

"You asked my father to forward a message to me? You wanted me to call?"

Cooper heard him take a deep breath. "There's no way to ease you into this, Cooper. Bridget wants to see you. She's dying."

He sat up straighter. "What?"

"Cancer. She's been fighting it like a trouper, but the days of the fight are over. We suspended chemo, hospice is here, her time is short. And she really needs to see you."

"Why?" he asked.

"Trust me, it's important. You need money for travel? For time away from work? Whatever it takes, I'll cover it."

"Spencer, come on—we don't have any unfinished business. That was all a long time ago. She told me she was happy with you."

"We had some very good years," he said. Cooper could hear the emotion in his voice. "This disease has been hell. Cooper, you have to come. She's hanging on and I don't think she'll let go until she sees you. Please. She's bad."

"Can't you tell me why?"

"She has some things to say to you," he said. "She wants to talk to you before she dies. And she doesn't have much time."

"God," Cooper said. "She's not even forty! This isn't about amends or anything, is it? Because we're square, me and Bridget. It wasn't meant to be, all right? There's nothing to work out—I could tell her that on the phone if it would make things easier."

"Cooper, I want her to have whatever she asks for. We're staying in her parents' house in San Antonio. All she wants is to talk to you. It might take a couple of hours, that's all. Where are you? Are you in a foreign country? Can you come, even if it's a quick trip? I'll pay the—"

"I got it," he said. "I just don't like mysteries and secrets, that's all."

"I feel ya, pal. We've been living with cancer for almost three years now. Talk about mysteries and secrets. I'll text you the address. You have my cell phone number—let me know when you can come. Hurry, please. And, Cooper? Bring a suit."

Cooper just sat and looked at his phone. He hung his head. He felt Sarah's hand on his back, gently soothing. He turned to look at her. "She's dying. Apparently soon. She wants to see me."

"Oh, Cooper," Sarah said. "Maybe she wants to clear her conscience about your romantic falling out or something."

"She doesn't have to do that."

"Well, apparently she thinks she does."

"I have this place to run," he complained.

"I'll help. Rawley can open, I'll come over after work. I have the weekend off. I'll let Landon hang out and help—he'll love that. It'll be okay. But I can't be here in the morning to explain things to Rawley—I'm flying tomorrow."

Cooper gave a half smile and went through his phone directory. He hit the call button.

"What's that?" she asked.

"I bought him a phone. Now let's see if he'll answer it."

"What?" came Rawley's gruff voice.

"Well, I'll be damned," Cooper said. "You didn't throw it in the ocean."

"It's late."

"I can hear your TV," Cooper said.

"That don't mean I'm awake."

"All right, sorry about the time. I just got a call from someone—an old friend is real sick. I have to go pay a visit. I'll be gone a couple of days and Sarah says she can help out. Can you handle things around here?"

"Don't I usually?"

"I'd like to think I contribute here and there," Cooper said.

"Just go do it," Rawley said.

"Listen, if there are complications or schedule problems, just hang a sign on the door—closed for family emergency. All right?"

"I'll handle it," Rawley said.

"Thanks, man. Hey, and you kept the phone!"

"It was inconvenient. But I got games, books and music on this phone. Decent contraption." And he hung up.

It was only minutes after Cooper called Rawley that Sarah left, promising to be there to cover for him the next evening. She took the Razor across the beach, going slowly to avoid any people who might be walking or sitting on the sand. When she was leaving him, he was understandably quiet. Melancholy.

Timing was an interesting phenomenon. She had just been thinking that it was time to let Cooper in on her secret, to talk to him about her pending assignment. But she hadn't, and then the phone call came. It was funny that Cooper had been anxious to clear the air about any lingering ties she might feel toward her ex-husband, Derek, but she had never considered that there might be relationships in his past that hadn't been fully dealt with. This woman, this dying woman…was this something that haunted him? Had he, like Sarah, harbored a feeling of failure, of grief? And he *had* told her, there had been two engagements….

There were more things to talk about than just her past marriage.

Sarah didn't fear having a rebound lover in Cooper, but she did fear leaving her career, putting all her eggs in his basket and then learning that despite all he said, he was the one who couldn't commit, couldn't make it last. Where would that leave her?

Suddenly her options shrank yet again. She tried to envision Cooper's reaction to her dilemma. He would tell her not to worry, to stay here with him, to enjoy the town, the beach, the business and Landon's senior year at Thunder Point High. And what if that didn't work out the way he expected it to, as his two previous attempts had not? And if she had separated from her Coast Guard career and found herself a year later not only alone, but also unable to support herself? Unable to help Landon with college?

Yes, Cooper had always seemed the transparent one while Sarah thought of herself as complicated. Yet wasn't it really the other way around? He'd been a loner, a wanderer and had twice tried to settle down with one woman. And had failed both times. Had there been more than two women he'd promised to love forever?

From the first time since she'd met him, since she'd fallen in love with him, she realized she was probably the better relationship risk. The truth of her situation was not exaggerated—the demise of her short marriage was not her failing. Her ex-husband was a serial cheater and she should have known, but turned a blind eye because she wanted a family life so much.

She would never do that again. And she would never close her eyes to reality again, either.

That woman in Texas, that woman who was dying and wanted to see him one last time. There was obviously some unfinished business there, something he had never thought to mention to her.

Sarah had a feeling she wasn't going to sleep soundly tonight....

There were a lot of beautiful cities in Texas, and San Antonio was definitely one of them. Cooper flew into San Antonio, which required two plane changes from Eugene. He put the address Spencer had given him into the GPS on the rental car and drove through the lush rolling hills to the suburb where Bridget's parents lived. He'd been to their house before, but he'd never have been able to find it on his own this many years later. He retired his torn jeans, T-shirt, leather jacket and boots and wore a white dress shirt, khakis and suede shoes. He felt as if he was going for a job interview.

He'd met Bridge when he was about twenty-five. Or was that twenty-six? He was at a lake party and, in typical Cooper fashion, he picked out the prettiest girl in sight. Cooper liked beach or lake parties because the girls didn't wear much. Bridge was blonde, stacked, green-eyed and sexy as all hell.

He was working for a civilian contractor who supplied helicopters to UN missions and private sectors abroad. They were "wet lease" copters, which meant they came with a crew. He had a high-level security clearance and when he was sent out on a mission, it could be for weeks at a time. At that time he was living near Fort Sam Houston because he liked the San Antonio area. He'd always loved the river walk, the Alamo, in fact the whole city was something special.

He asked Bridget out. He took her home from the

party. And he fell hard and fast. So did she, as far as he could tell. Until he got another assignment a couple of weeks later they spent every minute together at her apartment. For a while it worked. She even asked him if they could get married and he said yes. Why not?

He bought her a ring on one of his trips home and she loved it. She took him to meet the family—a brother and a sister, parents, grandparents. And then she said, "If we're going to get married, you have to find something to do for work that doesn't take you away six months of the year—especially away to scary places you can't talk about."

And then the arguing commenced. He was young; he wasn't ready to have lead in his shoes, and to put down roots. He was also selfish—he wanted it all. He was still hooked on adventure, but he didn't want to give up a woman like Bridget. He thought he might be ready for a nice suburban life in a few years. Eventually he came back from a trip to Somalia and she informed him, this just wouldn't work for her. She wanted a more stable family life. She was the first woman to tell him he had trouble with commitment, with real intimacy. She gave him back the ring, but they got together a few more times when he wasn't traveling.

In fact, that was the crux of it—they couldn't agree on anything out of bed. In the sack, *everything* worked. All he wanted was for Bridget to put up with his job, his traveling, welcome him home like the hot mama she was. All she wanted was someone she could depend on all the time. And it made her furious that she couldn't resist him.

It made him feel just fine, however.

Eventually, maybe six or eight months after the engagement was off and the back-and-forth had gone on too long she said she'd met someone. He remembered, he tried to cajole her into once more for old time's sake and she told him he was a pig.

Well, she was probably right. He was less piggish these days. He was a lot more conscious of the feelings of others. It was something he assumed came with maturity. He hoped so, anyway.

A few minutes later Cooper pulled up to the well-groomed, large ranch-style home. It was painted light green with white shutters and a dark green front door—the kind of house Bridge had wanted to live in, to raise a family in. There were a lot of cars and he felt his heart clutch. He hoped she hadn't died. He hoped she wasn't too near death to say whatever it was she had to say. He hadn't been a very good boyfriend or fiancé; maybe she just wanted to ream him out one more time before she crossed over. Who was he to deny her that pleasure?

He knocked on the front door. He was afraid to ring the bell—what if there was grieving. Mrs. Cunningham answered and God bless her, she had aged far more than ten years. Cooper couldn't even imagine losing a family member like this—dying by inches. He put out his hand. "Mrs. Cunningham, do you remember me?" he asked.

"Of course, Coop. Thank you for coming. I realize it's a lot to ask of you."

"I'm sorry you're going through this," he said.

"Is that him?" he heard someone ask. Then the man who must be Spencer came into the foyer. "Cooper?"

"Yes," he said, putting out his hand again. "Spencer?"

"Nice to meet you, Cooper. Can I get you a drink or something?"

In fact, Spencer looked as if he could use a drink. So did Mrs. Cunningham.

"No, thanks. How's she doing?"

"She's hanging in there. Hospice does a good job of keeping her comfortable. I don't know how to prepare you, Cooper—she's not the same girl you dated. Her appearance is—" Then he ran a hand around his sweaty neck. "We converted the sun porch into a hospital room so she could be here with the family. Our house is smaller and less accessible—two-story and all. I'm sure you want to get on with this. Follow me."

In fact, Cooper *didn't* want to get on with it. He wanted to bolt. But that ship had sailed and here he was. He walked through a family room. Mr. Cunningham and a couple of younger men were watching TV but the volume was turned low. There were three kids and a teenager playing a board game at the dining room table and two women puttered around the kitchen, whispering. The house had a pall of death over it—all subdued and respectfully quiet.

He had a sudden and profound understanding of wounded animals sneaking off into the forest to die alone and without an audience.

The room was large and while the blinds were partially closed, he could see that if opened, it would be a bright and sunny room. It was dominated by a hospital bed, the back raised and the woman in the bed was not his Bridget. This woman looked a hundred years old. She had only yellow fuzz on her head and she was slumped over, her bony arms appearing spidery, her fingers too long. She had an IV hooked up, and a woman who must be a nurse busied herself keeping Bridget comfortable. The accoutrements of illness were present—wheelchair, bedside table holding a couple of glasses of liquid, straws, basin, towels, bedpan. There was a cot beside the bed—someone slept there, close by her side.

Spencer leaned over her, kissed her forehead and said, "Honey, he's here."

Bridget roused slowly. "Cooper?" she asked.

Spencer stroked her naked head and she opened her eyes. They were no longer that bright, fiery green but pale and weak. She tried to sit up in the bed, but Spencer wouldn't allow her struggle. With strong hands under her armpits, he pulled her up. The nurse left immediately and Spencer backed away from the bed. Bridget patted the bed beside her, indicating Cooper should sit down and Cooper, feeling like the biggest coward alive, hesitated.

"Cooper, I'm sorry for all the secrecy," she said, her voice much stronger than he expected. "This is my fault, but I swear to you, I didn't know. Less than six months ago I learned something you need to know about. We did a lot of tests of everyone in the family and extended family in search of a bone marrow donor—I was too sick for my own bone marrow to be harvested. That was when we discovered something. Cooper, you have a son. My son. Spencer and I always assumed he was ours, but the testing showed… Cooper, I'm sorry. I really didn't think it was possible."

Cooper was stunned. He couldn't speak. She must be mistaken, surely. He said nothing because in his head he knew these must be the delusional ramblings of a very sick woman.

"I started seeing Spencer a few months after we

ended our engagement but you and I, we always had one last goodbye, didn't we. We just discovered this and it seemed logical to wait until later, after Austin was older.... But then I decided at the last minute, I couldn't leave this to them." She made a sound that was like a chuckle. "Last-minute. That's putting it mildly. Austin is ten years old and very smart and we explained it to him. I wanted to be the one to tell you. And to plead with you—know him if you want to, but please don't take him away from his father."

Take him away? Cooper thought. *I'm not sure I even want to have a kid.* Finally, fighting through the shock, he said, "You can't be sure."

"I'm sure. There's no other possibility. But you should have tests—DNA. We'll cover the costs, of course. I just can't move on unless my conscience is clear. I didn't know. I really didn't know."

"You didn't suspect, after we were together...?"

She shook her head. "When I first realized I was pregnant, you'd been gone for a month. Austin was born two weeks early and weighed seven pounds. Possibly he was actually two weeks late, instead. That aside, he doesn't have Spencer's DNA. And there is no other possibility." She reached for Cooper's hand. "I'm sorry. I never would have kept something like that from you."

"You're sure?" he asked.

She nodded. "He knows. We told him Spencer is his father of the heart, but he has someone else's genes. You and Spencer will have to work things out." She coughed weakly. "Please consider their relationship. I'm out of time, Cooper."

"All right, sweetheart," Spencer said. "You've done your part. I'm going to get Cooper here a drink and send

Mary Ann back in here to give you something. Sleep a little if you can. I'll be back soon."

"Thank you," she said to her husband.

But Cooper didn't move.

"Cooper?" Spencer said. "Come on, let's talk."

Cooper followed numbly. He passed the kids at the dining room table—two of them were boys in the right age group and he wondered if one of them was his biological son. Spencer led him into a study and closed them in.

"Mary Ann is going to give her a big load of morphine," he said, going directly to a small wet bar. "She's been holding off today, wanting to be alert when you got here. Scotch? Bourbon? Beer? Anything."

"Yeah," Cooper said. "Anything."

Spencer poured two scotches and handed him one.

"Austin?" Cooper asked.

Spencer laughed. "I'm from Missouri and was down here for a teaching job. I always expected it to be temporary, but it turned out to be good for me. Bridget and I escaped to Austin sometimes. It's a pretty town. I always thought she got pregnant there, but..." He shook his head. "Sorry you were blindsided, Cooper. She wanted to be the one to tell you. She didn't say so, but I suspect she hoped that her appearance would influence you into letting Austin stay with me, live with me. It's what he wants, but he's only ten."

Cooper took a sip of his drink and just shook his head.

"You're taking this pretty well...."

Spencer laughed and shook his head. "Yeah, right. Well, I didn't always take it real well. It took a lot of discussion, a lot of figuring the dates, a lot of jealousy on my part. Try to imagine finding out your son isn't your son."

"She didn't cheat, Spencer. She told me she'd met someone—she'd just started seeing you. She hoped it would work out better than it had with me. I didn't even take it seriously. I figured eventually we'd end up together, but the next time I got back to the States, she was getting married. I didn't know about the baby. She never said anything about that."

"I'll be honest with you, Cooper. I was disappointed. Pissed. But I've had six months to think about things. Six really tough months—Bridget has been so sick. All I want is to go easy on Austin."

"Why would I punish a kid by doing something like taking him away from the only father he knows?"

"Thanks. That'll give everyone some peace of mind, his grandparents being here, as well. Especially Bridge—she needs reassurance. And..." He turned away for a second, took a sip of his drink before turning back. "I can't even think about losing them both."

"I want to know him," Cooper said. "I mean, once we're sure..."

"We're sure, but I understand."

"Are there more? Kids?"

Spencer shook his head. "We tried. We were just starting some fertility workups. That's how we found out Bridget was sick. We did chemo instead. We thought we were beating the son of a bitch a few times."

"What kind of cancer is it?"

"Started as colon cancer, but it's just about everywhere now. Really, Bridget has been on borrowed time for a while. I'm sorry about this, Cooper. This is no way to find out."

He just threw back his drink. He believed her—that she didn't know. And how could he complain in the face of what these people were going through?

"Would you like to meet him?" Spencer asked.

Cooper just nodded. "What do I say to him?"

"Whatever you want. Maybe, 'Nice to meet you?'"

"Should we wait until there's a test to confirm this?"

"We'll get that done, too. We have the supplies—a kit. You could get by with a swab. We'll send it in for you. It could be as long as six weeks."

"Bridget isn't going to make it six weeks, is she?" Cooper asked.

"I don't think she's going to make it six days," Spencer said. "But she knows how this is going to come out, Cooper."

"Can I say goodbye?" Cooper asked.

Spencer smiled. "I think that would be nice. Let's go do that before morphine takes over." As they were leaving the study, Spencer put a hand on his shoulder. "You're a good sport, Cooper. I can't imagine something like this complicating my life right now."

The guy's going through cancer, losing his wife, and Cooper is a good sport? He was suddenly ashamed. When he got back to Bridget, he could see at once that some of the tension of pain had left her.

Cooper sat down on the edge of the bed and lifted her hand into his. "Bridge," he whispered. "Are you awake?" She nodded weakly. "Bridget, I know I wasn't a very good boyfriend or fiancé." She gave a tiny smile and squeezed his hand. "But I want you to know something—

that time we were together. That was good. I'm sorry it got a little messy, but no regrets from my end. And don't worry about Austin. I'm not going to interfere in his life. He'll be okay, Bridge. His needs will come first." He leaned forward and kissed her forehead. "Rest easy."

Before he broke down and cried like a girl, he stood up and left the room. He was barely out the door when, standing right in front of him was a handsome little boy. Kind of small for ten, just like Cooper had been.

"You him?" he asked. "You my real dad?"

Cooper smiled. "Not exactly," he said. "I'm kind of your alternate dad." Then he ruffled the boy's hair. "You have a pretty good dad on stage right now—I wouldn't want to get in the way of that. But if you need me..."

"He's a teacher," Austin said. "And a coach, too. He's good with homework."

"Excellent reason to keep him around," Cooper said. He looked up. All eyes were on him. Parents, grand-parents, siblings, kids.

"Come on, Cooper," Spencer said. "This will take two seconds, then you can do whatever you want. Stay, go, whatever."

He noticed Spencer had a small box in his hand—the kit.

"Let's just step back in the study."

Spencer gave the inside of his cheek a wipe with a swab, slipped it in a sterile tube and closed the enve-lope around it.

"Do you sleep on that cot by the bed?" Cooper asked.

He nodded. "Sometimes she's needs to be held. Sometimes just the opposite. I'm on a leave from work. I try to be around."

"I'm glad she found you, Spencer," Cooper said. "I'm glad they both did."

* * *

Cooper got himself a hotel room not too far from the Cunningham household. He went out for some takeout, a bottle of single malt, a bucket of ice and after eating something he made himself a stiff drink and called Sarah. He talked to her for an hour and a half without telling her about Austin. He lied instead—he said that Bridget wanted to talk about their past, make sure he was okay with everything and say goodbye. He had given this decision about five minutes of thought first, deciding that if the DNA test came back pointing to him, that was soon enough to explain. He did say that it made him very sad, that he couldn't imagine going through something like that. And it was Sarah who had many questions about his relationship with Bridget, how they got along, what their relationship was like before they broke up and he found that reminiscing actually seemed to help. It was late and he might've been a little drunk when he fell asleep. His cell phone woke him and the clock said 2:00 a.m.

"Sorry about the time," Spencer said. "Bridget is no longer with us. I thought you'd want to know."

"When?"

"About four hours ago. It takes a long time to have a body picked up, even when you're expecting it and all the arrangements are in place. Then there was her mom and Austin...."

"How's he doing? Austin?"

"He's finally asleep. I think he'll be all right. We're all just glad she can rest now. Rest without pain. She'll be cremated and we'll have a service on Monday."

"Is there anything I can do?" Cooper asked.

"I got it, Cooper. If you're still in the area, you're welcome to attend. And I understand completely if you'd rather not. It's entirely up to you. Service at St. Bethel on Anniversary Avenue and at 2:00 p.m. an open house at the Cunninghams'. And of course, I'll have the test results forwarded to you."

"Thanks. And Spencer, I'm sorry, man."

"We had some good years," he said. And then he said goodbye.

Cooper knocked around for three days. He drove to Ft. Hood and although he wasn't allowed on the post, he did visit some of his old stomping grounds—bars and restaurants he'd frequented when he was there. He went to the San Antonio River Walk and the Alamo, wishing Sarah was with him. It was no surprise that he remembered being on the walk with Bridget, eating at a sidewalk café, drinking beer or a latte at a small table on the walk, watching people and boats pass by.

He booked a flight back to Eugene for Tuesday morning, but he didn't go to the service on Monday. The memorial was for family and close friends; he didn't want to make anyone uncomfortable. Instead, he pressed his suit and dress shirt and went to the Cunningham house at about two-thirty.

There were cars parked all the way down the street and he caught sight of a couple entering the house, carrying what appeared to be a covered dish. Sitting on the front step with a baseball and glove was Austin, looking real down in the dumps. He went to the boy, sat down beside him and asked, "Hard day, huh?"

The boy shrugged. "It sure ain't no fun in there." He looked up. "I'm waitin' for my dad. I mean, my other dad."

"I bet he's kind of busy today."

Austin looked up at Cooper and identical brown eyes connected. "Did you ever wish't you married my mom?"

Cooper was stunned by the question, then wondered why he'd been surprised. Chances were good there would be lots of questions like that. He decided on honesty. "I did," he said. "It took me a long time to see that Spencer was the better man for her. He was ready to settle down, like your mom was. And I was sorry I wasn't ready for that kind of responsibility. I might've lost out, but at least you didn't, Austin. He's a good guy."

"My mom said you're a good guy, too."

Cooper shrugged. "I'm better now than I was ten years ago. Older. Smarter a little bit. Want me to throw that ball around with you?" he asked, nodding at the ball.

"You're all dressed up for church."

Cooper took off his jacket, tossed it on a bush and rolled up his sleeves. "I can adjust."

"'Kay." Austin jumped up and ran to the other side of the lawn, throwing Cooper the ball. "Were you mad when my mom told you? About me?"

"Nah," Cooper said, throwing it back. "Best news I had all day. All month."

Austin grinned. "You don't live around here," he pointed out.

"No, I live in Oregon."

"My dad says we need to get to know each other. How we gonna do that?" he asked, throwing again.

"Well, we can talk on the phone. Maybe we can Skype. I can visit sometimes."

"Can I visit you?"

"Fine by me, but we have to go slow. I think your dad is going to want to check me out, make sure I'm safe."

"Right," Austin said. "Make sure you're not a perv."

Cooper smiled, thinking of Landon. "I have friends you're going to like. My girlfriend's brother is sixteen, a quarterback, plays some killer football. My girlfriend is a Coast Guard search-and-rescue pilot."

That stopped Austin. "She is?"

"She flies a helicopter. Oh, I live on the ocean. I have a Jet Ski."

"Really?" Austin said, frozen for a moment.

"Really."

"Do you have a family?"

"Parents," Cooper said. "No wife or ex-wife or kids. Sisters and their kids. And Sarah, my girlfriend."

"Would they be my family, then?" he asked.

"I guess so." Then he grinned. "If your dad decides I'm not a perv."

That made him laugh. "Your sisters would be my aunts."

"Correct."

"I have plenty of those," he said with a sour face.

"I know the feeling," Cooper agreed.

A man cleared his throat. Spencer was leaning against the side of the house, watching them, a half smile on his face. His sleeves were also rolled up; his tie was loosened.

"How long have you been standing there?" Cooper asked.

"Long enough to hear the Jet Ski bribery."

"Well, since I'm not good at homework, I had to have something in the plus column. I also have a Rhino and a Harley."

"A *Harley?* Aw, *man!*"

"Pretty underhanded," Spencer said. "I have a canoe."

"Dad! A *Harley!*"

"I heard, Austin. Well, I guess if you have to have two dads, at least one of 'em has a Harley."

Ten

Ashley ended up staying in the hospital for almost a week. Five days, which was three longer than she had planned. The extended stay was largely to regulate her very mild anti-anxiety medication as well as to give her the benefit of inpatient group therapy. The doctor decided she wasn't suffering from clinical depression, but that didn't mean she wasn't all worked up about the events in her life. The kids in her group were sympathetic and an odd thing happened—she found out that lots of outcasts had been harassed in this way, through texts, social media, bullied by whatever means available. Before now, Ashley had never considered herself an outcast! The fact that she was considered this way only by Downy and his girlfriend didn't make it any easier to bear. It was shocking and revealed an entire universe to her that she'd never thought herself vulnerable to.

Going back to school was scary, even though her mother got her a new cell phone with a secret number and promised to rescue her immediately if there was any trouble. And even though Eve had her own issues with her mother's surprise return, she was still standing beside Ashley's locker, ready to be an escort and loyal friend. Landon was with her, of course. They'd brave being late to their classes just to make sure Ashley didn't have any trouble in the halls.

To her surprise, Frank Downy appeared after third period one day. "I'll get you to class whenever I can— we have a couple together."

"Frank, you don't have to," Ashley said.

"And if I want to? You shouldn't have had to put up with any shit because of Downy. Sometimes I just can't believe him…."

"I don't want to say anything bad about your brother," she said.

"You don't have to. Just in case you wonder whose side I'm on, wonder no more. He's a dick and everyone but Mom is real pissed off at him for what he did to you."

At the same time he was talking to her, Ashley wondered when Frank's complexion had cleared up. When did he start to shave? In fact, hadn't he been shorter than her? When did all this happen? Because she had known him since they were about five, too.

"Come on," he said, grabbing her elbow in a gentle escort. "History is next for us."

Then she realized he wasn't wearing his glasses. He'd always worn thick glasses, which had given him such a bookwormish look. She stopped suddenly and looked at his face. "Frank, did you have LASIK surgery?"

"Contacts," he said. He looked down at her. "I've had 'em about a year."

She was completely embarrassed. "I'm sorry, Frank. I didn't realize…"

"You've had other things to think about," he said, pulling her along to class.

Indeed. She'd thought of no one but Downy for longer than she could remember. She was confident it hadn't kept her from being a good friend to Eve, but there was probably a lot going on in school that she had been too distracted to notice.

They were almost to class when some boy she didn't even know very well said, "Hey, Ash, nice tits!"

In a flash, Frank was on him like a hound and shoved him against the lockers. Frank's forearm pushed against the kid's neck. Frank had muscles on his arms. From the look on the kid's face, this was a surprise maneuver. "Apologize," Frank ordered.

"Sorry," he said. "Just kidding."

"No more kidding," Frank warned, releasing him.

Ashley was rooted to her spot, stunned. When had Frank developed shoulders?

"Um...thanks," she said.

"No problem. Let's go," he said, steering her down the hall, around the corner to their class.

When she went to her group therapy later that week, she briefly wondered if all teenage support groups looked the same. Someone was having problems with their parents, there was a substance abuse in someone's situation, another kept getting in trouble in and out of school and was in danger of being expelled, one was being bullied, another girl's boyfriend dumped her, rather cruelly. Mostly it was social issues these kids couldn't cope with any better than she had. But no one in her current outpatient group had spent time in the hospital and they were all anxious to hear everything.

The one thing she wanted to tell them that seemed

even more important was what she discovered when she went back to school. The fact that Downy's younger brother, so gentlemanly and protective, had been completely invisible to her before her breakdown, and suddenly she saw a new Frank. Somewhere in the past year or two he'd grown up, grown tall and strong. "If I stop to think about it, Frank has always been a good friend. I've had to call him about homework and he talks me through it. He's so patient and never gets tired of explaining things—he's nice to everyone. He used to get picked on, but Downy was a great bodyguard so people left him alone. But he's not one of the jocks—he's going to be our valedictorian, everyone knows it. He's the smartest guy in our class. Maybe in the county."

"Is he a nerd?" someone asked. In fact, that was Bradley, who was a thick-glasses nerd.

"I used to think so, but he's all grown up now and I think maybe he's a Bill Gates."

"Bill Gates is a nerd."

"Okay, but nerd or not, any girl would date Bill Gates because of his huge brain. And Frank is confident. He doesn't care what anyone thinks of him—they'll all eventually ask him for help on their calculus."

"But he's the asshole's brother!"

As if she needed reminding. "Well, I'm sure he loves his brother, but he doesn't seem to be a big fan of Downy right now," she said. "The thing is—I still cry. I'm not going to make a fool of myself by calling Downy and I think he's a total jerk, but if he came crawling back all sweet and sorry, I'd probably give him another chance."

"May I ask a question?" Burt, Simone Ross's associate and the group leader, asked. Burt was a lot younger

than Simone, a man in his late twenties or early thirties. Talk about a nerd. He was kind of on the homely
side, very thin with heavy dark brows. Ichabod Crane-
ish. Aside from keeping them on track and maybe asking a question or two to get them started, he didn't say
much. Sometimes he took notes, but she saw the page of
his steno pad once and it was filled with doodles. That
gave Ashley more peace of mind—at least he wasn't
writing *"this one is crazy as a loon."* Burt was growing on her. In the same way she finally noticed Frank,
she was starting to see handsomeness in kindness and
intelligence.

"Sure," she said.

"If your best friend's boyfriend did to her what was
done to you, would you advise her to take him back?"

"Of course not. I know it's not smart," Ashley said.
"I know I shouldn't, but it's just a fact."

"When you were his steady girl, he never acted like
that, did he?"

"Never!"

"And neither did you," Burt said. "Because you're
a nice person who can think about the feelings of others. Is it possible you want the Downy you once knew
to come back? But not the Downy you know now?"

"Yes. Of course, yes."

"If he came back now, would you worry every time
he didn't take a call or answer a text?"

She looked down. "It's just that what he did still
hurts so much."

"It does. The pain can feel unbearable and I'm so
sorry, Ashley. I say this a lot in our teen groups, but I'll
say it again, anyway. This time in life especially, you're
designed to fall in love. It's part of your developmen-

tal cycle. It's emotions and hormones and a struggle to create an independent adult life for yourself—one that meets all your needs. Also, this process of falling in and out of love, sometimes very painfully, helps you to identify the kind of life partner you fit with best. Some people never do, I'm sorry to say. Some people will be unsuccessful at relationships with the right people. In fact, some people are inexplicably drawn to people who will hurt them. But others will learn valuable lessons and graduate to positive, long-term relationships with people who won't let them down or betray them. I'm not saying perfect relationships—I'm afraid there's no such thing. I'm saying positive, growing, healthy relationships that can get back on track after something derails them.

"It's very important," he went on. "It's a process that's all about developing maturity and wisdom. And, Ashley, I'm very sorry that it hurts every time it doesn't go well. Very sorry."

"And did you do that? Get your heart broken?" she asked, eying his wedding band.

Burt, not a member of the group but a facilitator, didn't usually answer questions, especially about himself. But he smiled and said, "At least a dozen times."

She thought he was *wonderful*. Tears gathered in her eyes. "Then I probably have eleven to go."

"They won't always be as dramatic and awful as this was. It depends entirely on the criteria you establish for yourself. I suspect that a few years from now you'll go out on a date or two and immediately see something in a potential boyfriend that you weren't able to see at sixteen. And the red flag will wave before your eyes and you'll say, 'No thank you. I deserve better than that.'"

"Well, thank you, but I need something today," she said.

"Who has something to say that might help Ashley today?" Burt asked the group.

"Protect yourself from people who have the habit of being mean," someone said.

"Take a long break from boyfriends until you get past this and can at least understand it," said someone else.

"Try to believe the next time will feel better. You don't have to think this was the first and last time you'll ever like someone that much."

She listened to a number of suggestions from her group. And as usual, when she left that afternoon, she felt so much better.

Mac's lawyer, Sidney Mikowski, met with him to discuss a call he'd recently had from Cee Jay's attorney. Briefly, he explained that she wanted to see her children. She wasn't asking for any custody or support, just a visit. Sidney informed Mac that it would look good for him to be friendly and cooperative, in the event something legal came along down the road. "What she's asking is reasonable. She doesn't have a police record or any legal entanglements. It's just a supervised visit she's asking for."

"If she wants visitation, I want child support," Mac said, feeling surly. "I've raised them entirely on my own for ten years. It hasn't been easy."

"You signed off on support," Sidney reminded him. "Let's be clear—you're not asking to change the settlement at this time. I would advise that you give her an hour of supervised time with the kids."

"*She* signed off on visitation," he said.

"Mac, reel in that temper. I understand the insult

you feel, but her request is logical and rational. It's also legal—she's not challenging their custody, just asking for a supervised visit. They're her children, too."

"Where would we do this?" he asked, remembering grudgingly that his kids also wanted to see her.

"It doesn't matter, but I suggest somewhere where you all have privacy, just in case it's emotional. My office or maybe your home? Oh, and she's not interested in seeing your aunt. I'm guessing there's bad blood there?"

Mac laughed. "Oh, you could say that. Cee Jay didn't just leave me. I had to beg Aunt Lou for help. First I had to tell her that I got my teenage girlfriend pregnant, then I had to ask for her help when Cee Jay left me. Now that Lou is completely bonded with the kids, guess who's back? Lou might find it hard to be welcoming."

"Then it's a good thing she's cutting Lou out of the visit. What we don't need, Mac, and what will not cast the most positive and convincing light on your efforts to cooperate is a confrontation. Can you convince Lou to excuse herself for an hour?"

"I suppose I can, but it'll cost me...."

"Let's have the meeting in your living room. I'll be there as I'm sure her lawyer will be, too. Can you engage the services of an off-duty deputy?"

"What for?"

"If you have to invite your ex-wife and her attorney to leave, I'd rather you not play the bad guy. This is a supervised visit, off the books so to speak, to show your willingness to be cooperative and compassionate. I recommend it because your children should see their mother and because, if push comes to shove, you've been the responsible party. In custody debates, that goes a long way."

* * *

The visit was set for Wednesday at six-thirty. Mac came home at five and found Lou dishing out pizza slices. The kids were at the table but even though it was their favorite dinner, they weren't scarfing it down. Ryan was taking small bites and Eve's was untouched.

"There's nothing to be nervous about," he told them. "I'm sure your mother just wants to see you, find out how you've been, that sort of thing. I'd like you to have a nice visit. And I'll be with you."

"Why do we have to do this in front of people?" Eve asked.

Mac had rejected the idea of a deputy on the scene— two lawyers were more than enough of a crowd. "It's a legal issue, Eve, there's just no getting around that. Since your mother's lawyer will be with her, my lawyer will be present also. That way there shouldn't be any questions afterward."

"But Aunt Lou can't be there, too?" she asked.

"Unfortunately your mother and Aunt Lou don't exactly get along."

"It's better this way," Lou said. "We'll avoid any silly disagreements if I'm just not here. It's okay—you can tell me all about it later."

"Are you still mad at her?" Ryan wanted to know.

Lou took a breath. "I don't want to be and I'm not going to act like I'm mad, but I was angry that she left and didn't call to check on us. I'm working on being forgiving, but I might be too old and mean…. But until I get to the forgiving part, I intend to act like I've forgiven her. And hopefully she'll act the same way toward me. Just not tonight, apparently. Now eat some pizza." And with that, she took a big bite herself.

"I'm not hungry," Eve said, leaving the table without permission.

"Eve," Mac began.

Lou held up her hand. "Let it go. Understandably there's tension. The pizza will keep."

Mac had never, in his life, felt an hour and a half stretch interminably. At six he went to his room, showered and put on a fresh shirt. He even splashed a little aftershave on his cheeks. He yelled in the direction of the other bedrooms. "Fifteen minutes, kids." No one answered. He hoped he wouldn't have to pry them out of their rooms. He got himself a cup of coffee from the kitchen and went to the living room, where his three children were lined up on the couch. They were looking spit and polished even though they were all still wearing their jeans. And they were sitting very close together, Eve in the middle. "Has Lou left?" he asked.

They nodded in perfect sync and he couldn't help but laugh at them. "It's not an execution! It's your mother, finally come to visit and see how you are. Try to make this a happy occasion. I'm sure she's not planning to stay long so take this opportunity to ask her anything you've wondered about."

"Why now?" Eve asked.

"Well, honey, she said she's missed you and wants to make amends," Mac said. "All you have to do is be polite. Once she's gone, I'll warm up that pizza."

The doorbell rang and all three kids stiffened as if they had heard a gunshot. Mac put down his coffee on the side table. "I'm sure that's just Sidney, our lawyer." He opened the door to two beautiful, elegant, richly dressed women. Cee Jay's attorney was a knockout. She was a blonde, a stark contrast to Cee Jay's dark hair. But here they were, young and beautiful and sexy, looking as if they came from the same world, as if they belonged to the same tennis and golf club.

The lawyer put out her hand. "How do you do, Mr. McCain. I'm Antoinette LeClair. Please call me Ann."

He frowned. She looked very familiar. "How do you do. You're a little early."

She laughed and looked at her watch. "My apologies. Mrs. McCain was, understandably, very anxious."

"Do I know you?" he asked, frowning. "Do you practice around here?"

"I've been up here a time or two, but my office is in San Francisco."

He leaned a little closer and spoke quietly. "It's Deputy McCain. And it's not 'Mrs.' Cecilia Jayne and I have been divorced a long time and the kids haven't seen their mother in ten years. Don't be presumptuous." And he watched as Cee Jay bit her lip and turned teary eyes away. Sadly, he thought about how jaded he was. He just couldn't give her the benefit of the doubt. He felt sure her emotions were an act.

"Come in," he said, standing aside.

Ann let Cee Jay enter ahead of her. She stepped into the living room, covered her mouth as tears ran down her cheeks and said, "Oh, my beautiful babies! Oh, my God! Look at you!"

Mac winced visibly. This was going to be so confusing to them—their mother gone for so long and then returning with all that gush!

Cee Jay sat in the chair that Mac usually occupied, his cup of coffee sitting next to her on the side table. Once again, she looked rich…and powerful. She had a large diamond ring on her right hand, a diamond bracelet on her left wrist, diamond stud earrings as big as peas in her ears. And her clothes were chic, no other way to describe her. Elegant. Sitting on the edge of Mac's old, worn recliner, the contrast couldn't have been greater. With impressive skill she implored her children, "Tell me everything. I want to hear what you're doing. I bet you're so smart in school."

They were clearly uncomfortable; so stiff and shocked and intimidated. It was a long moment before Ryan said, "I play ball. Baseball."

"Do you?" she said excitedly, swiping the tears from her cheeks. "Your daddy played ball in high school!"

"And football. With Pop Warner," hc added in a quiet voice.

There was a knock at the door and Mac let Sidney in. "Early," Mac explained.

Sidney gave a nod and merely stood inside the door as a witness. But what he was seeing was Cee Jay's passion for her children.

"I take dance class," Dee Dee said, so softly she could barely be heard.

"Oh, I knew it! I used to dance! And what else do you do, my darling?"

"Piano," she added. "Why can't Aunt Lou be here? She's the one who takes care of us. With Daddy."

"I'm afraid I was a disappointment to your Aunt Lou," Cee Jay said smoothly, looking down, looking ashamed. "We were close once, but not anymore."

Close? Mac thought. *When was that?*

"Eve, tell me about yourself," Cee Jay said.

"No," Eve said. "Tell me about *your*self. You look pretty good. Jewelry and everything. What kind of job do you have?"

"Oh. Um. Well, I've been living in Los Angeles so I've been doing some modeling, some work as an extra on movie sets, that sort of thing. Nothing very impressive."

"It must pay very well," Eve said. Mac thought, *That's my daughter—already investigating.* "The only other thing I want to know is *why*."

"Why?"

"Why you got up one morning and decided to leave us. Without telling us you were going. Without saying goodbye. Without ever calling or sending a card or visiting."

Cee Jay looked shocked. "Eve, I'm sure your dad told you about—"

"I want you to tell me. Why didn't you at least visit us?"

"Your father asked me not to," she said.

Mac scowled. "That's not true," he said.

She turned and looked at him. "You served me with divorce papers that severed my custody and visitation."

"They know that, Cee Jay. Five years after you left, I filed for divorce and custody, and you signed off. They know. They've always known that we hadn't had a conversation for ten years."

"So then?" Eve said. "Why?"

"I'm sure you're very angry with me, Eve, but I came home to tell you about—"

"I don't want to talk about it," Eve said. "I want to know why!"

"Eve," Mac said in a warning tone.

Her voice was more compliant when she looked at him with pain in her eyes and said, "That's all I want from this, Dad."

"I understand. Please, be polite."

She looked back at Cee Jay. "I politely request that you tell me why. I don't want to talk about it, I just want to know."

Cee Jay sat a bit straighter and her mouth was not set in a happy line. Her lovely arched brows furrowed unhappily. "I don't expect you to understand, but I was very young. I had too many small children to care for without any help, without the love of a husband, without enough money to keep the house decent or enough food on the table. I broke, that's all. I broke and ran, afraid I was losing my mind. I'm sorry. I know it was wrong, but I wasn't strong. And now I'd like to reconnect and make up for all I missed."

Eve stood up. "Thank you." She walked toward her bedroom.

"Eve!" Cee Jay stood. "Won't you give me another chance?"

With tears gathering in her eyes, Eve shook her head. Then she proceeded to her room.

"Can I be excused?" Ryan asked.

"Me, too," Dee Dee added.

Mac nodded, knowing they were going to go hide or at least lay low. He was going to have so much to explain to them, damage to try to repair.

Cee Jay turned blazing blue eyes on him. "What have you done to them?" she snapped. "They *hate* me!"

"I have to admit, I'm surprised," Mac said, running a big hand down over his jaw. "I knew Eve was angry, but I didn't realize... Look, Cee Jay, Ryan and Dee Dee were very young when you disappeared, and they don't remember the day you left. But Eve remembers every detail. I had to get her in counseling—she was a wreck. But you have to be realistic—it's not as though they didn't notice their mother wasn't here or that you didn't call or write or visit. I didn't have to point that out to them."

"You poisoned them against me!"

"What?" he said on a laugh. "You didn't ever think of calling, or ever sending a birthday or Christmas card? Did it never occur to you that not visiting once in ten years would do the job of making them angry with you? You think they needed input from me? Oh, Cee Jay, how delusional can you possibly be?"

"You bastard! You're happy they reject me!"

He took a threatening step toward her. "I'm probably going to spend the better part of the night, maybe the next several days, trying to convince my daughter your abandonment was not her fault, that it was no one's fault. I might be headed for more counseling, which is tough on a deputy's salary." Then he stopped, looked her over and said, "Modeling? Movie work?"

"I'm done talking to you," she said, turning to leave.

Mac looked at her attorney, lifting his eyebrows in question. She gave a little shrug. "Right now Mrs. McCain's sole job is trying to reunite with her family."

Mac's expression was deadpan. "It's not Mrs.," he said for the second time.

Cee Jay was out the door, down the walk and in her car quickly, her attorney following. Mac stepped outside, Sidney on his heels. Nothing was said while Cee Jay started her classy car and pulled away from the curb. He squinted toward the car, memorizing the license plate. There had been no exchange of business cards; Ann had never offered one.

Then he turned to Sidney. "That went well," he said.

* * *

Lou McCain went into Cliffhanger's, meaning to have a quiet drink at the bar while she waited for Mac to be finished with *The Visit*. Given it was a Wednesday at six, the place was kind of busy and, as luck would have it, there was only one seat available at the bar... right next to Ray Anne, real estate agent extraordinaire and Lou's long-time nemesis. And while Lou was in a pair of jeans that she'd dressed up with a jacket, Ray Anne was decked in a royal-blue silky suit, short skirt and very high heels.

Lou and Ray Anne weren't exactly enemies, nor were they actual rivals. Anymore, at least. But they grew up together and had issues that went way back to the old days in Coquille. Ray Anne liked men very much and it didn't matter to her if they were spoken for or not. In fact, Ray Anne, a cute, sexy little blonde in her younger years, had helped herself to at least a couple of Lou's boyfriends. Lou had a memory like an elephant; it took a lot to cause her to hold a grudge, but once she achieved it, it was even harder for her to let go.

Ray Anne had relocated to Thunder Point about fifteen years ago, but given that it was so close to Coquille, Lou still saw more of her than she had liked. Then when Lou moved to Thunder Point with Mac and the kids, it seemed as if every time she turned a corner, she ran smack-dab into Ray Anne. Ray Anne might not be the same cute little blonde she once was, but she acted as if she thought she was. Now she had big boobs to add to her charms. Lou had suspected, quite rightly, that a surgical intervention had been necessary to achieve that impressive bustline.

Every time Lou saw Ray Anne, she automatically

looked down at herself. Yup, sixty years old and still she looked as if she were wearing a training bra.

Yet, there was that lone bar stool. And Lou wouldn't take a table in a busy restaurant for just a drink. She took the stool next to Ray Anne.

"If I sit here, can we have one hour of no conversation?" Lou asked Ray Anne.

Ray Anne lifted her glass of wine. "That's a long time," she said, lifting one tawny eyebrow. "What's the matter? Man trouble?"

"In a manner of speaking," Lou said.

Right then, Cliff came over to Lou and smiled at her.

"Give me a brandy, Cliff. Make it a good one, please," she said.

"You got it, Lou."

"Wow. You didn't lose that hunk of a boyfriend, did you?" Ray Anne asked, referring to Joe.

"Not yet," Lou said. "But I can give you his phone number and address if you want to make a run at him."

Ray Anne leaned an elbow on the bar and rested her head on her fist. "You know, the way you pick at me—it gets old. Aren't you worried you'll really hurt my feelings?"

"I guess the fact that you call me a lesbian and an old maid wouldn't be considered picking," Lou said.

"Yes, but I'm kidding," Ray Anne said. "And you damn well know it."

Cliff brought Lou's brandy and disappeared quickly. Lou and Ray Anne had been prickly toward each other for as long as anyone in Thunder Point could remember. It had never gotten down to hair pulling, but they had such scrappy attitudes no one was ever quite sure it wouldn't result in that one day.

Lou took a sip of her brandy. "I declare a one-hour truce. This was the only bar stool empty."

Ray Anne looked at her watch. "One hour it is. What's got you drinking the hard stuff?"

"This is considered hard? This is a Christmas drink!"

"You're wigged out about something. You haven't even criticized my attire."

Lou gave her a long look. "How high are those heels?" she asked. "Seriously, no criticism intended, but how the hell do you walk in those things?"

"It's an acquired skill. Practice. Those wedgies of yours would probably give me leg cramps. Why are you out having Christmas drinks alone?"

"Well," Lou said tiredly. "You'll hear about it, anyway. Mac's ex is in town, wanting t0 see the kids. She's over there right now and it was agreed that I not be present since I might lose it and just kill her."

"Cee Jay," Ray Anne said in a breath. She had a rather stricken look on her face, her lacquered lips formed an O and she raised a hand to hover over her mouth.

"Yes, the one and only." Lou took another sip of her brandy. "God help us all."

"Oh, holy Jesus, that *was* her!"

"What are you talking about?" Lou asked.

Ray Anne turned her full attention on Lou, swiveling on her stool to face her. "She contacted me. She said she was looking at property in the area and asked about Thunder Point. She introduced herself as Cecelia Raines. She said the house had to be large and she wanted a view. I showed her the Morrison property that's in foreclosure, but she had a lot of questions about the town, the people, the *deputy!* I didn't put it together until ten seconds ago."

Lou turned toward her. "Seriously?"

"Seriously. I never met her until a few days ago and I thought she looked familiar. Now that I think about it, Eve looks just like her. Oh, my God, she's stalking. What does she want?"

Lou shook her head. "She says she wants to see her kids. But why now? She hasn't been in touch since the day she left and now she comes to town to see Mac? This is very strange. Now, after hearing what you've just told me, I think it's a little scary."

"She didn't give me any information about herself— she was a walk-in," Ray Anne said. "Happens all the time—there aren't very many agents in a dried-up old town like ours, so I wasn't suspicious of her when she arrived at the office. Besides, a lot of people have wanted to see the Morrison place, not that anyone actually wants to buy it. But she was sure turned out—looked like a million bucks. She looked as if she had money, that's why I took her out there. God, I hope I didn't do any harm to Mac and the kids. Or you, for that matter."

"Me?" Lou asked.

"You! I hate you," Ray Anne said. "But that doesn't mean I don't love you!"

Lou laughed at her. "You steal my boyfriends."

"I haven't done that in years," Ray Anne said. She lifted her hand to Cliff for another glass of wine. "Your boyfriends are too old for me."

"You're such a slut," Lou said, but she laughed.

"Oh, I'm not. I'm just flexible." Then she smiled. "And open-minded."

Lou's phone chimed and she picked up to read a text. It said, *The coast is clear.*

"That was Mac. She must be gone already. Oh, that doesn't seem like a good sign."

"Listen, if there's anything I can do to help, please let me know. Tell Mac I talked to her and I'd be glad to tell him anything he wants to know about our meeting."

"That's nice of you, Ray Anne," Lou said while she fished a ten-dollar bill out of her wallet. "I'll tell him."

Ray Anne covered Lou's hand that held the bill. "Let me," she said. "I probably owe you a drink." She shook her head and tsked. "I just can't imagine a woman leaving her children and not having any contact with them for ten years," she said. "I never wanted anything so much as to have a family. If I'd had a family, I would've been so happy."

Lou was stunned. Ray Anne had never acted like a woman who wanted a family. She behaved like a woman who wanted a man, and another man, and another and another.... "Is that so?" she asked.

"Of course. I was married three times."

"I know, but..."

"They didn't work out," Ray Anne said a little wistfully. "But it wasn't all my fault."

"Hmm. Well, I'll tell Mac you've seen Cee Jay, talked to her. Listen, I'd better run—I have no idea what I'm walking in to."

"Sure. Good luck."

Lou started to leave. She turned back, looked at her watch and said, "Next time we can go more than an hour on the truce. If you can behave yourself."

Mac checked on his kids, all tucked into their individual bedrooms, starting with Dee Dee. "Doing okay?" he asked her.

She nodded. "Do you think she's coming back?"

"I don't know, honey. Do you want her to?"

She shrugged. "It's okay. But she has to let Aunt Lou be here because Aunt Lou *lives* here."

He smiled. Can't get anything past kids. "I'll be sure to pass that on if I'm ever asked."

"Can I watch TV? For a half hour?"

"Homework done?" She nodded again. "Okay, then."

He went to Ryan's door and opened it. Ryan was laying on his bed, his hands behind his head, staring at the ceiling. "How are you doing, Ryan?" Mac asked.

Ryan sat up. "Why'd she come here again?"

"To see you, she said. To see all three of you. And for you to see her, since you haven't seen her in a long time."

"Are we done with seeing her now?" he asked.

"I don't know. I guess we'll find out if she calls again."

"Probably in ten years," Ryan said. "Can I get on the computer?"

"Homework done?"

"I did it at school. Can I?"

"Okay. Let's not talk about this visit on Facebook or anything. Family business, right?"

"I don't want to tell about it," Ryan said. "It's too weird."

Finally, he approached his eldest daughter's room knowing this discussion would be a lot more complicated than the ones he'd just had. He gave two knocks on Eve's bedroom door and then entered without an invitation. She was sitting cross-legged on her bed, her phone in her hands, texting. There was no question in his mind, she would be checking in with both Ashley and Landon. She looked up at him and he could tell all the wind had gone out of her sails.

"You okay?" he asked.

"I don't know," she said with a shrug. "Are you?"

"I hated that," he said. "Hated watching that."

"I'm sorry."

He sat on the edge of her bed. "I'm not mad at you, Eve. It was so uncomfortable. Something tells me your mother really wants a relationship with you kids. And I'm terrified."

"Why? Because she's lying?"

"I don't know if she's lying. I think our perspectives are completely different, as they are between divorced couples. She really believes I failed her. I really believe I did everything I could. How do you change that? The only thing I really want you to know—it was never your fault. Maybe mine, maybe hers, but never yours."

"I know," she said weakly. "But I don't care whose fault it was! I just want to know how you can love your children and not even send a birthday card!"

"Maybe no one ever sent her one when she was a kid," he said. "I don't know too much about your mother's childhood—she was in a foster home when I met her in high school. I never questioned that experience back then—seventeen-year-old boys usually don't ask those kinds of questions. Maybe she was ignored, maybe she had a real bad time growing up or something. A lot of the way we act as adults has to do with how we were treated as children. I might've had no idea what I was getting myself into, married at nineteen, but I know that once you arrived, you were like the center of my world. You and your brother and sister were always wanted. I wish I could fix it so you don't have any pain over this—you're innocent."

A tear rolled down her cheek. "I don't want to be like her—I don't want to run out on my children."

"Then you won't. Listen, I know it's not easy, but I think you have to just accept people as they are. That's the best Cee Jay's got, Eve. You don't have to spend time with her unless you want to, but you also don't have to carry her burdens. She's the one who wasn't here for ten years, no one pushed her away."

"I know."

"But it doesn't mean she doesn't love you."

"I know. It's just hard."

"It is that," he said. "Hard for everyone, I think."

"I don't want to spend time with her. But I wouldn't mind if she sent a birthday card or something."

"If she ever asks, I'll tell her," he said.

"And I might let her take me shopping some time," she said, smiling sheepishly.

Mac laughed. "She should probably take us all shopping."

Eve shook her head. "I was kidding, you know."

"I know," he said with a smile. "Have I told you lately how proud you make me?"

"But I was rude," she said. "You asked me to just be polite and I was rude. And I knew it."

He squeezed her hand. "You can work on that, but I'm not mad. What have I always told you? We all have our personal boundaries. You have your boundaries and I understand that. It always works best if you defend your boundaries by being firm but without losing your temper, but hey—sometimes if we feel threatened, we lash out."

"You think I was feeling threatened?"

He lifted an eyebrow. "Do *you* think you were?"

She thought for a while. "I don't want her coming around acting like she always missed us because if she missed us, she would have let us know that before now. I don't like it when someone just lies in my face and acts like it's the truth. She did *not* miss us. She came back, but she didn't tell the truth about why. I guess that's my boundary. The truth."

"Possibly we just don't have the whole story," he suggested.

"Then that's my other boundary. The whole story. Don't just come around acting like it was all a little mistake and hey, we're all over it now, so let's party. That isn't going to cut it."

He tried not to smile. One corner of his mouth lifted. "Like I said, we all have our boundaries. They're personal and they're ours. I respect that."

"What about your boundaries?" she persisted.

"Well, my personal boundaries are my business but, in this case, I had to think about the whole family, about all of us, and I did the best I could to be fair about that."

"You were fair," she acknowledged. "I should call Ashley. She's dying to hear about it."

He stood up. That was his cue to give her some privacy to do an emotional postmortem with her best friend. "If you need to talk about this anymore..."

"I'm fine, Dad. Sorry I was rude."

Eleven

For the first time since Sarah had known Cooper, his temperament was unreadable. He came back from San Antonio in a very quiet, distracted mood. He was so happy to see her, so grateful for her help in the bar while he was away, yet nothing she could say would get his disposition to brighten.

"It must have been so hard seeing Bridget like that," Sarah said.

"It was the saddest thing I've ever seen. Her family had a tough time letting her go. I hope to never see anything that sad again."

"I think you brought a lot of that sadness home with you," she said.

And he pulled her close, kissed her temple and said, "I'm sorry, baby. I don't want to burden you. We have a lot to be thankful for."

He wasn't done with it, apparently. Maybe he just needed a little time to process it all. Sarah was happy to have a full week of work to occupy her and keep her from worrying about Cooper every second of the day. By the following weekend, when they had a little more time together, she decided to pursue the subject again. They sat out on his deck under a very starry sky and bright moon, watching over a couple of fires on the beach, listening to the waves break on the shore. He had his evening beer, she had her wine. There were a couple of other people on the deck, also enjoying the spring evening, so they were mostly alone. At least alone enough to have a private conversation. "Did you ever figure out why Bridget wanted you to come to San Antonio?"

Again he pulled her closer as he did every time the subject came up, as if afraid she might slip away from him. "There were a lot of reasons—lots of talk about the past, making sure I never for a moment thought she was less than honest with me. But while it probably relieved her and allowed her to move on, it did something bigger for me. I failed her, Sarah. I was a poor excuse for a fiancé. I was a disappointment as a boyfriend. I wanted to marry her without making any real compromises in my own life. I was leaving the country for weeks at a time, and all she wanted from me was my promise to find a more stable lifestyle."

Sarah felt a lump in her throat. "Lots of regrets, huh?"

"Lots, but let's see if I can explain—it's better for both of us that it didn't work out. She married a good man and I'm so happy with you, here, now. This is the way it should be. But, damn, I don't ever want to be that kind of disappointment to anyone again. If I thought I let you down like that, it would just kill me. The whole thing—it's made me think real hard about the man I want to be."

"I want to ask you something. Try to be honest, okay?"

"I always tell you the truth. Not something I've always done, but always with you."

"You were engaged twice. Was the other woman before or after Bridget?"

"After. And it might've been a rebound thing—it was Patti, and I was never so relieved as when it didn't work out."

Sarah turned in her chair, facing him. "I can't wait to hear this."

He chuckled softly. "Try not to be too amused," Cooper said. "I was dating Patti. Same drill. I was the runaway boyfriend—in the States for a few weeks, away for long stretches, expecting the woman of the moment to be so thrilled by my occasional presence that she'd never think of asking more from me."

Sarah just shook her head and snickered. "You were such a dog. I've known a hundred guys just like you."

"Yeah, not really flattering to know I'm just another brute. Inconsiderate and self-absorbed. So, I was dating Patti and ran into, guess who? Bridget. At the grocery store, of all places. I hardly ever went to the grocery store. She was picking through tomatoes or something and she looked..." He just shook his head in wonder. "She looked amazing. Happier than I'd ever seen her. She had a rosy-cheeked one-year-old in her shopping cart and she was making him giggle. When she saw me, she gasped and laughed and threw her arms around me and said it was so good to see me. I knew she was married but I have to tell you, Sarah, the way I saw her that day? She was never that happy with me. We talked for about five minutes—she married a teacher, had a nice little house not far from her mom and dad, hoped to fill it up with kids. She asked me about how I was doing…I was doing the same thing. She had grown a family and I had grown a little savings account—contract labor outsourced by the Army was good money."

"And that was when you wanted her back?" Sarah asked.

"I don't know," he said. "I don't remember feeling that way. What I remember was thinking I hadn't been as smart as I thought I was. So, right after that I asked Patti to marry me and she was thrilled. What is it about women and the capture, huh? What did she have to be thrilled about? In two weeks I knew it was a mistake and we broke up. That's all there is to the Patti/Cooper story. I think I was trying to reach back in time—I think I felt like I'd been an idiot. A fool. I packed up and left San Antonio, went to the Gulf coast, got a job for an oil company flying equipment and people to off shore rigs. Right then I made a decision to live alone for the rest of my life." He squeezed her shoulders and grinned. "Until you came along."

"You grieve her," Sarah said. "You grieve Bridget and the life you might've had together."

He shook his head. "I don't think it's that simple, babe. I grieve the foolishness of my youth. But I'm grateful for all the things that happened, even the stupid things. I want to be here with you now and if I'd been smarter back then, this wouldn't have happened. So, I'm sorry I was an idiot and grateful I was an idiot? Does that make any sense?"

Derek Stiles, Sarah's ex-husband, instantly came to her mind. She had so wanted her marriage to work but now she was so grateful things had gone the way they had, allowing her to be here with Cooper. "I think I understand, Cooper. I'm just sorry you're so sad."

"She left a husband and young son," he said. "That just shouldn't happen."

"It happens all the time," she said. "It happened to Landon."

"I think about that all the time," Cooper said. "I know I can't ever be a father to Landon. But you know what, Sarah? If something terrible happened tomorrow and Landon was left alone, I want you to know—I'd never abandon him. Never." Then he laughed at himself. "I'd be his shadow. I'd stick with him."

Cooper got better over the next week. He might've been a little bit quiet, but he was lightening up. And then the following weekend, she could tell something had changed. He was as morose and preoccupied as he'd been that first day he had returned from Texas.

Sarah went out on the bay on her board while he had customers in the bar and planned what she was going to say to Cooper, because this had to be resolved. Later that day she didn't say anything and tried to ignore his mood until it was late enough for them to be alone. Sarah was sure that Bridget's death had opened his eyes—he must know in his heart that he'd been in love with her and was sorry he'd let her go.

When the last four people from town were walking back down the beach she said, "Let's get it over with. I want to know what's going on with you. And I want it all, right now."

He just stared at her for a second, shocked. Speechless.

"I know it has to do with me," she said. "Just get it

out. Stop with all this 'I love you so much' stuff and tell me the truth. What's eating you?"

He smiled slightly. "I was going to tell you tonight. I'm sorry you had to wait," he said. "Come here." He put out his hand and led her inside.

Once they were in the shop and there was sufficient light, he pulled out his cell phone and scrolled through the pictures, handing it to her.

"Bridget wanted to tell me before she died that I have a son. She didn't realize Austin was mine—it was an honest mistake that came to light when her whole extended family, including Austin, had blood tests to try to find a match for a bone marrow transplant. It revealed that Austin and Spencer, Bridget's husband, weren't a match. I had a DNA test while I was in Texas and was waiting for confirmation. The letter came yesterday afternoon. I'm a match. I wanted us to have some time to talk it over once I knew for sure."

She looked at the face of an adorable little boy. Then she looked at Cooper. "Oh, God," she said. "You feel like you lost your love of a lifetime!"

"No, Sarah. I feel like I have a son. I feel like I have more responsibility. To you, to Landon, to Austin, even a little bit to Spencer. Bridget asked me not to take Austin away from the only father he's had and, of course, I agreed to that. But I have to find a way to get to know him. I have to be a father, even if I'm not a full-time father. I have absolutely no idea how that's done." He took a breath. "Baby, how the hell did you do it? Take on Landon when you were just a kid yourself? How did you do such a great job at that?"

Her eyes welled with tears. "And that's what's been beating you up?"

"Isn't that a lot?" he asked. "I have a kid, Sarah. I have a family. It might be a part-time job, but Jesus. What if Bridget and I had known back then? What if we'd gotten married? I think Austin is lucky it worked out like it did. But I have no idea what to do next."

Sarah wiped the tears from her cheeks. "You have a family," she said.

"I know and it all feels kinda heavy for a guy like me. Am I going to get used to this?" he asked her.

"He has to come first," she said. "Even if he has a good father already, you have to put your son first. He's your first priority. That's how it's done."

And that, Sarah thought, *is going to make it even harder for us to be first to each other.*

Mac hadn't seen Cooper in a couple of weeks. He'd dropped into the beach bar one evening on his way home from work to discover that Cooper was away—some kind of family emergency that Rawley said Cooper would explain later. Mac left the bar thinking he would catch up with his friend eventually.

More than a week later Cooper walked into the deputy's office.

"Break time?" Cooper asked.

"I'll be damned," Mac said. "I thought you'd made good on your threats and just sold the bar and land and left us."

"Nah, I had business out of town. I wasn't gone that long."

Mac rubbed his neck, leaning back in his desk chair. "Right, but then I had a busy week and it seemed like you'd been gone forever. Well, good to see you. I heard there was some kind of emergency."

"Yes and no. It turned out that my ex-fiancée's husband was looking for me. She had cancer. Terminal. Time was short. I didn't have much notice."

"I'm sorry, man."

"I didn't know she was sick. By the time I saw her she was ready to go, just had a few loose ends and goodbyes to wrap up and then, thank God, she could just let go. It was hopeless and she was…man, she was suffering. I was one of her loose ends." He looked down and shook his head solemnly. "I'll be honest—that really screwed up my head for a while. Poor Sarah. She had to try to figure me out. I think she should've just slapped me a few times."

"You okay?" Mac asked.

"Yeah, I'm fine now. But here's the thing—you might be hearing from her husband and I wanted to give you a heads-up. The guy's name is Spencer Lawson and I suggested he call you. I suggested he do a complete background search on me and that you are a personal reference, but one with a real professional expertise." At the puzzled look on Mac's face Cooper got right to the point. "I just got confirmation—lab work confirmation—but it was just a formality. It seems I have a son. And none of us knew."

"Whoa! Cooper, you old dog!"

Cooper laughed in spite of himself. He pulled out his cell phone and showed Mac a bunch of pictures of Austin while he explained about the broken engagement, the bone marrow transplant work-up, all the details. "I'm going to have to figure out how to tell my family. My mom and dad, my sisters."

"Probably prudent," Mac said, but his grin was huge.

"I'm really surprised by how much I want to tell them, my dad especially."

"I suppose you'll be bringing him here to live with you?"

The smile left Cooper's face. "Well, no. Spencer is a good father. Austin just lost his mother. He wants to stay with Spencer and why would I screw with that? But I am planning to visit in a couple of weeks. I want to take in a Little League game, maybe go out for pizza. I'm not practiced at this, man," he said with an embarrassed laugh. "I haven't even been that great an uncle to my sisters' kids!"

"Oh, you're good with kids. You might even be a natural—I've seen you with Landon."

"He's a lot older. Austin is only ten," Cooper said. "Besides, I owe Landon. Through him I found Sarah."

"How's that working out?" Mac asked. "You and Sarah? Now that there's a kid in the picture?"

"She's completely afraid to get serious about me, but I'm wearing her down. I'm counting on Austin to soften her up a little. He's cute as the devil—obviously doesn't look that much like me," he lied. And the grin was back. "I'm hoping that once I check out, Spencer will let Austin come for a visit. He really likes the idea of a Jet Ski. You know what's so ironic? One of the reasons Bridget and I broke up was because I wasn't ready for an anchor. I wanted to get married, that was real—I was ready for a permanent woman. But all the stuff that went with it—settled, house, no more contract flying to warring countries, kids...I wasn't there yet. Little did I know."

"What if you had known?" Mac asked.

"Hard to say. I probably would've gotten married—I

was prepared for that. But I was the stubborn idiot who thought nothing had to change about my life. I'd keep doing whatever I wanted to do and Bridget would go along. Right? Isn't that what young men think?"

"Oh, man," Mac said. "You really would've been surprised."

"I think Spencer will call you. Be honest, Mac—this isn't a favor I'm asking. You don't have to tell me when he calls, what he asks. Austin's a good little kid. I want his dad to be careful, to know the truth."

"I don't know anything bad about you, Cooper. And there's a tradition that goes along with all this."

"Oh?"

"Gotta buy us a couple of cigars," he said. Then he put out his hand and said, "Congratulations, man!"

While Cooper had been dealing with the news of his surprise son, Mac had been busy with his own mystery. He'd been researching his ex, trying to figure out what Cee Jay was up to. Her car was registered to a Madeline Crofts from Los Angeles and that was the second time he'd come across a familiar name but wasn't sure why. There was no police record, just an L.A. address.

It hadn't occurred to him to look up his ex-wife's attorney until days had passed. When he finally searched the California Bar Association using every possible spelling, the name didn't pop up. A fraud? Could she be practicing without a license? Finally he looked up Antoinette LeClair on Google and had to go through pages of references until he came upon one that jiggled his memory—that was the name of a character on *Law and Order*. And she was played by none other than Madeline Crofts, formerly of Oregon.

Then he went to work on Cee Jay's history, searching under a variety of aliases, including Cecelia Raines and bingo. Cecelia Jayne McCain was married to Martin Raines six years ago. Almost one year before her divorce from Mac was finalized.

"Bigamy," Mac muttered.

The Raineses were divorced two years ago and the wealthy Mr. Raines left her a very large Laguna Beach home, two luxury late model vehicles, jewelry. He also paid two hundred and fifty thousand dollars a year in spousal support. Further research a few days later showed that the house was in foreclosure. It appeared that it was left to Cee Jay free and clear and she'd borrowed against it. Its value was two-point-four million.

What the hell?

Mac had bought his five-bedroom home for one hundred eighty thousand and had done all the necessary repairs himself. His Aunt Lou was also an owner—they bought it together. Their plan was to own it free and clear in another ten years.

How had Cee Jay gone through that amount of money in such a short time? She was well-dressed, but how much money did that take? And if she had resources like that, what was she doing back here, trying to get reacquainted with her children? He had trouble believing it was sincere motherly love.

This all made no sense to him.

He called Sidney and asked him to get in touch with Cee Jay's attorney to set up a meeting. Sidney called him back a few hours later to tell him that the number he had for Ms. LeClair was not in service. "Not a listing anywhere," Sidney said. "And I can't find her in the directory of California attorneys."

"Neither could I," Mac said. And then he told Sidney what he'd found on a computer search of public documents.

"I don't recommend a meeting with the 'so-called' lawyer right now even if we could locate her," Sidney said. "And, frankly, if I'd known all this, I wouldn't have agreed to that meeting with the children. I don't know what's going on here, but I'm pretty sure it's not legal. It's certainly not responsible. There are the feelings of children involved!"

"I couldn't agree more," Mac said.

Mac didn't discuss this conundrum with anyone else, not even Lou. Instead he called a colleague in L.A., who recommended a private detective with a good reputation. Mac hired him to gather background information on Cee Jay. He was primarily interested in where her money was and where her ex-husband had gone. Marrying and divorcing him, obtaining a very large settlement when she hadn't been divorced and free to marry in the first place was fraud. She'd be lucky if she didn't go to jail.

The very idea of the mother of his children in jail chilled Mac to the bone.

With the way things had been going with Ashley, Gina did something she thought she'd never do—she phoned the parents of Ashley's biological father, Eric Gentry. She had no idea where he lived now and she hoped she could get a current address from his parents, whom, she knew, were residents of a retirement community outside North Bend. Without wanting to get into a lot of detail with them Gina fabricated a little white lie. She said she worked for an auto insurance company and had a large refund check for Eric Gentry, but had no current address for him. "Since he hasn't been a client of ours for over fifteen years, we don't have his address and the check was returned. I can't send it to you—it will have to be signed for. Would you be able to give his contact information?"

Mrs. Gentry, gullible as many seniors are, gave Gina his current address. It was a business address in Eugene, Oregon.

It took Gina about fifteen minutes on the computer to learn that Eric Gentry owned a body shop in Eugene, which was relatively close to Thunder Point. She'd bet her last tip that he'd stayed clear of Thunder Point ever since he'd left town almost seventeen years ago.

Gina was reluctant to be very far away from home these days, but she thought her reasons for wanting to see Eric after all this time were important enough to pursue. She needed to ask Eric about the medical history on his side of the family.

She wasn't going to tell Ashley about this plan—at least not yet. She wasn't sure how her daughter would react to the news that Gina was going to try to talk to her father. She might even ask to go along, and that 'twas not going to happen. What Ashley did not need right now was one more unstable relationship in her life. So Gina told her she was going over to Bandon to the doctor's office for her annual exam and since she had to take time off from work to do it, she thought she might shop a little. Ashley was told to call her grandmother if she needed anything.

On the drive to Eugene, Gina wondered what Eric would be like. She expected him to be a slightly older version of the boy she'd known. The fact that he now owned his own small business kind of threw her; she did not exactly remember him as being responsible.

His body shop—*Gentry's*—wasn't in a particularly nice part of town but it was large, on a clean lot surrounded by a cyclone fence and a couple of signs that said there were guard dogs on the property. She shivered. There was only one small reception counter inside the front door—the place where people dropped off their keys and phone numbers—and the rest of the building was all garage and service bays. She peeked in—there were at least eight work bays and there looked to be six employees working on cars. She saw brutalized bumpers, crunched-up sides, but also vintage and classic models undergoing restoration. And the garage was spotless.

A young man came to the counter, wiping his hands on a rag. He had his name, Rafael, sewn on his work shirt. "Can I help you?"

"I'm looking for Eric Gentry," she said. "He was recommended."

"That's great—what do you need done?"

"I was told to only talk to Eric," she said smoothly.

"I'll see if he's available." And the guy disappeared.

Not two minutes later Eric walked through the door from the garage, wiping his hands on an identical blue rag. And it was like stepping back in time. He was the same guy, just older and more mature. He'd have to be about thirty-six now and his red hair was a little darker, but those green eyes, Ashley's green eyes, were just as breathtaking. He still had that bad-boy aura that had once put her afire. And he recognized her immediately. His eyes grew wide and his mouth formed a handsome O of surprise.

"Don't call the dogs," she said, putting up a hand. "I don't want anything from you. You're not in trouble or anything. I just have to ask you a few questions. Health questions. For my daughter's health."

"Daughter?" he said, as if he didn't know.

"Yes, daughter. Do you have fifteen or twenty minutes? I won't keep you long, I promise. And there are no wrong answers—you're not at risk. It's medical history stuff and it's important for her, so she gets the best medical care."

"Is she sick?"

Gina allowed a small smile. "It's one of the first things a doctor asks when you need medical attention and we don't know anything about the medical history of your side of the family. Is there somewhere sort of private we could talk?"

"There's a Denny's a few blocks away. I'd be happy to buy you a cup of coffee. I'll just let my guys know I'm leaving."

"Should I follow you?"

"That'll work. Give me a couple of minutes—I want to wash my hands. I'll be backing out of the lot in the tow truck."

"I'm in the old Jeep," she said.

Gina left to wait for him in the Jeep. While she sat there she wondered what her next move would be if he bolted again. But he had a business—surely he wouldn't run now. When he ran at eighteen, he'd had nothing to hold him. He couldn't possibly believe she'd be coming after him now for support, or to charge him with statutory rape! At this late date? But then, the big tow truck backed out and she put her Jeep in gear and followed him.

Eric parked around the back of the restaurant and Gina parked in front. She had the passing thought that Denny's was certainly getting a workout lately—Mac had met with Cee Jay in a Denny's. Gina hoped this conference would be much more productive.

She waited for him inside the door and once he was there, the waitress appeared, all smiles.

"How's it going, Eric?" she asked.

"Great, Jenn. Can we have a booth?"

"You bet," she said, grabbing menus and showing them the way.

They settled in, menus closed and Eric immediately asked, "Is she all right?"

"She is. She's had some challenges lately, as all teenage girls will, but the only thing I could use help from you with is a medical history." She pulled a slip of paper from the side pocket of her purse. "Like—any history of cancer, heart disease, mental illness, epilepsy, diabetes? Any chronic illnesses or hereditary conditions I should know about? Kidney failure? High blood pressure? Breast cancer, uterine cancer? How about clinical depression or bipolar disorder?"

He frowned. "My dad had bypass surgery, but I'm pretty sure it was more about fried foods and no exercise than genetics. Mental illness? My mother's pretty crazy, but I think it's just that she's pretty crazy, not mentally ill."

"Pretty crazy how?" she asked.

He gave a shrug. "She complains constantly. She's manipulative as all hell. She's seventy-five and still angry about everything. It might be keeping her alive."

"That's right, your parents were older when you were

born. Didn't your dad retire right about the time we knew each other?"

He nodded. "They had two children. My sister is eighteen years older than I am. My dad is a retired postal carrier—he retired at sixty. My sister and her husband built a guest house on their property and my folks live in it." He smiled. "God bless her."

The waitress appeared and Eric said, "Two coffees, please." And then to Gina he said, "Would you like something to eat?"

She shook her head. "I take it you're not close to them?" she asked. "Your parents?"

"Unsurprising, if you think about all the trouble I gave them. We've been closer the last few years, but they have relentless memories. I hope…I'm sorry—her name? Your daughter?"

Your daughter, too, she almost said. "Ashley."

He smiled. "I hope she's easier on you than I was on my parents. Ashley."

"She's a dream come true."

"That's a pretty name. I wasn't sure. You know?"

"Sure of what?"

He rubbed his hands over his face. They were callused hands; hardworking hands. But clean. Even his nails were clean.

"Well, if you really were pregnant. If you had a baby. Or maybe decided not to take a chance on one, given the father. I thought about contacting you. Then I thought better of it. I didn't want to stir up any bad memories for you. I thought you'd be better off, you know?"

The waitress put the coffees on the table, but they both ignored them.

Gina shoved her list back in her purse, a little angry. "Better off, how?"

"Look, Gina, I know what I did to you was low. It was so wrong nothing could make it right. I wanted to say I was sorry, but sorry was so lame I couldn't even choke it out. By the time I could've apologized, so much time had passed, I figured I'd be like a bad dream. And you didn't need that."

"Is that so?" she asked. "So, checking to see if you actually had a child, you thought that would be a bad idea. You thought—"

"I was in prison, Gina."

Well. Gunshot to the heart. She felt all the color drain from her face. "Prison?" she asked weakly.

"Armed robbery. Seven years and I served five. I'm not making excuses here, but I was kind of along for the ride. I made a few bad friends and at that time in my life I thought bad was very cool. I think someone dropped me on my head when I was a baby. I'm sorry, Gina. I'm really sorry. You're just one of many people I disappointed."

She was stunned silent for a moment. "Right," she finally said. Hands shaking, she pulled her list out again. "Diabetes?" she asked. "Metabolic issues, like Crohn's disease?"

He covered her hand. "I'm not a dangerous person," he said. "I've turned my life around. But to a kid, that news wouldn't be important. I wouldn't want the reputation that goes with having a con for a dad. I won't bother you. Or your daughter."

"You seem to be doing okay for yourself now," she said.

He gave a nod. "When you're an ex-con, getting work

is almost impossible. My brother-in-law helped me land a job in a run-down body shop. It went into foreclosure and he helped me buy the auctioned property. I was probably too young and inexperienced for it, but it was a lot better than begging for a chance, a break. So, I worked hard, ran it for a few years with ex-cons I knew were okay and we turned it around. What you see is a rebuilt and highly leveraged business, but an honest and dependable one. The last couple of years, even in this economy, have been good years." He took a breath. "I haven't been in trouble since. You can check that."

"I should probably just go...."

"I have some money put aside. No other children," he said, shaking his head. "If you can use a hand...let me know. You wouldn't have to tell her where it came from."

"I don't need anything," she said. "I just wanted to know about the medical history."

"And now you probably know way more than you wanted to know."

She nodded. "Wow. I knew you were trouble back then, but I never..." Then she blanched. "I mean..."

"I know exactly what you mean, Gina. Listen, I realize I have no right, but can you tell me about her? I promise not to bother her or you."

Gina thought about this for a long moment. Then she pulled her cell phone out of her purse, clicked on the picture gallery and passed it to him. The first picture was one she'd taken at a Thunder High basketball game. Ashley was smiling, red hair shining, green eyes twinkling, her pom-poms under her chin. She was stunning.

And she saw him almost crumble. He cradled the phone in both hands, a look of wonder came over him.

He had to glance away briefly to compose himself. "She's so beautiful," he said in a strained whisper.

"There are more. You can scroll through."

He took his time with the pictures and awe was obvious on his face. She had about a hundred pictures— Ashley fooling around with friends, sleeping, laughing, cheering, studying with Eve, hugging her grandmother, sitting at the counter at the diner. It was a long while before he stopped and looked at her. He laughed uncomfortably. "I better stay out of Thunder Point or the whole town will know who I am."

"Her resemblance to you is unmistakable, that's for sure."

"Are you married now? Do you have someone?" he asked.

"Not married, but yes, I have someone. You?"

He nodded. "A fiancée. She's thirty. A web designer." He laughed. "Hard to pull her away from the computer and out of the house. But she's amazingly talented. She wants her own company. Who is your guy?"

She couldn't help but laugh at the irony. She grinned. "The Deputy Sheriff."

He smirked. "Figures. Well, I'm not in trouble anymore. Tell me more about her. About Ashley. Something happened. There's some reason you're here asking about diabetes and Crohn's disease."

"She had a breakdown," Gina said simply. "She had a serious boyfriend, first love, and he dumped her and I could barely get her out of bed. She was saying things I couldn't deal with—like that she didn't even want to live. And then—" She stopped. She swallowed. Was this the kind of private stuff you don't tell a stranger, even if he's the father of your child? And without thinking any further she said, "And then the mean girl he's now dating used Photoshop on a picture of her with naked boobs and texted it to everyone on his phone list. It was up on the internet. She collapsed. I had to have her hospitalized."

His face darkened, then grew crimson. He steepled his fingers to keep his hands from shaking. Then he pursed his lips.

"We were afraid we could be dealing with clinical depression, but the doctor is convinced she was just in crisis. She's home now, doing much better. Except for some emotional disappointment now and then, she's getting her strength back. But it was that crisis that led me to search you out, to ask about family medical history. I was scared to death, I don't mind telling you that."

"Who would do something like that?" he asked in a whisper.

She actually laughed, but it wasn't a happy laugh. "A mean and jealous teenage girl would. Really, Eric, you have no idea how cruel people can be." And then she thought about what she'd said. The man had spent five years in prison. Chances were he knew.

But he was gazing at her with serious eyes. "It must have been so hard," he said softly. "Raising her alone."

"There were hard times," she admitted. "But I had my mother. And like you, I've made a good life for myself. I have strong relationships in Thunder Point and Ashley has a very solid support network and good friends. And I'm watching, I'm always watching. I won't let anything happen to her."

"If there's anything I can do. Any way I can help. Like I said, I have a little money set aside and she wouldn't have to know her father is a—"

"When Ashley is older, when I'm sure she's stable and feeling good about herself, I'll tell her about you. I mean, the new you—I've been honest with her about my past. Right now? I think we just leave it alone. No, I don't want your money. But thank you for offering."

"I only ask one thing, Gina. One small thing." He pulled a card from his shirt pocket. "It's my cell phone number. If there's ever anything I can do for her. Anything. Will you call me?"

She stared at the number. "If I'd come around five years ago and asked for help, would you have been this receptive?"

"I changed my life," he said. "I had to. The path I was on, I was going to die ugly and young. And hard as it is to believe, I didn't want to. Five years ago? Yes, I think I would've tried to help—I was well on my way to a better life by then. But I'm sure now, beyond a doubt. If you need me, if Ashley needs me, I can do my best. If I could meet her someday... Ah, I'm not pushing on that. That's just fantasy. But if she ever needs help, just call me."

They talked for another half hour—she gave him news of the town, he told her about his family and some of his misadventures. Gina cried a little on the way home. It was not about regret. It was about gratitude. Her mother always said things happened the way they were supposed to. If she'd found a way to strap Eric to her seventeen years ago, she'd have found herself stuck with a felon; an irresponsible and heartless bad boy. But the world had done its job to shape him while she and Ashley were busy building their family together.

And now, unless she was no judge at all, he really had rebuilt his character and his life.

She was lucky. She had Mac, the love of her life. And a phone number for emergencies.

Twelve

Cooper had to force himself to call Austin to start a dialogue and he had never found anything so unnatural or difficult. Making small talk with a shy ten-year-old was torture. Cooper asked him about school, about his grandparents, his dad, baseball. Austin responded with one-word answers then, invariably, Cooper would ask for Spencer so he could get the lowdown on how Austin was holding up since his mother's passing.

"He's doing well," Spencer said. "He's resilient and I think he was more than ready to start thinking about normal things. The last few years have been really hard on him."

"And how about learning he has a new biological father on the scene?" Cooper asked.

"It's news to you, Cooper, but we told Austin months before Bridget passed. He's ten—if he was going to have another dad on the scene, all he hoped for was a cool one. You passed the cool test with your Jet Ski and Harley."

About ten days later, Austin was more relaxed on his

call with Cooper. He used more than one-word answers and even seemed to enjoy the conversation a little bit.

Soon after making regular calls to Austin and Spencer, and at Spencer's invitation, Cooper packed a duffel and headed to Texas for a weekend visit. Spencer and Cooper took Austin and one of his friends, James, out for pizza on Friday night. Cooper realized that what greased their relationship best was James. The boys got to laughing and screwing around, eventually running off to play video games in the pizza parlor.

"You're a genius," he told Spencer. "Bringing James along made it so much easier."

"Austin has been drowning in adults for months, especially while Bridget went through the last of her illness. He'd almost forgotten how to have fun."

"How's he doing back at school?" Cooper asked.

"He seems relieved to be there. Like he's so goddamn tired of being serious, of being sad. It's awful seeing a ten-year-old act like an old man."

"You did a better job with him, especially through all these adjustments, than I ever could have. I wouldn't have known where to start."

"You would if you'd had him in your life since he was born," Spencer said. "I think you're doing fine."

"Listen, something's been on my mind," he said, looking at Spencer. "Bridget wasn't cheating on you or anything. You're comfortable with that now, right?"

"Now, yes. I admit it took me a while. I know how it was. At least I think I do. You broke up. She started dating me a few months later, but we were taking it slow. She was trying to make sure it wasn't a rebound thing. Finally she was ready to get more serious. I'd been ready first, that's the fact. We were both pretty surprised by the pregnancy. We both thought it happened the first time...."

"I was having trouble with all the things that went along with the commitment. I was good with the fidelity part. I loved Bridget, or at least I thought I did at the time. But I wasn't ready for stability and family life, and she was smart enough to get that. I wasn't willing to give up anything to make us work. That's why we broke up. But I kept coming back. We had history, that's all it was. It was comfortable and familiar. Then I came back too late—I called her and she told me she was through fooling around, that she'd met someone who could actually make compromises and she was in love." He gave a shrug. "I was pretty pissed, to tell you the truth. I didn't contact her again for six months. And you know the rest."

"She was married and pregnant," Spencer said. He shot Cooper a melancholy look. "And said she was happy."

"She *was* happy. We were over before she moved on. Bridget was a good woman."

"You don't have to sell me on that, you know."

"I'm going to have to tell my family about Austin. And they're going to want to meet him at some point."

"I know. You tell me when and I'll take him. It's not that I don't trust you with him..."

"Listen, let's be straight about this, about anything that has to do with Austin. I don't want Austin scared or overwhelmed. I *want* you to be with him. He's just a kid for God's sake. Until he's ready to visit me or go to my family without you, I want you there with him. I'll try to work out a time with my family and check it with you. I'll pay the fare. Maybe after school is out? They're just over in Albuquerque—not a bad flight for you."

Spencer chuckled. "You're something, you know that? You could be a complete asshole about all this."

"I've been a complete asshole here and there, which might be one of the many reasons Bridget broke up with me," he said, slapping Spencer on the back. "But I'm trying, man. I'm trying. There's sure nothing in it for me if Austin grows up all screwed up."

"Let's hold off on the family visit in Albuquerque," Spencer said. "First, I think Austin and I should come out to Oregon to visit you. On your turf. Is there a hotel in town?"

Cooper smiled. "Even better. I live on the second floor of my business, but I have an RV and a hook-up on the property. It's nice. You and Austin can have it for a weekend. You'll have fun, I can almost guarantee it. It's a nice little town." He grinned. "And I have that Jet Ski."

Right then the boys came running back to the table. "Dad! Dad! We need more quarters!" Austin was flushed and sweaty and smelled gamey, like a happy little boy should.

"I got it," Cooper said. He reached into his pocket. He pulled out a five-dollar bill. "When you get change, count it and make sure you've got the right amount. Got that?"

"Got it!" Austin said. And they turned away.

Austin's friend, James, said, "Who's that again?"

"That's Cooper," Austin said. "The bio-dad."

It wasn't unusual to see Landon on the beach with Hamlet in the afternoons. After school he was often with other high school kids or Eve, but today he was solo, throwing the ball for Ham all the way across the beach. Seeing Cooper up on the deck he headed over and ran up the stairs with Hamlet on his heels. Ham went straight to Cooper for a little scratch behind the ears. "What's up, my man?" Cooper asked Landon. "Coke?"

"Yeah, thanks," Landon said. "I'll get it."

A minute later he was sitting next to Cooper in the same relaxed position, feet up on the deck rail, chair leaning back, looking out at the ocean. It was a few minutes before Landon said, "Coop, do you understand women?"

Cooper turned to look at his profile. He grinned. "Not that often." When Landon didn't say anything, Cooper asked, "Girl trouble?"

"All over the place," Landon said. "Maybe not trouble, exactly. More like confusion. Does it seem like Sarah's in a bad mood these days? And Eve...she's got all that stuff going on—sometimes she's just plain pissy. Sometimes she's crying about nothing or laughing about nothing."

"Sarah seems okay to me," Cooper said. "Maybe a little quiet now and then. She said she's got work stuff going on—stuff that should be resolved soon. I don't know anything about Eve's mood."

"She's been upset about Ash and Downy—that went down badly. It freaked Eve out—she was afraid we'd get all serious and then I'd do something that nasty to her. Then Eve's mom showed up after ten years and that had her all upside down. And I think Sarah's been weird lately."

"Landon, you gotta be patient, man. There are cosmic forces that have nothing to do with me and you. Like PMS. Ever think of that?"

Landon winced. "I try not to think about things like that."

"I don't blame you, buddy. And for God's sake, never ask! That's the kiss of death." He took a sip of his coffee. "I think Sarah was a little worried about my trip to Texas. I think she doesn't know what to make of this situation I'm in—all of a sudden I'm a father. I just try to reassure her—it doesn't change anything between us. It's gotta be a shock, though, huh? So if she's moody, it's probably because I threw her a curve...."

"You think she's jealous or something?"

"Nah. I think she was worried enough about taking me on, now she thinks she has to take me *and* a kid on. It's not really like that, though. Austin wants to live with his dad, Spencer. He feels safe there. I'll just visit from time to time and they'll visit here. You don't show up in a kid's life when he's ten years old and take over. I mean, if he was in trouble I would. But he's not in trouble. Spencer is a good guy."

"How'd you end up with a kid?"

He shrugged. "Who knows? Since we were specifically trying not to have one, something obviously went wrong. But when you see that kid it makes you think maybe something went right...."

Landon shuddered. It was unmistakable.

Cooper pulled his feet off the rail and turned in his chair. "You want to talk about something?"

"No," Landon said, but he didn't make eye contact. "Did you have a girlfriend when you were in high school?"

"Not exactly," Cooper said.

"What does *that* mean?"

"Well, like every kid that age, I was in love just about all the time. I lusted after a lot of girls who didn't appear to lust after me. I had some dates. Most of them were first dates. I think there were a couple of girls I dated a few times."

"So, when did you first, you know..."

"What, Landon? When did I get laid? Do we need to talk about the birds and the bees?"

Landon finally looked at him. "You trying to piss me off? No wonder Sarah's cranky."

"I was older than I wanted to be. I don't know. Maybe seventeen, but probably eighteen. I didn't have a girlfriend I'd been with for six months, that's for sure. Now, what's going on with you and Eve? We got problems?"

He shook his head. "It's just that... Well, I don't want to lose her. She's really special. Perfect. I could never want a better girl. But I don't want to... You know about her mom and dad, right? How they had to get married because Eve was on the way? And they were just kids? Eve's mom was younger than Eve is now. Holy shit is all I have to say about that!"

"Guys don't usually talk about things like that, but I'm capable of math," Cooper said. "You and Eve getting a little too serious?"

"Not yet," he said, and Cooper couldn't tell if it was remorse, disappointment or fear behind those words.

Cooper leaned back and put his feet up on the rail again. "Okay, here's what I have to say about that. You can probably save yourself a lot of heartache by being real careful, by which I mean lots of protection. But hear this from Papa Cooper—there don't seem to be any real guarantees. Any time you want to talk about it..."

"Did you ever feel, you know, like you really loved someone?" he asked.

Cooper smiled at him and he hoped he smiled gently. "I feel that way right now," he said. "I've felt that way before, as a matter of fact—times it didn't really work out. And now I'm kind of glad it didn't. I don't mind telling you, Sarah's the best thing that's ever happened to me and I waited a long time to find her." He clapped a hand on Landon's shoulder. "It's okay to feel like you love Eve. Nothing wrong with love, Landon. Some people find it young, some people have to wait awhile. But what you have to guard against is letting a little love make you a lot careless."

"You can't tell Mac about this conversation," Landon said.

"I wouldn't do that," Cooper said.

"Or Sarah."

"Or Sarah," he repeated. "Now here's what you do, son. You're both, what? Sixteen?"

"We're both seventeen this summer. Eve's seventeen in July."

"Right. You're looking at your senior year and right around the corner will be college. Yep. Here's what you do—you make sure you're protected. Safe. Both of you. Just in case, you know, you get a little crazy. I'm assuming you have—"

"I'm good...."

"Well, that's one of you," Cooper said thoughtfully. They met eyes for a long moment.

Then Landon turned his chair back toward the ocean. They both put their feet up again. And Landon said, "So. How about those Yankees?"

Cooper laughed. "You know what, Landon, old man?

I think you need an after-school job. And a summer job. Keep you out of trouble while Sarah's working."

"That's a good idea. You pay anything?"

"We'll negotiate if we have to," he said.

The *Oregon Dispatch* was a regional newspaper that came out once a week and covered news from the many small towns in Coos County. There were also coupons for local businesses and groceries—a dying tradition as people could download many of these coupons from their computers. But when there was exciting local news or big events, the *Dispatch* was always there. And this week there was a news story from Oregon State University and Thunder Point. It was rumored that Crawford Downy was going to be a first round major league draft pick. A freshman! A couple of scouts had admitted he was a hot property and if he continued to play as well as he had been, he'd be in the majors in no time at all.

Yes, this was the boy who was one of the favorite sons of the town. Perhaps the favorite of all. A brilliant athlete.

It was all the talk at the high school and so Ashley couldn't escape the news. Then she saw the article. There was a picture, of course. Smiling, broad-shouldered Downy with his mitt in his hand, his sandy blond hair lifted by the wind.

Also in the picture was a female shoulder and arm. He had his arm around a girl who was apparently cropped out of the picture.

Was it the same girl? Or a new one?

If he was going to be a pro athlete, Ashley imagined he could have a new girl every week. It depressed her, but she was now completely unsurprised. This guy did not feel like the Downy she had known. She hadn't thought of her Downy as shallow or ego-driven, though he did love the attention in sports. He had been sweet and loyal. No longer, she thought. She threw the paper in the trash.

She went home after school, changed into a pair of shorts and walked down to the beach. Spring was a little lazy finding the northern coast, but the weather was getting so nice. The hillside on what Ben had called his bird sanctuary was covered with blossoms and the green of the trees and bushes was brightening. The sun was out almost every day and the water on the bay was as blue as the sky. People had been paddleboarding a lot lately.

Ashley sat on the sand, knees raised and her arms around them. How many summers had she spent on this beach? How many nights with Downy, partying, making out? She had predicted he'd lose interest in her when he went away to college, but he had said, "Where am I ever gonna find a girl prettier than you? Or sweeter? Come on!"

She thought that was going to be the truth, that he was committed. But now as she looked back, during fall and winter he was just some lame freshman, some second string football player who never got to play. He was a pledge, a plebe.

Then came baseball and Downy had an atomic arm. He not only started every game, but he also caught everything, hit anything and ran like the wind. They used him as starting pitcher and tried him on first base, as well. His batting average was solid; he had a college and alumni following. He was going to take them all the way to a championship. A freshman!

Downy was hot shit. And he probably had his pick of girls. And that was all it took.

"Ashley?"

She looked up to see Frank standing nearby. Oh, poor timing, Frank! She blinked away some tears that were close to falling. She had just been mourning Downy's absence.

"Hi," she said, hearing the sadness in her own voice.

Frank sat on the sand, facing her. "You see that article today?"

"I couldn't miss it. It's got Downy's fan club pretty excited."

Frank shook his head. "It got me thinking about something. I bet you counted on Downy taking you to the prom this year."

She laughed. "I promise you, I got over that idea a while ago."

"Well, I know. But I'm not taking anyone. I'd love to take you."

She was speechless. She thought it possible he had a crush on her, but even so, what a sweet thing to do! "Are you sweeping up after Downy, Frank?"

"Oh, hell no," he said with a bitter laugh. "I think he's an idiot. He's an idiot getting ready to be a bigger idiot!"

She frowned.

"Do you know if he's a high draft pick, he'll drop out of college to take it? Like he's invincible and doesn't need an education or a career other than baseball."

She sat up a little straighter. "Seriously? What do your parents say about that?"

"They're being idiots about it, too. But they don't really appreciate the value of education—neither of them went to college and they're pretty satisfied with things. Dad says the union did more for him than an education ever would." He shook his head. "They think Downy's going to make millions and build them a big house on the ocean. Crazy."

She laughed lightly. "Where did you come from?" she asked, shaking her head.

"The cabbage patch, I think. Doesn't Downy get that that his whole life is only as good as his rotator cuff or his elbow if he goes with baseball?"

"You know what, Frank? He was born to take that on. Athletics has always been the most important thing to Downy. Any sport. He lives that way—it's his life. Being a star athlete—that was more important to Downy than anything else. And you? Learning is most important to you. I think you're both going to do well in life, that's what I think."

"I hope you're right."

"I bet you already have scholarship offers," she said. "Just based on your SATs."

He shrugged.

She laughed. "I knew it! Well, I guess there's a lot more to the Downy family than people know. Your folks might not have big flashy degrees, but they have some talented kids."

"Sure. Thanks. Back to the prom..."

She reached out and touched his arm. "You know what, buddy? If I didn't have a lot of crap to deal with, I would totally accept that invitation. And it isn't just about Downy being your brother, either. It's just that this year, even though I was really looking forward to it, I'm not going. With anyone. Justin Bieber could ask me and I'd say no thanks."

"What good is it going to do to skip it just because my brother acted like such a jerk?"

"It's not about him anymore, Frank. It's about me. I was so into Downy, it was almost like he absorbed me or something. It seemed so cool to have this popular senior like me, promise to love me forever.... Then when he left me, I couldn't find myself again. I was so broken. Now my work is to figure out who I am. I want to go back to who I was—I want to be that strong girl again."

"You've always seemed strong to me," he said.

"I was, back before Downy decided I was the anointed one. Then having him became more important to me than anything else. I didn't realize it at all, not until he was gone and all I could feel was so empty and lost I couldn't get out of bed. Did you know I spent a week in the hospital?"

"I think everyone knows that, Ash."

"Do you know why?"

He tilted his head. "Depression?"

"Yeah. Depression and feeling like I didn't want to live. It scared my mom so much, she called the counselor. And while I was in the hospital I met a girl who had the same issues and she tried to fix her boy problems with a razor blade." She shook her head and shuddered. "You just can't mess around with those kind of thoughts, Frank. I'm never losing myself like that again. I had wanted to go to the prom. But I'm not letting a fancy dress or a popular boyfriend be more important to me than living. For God's sake!"

He gave her a wan smile.

"Now why would you smile at that?"

He reached for her hand. "I guess because you know what you need now. You're going to be all right."

"I'm still struggling," she said. "I felt so left out that I couldn't celebrate the draft rumor with him. I would have encouraged him to stay in school, but still..."

"He's such a fucking idiot," Frank muttered.

"I don't want you to hate your brother because of me," she said.

"Look, Downy took good care of me when I couldn't take care of myself. When I was skinny little kid who'd rather read than play soccer or sandlot ball. I'll always owe him for that. I'm not going to feud with him over this, but I have my own opinions. He's not my hero at the moment."

"I still cry," she whispered, as if it was a secret.

"Yeah? Me, too."

Her eyes grew large with the question.

"I had a dog. The only thing in my family that was really mine. I lived in a house full of jocks and I was the runt. I couldn't see to get out of bed without my glasses, but Dodger loved me. He died last fall. He was fourteen—long for a Golden, actually. He's better off—he'd started dragging his hind quarters and I helped him outside to go to the bathroom. No life for a rabbit-chasing, happy, fun-loving dog. But if I think about him, I can still cry. I think loving someone and losing them can leave a hole in your heart. For a while, anyway." He pulled her hand into his and rubbed his thumb over the back. "But scars are much tougher than virgin skin. Right?"

Another thing Ashley hadn't thought about at all— the Downys' dog had died. It never occurred to her that he was Frank's dog. That Frank was grieving.

"You should get another dog," she said.

"You should get a better boyfriend. One with an IQ higher than a turnip."

"Not yet." She laughed. "I think maybe some good came out of this mess."

"Yeah?"

"Well, I feel closer to you. You've been so nice."

He looked down briefly. Shyly.

"Listen, could you please not tell about the hospital? I think my reputation as a lunatic is going to be hard enough to get over."

"I would never tell anything you tell me," he said.

They talked for an hour, off the subject of proms and Downy, and on to what colleges they were interested in, what they'd like to do for careers, where they'd most like to live. Frank wasn't sure what he would study, only that it would have a lot to do with math, and his dream career would be as an inventor. He had questions for her about her goals, none of which she could answer. She had always wanted to follow Downy to college and she hadn't thought she would ever leave Thunder Point. She had no real career ideas besides being a wife and mother. Things with Downy had changed all that.

Gina had been helping in her mother's deli for a good twenty years. Carrie did all the baking and experimenting with new recipes, but Gina could slap together deli sandwiches in record time. If she had time after leaving the diner, Gina would go across the street and give her mother a couple of hours and when Carrie had a party or wedding to cater, it was usually Gina—and sometimes Ashley, as well—to help her serve and clean up after the event. It was rare that neither of them were available, but on those occasions Carrie had a few friends who didn't mind making a little extra money.

Carrie's business had grown lately, which kept Gina busier than usual. People were already ordering graduation cakes. Cooper had made a contract with Carrie for her wrapped and premade deli items for his bar and, with the weather warming up, summer coming and more people on the beach, especially on weekends, he was doing a bigger business—and more food was needed. While Ben, the previous owner, had been happy with simple sandwiches, Cooper encouraged her to try out some new things. She came up with some turkey, ham and salami wraps dressed with spinach leaves and sweet mustard, crab cakes that Cooper could just warm up, shrimp salads, big tomatoes stuffed with shrimp or crab salad, and her special pizzas all made up and ready to pop in the oven for twenty minutes. She had sausage rolls, crab rolls, Caesar salads, fruit plates. All these things could be made ahead and they lasted for three days. Cooper was thrilled and bragged to his friends constantly about the awesome food he served.

Carrie entered the diner in the midafternoon, right before Gina was finished for the day. She was holding her battered notebook, which usually meant she wanted to brainstorm menu ideas with Gina. Carrie had a few events coming up—a wedding, a baby shower, an anniversary party and the grand opening of the new clinic across the street.

"Coffee, Mom?" she asked.

"Please. I'm trying to come up with some new ideas for the same old chicken reception dinner and want your opinion."

"Just chicken, huh?"

"If they'd spend another fifty cents per plate it could be chicken and salmon, but like most young couples, they want to keep the price down. I can actually save them money with this chicken stroganoff recipe."

"I *love* that," Gina said, mouth watering.

"I can get by with a little less meat...."

The door to the diner opened and in walked Marjorie Downy. She was the client who was throwing herself a twentieth anniversary party. Thunder Point people seldom went all out like this, hiring a caterer. But Marjorie was quite proud of this anniversary and Gina had heard she was planning on renewing her vows with her husband.

"Hello, Marjorie," Gina said.

"Well, hello," Carrie added.

But Marjorie glided forward with a look on her face as though she might have a problem. "I guess it's best that I caught both of you together, though I tried the deli first. I was going to just take this up with you, Carrie."

Carrie closed her notebook. "We can walk across the street, if you like."

"No, no. This actually concerns Gina, as well." She took a deep breath. "Party time is coming up. I know you rely on Gina and Ashley to help cater events, but I think this time it might not be the best idea. Crawford is coming home for the party."

Gina was flabbergasted. "Marjorie, you can't possibly think I'd let Ashley serve at your party when her ex-boyfriend will be there! This has been hard enough on her!"

"Oh, my," she said, hand to her breast. "I should have known you'd understand, Gina." Marjorie wasn't a particularly pretty woman; she was very plain and would be more attractive without so much makeup, and with a more flattering haircut and color. She was hooked on perms and her hair tended to frizz. Her natural color had been dark but with the onset of some gray, she took to yellow streaks. Not blond. Yellow. It appeared striped and the girls in town joked that she was the bride of Frankenstein.

Her appearance wasn't the problem, of course. She was jealous and insincere by nature and this is what people found most objectionable about her.

"Of course you heard about the possibility of being a first round draft pick for Crawford?"

And uppity.

"Of course," Gina said. "I guess congratulations are in order."

"Yes, thank you. And he'll be bringing Selena home. It's getting more serious. She comes from such a nice family. Her father works for a congressman. He's a lawyer."

Gina ground her teeth. "You must be looking forward to that."

She laughed a little bit. "We are. Yes, indeed."

"Well, rest assured, Ashley won't be at your party, serving or in any other capacity."

"I compliment you, Gina. You and your daughter have both handled this situation so well. Rejection can't be easy and Ashley has been so mature. A credit to you, of course."

"And will your parents be attending the party?" Carrie asked.

"My parents?" she asked. "They don't live around here."

"Oh? Have they moved?" Carrie asked. "Didn't they

used to live between here and Bandon? Your dad worked on a big commercial fishing boat—he was a crabber. Your mother took in sewing and ironing. Right? Because I was just getting my business off the ground while still working here at the diner and they bought one of my first graduation cakes."

"They wouldn't come here for a cake," she said, laughing nervously.

"I advertised," Carrie said. "I ran coupons. I still have a picture of that cake. And they showed me your picture—so proud of you when you got your diploma. They wanted a flute on it—you played the flute. Nineteen years ago."

"No," she said, shaking her head. "That would've been twenty-*two* years ago."

Carrie shook her head. "I was disappointed they didn't try me for a wedding cake. I so love making wedding cakes. It's not my specialty, but I think I do a fairly decent job."

"You're mixed up, but no matter. No, my parents won't be coming. They're not doing very well."

"I'm so sorry to hear that," Carrie said. "Please, give them my regards. I'll be bringing some other servers to your party, not my girls. Anything else you want to check? Still happy with the menu?"

"It's fine," she said a bit sourly. "I'd better finish my errands...."

"Till later then, Marjorie," Carrie said.

When she was gone Gina turned to her mother. "What was *that* all about?"

"This isn't her twentieth anniversary. It's her nineteenth."

"But Downy is nineteen!"

Carrie shrugged. "Must have taken some time to sort out. I know she didn't graduate with her class. Her mother told me she dropped out and got a GED. She got pregnant in high school and didn't marry her husband until after the baby was born."

Gina was speechless for a moment. "After all the cruel things she's said to me and about me?"

"I'm sure she thinks no one knows, she's been lying about it so long. And when was the last time you saw Downy's grandparents in town? They go visit them, they rarely, if ever, come here. But some of us have been around here a long time."

"You've known this all along?" Gina asked. "And never said anything?"

"It's not a good idea to make bad karma. It'll bite you in the ass eventually. But I slipped—she just pushed me too far, bragging on that girl who sent texts of that awful picture of Ashley. In fact, I wouldn't have taken on this job, but I can't afford to turn away neighbors in a town of only fifteen hundred. And if they're decent, I can keep their secrets, but Marjorie tries my patience."

Gina let a huff of laughter escape her. "All this time...how on earth did you remember? Dates and everything?"

"I never forget a cake," Carrie said with an innocent shrug.

Thirteen

Cooper set up the RV for Spencer and Austin to use on their upcoming weekend visit. Sarah helped him wipe down the dusty surfaces and she changed the sheets on the bed while he cleaned the bathroom and stocked the refrigerator. "If the boy is going to visit sometimes, he should have a house," Cooper said. "He has a house in Texas."

"Don't be so jittery," Sarah said. "He'll love this."

"It's a tin can," Cooper said. "Why have I never had a house?"

"Because you're shiftless," she told him with a laugh.

Not only did he make sure Rawley was on board to help him cover the weekend, but he also asked Landon to be there. He couldn't serve drinks, but he could serve food and help with clean up. And Landon, trying to get ready to take his girl to the prom, was more than happy for the extra work.

Friday afternoon finally arrived and Spencer drove his rental car down the road to the bar. After parking the car, he and Austin headed to the deck surrounding the property. Spencer looked around the bay and promontories, took a deep breath of the coastal air and smiled. "You're a lucky man, Cooper," he said.

Austin was quiet, seeming very shy about the whole visit idea. He met the welcoming party—Sarah, Rawley, Landon—politely. He viewed the bay and ocean passively. "Are we going on that?" he asked, pointing to the Jet Ski.

"Sure, I'll take you out on it," Cooper said.

"What else will we do?" he asked, looking completely unimpressed.

"Well, we can take the Rhino into town. I can show you how to paddleboard. We can fish off the dock. We'll find stuff to do." Cooper felt as if he was drowning—this was not going to be easy.

Then Austin pointed at the toy hauler and asked, "Is that where we're staying?"

"Well, it can be. Or, if you're more comfortable in the bait shop, there's a very small apartment upstairs—big enough for you and your dad."

"Bait shop?" he asked.

"It used to be a bait shop with a bar in it and now it's a bar without any bait. Let's take a look at the RV first." Inside, Cooper's heart sank a little bit. He didn't have anything good enough for a son and he felt unprepared and a little like an underachiever.

They grabbed the luggage and headed over to the RV. Cooper opened the door of the toy hauler and let Austin step in first, followed by Spencer.

Austin stood in the middle of the living room and turned full circle, looking around, taking it in. Cooper was prepared for him to say something about it being a *trailer,* which it was. Then he turned to Cooper with bright eyes and said, "This is *awesome!*"

* * *

The weekend went better than Cooper had dared hope. The weather cooperated and they spent a lot of time on the water. Despite sunscreen, Austin got himself a little color. The toy hauler was full of sand from all his running in and out and so was the bar. Cooper's upstairs apartment was like an indoor beach. They were going to have to revisit foot wiping. Austin not only loved the Jet Ski, but also bonded with Hamlet, who spent a lot of time at the bar over the weekend. Austin got to drive the Rhino across the beach with Landon as co-pilot. At night, they had a fire on the beach and roasted marshmallows.

"I don't know if I can compete with this," Spencer said.

"I didn't think I could compete with ten years of history so let's go ahead and write up a noncompete clause," Cooper said, only half-serious.

Cooper hadn't even considered the importance of having fun himself—he felt a huge responsibility to *give* fun. But, in the end, the weekend was satisfying. Spencer took off on his own a couple of times, exploring the general area, leaving Cooper and Austin on their own.

Once the weekend was done and he was back on his own, Cooper settled in to do the thing he'd been working up to. Knowing his parents were early risers, he phoned them early Tuesday morning—it was barely 7:00 a.m. in Albuquerque.

"Hey, Dad," Cooper said. "You and Mom both up? Had your coffee?"

"Up and caffeinated. How are you, son?"

"Excellent. Listen, can you get Mom on the phone or put me on speaker? I have something to explain to you."

"Okay, you're on speaker." Then his father said to his mother, "He has something to explain."

"Cooper, are you all right? You're not sick are you?" his mother asked.

"No, I'm fine. Perfect. Listen, this surprised the hell out of me so I know it's going to really shock you. Um. Remember Bridget...?"

On a sunny Saturday afternoon in May Frank Downy walked a few blocks to Ashley's house. He had a back-pack and a soft cooler. When Ashley came to the door he asked, "Are you busy?"

"Not really. I was helping my grandma make cookies. Want one?"

"Yeah. And how about putting a few in a baggie and come with me."

"Where?"

"Just to the beach and the south promontory," he said. He lifted the cooler. "I came prepared for a little adventure."

She eyed him suspiciously, but she couldn't help her smile. She had no idea little Frank would grow into his looks and become a hottie. "What are you up to, Frank? Shouldn't you be going to the prom?"

"I'm not going to the prom, Ash. Why would I? You'll need tennis shoes—we're going to take a little hike. You'll like it, I promise."

"You're just trying to take my mind off the prom. You don't have to," she said. "Landon even offered to have two dates, but I'm still happy with my decision. I don't want to go this year. Next year, maybe. Not this year."

"Well, I'd love to take credit for doing something

so chivalrous, but it's a total coincidence. I was down on the docks this morning talking to a couple of the crabbers—the gray whales are running heavy. One of them said yesterday they saw several breach. They're feeding on crustaceans close to shore on their way back to the Bering Sea from Baja. One of the guys said he thought more than the usual number is hanging around our coastline and not migrating this year. I thought we'd go out to Ben's point."

"Oh, that's private...."

"I asked Cooper if he'd mind. We won't disturb anything. Dusk is a good time." He turned around. "I have everything we need. Blanket, binoculars, flashlight for getting back, Duraflame for the beach afterward. There's a path out to the point. Not a good one, but a path. Come on—the flora is in bloom out there. Let's go."

"Flowers." She laughed.

"Flowers, plant life, flora—whatever. And the birds are all in love, I can tell you that much."

"What about the whales? Are they in love?"

"They took care of that in Baja," he said with a grin. "I'm going. Want to come?"

"Yes," she said, smiling.

"Put on some long pants and grab a sweatshirt," he said. "There are lots of berry bushes out there. They'll scratch up your legs. And you know, when the sun goes down—"

"I know, Frank. I've lived here my whole life. Should I make us a couple of sandwiches?"

He lifted the cooler just as Gina was coming up behind Ashley. "I did already. We're set. Sandwiches, chips, case of beer…" He smiled at Gina. "Kidding. Diet Coke and green tea."

"Just give me a minute," Ashley said, whirling off to her room to get changed.

Gina stepped toward the front door. "This is very nice of you, Frank."

"Thanks, but I was going out there, anyway. I went from the marina to the bait shop to ask Cooper if he'd mind if I hiked out to the bird sanctuary, and then I thought, maybe Ashley had nothing to do." He could feel a little color on his cheeks. Being sixteen could be a royal pain. He'd been killing himself trying to think of something that might distract her on prom night and just lucked into the whales.

"Well, come inside. Let's see what else we can stuff in that cooler," she said.

But he had it pretty well stocked. In addition to the sandwiches and chips he had veggies and fruit.

Carrie grinned when he came into the kitchen as she'd obviously heard the exchange at the door. "Here you go," she said, handing him a bag of cookies. "And is there room for this?" she asked, pulling a small, disposable plastic container out of the refrigerator. "Pasta and crab salad? Just fresh today."

"Thanks," he said.

She handed him two plastic forks. "Do you have napkins?"

"And wet wipes," he said with a shy smile.

"You're a dream date," Gina said.

"I'm not a date," he said. And he thought, *I'm not a date, thanks to my idiot brother.*

"I could call my friend Sarah and borrow her Razor and you could drive across the beach," Gina offered. "If you left it by Cooper's while you go out on the point, it would be safe."

"Thanks, but I'm up for the hike. If Ashley is."

She came bouncing into the room, jeans and tennis shoes on, hoodie tied around her waist. "Of course I'm up for it. I can't wait."

"We need to move it. I don't want to get out there too late. Once the sun sets, the show is over. Let's go."

"Let me carry something."

"I got it. When we have to go uphill you can have one of these handles." Then he looked at Gina and said, "I don't think we'll be late."

"Ashley has her phone," she said. "Just be careful and have fun."

Gina called Cooper. "Hey, it's me, Gina. Frank came by and said he asked if he could go out on the point to look for whales."

"Affirmative," Cooper said. "Permission granted."

"He has food, a blanket, a Duraflame.... The log is for the sand, not the point, I take it. So, I think this is great—something for Ashley to do on prom night. But I'm just saying..."

"I'll be here all evening, Gina," he said. "After Sarah takes pictures of Landon and Eve before they head off to prom, she's coming over. I see some deck time coming my way. I'll keep my eyes and ears open."

"I'm not really worried about her. She has her phone," Gina said. "But it's been a real rocky spring."

He laughed. "Tell me about it! The whole world tilted on its axis!"

"I guess it did, didn't it? Have I said congratulations yet?"

"A couple of times, I think. Don't worry about Ash. Downy might be a dipshit who's going to regret his manly moves, but I think Frank's a standup guy. And for the record, I don't think he's just cleaning up Downy's mess."

"I think you're right."

"Did you know he can name every plant and bird on that point?"

She laughed. "I'm not surprised."

Ashley had been on picnics all her life, but she'd never been on a picnic with Frank. It was like a biology class, but more fun.

Instead of climbing the stairs to Cooper's deck, they walked up the drive, then out toward the point.

"I haven't been out here in a while," Frank said. "This place is covered with pine and manzanita, but there are some beautiful plants—wild ginger, salal, iris, ocean spray and even swamp rose, which is typically an east coast plant. The last time I was out here I counted ten types of fern—deer fern, chain fern, maidenhair, lady. There are several lilies, including mariposa, and that usually grows on the mountainsides."

"You know all these plants?"

"I looked them up," he said. "That's a flowering currant and that's Pacific blackberry."

"Wow."

"I know. Geek, right?"

"No! It's cool," she said.

"Ben was more interested in the birds—the loon, eagle, belted kingfisher, cormorant, merganser. I think he counted all the different birds he'd seen out here."

"Are you into birds, too?" she asked him.

"I'm better with stars," he said. "I should say I'm more interested in them. Here we go," he said, reaching the end of the point. He dropped the cooler and backpack and pulled out a blanket to sit on and the binoculars, which he gave to her. "I'm counting on you to sight the first breach."

She grabbed the binoculars and trained them on the sea. She was quiet for long moments before she said, "I saw a spout, but it's a million miles out there."

"I hope some come closer," he said. "It's a good day for it."

"Do you do this often? Whale watch?"

"Spring and fall," he said. He took an apple out of the cooler and offered it to Ashley. When she shook her head, he bit into it. "Sometimes I'd hitch a ride out with a fisherman. Nobody minds me. I'm quiet. Sometimes I'd come out here. Ben didn't care because I was careful not to disturb anything. Sometimes he came with me. Before Dodger's arthritis got bad, he'd come, too."

"We haven't had a dog since I was four," Ashley said. "She was my mom's dog. She was real old even then."

"And you didn't get another one," he pointed out to her.

She shook her head. "I'm not sure why."

He laughed. "I hope you don't feel that way about boyfriends."

"I do right now," she said, but she smiled at him. "It's going to be a long time. And I'm going to be much fussier. I'm not hooking up with some big dumb jock who has an ego the size of California."

He just smiled. Then he pointed. "Spout. It's much closer."

She went back to watching, but without the binoculars. She scanned the horizon and saw another spout, a few minutes later. After about an hour, they each had a sandwich and a cookie, broke out some drinks, saw a few more spouts.

When the sun started to get a little lower over the Pacific, Ashley spotted a few dark humps in the water and wordlessly pointed.

"Here we go," Frank said. And no sooner had he said that than there was a big breach, all the way up out of the water, not too far off the coast. "That's what I'm talking about!"

Ashley had never done anything like this with Downy. If they were together, he wanted to be either throwing a ball or making out. But they had talked on their phones all the time—they even had to get a special plan for exchanging calls so they wouldn't have such high monthly call charges. Several calls and many texts passed between them every day. Her grandma would say, *"You young people text each other when you're in the same room together. Don't you realize you have to communicate to have a relationship?"*

"Frank? Do you text many people?"

He gave a shrug, his eyes focused on the ocean. "If there's a reason. By the way, that text that went around? I knew that was a fake."

"You did?"

He looked at her. "Ash, you have a nice figure but that obviously wasn't your chest." And he colored a little.

"No joke," she said with a laugh. Oh, my God, was she laughing at that horrible incident now?

"Everyone knew, except idiots," he said. "There. Look out there."

And sure enough, a pod. Close to shore. There were a couple of tail splashes and another breach. As Ashley knew, you could go whale watching for hours and never see anything.

"Do you date at all?" she asked Frank.

"I've been out a few times. Nothing special. I mean, nice girls."

She laughed at him. "Who?"

"Paula from science club. We doubled with Kurt and Lynette. Paula is *not* very happy with me."

"Why not?"

"I told her I just wanted to be friends," he said. "I think she wanted to get married."

Ashley crumbled into laughter.

"I didn't think it was that funny," he said.

"I know, I know. But that's the thing about girls," she informed him. "We all want to live happily ever after. And the sooner, the better. Even the ones who want some major career achievement still want to be adored forever. Believe me, Frank, it causes a world of trouble."

"Did you? Want to marry Downy?"

"Oh, absolutely! We even talked about it—made crazy promises to each other about forever. We had plans—right after college he was going to go pro and we'd have a big wedding and I'd follow the team to games." She shook her head. "So much for that idea."

"And now?" Frank asked.

"I want to punch him in the face," she said. "With a brick."

Frank's smile was *huge*. "I think it's time to move this party to the beach," he said. "I have a log. I'll show you some popular constellations. If you're up for that."

"I'm up for it," she said. "I might have to make a

stop at Cooper's. And, Frank? Am I getting credit for this course?"

"You get anything you want, Ash. How many whales did you see?"

"I don't know! Twenty?"

"Nine."

"Do you remember everything?"

He shook out the blanket to get the dirt and dried pine needles off. "Sometimes it's a curse."

The sun was setting a bit later over the ocean and it was Saturday night, big night in Thunder Point. Cooper had been busy, but by eight-thirty there was just one couple sitting on the deck, a candle on their table, a beer and a glass of wine before them. They'd come across the beach in their golf cart and would go back the same way. Cooper wiped down the bar and took a glass of wine out to the deck for Sarah, bringing a beer for himself. There was a small fire out on the beach—Ashley and Frank. They were lying on their backs, looking up at the star-filled sky. Before sitting down he said to his last two guests, "Let me know if you need anything, folks. I'll be right over here."

"Thanks, Cooper."

"My pleasure."

Then he joined Sarah. He leaned back and propped his feet up on the opposite chair.

"I think you like this life," she said.

"What's not to like? A night in May by the ocean. And you right beside me." He looked at her. "Landon will be out late. We can sneak upstairs." He gave her a purely lascivious grin. "For a while."

"You haven't told me how your family reacted to your news. I'm dying to hear about that."

"Oh, right." He sat up straighter. "It was classic. My father was speechless and my mother started to cry. Austin is the same age as one of my nephews. Our conversation was a little awkward—they wanted details on how Bridget got pregnant six or eight months or a year after we broke up. I did the best I could with that—told them we'd called off the engagement but still saw each other sometimes. You know—old habits are hard to break. My mother said, 'Henry Cooper!' at least once. I tried to put Spencer in a good light—he and Bridget had been dating, but hadn't gotten too serious until... Well, you know. But word spread and my sisters got in touch. They were ruthless—each one of them called me. They wanted all the intimate details of everything! They wanted to know who was sleeping with whom and when." He chuckled and shook his head. "I told each one of them that the only really important things is that I was never, at any time, sleeping with Spencer. If you come from a family like mine, it is impossible to have a personal life."

She pulled up her feet, circling her knees with her arms and resting her chin on her knees. "Are they happy with the news?"

"I think they're a little too intrigued by the biology of it all. I promised to take Austin to meet them sometime. Probably this summer."

"Aren't you a little intrigued with the biology?"

He shook his head. "I have it figured out. The important thing is that Spencer has it figured out, too. Our engagement had been broken off for over six months and even though I blew into town sometimes, she was moving on. I knew that even if I didn't take her seriously enough. She'd been dating—she'd met someone she really liked a lot. And if you knew the Bridget I knew... She was extremely straightforward and honest, almost to a fault. Had she known, she would have told us both."

"But have you wondered about—"

"I was tested, Sarah...."

"No, I mean, others? Have you wondered if this is the only time, the only one?"

He leaned back and laced his fingers behind his head, looking up at the sky. "The truth is, I did a memory check. It's possible there was a miracle before I met Bridget, and I say miracle because I was always careful. Responsible. Not because I'm some angel, but because I wasn't looking to get tied down. And I know this is probably hard to believe, but I never liked one-night stands. Seemed like I either had no woman in my life or I specialized in brief engagements. That all came to an end after Patti. I was a monk after that one."

"Oh?" she said, peering at him.

"It didn't feel good, Sarah. I can't blame anyone but myself, but it wasn't... Hmm, how do I put this? An optimal experience?"

"You get over that?"

He reached over and gave her back a gentle rub. "Oh, yeah. I think it's highly improbable there were any other unknown children from my past. You know what I think about a lot more? That I might've never known about him. If Bridget had lived a long and happy life, they might not have known. Or even under the circumstances, they could have decided not to tell him. Or me. Most families are notorious secret keepers if not outright liars. Everyone in my family hides Aunt

Mercedes's tippling and we don't talk about Grandpa's earlier years—the ones where he had this other family, the one he left to make *our* family."

She laughed. "Are those some of your family secrets?"

"They're not secrets, they're just things we don't talk about in front of Aunt Mercedes or Grandma and Grandpa. And I'm sure there are lots more—I have three sisters. My mom and the girls—they love that stuff. They trade in secrets. Dad and I are kind of..." He shrugged as if to say *Who cares?*

"He's cute...Austin. What a happy kid. I mean, after all he's been through lately, he sure knows how to have a good time."

"You have to remember, he's known about me for months—Bridget and Spencer told him long before they told me. And that other awful thing—losing his mother. He'd been losing her for a long time. On some level it might have been a relief for him to be a kid again, not worried and sad every day."

"He reminded me of Landon at that age."

"Really?"

"It was probably the hardest time of my life and yet the most fulfilling. He was only five when we lost our parents. I wrestled him away from mean old Aunt Frances when he was six and I struggled adapting to the life of a single mother who was also a Coast Guard pilot. It was so hard to keep up with everything—so hard to take care of him, be a parent, get to the school and sport events, find the right people to keep him overnight or after school. But he was the light of my life—so funny and smart and...and...he just *loved* me so much, even when I was inadequate. Oh, and I so often felt inadequate!"

Cooper laughed softly, stroking her back. "I bet you were not even close to being inadequate. Look at him now. He's amazing. Austin followed him around like a puppy all weekend."

"They were kind of cute together."

"A few months ago you told me that you had this dream of having a kid of your own...."

"A silly thing," she said with a shrug. "Let's face it, Landon is as much my own as any baby could be. Don't worry about that. That's never going to happen...."

"It isn't?" he asked. "You've given up on that?"

"I'm thirty-three with twelve years toward retirement responsible for a kid who's going to be a senior in high school and then looking at colleges. I think the die's been cast."

"You never know. The right man could show up and then everything looks different...."

She laughed. "Hah. I've been taking care of myself and Landon for a long time now. It's a habit and a personal priority—I support myself. I'll always support myself."

"Yes, you do," he said with a smile. "I have an idea. Let's sneak upstairs while Landon's at the prom and see if...ahem...the right man shows up and makes things a little different."

"You lobbying for another family, Mr. Cooper?" she asked. "You still have two customers."

"I'll kick them out," he said, leaning toward her.

She let him have a chaste kiss, but she pushed him away. "When you're closed for the night, I'll sneak upstairs with you for a little while. But don't get the idea you're going to change my life."

He grinned at her. "You know the problem with you, Commander Dupre? You just don't keep an open mind. I could take you to bed and change everything. You could discover you just can't live without me."

She ran a finger down his scruffy cheek. "And the problem with you, Mr. Cooper—you think you can solve everything with good sex."

His grin broadened. "It is good, isn't it, Sarah." It was not a question. "Well, one thing at a time." He threw a glance over his shoulder at the couple down at the end of the deck. "Should I tell them it's time for them to go?"

She lifted her glass and said, "Just get me another glass of wine and leave those nicc people alone."

Fourteen

In a place like Thunder Point there were several key locations to run into friends and acquaintances—Cooper's beach bar, being one. In the time he had been here, Cooper had met a lot of people. The beach in general found people walking, jogging, fishing off Cooper's dock, kayaking, just sitting on the sand or a handy rock, enjoying the view. The diner in town was a convenient gathering place, and so was the main drag through town.

But today was the first time he'd ever been called and asked to meet someone. Mac McCain rang him up and said, "You free to come over to Cliffhanger's for a beer? There's something to talk about."

"Sure," Cooper said. "As long as I can get back here before it gets busy this evening. Anything in particular I should prepare myself for?"

"Nah. Just bring your laid-back self."

While Cooper was crossing the beach on his Rhino, maneuvering around the big rocks that dotted the landscape, he pondered that statement. Laid-back. Huh. That was the funny thing—he actually had not seen himself that way. At least not until he'd taken up residence in Thunder Point, which was, in so many ways, just a simple, easy place. There was no shortage of challenges. In fact, his closest friends were having the greatest challenges at the moment. Mac's ex-wife had been lurking, making him wonder what she was up to and Gina was worried about her. And Sarah...ah, Sarah! She'd been worried about some work issue she had yet to share, but this talk of hers that she'd always support herself had an independent ring to it that made him nervous. And even with all that, Cooper couldn't help but think that as long as they had this—the sound of the sea, the compact cocoon of a town and the reliability and loyalty of its people—things would work out fine.

Yes, he was now laid-back. Prior to this he'd always been a little high-strung, working things over in his mind, thinking too much or too hard. Worrying about what the future might bring or where it would lead him.

He parked the Rhino at Cliff's and went into the bar. He saw Mac, the football coach and Cliff sitting at a table in the bar. He walked over.

"Looks like a board meeting," Cooper said.

All three men stood. Mac put out his hand. Mac was in uniform and had a cup of coffee in front of him while the other two men were nursing beers. "Thanks for coming over, Cooper. Coach Rayborough, this is Cooper. He's the newcomer here. Have you two met?"

"We've met in passing," Cooper said, shaking the man's hand. He hadn't really thought of himself as the newcomer, but that was probably accurate. He was no longer someone passing through. He'd settled in, made himself a part of the town. It seemed as if every other place he'd lived before this, he'd always been thinking about where he'd go next. That had definitely changed for him and there was only one caveat—Sarah. "Of course, we've seen each other at games and around town," Cooper added. Then he shook Cliff's hand. "How's it going?"

"Good," the man replied. "A beer's on the way over. Take a seat."

"This looks downright ominous," Cooper said, pulling out a chair. And before they could get down to it, his beer arrived.

"When Cooper showed up in town, he looked like some kind of jet jockey—leather bomber jacket and boots and short hair. Now he's starting to look like a beachcomber," Mac said with a laugh.

Cooper looked down at himself—soft scrubbed jeans, sweatshirt, well-worn topsiders on his feet. His hair had got a little long and he needed to take time for a haircut. As far as he was concerned, he was attired in the uniform of the day.

"There's some news coming our way," Mac said. "Coach?"

The older man cleared his throat. "It's been a rough year, but I don't have to tell you that. You're here because you lost a good friend—Ben Bailey. And you're good friends with Landon Dupre. We all know he went through some hard times when he first moved here.

"I expected to teach and coach till I'm seventy-five," the coach said. "I've been here a long time. Been growing up the young men in this town for decades. I'm sixty-five. I think it's time for me to step down, let a younger man take over, if one can be found." He shook his head sadly. "I missed so many warning signs—I was coaching a kid who had been a lethal bully for years and I never saw what was happening."

"As I've told the coach, there were a lot of us who regarded Jag Morrison as a spoiled pain in the ass, but never realized he was capable of taking that to the next level," Mac said, referring to the kid who was now in detention for manslaughter. Mac lifted his coffee cup to his lips.

"You can't hold yourself accountable for him, Coach," Cliff said. "No more than I can. I've been friends with his dad, Puck, for years and I couldn't stand the way Jag treated his folks or the folks around town, but I never said anything. I never did anything."

"What could you have done?" the coach said. "I was in a position to take a stand—he was my player." He turned his attention to Cooper. "I've written a letter of intent to the school board and they'll receive it tomorrow. I'm resigning as athletic director and head coach effective the end of the school year. I can stay on as a consultant to a new coach—I know the town, I know the boys. But that's the best I can do. I think the team needs better instincts, younger eyes."

"You took the team all-conference last year," Cooper pointed out.

Coach Rayborough shook his head, looking down. "There's more to it than that," he said. "I've always tried to impress on the kids that there's more to it than just winning. It's about making your school and your parents and your town proud, and that goes beyond the field."

Cooper took a drink from his beer. Then he asked, "Have you thought this through? Maybe you're just disappointed. You have a right to be—you were as let down as anyone in learning that your team captain was felonious. But the boys—they held it together through some pretty rugged stuff."

"I went to his sentencing hearing today," the coach said solemnly. "I watched a boy not yet eighteen sentenced to prison and he still smirked and laughed as he was being led away. There's evil there. And I never saw it."

"What does this have to do with me?" Cooper asked.

"Dupre, for one," Coach said. "The kids in this town need good coaching, good role models. Most of 'em come from simple families—fishermen, small business owners, folks with jobs out of town, public servants. These aren't rich folks. Their kids need scholarships if they can get 'em. They all work, with few exceptions. They get through high school struggling for the best grades, hold part-time jobs and if they're athletic or musical, they put a lot of time and heart into developing those skills to help them land scholarships. We've been real lucky—we've turned out some damn fine athletes. There have only been a couple of pros out of Thunder Point, but there have been a lot of college degrees."

"Cooper," Mac said. "How's your game?"

His eyes widened and he snapped to attention. "*My* game?" He laughed. "First of all, I have a year and a few credits of college and that's it. I could teach just about anyone how to fly a helicopter, but not much else. Second, I played sandlot football—I could catch a ball if someone walked across the parking lot and handed it to me. Is that why you wanted me to come over? Hoping I could step up? Because, man, I love the game but... but I love the game enough to stay the hell out of the coaching business."

"Actually, I wanted to call you because of Landon," Mac said. "He's got a lot riding on his senior year."

"No kidding," Cooper said. "What's that got to do with me?"

"Well, you're his mentor," Mac said. "You're his closest adult male influence. He probably can talk to you about things he can't really talk to Sarah about. He might be in the market for some serious moral support. I'm sure he's counting on the coach being there."

Cooper shot Coach Rayborough a look. "Listen, I get that you've had about enough. I understand, seriously. But if there's not a decent coach on scene..."

"I'll do what I can," he said, but he was shaking his head. "My best just isn't so great these days. I thought you could bring this up with Sarah. Of course, she and Landon should call me if they want to talk, but there's plenty of time before practice starts at the end of summer for them to look around. There are other schools and even private schools in the general area and if—"

"Like you said, Coach—Landon had a hard time settling in here, but now he's established. He has good grades, the boy's got serious game and there's the girlfriend, not to mention other friends." He shook his head. "I don't see him volunteering to change schools for his senior year. Matter of fact, I had to do that because of my dad's job and I still remember how tough it was." He drank some of his beer. "We'll just have to hope for the best. You probably know every coach and teacher in the county and beyond. You have any ideas?"

"There's some talent out there, but even though we're a good school and a tough team, we're small. Starting pay isn't impressive. I'll start doing some serious asking around, but we're probably going to draw attention from young men without a great deal of experience or an exciting track record. Those folks tend to head for the colleges, then the bigger universities."

"And why didn't you leave, Coach?" Cooper asked.

"I like it here," he said with a shrug. "I like the high school kids—I like taking the raw talent with minimal funding and working it hard, molding it into something bigger than this little seaside town. I like watching those kids come off the field like rockets, all lit up after they've taken down one of the big schools—big schools from districts with money to spend. When we do it, it's harder. But it means more."

Cooper leaned toward him. "You shouldn't quit until you find the right person to take over."

"I won't let the town or the school down, but I hope it doesn't come to that. I'm discouraged. I don't mind telling you—I'm tired. It takes a lot of positive energy to crank up those boys. I'm better off assisting, not trying to lead. Not right now. Now you just talk to Landon and his sister. Tell 'em to call me if they need to, but fill 'em in. Landon—he's a leader. If he chooses to stay at this school, on this team, he could make a difference. If he chose another team, I'd understand. Anyone would understand."

"Let me just ask you something," Cooper said. "Why do you want me to talk to him? Why don't you just talk to him?"

"Because he'd see in one second that I'm giving up. That isn't the best message for a kid who's gonna have a lot on his shoulders if he picks this town. But you can do it, Cooper. Mac says the boy relies on you. And I know he's got the heart if he has the backing."

* * *

Cooper finished his beer. He regretted that he'd given Landon the job—he'd be at the bar, washing dishes, sweeping up, running food to tables, serving up sodas or bottled drinks, smiling like a kid who'd won the lotto. And after the heavy lifting was done for the day, Cooper was going to tell him his coach was quitting and break his heart.

When he got back to his place, Landon was sitting at one of the tables in the bar, apron on, books open. There were a couple of people out on the deck and they'd been served. It had been Cooper who suggested that if things were quiet and Rawley was caught up, he use the time to get some of his homework done. Soon enough they'd hit their busy time when the sun started down over the Pacific and Landon would be on his feet.

Wouldn't it be nice if he could put off this news about the coach until school was out for the summer. But, if Coach Rayborough was giving a letter to the school board so they could post the job and get busy looking at possible candidates, word would get out. Mac was going to tell Eve that night; Cooper should tell Landon so he'd have time to think.

And then as if the universe conspired, Sarah showed up at about eight o'clock, just as the last of the customers was leaving.

"Maybe we could heat up a couple of pizza slices or something?" she said. And then she immediately said, "What's wrong?"

"Nothing is wrong, but I have to talk to you and Landon. Is everyone gone from the deck?"

"There were a couple of people leaning on the deck

rail, looking at the bay, but I think they're about to go. Landon picked up their glasses and dishes. What's up?"

He was behind the bar; she was sitting up on a stool facing him. He poured her a glass of wine while Landon bustled his dishes back to the kitchen.

"I had a beer with Mac and Coach Rayborough this afternoon. The coach—he's worn down by all the trouble last year, by the fact that he had a player in trouble and missed all the signals. I think he's just worn out, to tell you the truth. He's getting on in years and the kids kind of—"

"Cooper!"

He leaned on the bar. "He's going to retire, Sarah," he said. "It's not public yet, but he hopes there will be a new coach in place by the end of summer and he was real honest—he's too tired for this. A new coach could be inexperienced and young. Rayborough could assist, but he'd rather just move on. He suggested that you and Landon might consider other schools, even private schools, where Landon could get the most and the best—"

He stopped when Sarah closed her eyes, tilted her head back and her lips took on that twisted, tortured look of someone who was fighting tears. She lost the fight, of course—a couple of big ones escaped and she wiped at them furiously.

"Baby?" he asked in a whisper.

"God, could the kid catch a break?" she whispered back. "Just when he's weathered some of his toughest days, the winning coach who's going to bring him out as quarterback for his senior year, showcase him and set him up for a scholarship..."

"It's not the only game in town, Sarah. Plus there's

scholarship and grant money out there—there are good loans at the moment. And hell, I'd help. You know I'd..."

She just shook her head. "Napkin?" she asked. He handed her one and she blew her nose. Then she fanned her face with her fingers. And then Landon was back from the bar.

Landon had taken off his apron and had his backpack over on shoulder. "Need anything else, Cooper?"

"Yeah, just one more thing. I have some news to pass along. I'm glad your sister is here because I said I'd tell her, too." Then he went through the details, the suggested options, the challenges and possible changes. "The coach said if you have a lot riding on this season, you should at least consider other schools...."

"I'm not going anywhere," he said, shaking his head. Then he looked at his sister. "Not unless we have to, but God I hope we don't have to."

"Landon, if you don't have a good coach or a solid team, it could really affect your ability to get noticed, to get help with tuition...."

"Then I'll borrow money. Hey, maybe I'll go Coast Guard or Army or something. But if I don't have to, I'm not leaving town. We have a good team—we have a good little town. I have friends here. There's Eve..." Then he looked at Cooper. "Is Coach all right?"

"He's okay, Landon. He's been coaching forty years now—he's a little worn out. Last year was a bad year for him—he took things with Jag real personally. He said he'll hang close to help the new coach. He said if you don't consider your options, you're going to have one helluva load on your shoulders. Teammates will expect a lot from you. He also said to call him if you want to talk about it, but he asked me to tell you because we're…" He stopped for a minute. Then he shrugged. "Because we're friends and I never miss a game." He smiled.

"Does Eve know?" he asked.

Cooper nodded. "Mac's going to tell her, but listen— it's not official. You can talk to Eve, but you have to sit on this for a little while, okay?"

"Okay. I'll talk to Eve. Then I'll call Coach. It's okay. I bet he doesn't go anywhere. I'm not going to freak out. We have a good team. I know that. I know it." Then he looked at Sarah. "I'll leave you the Razor to take home. I need the walk. And the think."

"Want me to come with you?"

"I think I'd rather not talk about it yet. But it's okay. Really, it's going to be okay."

When Carrie asked her closest friend, Lou McCain, if she could help cater the Downys' anniversary party, Lou smiled. "I'd much rather serve than attend as a guest."

"Oh, I'm sorry," Carrie said. "Of course, if you've been invited, you have to go! I'll find someone else."

"Don't be silly. I *want* to serve. That noodle-head Marjorie sent an invitation to me and another to Mac— both said *no additional guests.* She knows perfectly well that Mac and Gina are a couple. Does she think Mac wants to go with his old-maid aunt? I think she's getting a little too big for her britches."

"She hasn't been very nice to Gina," Carrie said.

"Because she's a fool. People around here would much rather spend time with Gina than Marjorie. If she had a brain, she'd suck up to Gina."

"Is Mac going to go?"

Lou gave a laugh. "Well, he's a public servant. He doesn't discriminate, so he tries to be everyone's friend, especially in the good times. He's going to stop by, in uniform, drink a cup of coffee and run for his life."

"If you're sure," Carrie said.

"I'm sure."

"I just need one more person," Carrie said. "I wonder if Sylvia—"

"Ray Anne," Lou said. "Let's ask Ray Anne."

Carrie scowled and lifted one eyebrow. "Ray Anne? She's never helped me. Ever."

"I'll show her what to do."

"You hate her!"

"We have a little truce going. I had a drink with her when I was banned from the house so Cee Jay could see the kids. We may not like each other but we have a very nice understanding. Sort of."

"Right," Carrie said with a laugh. "And how long will that last?"

"We're good. It'll be fine. She can wear her satin, low-cut, supershort waitress uniform with the seven-inch heels."

"What if you squabble and snipe at each other?"

"I'll pass that by her, tell her you're worried about that," Lou said.

"You *talk* to her?"

"We've had the occasional glass of wine, nothing big. So?"

Carrie narrowed her eyes. "If you start to bicker, I'm going to hurt you."

Lou laughed.

"You're an invited guest," Carrie said. "I don't feel right about this."

Lou laughed again. "Don't worry about it. I'll hit the next twentieth anniversary party in a couple of years."

Carrie gasped. "I didn't say anything about that!"

"Did you think I didn't know? She's been fudging that for a long time now. Everyone knows. So what? She got caught. It's been known to happen."

"But you've only lived here four years! I've been here since before they moved to Thunder Point!"

"Carrie, everyone knows. See, here's the lesson—if you have secrets to keep, at least be nice so people feel like helping you keep them. Marjorie has been a pain in the ass because she thinks she's going to buy the world with her son's future in pro baseball." Then she reflected, looking up. "The kid is amazing. I bet he's going to kill 'em with that arm." Then she grew serious. "Marjorie should remember, it's not *her* arm."

"Well, much as I'd love to give her a large piece of my mind, I have a business to run and my only goal for this party is that it be perfect. If I were rich or even more comfortable financially, I wouldn't have taken the job, even though she asked me before Downy and Ashley broke up. The truth is, in a town of fifteen hundred, I can't afford to be too picky about catering contracts. I have a reputation to uphold—I won't shortchange a customer because I don't personally like them. If you're not on board with that—"

"I'm on board, I'm on board," Lou said. She reached out and put a comforting hand on Carrie's forearm. "You're my closest friend. Even though I pretty much want to shove Marjorie and her precious son in a hole right now, no one will ever know it!"

* * *

Carrie put out a beautiful spread and her presentation was, as always, fetching—a long buffet and refreshment table garnished with roses and baby's breath that she drove all the way to her favorite nursery east of Bandon to buy. She served crab and salmon canapés, deviled eggs garnished with caviar, though not the most expensive brand, tapenade on small toast rounds, stuffed grape leaves, hot artichoke dip with thin sliced baguette, bite-size beef burgundy and a variety of relishes. There was also a beautiful white cake that said Happy Anniversary in silver frosting. She brought her champagne flutes for a toast and set up a wine bar at the end of the dining room. And Marjorie looked very nice in a new dress for the occasion.

Her husband, Crawford Senior, who everyone called Ford, had other ideas about the party. He ran some Christmas lights between the trees in the backyard and put out a couple of coolers of beer along with a bowl of chips and salsa on the picnic table. It seemed most of the guests, especially the men, preferred to be out there. Many of them loaded up on hors d'oeuvres and took their plates outside to mix them up with chips and beer. The women appreciated the wine bar and fancy nibbles, content to sit around the living room, gossiping. Nothing Marjorie could do would coax the men inside.

Downy brought his new girlfriend, a beautiful and tiny young thing dressed for sex with a very short skirt, high shoes, see-through blouse not covering her purple bra. Her long black hair was loose and flowing and she was stuck to Downy like lint. They pawed each other and drank too much beer, although they were underage and everyone knew it, so when the deputy showed up,

Ford told them to go hide in one of the bedrooms. Not ten minutes later there was a scream. One of the women at the party went looking for her purse, opened the bedroom door and found them stark naked, *in flagrante.*

Carrie had a helluva time rounding everyone up for a champagne toast after that but managed to convince Ford to do this one thing for his wife. Carrie, though not exactly commissioned to do so, took as many pictures of them toasting and cutting the cake as she could grab.

Then Ford was back outside with a box of cigars.

By eleven Carrie, Lou and Ray Anne had cleaned up, put the rest of the hors d'oeuvres on disposable but attractive plastic plates, washed out the chafing dishes and serving utensils and loaded everything in Carrie's van. Carrie told Marjorie good-night and Marjorie said, "Thank you, Carrie. I think it went very well." And Carrie wondered if the woman was being brave or delusional.

Once in the van she said, "I need a glass of wine."

"I could use something stronger," Lou said. "I'm completely exhausted."

"Not at my house, where Gina and Ashley will probably be waiting for a report. Not at your house, where Eve will be listening and will report to Ashley." They both looked at Ray Anne.

"All right," she said. "All right. My house."

There was no talking in the van as Carrie drove them to Ray Anne's little bungalow on the hill, just ten blocks from the Downys'. Like everything in Thunder Point, it was close. It was only five minutes to get there and eight minutes before Ray Anne was opening a cold white and pouring it into three glasses. They sat in the living room, kicking off their shoes. They sipped their wine and just sat quiet for a moment.

"I've seen it a hundred times," Carrie finally said. "It's the hardest part about this work—people with huge expectations are always disappointed."

"I like Ford, but he's an ass," Ray Anne said.

"Well, I can't stand Marjorie, but I think I feel sorry for her," Lou said.

"It gets to the point that when you have an event that didn't disappoint, you want to give a discount," Carrie said, rubbing her foot. "The worst is when a young bride doesn't get the reception she always dreamed of. It's rarely about the venue or the food, but usually some relative or guest with bad manners."

"I bet you don't often see renegade fucking at wedding receptions," Ray Anne said.

"That's where you see it the most," Carrie said.

"Really? I thought that was just me...."

"No, there's something about a wedding that makes people amorous. And reckless. But I have to say, I've never seen it happen at an anniversary party. By the son of the couple. In their bedroom. In the middle of the party."

"Coolers of beer and cigars...I bet Marjorie wanted to die. Here she was all dressed up and Ford's wearing his Seattle Mariners cap."

"Yeah, I bet that dress cost her forty bucks," Ray Anne said meanly.

"Get it out of your system," Carrie said. "Because you are not to gossip about this! To anyone!"

"I didn't sign a confidentiality agreement," Lou said. "Besides, everyone is going to be talking about it. Especially Pat, who got a close-up of Downy's naked ass."

She took a sip of her wine. "And all you did was pull the door closed!"

"It was that or throw a bucket of cold water on him," Carrie said. "I know he broke my baby's heart, but I'm glad she's moving on. Hopefully to someone with some manners. If not class. Jeez."

And then the three of them looked at each other and burst into hysterical laughter until they were crying and couldn't sit up straight.

Frank knocked on Ashley's door at nine-thirty. Gina answered, looking surprised. "Frank!"

"Hi. Is Ashley home?"

"Um, yes. I think she's plugged into her iPod. Or on the phone. I'll check. Come on in."

He stepped inside while Gina went down the hall and tapped on Ashley's bedroom door. When she came out, wearing a perplexed frown, her iPod earbuds were dangling over her shoulders. And Gina went in a different direction, leaving them alone.

He smiled and said, "Hi."

"What are you doing here? Shouldn't you be at your parents' party?"

"I stayed for the toast and the cake cutting. That's long enough. I'm sure they'll think I'm in my room or something."

"But what are you doing?"

"I'm going to the beach to look for stars and constellations and meteors. It's clear and cool." He half turned, showing her his backpack. "I have a log and a couple of drinks."

She crossed her arms over her chest. "You don't have to keep doing this, Frank. I mean, it's nice of you, but

I am managing not to feel like total toe jelly knowing Downy's in town with his girlfriend."

"Well, good. So, the internet says there could be a mild meteor shower tonight. And I did this, as you say, because no one else would be interested. And the party is not for me. My mom is semihappy—my dad gave her a necklace. And now he's getting hammered with some of his buddies on the patio. So—"

"Getting hammered? I thought it was a fancy party!"

"That is fancy for my dad. He put out two coolers full of beer." Frank grinned.

"What if someone's looking for you?"

"I left a note on my computer—gone to the beach to look at stars. I've done it before. They won't worry."

She sighed. "I'll sit on the steps with you for a little while, but I don't want to talk about Downy."

"Good, because I don't have anything to say about him. But turn off the porch light, in case there are meteors. I want to see them."

She flicked off the light, turned off her iPod and pulled the door closed behind them. She sat down on the top step with Frank.

Frank shed the backpack, opened it and pulled out a couple of drinks, handing her one.

"Let's be sure we have something straight," she said. "We're just friends. We're going to stay just friends and not because of Downy or the fact that you're a Downy or anything. It's because I'm not dating. Got it?"

He twisted the top off his drink. "I think we already had this conversation. I get it. And I'm real sorry my brother hurt you but I'm not sorry it gave me a chance to get to know you on a different level. While you were with Downy, we only talked if you had a math crisis.

I'm not looking for anything, Ash. I'm not dating, either. I have a lot I want to do."

"Like?" she asked, opening her drink.

"I have to ace a whole bunch of classes, for one thing. I'm not going to be getting a football scholarship."

"Hmm. So, where do you think you're going to college?"

"Harvard."

"Whoa. That's gonna be expensive."

"There are whole websites and blogs dedicated to tips on how to get in and pay for it. You could fill a phone book with the scholarships and grants available. Not to mention loans."

"Isn't there anything closer?"

"There are lots of good universities that are closer, but I want to go to the east coast. There's a lot out there I haven't experienced—museums, libraries, galleries, theater, observatories. Not only does Harvard have a lot to offer but the whole area is a cultural mecca. Not to mention—I just want to spend some time in New York City. And D.C. I've never seen the monuments. And the National Air and Space Museum. I guess you already know—I like space and numbers."

She was mesmerized. "You are going to be Bill Gates…."

He chuckled. "Bill Gates is taken. I'll just be me."

"Would you drop out of college?" she asked, thinking of Gates.

"If I had ideas that were bigger than what I could get in college, I might. That hasn't happened yet. And I don't see it happening soon. I'm more excited about the classes I'll get to take than the prospect of getting out of school and making money. I have a long way to go."

"You don't have as far as everyone else," she pointed out. "Show me the constellations again," she said, leaning back and looking up.

He leaned back. "See the Big Dipper? Ursa Major. And right across from that is Cassiopeia—the Lady in the Chair. See it? Shaped like a W. And see the North star? The last star in the handle of the Little Dipper." And then two burning stars shot across the sky. "Whoa," he said. "Nice."

"Make a wish," she said.

"Don't I get two?" he asked. "There are going to be more. It's the perfect night for it."

She laid back on the porch, her legs hanging down the stairs. "I love summer nights in Thunder Point. Tell me what you want to see in Boston, in New York."

"Everything—revolutionary landmarks all over New England. And there's the Museum of Fine Arts, the biggest art museum on the east coast. The Freedom Trail. Fenway and Boston Harbor."

"Fenway?" she asked with a yawn. "So you are a baseball fan?"

"You don't grow up a Downy without being constantly immersed in sports. I'm not as obsessive about spectator sports as everyone else, but I enjoy them. I've never been very athletic, but I like to sail. I have a friend who has a small sloop and we've taken it out on the ocean when the weather is decent. I like biking, which is probably a good thing since there's no way I'll have a car in college. In fact, I wonder if I can get a messenger job—that could be fun, biking through traffic, not that a good old Oregon boy knows much about real traffic. There's a great observatory at Boston University. They have nights open to the public and seminars. That's Coit

Observatory. Harvard has a great observatory, too—
and the Smithsonian Center for Astrophysics. Did you
know it was founded in the eighteen hundreds?"

A soft snore answered him.

He chuckled and laid back, watching the sky. "Big
surprise, I put you to sleep. Don't feel bad. It happens
all the time. And I didn't even get to New York or D.C.
yet. My mother says you should never ask me a question. If you visited me at Harvard, there are about a
million things I could show you. We'd take the train to
D.C. and spend a whole day on the mall, go to all the
museums and monuments, check out the Naval Observatory, spend a day in Georgetown..."

Undeterred by her sleeping, Frank just kept talking,
though softly. He knew he missed a lot of meteors because he had turned his head and was looking at her.
She slept with her lips parted just slightly and her rusty
brown lashes, so thick, fanned over her high cheekbones
and he wondered why she bothered with makeup at all.
Her lips were peachy and full, her skin so smooth and
ivory. She was so much more beautiful than Selena it
just made him laugh inside—Selena was going to be
the emotional death of his older brother. But then that
was Downy, so egocentric, thinking with his dick. With
Downy he was either watching sports, playing sports or
angling a way to get laid. It was a miracle he got into
State, he could barely maintain a B average and that was
taking classes that didn't require much study.

Ashley, when she was only a sophomore, had helped
Downy with his homework. Sure, she had called Frank a
few times to ask him questions for her math assignments,
but he was sure she had no idea how smart she was.

He wanted to touch her, but if she caught him it

would send the wrong message. "If you wanted to, you could make it to an Ivy League school," he whispered. "You could do anything. Be anything."

He just looked at her for a while, letting about twenty minutes of silence pass. Then he gave her arm a soft jostle. "Ashley?"

She opened her eyes. "Did I fall asleep?"

He smiled and nodded. "Were you dreaming of some geek going on and on about observatories and museums and libraries?"

She shook her head. "I didn't realize I was so tired."

"Why don't you go to bed," he said. "I'm headed for the beach. Just for an hour or so."

She yawned deeply. "Want me to go with you? So you're not alone?"

He smiled at her. "No. I don't want to have to drag you home. Go to bed."

"I think I will," she said. "Thanks for coming over, Frank." She rose, stretched, gave him a wave and went inside.

Ashley went to her bedroom, slipped into the boxers and T-shirt she slept in, put her earbuds back in and crawled into bed. *You could do anything. Be anything.*

No one had said that to her before. Well, her mother had, but mothers don't really count—they have to say that to their kid.

She hadn't been asleep the whole time. She had nodded off for a minute, but when she heard Frank talking about the train to D.C. and all the museums and monuments, she just listened to his comforting voice, eyes closed. She had never appreciated him before—he was more than just smart and good-looking, he was kind and gentle and fearless. Somewhere along the line he had developed a strong, beautiful body without being a jock, without seeming to be aware of it. Yes, she was discovering there was a lot more to Frank Downy than met the eye.

Fifteen

It had been three weeks since Cee Jay had visited her kids at the meeting that had ended so unpleasantly. It had been three weeks since Mac had hired a detective to get more information about what her life had been like over the past ten years in the hopes of getting a better grasp on what she might be after now. He'd called the detective a few times and had been reassured they were still in the data-gathering process.

It had been hard to be patient. He kept waiting for the other shoe to fall.

Finally a FedEx package was delivered to his Thunder Point office. It was filled with information, call logs from the detective's office, a few pictures, some of the same public records Mac had accessed—records of marriage and divorce—and a bill. Seventeen hundred and eighty-seven dollars.

He gulped.

Then he sifted through the material. And just when he thought he couldn't be surprised by anything, he was blown away. But there was one important thing missing. He called the detective's cell phone. "I looked through all your material and sadly, it all makes sense. But where is she?"

"Is there a casino within two hundred miles?" the detective replied.

"What makes you think she's still in the area?"

"Both women—Cee Jay and Maddy Crofts—came from the area and she's not turning up anywhere else. She used a credit card in North Bend a week ago."

"There's a casino there," Mac said.

"Want a wager?" the P.I. asked, laughter in his voice.

Mac wasn't laughing. "I'll pass. What does she want with me? Or the kids? We don't have anything."

"I can't answer that, buddy. I can only tell you where she's been and what she's done. Good luck."

So, was it *all* about gambling? Mac had considered many possibilities but never that one. How that could possibly involve him was a mystery. But, he'd have to know. He called the casino hotel in North Bend and asked for Cee Jay or Cecilia McCain and was told there was no one there by that name. He asked for Cecelia Raines and again came up empty. On to Madeline Crofts—no, again. But he struck oil with Antoinette LeClair, the fictional attorney.

"Let me talk to Cee Jay," he said when she answered the phone.

"Who's calling please," she replied.

"Coos County Sheriff's Department," he said.

And then he heard her say "Cee Jay, it's your husband."

"What do you want?" she asked impatiently when she came to the phone.

"I think we should talk, Cee Jay."

"And I think I'm all talked out."

"We should meet. Or my next call could be to the Los Angeles County District Attorney."

"I haven't broken any laws!" she shot back.

"Oh, yeah, you have. And even if he doesn't want to prosecute, at the very least he'll sign out a warrant and let poor Mr. Raines know he's not obligated to that alimony. So, would you like me to come to the hotel?"

Silence answered him. At long last she said, "I'll be in the hotel restaurant."

"I'll be there in less than an hour. And don't bring your attorney—no one's filming *Law and Order* episodes today." And he hung up.

He called one of the deputies who worked for him and asked him to cover the town. Then he texted Lou— he said he had to drive up to North Bend on business and asked her to cover the kids if he was tied up. And then he drove and was glad it took a while; he had to think.

In police work, he always had a strategy, a method of approaching a situation or suspect. A lot of his strategy was following policy, but some was pure instinct. But he knew so little about gambling and less about his ex-wife. He had three images of her—the young girl he'd once loved, the pretty young woman who'd left them so coldly and the beautiful and sophisticated woman who turned up a few weeks ago. He wasn't sure who she really was. And while he could assume her appearance in Thunder Point had something to do with money, probably with a debt, he wasn't sure of anything else.

As for gambling, he'd been to a few casinos. He'd even taken his Aunt Lou. Lou liked the nickel slots because she could play for hours, get mesmerized by the rolling cherries and other fruits, and do it on five bucks. He liked blackjack, but he never lasted long. He thought he had an exceptional memory and tried to remember card play to get to twenty-one, but the house beat him every time. But Cee Jay had obviously gone through millions in a few years. She wasn't doing that at the nickel slots or two-buck blackjack table.

He drove through the parking lot surrounding the hotel casino, passing down each lane slowly. Twice. Her girlfriend, the fraudulent attorney, must have gone somewhere—there was no sight of the fancy car.

When he walked into the hotel, people reacted. They stiffened, stared, watched. Dare he even hope Cee Jay would be intimidated by the uniform? She hadn't been the last time, when they met at Denny's. He went to the restaurant and spoke to the hostess. "I'm meeting a woman here, early thirties, dark hair, very blue eyes...."

The hostess smiled and sent a graceful arm and questioning glance into the sparsely populated dining room.

"Yes, that's her. Thank you."

Cee Jay seemed to be studying the menu until he neared, then she looked up and dazzled him with a stunning smile. *Oh, you think I don't remember?* he thought. It cut through him. That beautiful young girl who once loved him, there she was. She'd been new at school and it hadn't taken her long to single him out and even though she was much younger, to him she was the epitome of beauty and innocence. He fell in love with her immediately. A year later she was pregnant and he was married. And everything about his life changed.

She stood and by the lift of her arms, she intended to embrace him. He quickly put out a hand, indicating she should take a seat. She did so with a laugh. "Well, that was awkward."

The waitress was there instantly. Something about a police uniform usually produced service right away. He was very uncomfortable sitting with his back to the room but tried to tell himself he wouldn't be here too long and the casino had security. Still, even though he had no reason to expect trouble of any kind, his hand rested on his thigh, near his gun.

"Just coffee for me," he told the waitress.

"I'll start with a coffee," Cee Jay said.

When the waitress had gone, Mac said, "Nice hotel."

"It's the nicest one in the general area. How did you find me?" she asked.

He lifted a brow. "I looked."

"That doesn't quite answer the question."

"I know. So, what's your game?"

"I beg your pardon." She was indignant. She stiffened.

"What do you play?" he asked.

She seemed to be undecided whether to answer. "I just dabble," she said, visibly tense.

"Cee Jay, I know everything. So, what do you dabble in?"

"Penny ante," she said with a shrug, meeting his eyes dead on. She'd been through this before. She could pass a lie detector and he knew it. It scared him, as a matter of fact.

"I don't think so," he replied, shaking his head. "It appears you're having some bad luck."

"Not much." She shrugged. "Just lately. It's just for fun, anyway. I'm actually ahead."

He might not know anything about gambling per se but one thing he knew, gamblers always claimed to win. Always. And they rarely did. Big fancy casinos and casino resorts were not built on charity. "Is that right? Good for you. So, what does this have to do with us? Me and the kids?"

"I thought..." Her voice trailed off. "I told you. I thought maybe we could reconnect."

"There's more to it than that," he said.

She just shook her head. "Those years we were together—they were very hard, Mac. Very hard. And I didn't really have the tools to deal with what I'd taken on—I was a young fool. So I ran. But I kept looking back to those years, difficult though they were, and realized that was one of the few times in my life I felt safe and loved. I started to regret leaving almost immediately."

"Yet you didn't even call to ask how the kids were?"

She lifted her chin. "I was determined to improve myself in some way before getting in touch. I never brought anything to the table. I wanted to bring something. I thought I could contribute in some way, be valuable. Valuable enough to be welcomed back."

He frowned slightly and leaned toward her slightly. "What the hell happened to you, Cee Jay? What happened that made you feel being the mother of our children wasn't enough?"

"It was just more work and greater deprivation than I could—"

But he was shaking his head. "What happened in your childhood to make you think you had to have more? Be more? I want to understand, but I just don't get it. You said you felt safe and loved. Did the fancy car and jewelry make you feel safer? More loved?"

She let a huff of laughter escape just as two cups of coffee and cream were delivered to the table. Mac noticed her eyes had welled with tears but he couldn't trust that they were real.

"Growing up wasn't pretty," she finally said. "I was raised by a single mother who had four kids by four men. She moved us every time the rent was overdue, virtually ignored us and left us on our own to raise ourselves. I lived in dingy little apartments and motel rooms—there wasn't always food and we picked through scrap piles for clothes. I was molested when I was small, abandoned all the time, hungry most of the time, missed whole months of school and was always terrified. When I was eleven the four of us were split up into four different foster homes and I was moved every year. When I met you all I wanted was a family and a home."

He was silent. Was this some story concocted to get his sympathy? How could he spend seven years with a woman and never know any of these details? It could be as simple as young men don't ask, or a young man working day and night never thought about the details, or as complicated as Cee Jay making up a story that would get her a second chance.

"And yet you would leave that family and home?" he asked.

"It doesn't make sense, I realize that now. But I wanted things. We had a family and a house, but I was still scared all the time. Afraid of being abandoned, of turning into my mother—a young woman with a passel of kids and no money and no husband and no way to take care of them or myself. In hindsight…" She gave a wave of her hand.

Actually, it did make sense if it was true, Mac thought. Abused children often grew up to abuse their own children, so this history could explain a lot. But that didn't make it right. "Well, it appears you have what you needed. Money. Security. And don't worry, you're pretty and know how to flirt. You'll find another husband."

"Well, except that I've had a little setback recently. Nothing serious, but it kind of showed me how much I'd left behind when I left you and the kids and I hoped we could start to know each other again. You know— see if it was as big a mistake for you as it was for me. I knew the odds were not in my favor, but I had to try."

He just shook his head. "I told you, I have someone now. It's serious. Besides, you'll do all right."

"I have some debt to clear," she said.

"Cee Jay, I know about the house, the cars, the alimony, which incidentally was acquired fraudulently. You've gone through a fortune."

"Well, a person with my upbringing doesn't really know how to manage all that and it didn't take long before I mismanaged it. And lost it." She shrugged and looked away. "Bad investments, being taken advantage of by con artists, lots of things I just wasn't prepared to handle...."

"No, Cee Jay, you gambled it away. The house was free and clear and you borrowed against it. Millions. So, cash in a couple of rings and sell the car...."

She scowled at him. "The car isn't mine and the rings are fake."

He looked at them with lifted brows. He'd never have known the difference. "Good fakes. And where's the car? It's not here."

"It went away," she said sourly.

"And Madeline? Aka Antoinette?"

"Upstairs," she said.

"You must have a very unique relationship," he muttered. *Partners in crime,* he thought.

"We have similar backgrounds," she said. "We can trust each other."

He immediately thought he knew how to learn more about that. He could spend a lot of time investigating. He might look into Cee Jay's childhood if only to know if she was lying or telling the truth, but he couldn't care less about her girlfriend. And if what Cee Jay told him was meant to explain her adult behavior, his kids were safe from that kind of legacy. They hadn't been treated that way.

"Where did you grow up, Cee Jay? You always said it was Oregon."

She nodded. "I didn't know what I was walking away from, but I was unstable. Damaged. I haven't had a real happy day since."

"Poor Mr. Raines will be heartbroken to hear that."

She laughed. "Poor Mr. Raines is a penny-pinching, mean-hearted old man! I wouldn't have gotten anything in the divorce except for the prenup! I got exactly what was outlined—a house, car and limited alimony. He blows more than that in a weekend."

Mac leaned toward her. He lowered his voice. "Cee Jay, you weren't legally married. You didn't deserve anything at all, except maybe jail."

"I didn't think you'd ever look for me. I signed those divorce and custody papers because of Raines. I was trapped. I know, I know—I did it to myself. But still… I meant what I said, Mac. I missed the kids. I missed you. Missed us. If you weren't involved with someone, we might be trying again…."

"No, that would never happen. I'm no good to you. I'd probably never buy you a fancy ring or new car. The most you'll ever get from me is a cup of coffee. And there's no way I can help clear your debt, so you should keep looking."

She lifted one brow. "You have a house," she pointed out to him. "I bet you even have a retirement fund and some college savings. You probably have money you don't even realize you have."

Mac didn't react, but inside he felt shattered. And when he thought about this later it might make him cry. She'd do that? Take the equity in his house? The roof over his kids' heads or their college savings? What little security he had? He thought he knew what she'd do with it, and she wasn't going to pay down her Visa bill.

"How much is your debt?" he asked.

"It's not very much. Just a few thousand."

"How many thousands?"

"I don't know," she said, smoothing her hair. "Eight or ten. Maybe eleven. But even five would help. And I'd pay you back, of course. Right away."

"And how could you do that? Pay me back right away?"

"I'm going to work," she said. "I have several modeling and acting opportunities that I just haven't been able to pursue, but they pay very well."

"Which begs the question, why not work to pay off your debt?"

She sat back in her chair. "It's complicated."

He gave her a slight smile. "I have to admit, I'm dying of curiosity. I know you didn't get in this spot on quarter slots at little casinos. Vegas? Monte Carlo? High stakes poker? Ponies? What the hell have you done to yourself, Cee Jay?"

"I just got a little behind, that's all."

"Right. Behind enough that you'd take your children's college savings and try to roll it into a big payoff? What are you going to do—put it all on black at the roulette table?"

"If you're not going to help me, just say so."

He rested his forearms on the table and looked at her with sympathy. He looked into her eyes and knew that the young girl he'd loved was just not in there. "Yes, I'm going to help you," he said. "First of all, I have to give you advice. This comes from Eve, actually. If you find yourself missing your children, they'd love to get a note or card. Maybe on birthdays or holidays. You could send a gift, and it doesn't have to be expensive—just a token to say they're remembered, that would be welcome. You can't just show up in their lives after a decade and expect a warm reception, but you're their mother. They can't help the fact that they'd like to know you.

"Second, if you borrowed from someone who isn't exactly in the legitimate loan business, I'd be happy to help you file a complaint. I know all the right people. And third, I would be happy to locate a Gamblers Anonymous meeting and give you a ride. No questions asked."

She scowled at him. There weren't any tears, either. "Just get out of here and leave me alone."

"And fourth," he said, standing. "I'll pay for your coffee, and this is for the last time. Good luck, Cee Jay."

She just looked at him with weary eyes and a sarcastically twisted mouth. He noticed that she'd tried to cover up the dark circles under her eyes, but the makeup had failed.

"Listen, let me say something. As hard as the last fifteen years have been, I have to thank you. For giving me my family, I mean. They're great kids and they're the life in me. I'm sorry things have been so awful for you. My life has been spare—no fancy houses or cars. But it's been perfect in every way. I can't think of a person on earth I'd trade places with."

"Good for you," she said tiredly, resting her head in her hand.

He didn't leave money on the table. He wasn't sure how bad off she was. She might grab a ten-dollar bill and race to a craps table and try to turn it into a hundred, which she'd then try to turn into a thousand, which would turn into nothing in no time. He went to find his waitress. "I'm leaving," he told her. "What's the tab for the coffees?" He paid her and gave her a nice tip. "Thanks," he said.

One of the perks of wearing a uniform complete with weapons and driving an official car, the valets were more than happy to let him leave the vehicle in front of the hotel, locked. He tried to pass the valet a five, but the kid waved him off. "Forget it, Officer. We're good," he said.

"Thanks for taking care of the car, son," he said. "Have a good day."

At nine o'clock all was quiet at the McCain house. Eve was in her bedroom, either studying or whispering scary love-words to Landon over the phone, Dee Dee and Ryan were supposed to be having quiet time prior to sleep. Mac tapped on Lou's door and she said, "Come in."

She was sitting on her bed, her TV turned low, her cell phone in her hand.

"I'm slipping out for an hour or so," Mac said. "I'm going to Gina's. I've got my phone."

"I'll watch the nest, but I'm going to sleep soon."

"I won't be late. She has an early morning."

Less than ten minutes later he was parked in front of her house and he went to the front door. He knocked and she answered. He held up two bottles of beer in one hand and smiled at her.

She was drying a pan. Her hair was piled on top of her head, held with a clip and she wore those plaid pajama bottoms that were so worn in some places the Goodwill might reject them. No makeup. Fitted tank top. She had a wholesome look about her; accessible and genuine. She was a hardworking woman who saved her money and didn't splurge on superficial things. And she looked so beautiful to him, she took his breath away. He wanted to gather her up in his arms and hold her.

"What are you doing here?" she asked with a smile.

"Come out on the porch with me. Have a beer," he said. "I had a long day. I saw Cee Jay."

Gina was clearly shocked. "She called you?"

He shook his head. "I tracked her down."

Gina threw the pan and dish towel into the chair by the door and joined him on the porch. They sat on the top step and he twisted off the caps on their bottles. He leaned back against the porch post, one long leg stretched out on the porch and bent at the knee, the other rested two steps down. He patted the space between his legs and she slid over. She smoothed the fabric of his jeans over his hard thighs.

He bent and kissed her neck, inhaling.

"You're fresh out of the tub."

"I had a serious case of waitress legs today. Sore. Tell me about her."

He sighed. "She's messed up." And then he unclipped her blond hair and let it fall to her shoulders.

"She sure doesn't look messed up. All you have to do is mention her name and I start to feel shabby and poor." She stretched her hands out in front of her face, looking at the short, cropped nails. "She's so glamorous."

"You're not as poor as she is, honey," he said.

"She's got a good cover going, then."

"She's in trouble."

Gina turned to look up at him, questioning him with her eyes.

"I investigated her past and what I couldn't learn from public records, I hired some help to dig up. I felt that was important, to keep the family safe. She married someone else before we were divorced, then divorced him with a sizable settlement that, of course, she didn't deserve because she was never legally married to him. She could be prosecuted for that."

"Will you turn her in?"

He shook his head. "I don't think so. But if anyone runs a records search, if they look at Oregon docs and California docs, it jumps out. And that's not just bigamy, it's fraud. She knew she wasn't free to marry. But with all she's up against, that's not really her biggest worry—she has a gambling problem. A doozy. She's run through a fortune and she has debts."

"Don't you have to turn her in?"

"I'm not obligated to snitch on every person I've ever known who once did something wrong, not even in my jurisdiction. In fact, I probably did more damage to her just by telling her I knew. I offered her a ride to a Gamblers Anonymous meeting. Daggers shot out of her eyes. She's not ready to admit to that. In fact," he added with a humorless laugh, "she suggested I could help her with that debt."

Gina leaned back against him. "Really? You have a stash somewhere you're not talking about?"

"Uh-huh. I have a house, half a house, actually, a retirement account and a small savings for the kids to help with college."

"No!" she said. "She would do that?"

He ran his fingers through her hair. "I believe she would do that. She said she could pay me back immediately. She's staying at the casino hotel in North Bend. I think that means if I gave her money, she'd put it all on the table, trying to double it or triple it."

"She ran through a fortune? Did you point out to her that she once had a fortune and she never sent a dollar of it to her children?"

He put his hands on her shoulders and gently turned her. "No," he said. "I looked into her eyes, her beautiful blue eyes, and they were dead. She has so much she could do, but she has killed her own spirit. It's very sad. I hope she gets help for that, but it's not going to happen today." He leaned toward her and gave her a brief kiss. "Our lives are richer in every way." And then he pulled her in for a deeper kiss.

And then he let her slide back into her position between his long legs. "Will you tell the kids?" she asked.

"Eventually," he said. "I guess they'll have to know,

but I want to make sure they're capable of understanding. I think Cee Jay will probably leave the area now—she knows I know everything. I told her if I wanted to, I could make a call to the Los Angeles prosecutor's office. I pity her, but I'm not screwing around with her anymore. There's nothing I can do for her. She's on her own."

He slid an arm around her from behind, holding her, her back comfortably at rest against him. He took a drink of his beer, then nuzzled her hair. She was so soft and fresh. And for a woman who had so much going on in her life, she was so uncomplicated.

They sat in silence, just having a beer together. After ten or fifteen minutes of peace and quiet and a half beer each, she asked, "Tell me what you're thinking, Mac."

"I'm just thinking how ready I am to move on."

"Well, your ex-wife is pretty unpredictable. It's a thing you might never get completely resolved."

"You're right about that. If I'm not real lucky, I might have to deal with her from time to time, but I still want to move on. Because she may have more surprises in store for me in coming years, but I'm all done with her. I think the kids and Lou are safe from her manipulations and plots. If Cee Jay proves to be a problem from time to time, it won't be because any of us is vulnerable. I hope I'm not being overly optimistic in thinking she's starting to understad that."

"I think she's going to be lurking in the back of your mind forever...."

"No, babe. Not in my mind—that's on a different track. She could make attempts to mess with my peace of mind, but I'll be vigilant. Hell, that's how I am, anyway. It's hard to uncop a guy, if you know what I mean.

The worst part about my meeting with her today was that I sat with my back to the room in the hotel restaurant." He laughed and shook his head. "But I'm turning my life over to you. I've given this issue all I've got to give it."

She turned and looked up at him. "And what am I supposed to do?"

"I think we should put our heads together and make some plans for our own future. I know it's complicated, but there must be a way we can get married. Maybe not next weekend, but the sooner the better."

She turned to look up into his eyes. "Are you sure that's what you want?"

"More than you can know."

She turned around and knelt between his legs, her hands on his shoulders. "Do you think Lou and the kids can deal with it?"

"Lou's been telling me I need a woman in my life for years, but I'll sit down with her. As for the kids, the most stable thing our girls seem to have is each other. But—once Lou's on board, we should try to figure out the details. We have to combine our families."

"Or we could wait a year and a half, when our girls go to college," she said.

"I don't think I can wait that long." He pulled her into his arms. "The best place in my life is when I'm near you, when I'm holding you, when I'm spooning you in bed. That's my peace. That's my anchor. And you know what? I don't think it's going to be hard. I think it's going to feel like a huge relief."

"This is not going to solve all your problems, Mac."

"It's going to solve at least one. I need to be with you."

Sixteen

Gina was sitting on the front porch with her newspaper opened in front of her when Ashley came up the walk after school, her backpack slung over one shoulder. "My last big test," she said. "Done!"

"How do you think you did?"

"I think I did great, as a matter of fact. The only major thing left for me is a book report—mega book thesis—for English. And I did it already. I hate to brag but it's the smartest paper I've ever written. School's out in a week and I'd like to work this summer. As much as possible. I have to save some money. So, who do you think will hire me? You or Gram?"

Surprised, Gina answered, "Well, do you want to wait tables, or cook and do dishes?"

"I might have time to do both over summer—two part-time jobs. What do you think?"

"I'll ask Stu at the diner and you can talk to Gram."

"If I can manage to work and cheer in my senior year, I might want to do that, too."

"Suddenly very ambitious, aren't we?" Gina said with a smile.

"Well, I am. I've been thinking college is getting close. I used to think of Downy when I thought of college without even considering all the other things it could mean. I had no idea all the things I was interested in until I started listening to Frank talk about everything he'd like to study and I thought—hmm, I kind of like the idea of psychology. And how about physical therapy? Or education? Or biology? Or—"

Gina laughed. "How about all those things?" she echoed. "What brought this on?"

"I'm sick of hearing about the wonderful Downy and his atomic arm. Good for him, but I have a life, too, and I just am not about to waste it on some jerk."

"God," Gina said. "Why didn't I have your brains when I was your age? Sit down with me a minute. There's something I've been planning to talk to you about and with all you've had going on, I didn't want to overburden you. But—it's kind of because of all you've had going on. When I checked you into the hospital and filled out all the forms I realized that since you were born the 'paternal' side of the health history was always unknown. If we ever had a real issue—like if there was something hereditary we should know about, then... The thing is, Ash, I searched out your biological father specifically to ask those questions. And I found him. Not very far away."

The look on her face was one of sheer shock. "Holy crap."

"Yes, I found him, I talked with him, I asked him medical questions. And I found that he hadn't even been certain whether I was definitely pregnant, whether I'd gone through with the pregnancy, had you adopted, whatever."

Ashley leaned back on the porch post. "Wow. That's almost creepy. Especially at the same time Eve's long-lost mother shows up unannounced."

"Pure coincidence and entirely different circum-stances. It turns out your father didn't exactly run out on you. He did run, though, and I think we can all agree that worked out a lot better for us than it did for him."

Gina told her the whole story, including the fact that Eric had gotten in trouble, served time in prison and then seemed to have turned his life around. She had had Mac check him out and learned that he had not only been a model prisoner, determined to get out as early as possible, but was now a model citizen.

"Is he nice?"

Gina nodded. "Seems to be. In fact, lots nicer than he was at eighteen. He seems to be responsible and kind of successful with his own little business."

"Do you like him?"

"I like him more now than I had."

"Am I going to meet him?" Ashley asked.

"Do you want to?" Gina responded. "Because you shouldn't have any fantasies about him—he's no knight in shining armor. He's just a man—he does auto body work. He's got a girlfriend but no family and, he and I?" She shook her head. "Never. I think we're both pretty relieved he didn't step up seventeen years ago—it would've been a disaster. For that matter, I don't know that you can expect him to be a father, Ash. I think that time has surely passed. You might not even like him."

"I wouldn't mind seeing his face. Finding out what kind of person he is. I already know what kind of per-son he *was*."

"I can probably arrange that, but I want you to think

it over for a couple of days and be sure that's what you want. He gave me his word he won't push himself on you."

"Couple of days?"

"I think it's reasonable to think it over first. Don't you?"

"Sure. Yes. Wow—I always thought if I ever ran into him, he'd be a horrible person."

"He doesn't seem to be."

A couple of days after that conversation, Gina pulled the business card with the cell phone number out of her pocket and called Eric. "Hi," she said. "It's Gina. Ashley's doing very well after a real challenging spring. She had some major heartaches, but she's so smart, so strong. And I told her about you. Eric, I think it's time. She'd like to meet you."

"Do you have a date tonight?" Mac asked his Aunt Lou.

"Why? Do you need me for something?"

"I want to take you to dinner."

She backed away from the kitchen sink, put a hand on her hip and looked at him suspiciously. "Now this has never happened before."

"I'm sure it has," he said. "Hasn't it?"

"I don't think so. And the kids?"

"Let's throw a pizza at them—they'll be fine. I want to talk to you alone. It's about me and Gina."

"Oh, dear God, you haven't screwed that up, have you?"

He made a face. "Do you ever get tired of being so judgmental? No. I didn't screw up, just the opposite. It's time to talk about the future, which happens to link to your future. We have to get on the same page, you and me."

"Are you at least going to take me somewhere nice?"

"Will you settle for Cliffhanger's?"

"If I can sit at a table," she said. "I'll need thirty minutes. Lucky for you, Joe's working tonight and I'm free." And then she pulled a couple of frozen pizzas out of the freezer, set the oven, opened the boxes.

"That's a lot of pizza."

"If Landon doesn't show up, hell has frozen over. I should speak to Sarah—her brother clearly has a tapeworm."

Forty minutes later they were seated at a table in Cliffhanger's and Cliff was at the table personally to take their drink orders. "Bring Lou a white wine and I'll have a beer," Mac said.

"Hold on," Lou objected. "I want a mojito. Do you know how to make a mojito?"

"Yes," Cliff said tiredly. "I went to bartending school."

"Excellent," she said. "He's buying. I'm not pinching pennies here."

"Really?" he asked. "Are you sure I haven't ever taken you out to dinner before?"

"Like this? A completely adult dinner? Just the two of us? I can't remember a time."

He just shook his head. "You've done everything for me. I haven't done anything for you."

"You gave me a home," she said softly.

"You had a home."

"I had a house, Mac. I had two great nieces and a nephew I rarely saw because you were married to a woman who hated me and considered me an interfering old crone. I never once wished your marriage would fail, I hope you believe me. But in spite of the pain of it all, I had a family again."

Mac reached for her hand. "You will always have a family, Lou. You'll always have a home. I swear to you."

"I'm not worried that you're going to throw me out, Mac," she said. Their drinks arrived and they ordered dinner. Then she lifted her mojito to his glass of beer. "Cheers, Mac. Congratulations."

"For...?"

"I assume you're getting married."

He put down the beer. "We have to get the families together. I'm not sure how we're going to pull this off. And what if someone protests?"

"Who would protest?"

"Well, when Eve first found out about me and Gina, she got a little crazy. Afraid she'd be put through another traumatic situation, like when she was little and Cee Jay left."

"She panicked, that's all. If she takes three deep breaths, she'll realize this isn't the same thing at all. She loves Gina. And Gina loves her. Besides, Eve is in a serious relationship, like Ashley was last year. She might not admit it but Landon has become a priority."

"Where are we all going to live?"

"We could squish everyone in our house," she said. "It would be crowded for a while, but not forever. A year and three months from now at least one of those older girls will go off to school, maybe both of them, although I've been working on Eve to do her first year of college at community college. Or, maybe I'll move out. Not far, just out."

"With Joe?" he asked.

She laughed. "Oh, he'd love that. I've been trying to save Joe from being stuck with an elderly woman when he's still young enough to have fun, but he might be the one to bite the dust first. Not only is he a trooper, his blood pressure and cholesterol tend to be high and he's pretty lazy about it, too. Have you ever seen a man who enjoys butter more than Joe?" She shook her head. "I think his arteries might be completely clogged by now."

Mac smiled. Joe ignored her just as he did.

"Maybe Carrie would take me on."

"That sounds awful," he said.

"Seriously?" She laughed. "Two working women of a certain age who are tidy and like the same wine? One of whom loves to cook? A room of my own in an adult household where my boyfriend can spend the night without destroying the values of the younger generation? Please, Mac. You must think us so boring. Besides, I don't want to discourage you in any way, but I might not be completely interested in a household of seven. I had my own small house in Coquille, remember. I took you on when you were ten, and when you were twenty-six, I got you and three small children. I'm surprised the walls of that little house didn't blow out."

He grinned at the memory. "We sure worked hard back then, didn't we?"

"It was horrendous," she said.

At first, right after Cee Jay left them, Mac was so hopeful that she'd just return, he worked his two jobs—four days a week as an armored car guard, four nights a week as a new cop, not one day of the week without a job to do—and since Lou was teaching, they filled the gap with sitters. Lou ran back and forth between her house and Mac's, feeding, bathing, walking the floor, sleeping on the couch. Both of them were sleep-deprived and emotionally distraught. Finally Mac gave up hope; he and the kids moved into Lou's small house. All three kids had one bedroom, Mac had one, Lou had one—but one kid or another crawled in with them every night.

And Mac had been so broken. He'd been in pieces.

It never did get easy, but Mac had to quit the second job even though they needed the money—Cee Jay had left behind bills that had to be paid. They did get into a routine once they had child care nailed down and their schedules were at least the same every week. Once they moved to Thunder Point and all the kids were in school, life became more manageable. Not simple or uncomplicated, but definitely manageable.

"Honestly?" she said. "I don't know how we did it."

"We worked together," he said. "We had a common goal. Lou, please know I've never taken you for granted. I'm grateful for what you've done every day of my life. And you will never be alone or without a home. Never."

"That's very sweet, Mac. But if it's all the same to you, alone for a while might be just fine. I can still help out with carpooling, et cetera, but a nice little house or apartment...?" She smiled and gave him a shrug. "That might be pleasant."

"Gina and I have to talk to our kids. Everyone needs to have a chance to air their concerns. We have to get a consensus on how we're all going to live together. It has to be unanimous. And everyone should have time to adjust."

She just smiled at him. "You don't want to wait."

"I don't want to wait," he said. Then in a voice lowered to be private he added, "It took me so long to act on my feelings, Lou. I just want to wake up beside her in the morning. I don't care how crowded it is or how complicated, as long as she's by my side."

She sipped her mojito and smiled. Mac might be her nephew, but she'd been responsible for him for ten years when he was growing up, another ten after his wife left. He was more of a son than nephew; his kids were like grandchildren. They were her life. "This is what I've always wanted for you," she said, her eyes misty. "Cee Jay and I were like oil and water. I hoped she'd grow up and be the wife and mother you deserved. And now that you've been treading water for ten years, all I want for you is a life partner who loves and respects you as much as you do her. Mac, you're still a young man— marry your girl. Build a life with her. Be happy."

"You're the greatest woman in the world, you know."

She sipped her drink. "Yes, I know. About time you realized that."

When they got home, the household was in full chaos. Ryan and Dee Dee were fighting over control of the Xbox, Eve was screaming at her little brother for making so much noise that she couldn't hear her music, throwing couch pillows at him. Landon was sitting at the kitchen table finishing off a pizza with a tall glass of milk.

"You didn't get dinner?" Lou asked.

"I had dinner," Landon replied, stuffing another big bite in his mouth.

"What the hell's going on here?" Mac thundered at his kids.

Lou walked serenely to her bedroom. She hung up her jacket and pulled her cell phone out of her purse. She sat on her bed and hit the speed dial for Joe while simultaneously flipping on the TV. On her nightside table was her electronic reader and a couple of print books; on the other side of the bed, lotion, brush, lip balm and a glass of water from the previous night. Her cave.

She expected to leave a message, but Joe picked up. "Hey, babe," he said.

"Hi, Joe. Well, I've been laid off. Mac wants to get married. As soon as possible."

A low rumble of sexy laughter answered her.

There was just a week left of school and most of it was just a waste of time. There would be senior skip day, graduation rehearsal for seniors, a couple of tests and virtually no new assignments as the end drew near. Landon was determined to do very well on the last final of the year so he was hitting it hard, spending that last weekend studying. Next Friday night was graduation for the seniors. Juniors, like Landon and Eve, would celebrate by taking over the school as seniors in the fall.

The sound of the doorbell broke his concentration. He opened it to Eve. "What are you doing here? I told you I'd be over later."

Her eyes welled up with tears. "I have to talk to you."

He opened the door so she could come inside. "Are you breaking up with me?" he asked.

"No, but maybe I should. Let's sit down. This could be bad."

His heart skipped a few beats. "Spit it out," he said, leading her to the couch.

"Remember that time a couple of weeks ago when we got a little carried away? When we got a little...*close?*"

"It wasn't that close," he said, but it had been. He

was ready to grab the condom and go for it, but he held back the best he could.

"It was closer than usual. And my period didn't come. Rumor has it, those suckers can *swim!*"

Landon died on the spot. She was going to have to give him mouth-to-mouth and pound on his chest. He could feel all the color drain from his face. Then he felt his face get hot. "Huh?" he said so eloquently.

"I'm late. Five days. Or so. I'm never late, Landon. Never."

He knew this. He was not allowed to get her worked up at period time—she felt insecure about it. He, on the other hand, thought that might be the best time of the month if there was an accident, based on what he'd read.

"What are we supposed to do now?" he asked.

"I need a test. One of those pregnancy tests. But I can't just go buy one at the grocery store or drugstore where everyone knows me. And I can't borrow the car to leave town—my dad's working. If he saw me, he'd kill me for sure."

"I'll take you. Where should we go?"

"I'd like to go to the moon right now, but maybe Bandon's far enough away. Will you really take me?"

"Sure. Of course," he said.

"Then I'm going to have to stop in a bathroom somewhere—like a gas station or something. I can't take a pregnancy test home! Lou has the nose of a drug dog."

"We can come right back here. Sarah's sitting alert tonight."

"But what if she sees it in the trash?"

"I'm the trash man, Eve. I guarantee you, Sarah has never looked in the trash because I toss Ham's yard apples in there, too. And I always have it done before she gets home from work so there's nothing to complain about. Now, how'd you get over here?"

"I borrowed Aunt Lou's van. But I promised her I'd be less than an hour."

"Let's take it back to the house and drop it off. You tell your aunt we're running into Bandon to the sporting goods store. I want to look at running shoes—we'll start football practice in a couple of months and I want to get ahead of it. And you want to pick up some wax for your board."

She smiled. "I think that should work," she said a bit tremulously.

"Stop worrying. It's going to be fine. It would be more fine if they sold pregnancy tests at the sporting goods store. But we're going to take care of this."

Landon thought he'd been pretty smooth when Eve brought him this problem, but in fact his insides were trembling like a five-year-old on the high diving board. They didn't talk much on the way to Bandon. Every once in a while he grabbed her hand in his and gave it a squeeze. He tried very hard to be cool.

He went in the store with her, but left her to do the shopping by herself. He pressed a twenty into her hand and said, "Don't just buy the cheapest one." And then he went to the paperback and magazine section for ten minutes and left, empty-handed. He met her back in his little truck and all the way home, she read him the directions.

"What if it's too early?" she asked.

"It says it's not. But if it's negative and your period still doesn't come, we'll get another one next week," he said. "Look, we don't have that many choices. And I really don't think you're pregnant. I don't."

When they got to his house, she immediately headed for the bathroom with her package and Landon paced. Then she came out with a big grin on her face. "Was it a no?" he asked.

"I didn't have to take it," she said. "I just got you know what."

And Landon fell flat on his back on the living room floor. "Holy crap!"

She laughed at him and knelt down beside him. "It's okay. I shouldn't have panicked."

"Eve, we gotta get ahead of this. You have to talk to Aunt Lou."

"Oh, I'm scared to."

"Then I'm not going near you! We're not making out one more time because we both get a little crazy and one of these days... I love you like mad, but I want to be a little older before I start a family. I don't want one thin layer of latex between us and the next generation. And you shouldn't, either!" He pushed some of her pretty dark hair over an ear. "I'd like to be with you forever, but I don't know what you're going to want in a year or two. I don't want to have a baby at seventeen."

"We need to cool it down," she said.

"We can do that, too—whatever you want, but we can't get this scared again," he answered. "I'm willing to—"

The back door opened suddenly and Sarah popped in. Landon's school books were still covering the kitchen table and he was cuddled up with Eve on the living room floor. "Oh, hi, Eve," she said. "I didn't know you'd be here. I forgot my e-reader and didn't have a book with me," she said, passing through the living room on her way to her bedroom. She turned back to them and smiled. "I'm not going to sit up watching TV all night with the guys—I'm in the middle of a good book." And then she darted into her bedroom.

And then she darted out, e-reader in hand. "Sorry I can't stay and chat—I grabbed an hour to run down here and get this, but I have to get right back."

And then she walked into the bathroom, shutting the door.

Eve sat straight, folding up her legs. "Landon…"

He sat up, as well. "Where did you leave it?"

A shriek came from the bathroom. The toilet flushed. Sarah came out, e-reader in one hand, pregnancy test box in the other. Her face was in a scowl. Her eyes were narrowed. "Have we taken the test yet?"

No one spoke for a second. Finally Eve said, "It turned out, it was unnecessary." And her cheeks were so bright red, heat burned off them.

Sarah stepped into the room. "All right, you two. I know I can't control you, but there are two big rules. *Huge* rules. First, safety. And second, discretion. To live in polite society you have to not shock and dismay people. No embarrassing PDA. Public displays of…."

"We know what it means, Sarah," Landon said.

"So." She stared pointedly at Eve. "You on the pill?"

"Sarah," Landon began.

But Eve shook her head.

"Do you need me to take you to see a doctor? Because you should never have to buy another one of these," she said, lifting the box.

"I…ah…"

"We got it, Sarah," Landon said, more than a little furious with his sister.

"You have two days," Sarah said. "You either go to the doctor or clinic or talk to someone in your family and tell them it's not a good time to take crazy risks or... Or I will. Are we clear? Because I want to hear from your parents—either Lou or Mac, that is—or see evidence there's a prescription in place." She zeroed in on Landon. "And I'm counting on you, Landon."

"Sarah, stop it!"

She took a step toward him. "I want you to imagine yourself having a daughter next year. And I want you to imagine her at sixteen—and she just bought a pregnancy test kit and I want you to ask yourself, would you ignore this and leave it up to a couple of kids to make a mistake that could really mess up their lives or would you say something. When you have an answer to those questions, I will indeed *stop it!*" They both just stared at her. She turned on a heel and went back to the bathroom, putting the kit back where she found it. Then she faced them again. "I hope you don't have any big plans for your future life, Landon, because Mac might kill you! Love is grand. It's also been known to kill a lot of brain cells. Talk among yourselves."

And she left.

"I'm going to kill *her*...." Landon muttered.

"She's right," Eve murmured. "I'm just scared to face it."

"*You're* scared?" he asked. "Your father is going to kill me."

"Landon, it was both of us."

He smoothed her thick, dark hair over her shoulders. "You're not afraid your aunt Lou will chew you out, are you?"

"No telling," she said with a shrug. "She's the best, but she has a double personality and the other one is pretty growly."

He laughed. "Don't they all."

Three hours later, after the McCains had dinner and Aunt Lou had closed herself in her bedroom for alone time, Eve cautiously tapped on the door. She started with, "Can we talk for a minute?" and then said, "Landon and I have been dating for nine months or so and things are getting kind of..." She shrugged. "A little serious."

"Come and sit down by me, baby," Lou said. "Here—" She patted the bed. Then she turned Eve around so she faced her back. She massaged Eve's shoulders and talked softly.

"When I was seventeen, I had the hots for a guy at school. I was so crazy about him, I could've died. Of course we were very involved—we dated the last two years of high school. We were steadies. Back then there were no clinics and, in fact, birth control pills were pretty new and kind of scary. Everyone was supposed to wait. Save it for marriage. I went to a small high school but near as I can figure, four girls dropped out because they were pregnant. And hardly anyone with a steady boyfriend for more than a year waited."

"Four?" Eve asked. "Wow. Wild crowd?"

"Normal crowd. You probably think sex was invented four years ago."

"But didn't you guys hang out at the soda shop, wearing your bobby socks and poodle skirts?"

Lou turned her around. She looked deeply into her eyes. "It was the sixties. Free love. Anyone who could hung out at Haight-Ashbury or Woodstock." She turned Eve back. "By the time your mom and dad were in that 'pretty serious' place, there were clinics and even sex education, but it still wasn't easy to make that decision. That decision that says, I'd better make sure I'm safe and don't get STDs or pregnant. It's still one of the hardest things to come right out and say when you're a teenager."

Lou started running her fingers through Eve's hair, loosely braiding and unbraiding it. She said to Eve, "I'll take you for a checkup next week. You're free to ask the doctor for whatever you need—it will be confidential. She's probably going to want to check you for disease and maybe even do a blood panel for your general health. The first exam can be a little uncomfortable, but it's like that for everyone. Then you go for a checkup every year and it gets easier."

Eve got tears in her eyes. "I'm so scared to be doing this."

"Eve, you're a McCain. McCain women are very brave and we take care of our bodies. Just because you have protection doesn't mean you have to go along with what your boyfriend wants! You decide, you hear me?"

"Dad's going to be so disappointed. He really thought I'd stay a virgin till I'm thirty." She sniffed.

Lou laughed. "No, cupcake, he hoped for that, but no one knows better than Mac how unrealistic that idea is. In his secret heart, he wants you to know love just like everyone else does. Of course, he never wants you to be hurt."

"Can he not know about this?" Eve asked.

"He'll see the prescription on the insurance papers—there are no secrets. Especially from a cop, God bless him. However, you can tell him it's for cramps," she said with a shrug. "Then he can wonder, but not necessarily know for sure. Because, little madam, you don't to have discuss your personal life, your sex life, with anyone. You don't have to tell me or your dad every detail. In fact..." And Lou shuddered.

"Creeps you out, huh?"

"We'll head you off if you seem to be moving in an unsafe direction—like if we think you're into drugs or drinking or speed racing down country roads or throwing keggers. But trying to spy to embarrass and expose you?" She shook her head. "You can come to me with anything, honey. Anything. And I'll do whatever I can to help you. Your health and safety come first. I could *not* live without you."

Eve hugged her. "Thank you for understanding."

"I understand completely," she said, hugging back. Then, holding Eve away and looking into her eyes, "And stay far away from him until you're safe. Got that?"

"Got it," she said with a laugh.

Seventeen

Eric Gentry hadn't seen Thunder Point in over sixteen years. Yet here was the town, looking almost exactly as it had all those years ago. Gina was working in the same diner that her mother had worked in. It amazed him that things could remain so unchanged. He briefly pondered whether he pitied them for their lack of imagination or envied them the continuity of their surroundings and friends.

He went into the diner and found Gina standing behind the counter with a laptop open in front of her. She smiled at him. "Hello, Eric."

"Hi. This place hasn't changed at all."

"I know," she said. "Upgrades come slowly in Thunder Point. Stand by—let me ask Stu to cover for me for a bit and I'll take you to meet Ashley. She stopped by here about a half hour ago and said she was taking a walk down to the beach."

"Wait a sec," he said. "She knows I'm coming, right?"

Gina nodded. "You said sometime this weekend, whenever you could get away for a few hours."

"Is she nervous?" he asked, hands in his pockets.

"She's very curious. Are you? Nervous?"

"Nah, not me. I'm just terrified."

She tilted her head and lifted a brow. "As I recall, you're very good with teenage girls."

He winced. "I guess I had that coming."

"It'll be fine. Let me go talk to—"

"Nah, you stay here. Let me just go by myself. If she wants to, we could walk back here and have a Coke or something."

"Okay. You know the way, right?"

He tapped his temple. "Burned into my memory."

"Good luck, Eric."

He turned to go, then turned back. "Gina, I appreciate you giving me a chance here. That you trust me."

She smiled at him. "I don't trust you, Eric. I checked you out. My boyfriend is a cop and I ran a background search on you. You were very nice at our meeting and you haven't had a black mark against your name since you were a kid. But if you hurt my daughter in even the slightest way, you will regret it. I promise."

"I won't hurt her, Gina. And I promise."

He walked down the street, turned onto the beach road and spotted her immediately even though she was on the far side of the beach. Her red hair was pulled through the back of a baseball cap and she sat on the sand, knees pulled up with her arms circling them. There was one kid out on the bay on a paddleboard. Closer to the town side of the beach, a couple of young mothers sat on towels while their little ones played in the sand at the water's edge.

There weren't many places like this, he recalled—a long stretch of beach, a natural and untouched promontory, a calm bay without the presence of a lot of large businesses and hotels. Most of the coastline, at least parts the public could access, was busy with establishments that catered to beach combers and tourists. He remembered the bait shop; it looked as though it had been improved since he'd last seen it.

Ashley didn't notice him approach until he stood right beside her and she looked up at him.

"Hi, Ashley. I'm Eric Gentry."

Her mouth dropped open as she looked at him. She slowly got to her feet, brushing the sand off her butt. "Wow," she said in a breath. "I look just like you."

He chuckled. "You're much prettier, but you inherited the red hair and green eyes."

"My mom didn't mention that. I think she told me everything else, though."

"She said you've been having a terrible time lately," he said. "Go ahead, sit down."

"That's okay. You don't want to mess up your pants."

He looked down at himself. He wasn't dressed up by any means, just a pair of Dockers, a shirt, topsiders on his feet without socks. "I'm good," he said, lowering himself to the sand. "I'm sorry life has thrown you some curves, Ashley. Is there any way I can help? Anything you want to know about me or my family?"

She sat down, lifted her bottled water and took a slug. "Well, how about, where have you been?"

He knew that wasn't a literal question. "Well, I figured if I was my kid, I wouldn't want to know about me. I'm not exactly anyone's hero."

"Mom said you used to be a real hoodlum, but straightened yourself out."

"I served time, Ashley. She told you that, right?"

She nodded. "You must'a been a badass. What screwed you up?"

"Me. I screwed me up. I wasn't kicked around as a kid, my mother washed my clothes, had dinner on the table every night and my dad tried to get me interested in sports, but I fell in with a fun crowd and thought I was smarter than everyone else because I had a job that paid nine dollars an hour. I dropped out of school to work more and spent my money on cars, liquor and dope. When I heard I'd gotten my girlfriend pregnant, I ran and found another good-paying job as a grease monkey and a bunch of cool friends who not only drank and doped, but found an interesting way to improve themselves—they robbed convenience stores and liquor stores. That's pretty much the quick summary."

"I take it you got caught," she said.

"I drove the car," he said. "First time out, I got caught." He closed his eyes briefly. "Listen, there's no reason you have to tell anyone that your biological father is an idiot and an ex-con. Your secret is safe with me. I don't want you to be embarrassed."

"I'm not embarrassed, Eric. I'm not the ex-con." Then she looked out at the bay, at the guy on the paddleboard. Then back at him. "I bet you have a lot of regrets."

He pulled his knees up and looked out at the bay. "Kind of, kind of not. The thing about the hard times, the stupid times, they make you who you are. And regrets— I look back and ask myself if I didn't do a certain thing that I'm really ashamed of, how would that change the present? What would it erase from my current life? What if I hadn't been such a badass idiot back then? Would I have learned the cost of that recklessness? Would you be here? There are things I'm totally ashamed of that I wouldn't change. I ran out on your mom, but if I had stepped up and married her, oh, God, would she have gotten a bad deal. I was such an irresponsible asshole."

"And now?" she asked.

"I'm all right," he said with a shrug. "I abide by the laws. I have a little business and a girlfriend. My folks are starting to forgive me. I treat people right. I don't drink or do drugs. I'm nothing special, but at least I'm not unsafe. I've learned a lot."

She sighed. "Me, too."

"I hope you don't mind, but your mom told me some of what you've been through. Specifically, the boyfriend, the hospitalization..."

"She told me she did. She was looking for medical history, like does hearing voices run in your family...."

He couldn't help it, he chuckled. "No official mental illness that I'm aware of, but that doesn't mean I don't have crazy people in my DNA. Probably starting with me. So, Ashley, how are you getting along now? How are you feeling?"

"Oh, I feel kind of emptied out. I had a boyfriend dump me, but I'm not pregnant or in jail. I've been in therapy and group therapy and I'm very tired of seeing pain everywhere. When I was in the hospital, one of the other patients was my age and had tried to commit suicide, over a boy. It was shocking to think how dangerous that could be, how far something like that could go. I wish I'd never met her so I wouldn't have to think about how hopeless she must have felt to do that to herself. And I'm so grateful to have met her so I could see how far something like a broken heart could go, how much destruction there could be if we're not careful."

"I'm so sorry, Ashley. So glad there was a positive message in it for you."

She lifted one shoulder and looked down. "The worst part is that I felt that way for a little while myself, but I just didn't follow through. I just couldn't do that to my mom and Grandma. I wonder if that girl ever thought about that, about how people would feel."

"You felt that way because of the boyfriend?" he asked.

She nodded.

"What did your mom say about that? About the girl you met?"

"She said we don't all have the same number of tools in our tool belts. That she did the best she could with what she had. And I do the best I can with my set of tools."

"Your mom is pretty smart," he said. "I hope you have a tool for telling the ex-boyfriend to go pound sand."

She gave a soft laugh. "Oh, I still want things back the way they were, but I'm not dumb enough to take that kind of chance. I might never get over him, but I'm done with him."

"Things almost never go back to the way they were, Ashley. That's one of the hardest lessons—that you can't undo things and you can't unsay things. When you pass through something like that, you have to build something new."

"So people don't get back together?"

"Sure they do, but if they operate under the old rules

they'll revisit the old problems. You can't keep doing the same thing over and over and expect different results."

"Yeah, my mom said that, too." She turned to look at him. "You must have had to make a lot of changes."

He laughed without humor. "Yeah. I hate when that happens." The young man on the board was coming in. Eric watched as he dragged the board out of the water. "We only lived here a couple of years when I was a kid. I never learned to do that."

"Popular sport around here," Ashley said. "The bay is a great place for it—it's almost always calm. Sometimes when the tide is out you can even get on the ocean. Want me to teach you sometime? Cooper, the guy who runs the bait shop now, he doesn't have bait anymore but he has some paddleboards and kayaks instead. He rents 'em. And my mom and I—we have boards."

Eric smiled. "How about now?"

"You're not exactly dressed for it," she said. "You could get wet, unless you're like a natural. And I bet you're not."

He laughed loudly at that. "I can almost guarantee I'm not. But if I get wet, I'll dry. Let's go get a couple of boards."

"You're sure?"

"Why not? I've been trying to think of something we could do. I mean, you probably don't like popping dents out of cars or sanding them down and painting them. And you know—I always used to envy the kids who had their boards or skiffs out on the bay."

She grinned at him and his heart melted. "You're kind of goofy."

"One of the things I changed. I exchanged idiot for goofy." He stood up. "Come on, we'll give it ten minutes. And if you're not completely sick of me, maybe I'll come back at a prearranged time and wear a pair of shorts."

She stood. "All right, but don't say I didn't warn you."

Gina's shift should have been over before three, but she hung around the diner waiting for Ashley and Eric to come in for a Coke. An hour had passed. She hoped they'd gotten caught up in talking. She beat down the fear that something had gone terribly wrong. She knew Ashley wanted to meet him, believed that Eric was a safe man, but still…

Finally, unable to bear the suspense, she said good-bye to Stu and the teenage waitress on duty and walked down to the beach. What she would give for Ray Anne's binoculars! They didn't seem to be on the beach and a glance at Cooper's deck showed that place didn't seem occupied. Where could they have gone?

Then she heard a distant laugh that was clearly Ashley's. She looked out on the bay and there they were. Eric had removed his shirt and shoes, his pants were rolled up to his knees and he was trying to paddle the board, very clumsily, very slowly. And—he was soaking wet. His burnished red hair had curled up just like Ashley's did, water was dripping off him. His balance wobbled and, with a giant splash, in he fell into the sound of Ashley's wild laughter.

Gina wanted to sit on the beach and watch them, but she turned and left. This was something her daughter had never had in her life—a man in the family. No father, no grandfather, no steady guy. Mac had always been there for the girls, just as Gina had been, but this was different. And what were the chances that that irresponsible jerk could turn into someone decent? She didn't have any illusions that this could turn into a powerful and intense father-daughter relationship, but even if Ashley could have the knowledge that she didn't come from a total loser, Gina would be so grateful.

She looked upward and said, "Oh, thank you, God. Thank you. And please let it be real."

It had been about two months, but Ashley had finally gotten to the point she could resist reading about or listening to stories of her ex-boyfriend's grand achievements in baseball. About the same time Thunder Point High School was celebrating graduation, Oregon State was making it to the playoff championships. She was one of the few not planning to follow the playoffs or trying to attend home games.

Ashley was, however, concentrating on work. She wanted to earn money—her future depended on it. There were very few Thunder Point kids who didn't have to work to pay for their own activities or cars or car insurance, not to mention saving for college. In fact, most of Ashley's friends used their part-time job or babysitting money to buy their clothes or cheerleading uniforms or prom formals.

Ashley worked afternoons at the diner, relieving her mother, and some mornings she worked with her grandmother at the deli. All her friends were working— Landon was helping at Cooper's almost every day and Eve had gotten herself a part-time job at Pizza Hut. They wouldn't be spending the long days of summer on the beach this year, but rather catching moments here and there to hang out. And even finding time to spend with her mom and Gram wasn't easy. Sometimes they met at the diner if Ashley went in a little early for her shift and Carrie took a break from the deli before heading home.

She started at the diner on Memorial Day weekend, the end of May, and she'd only been there a week, the third generation of James women to work there, and she loved it. Gina trained her herself and just based on that and what she already knew from her mother, she was excellent at the job. In fact, although her previous plans had included going to State, living there in a dorm or apartment, she was reconsidering. It might be a better idea to stay in Thunder Point for her first year of college, borrowing the car to drive to Coquille to the community college and keeping at least one of her jobs. It would not only give her a chance to get used to the whole college experience, but it was also far cheaper and she could sock away more money.

She enjoyed the job of serving and cleaning up at the diner, and she saw lots of familiar faces every day. Friends and neighbors dropped by often and she realized that by being there, she never missed a thing that was happening in town or on the beach.

The new doctor in town, Scott Grant, would finally open his clinic across the street soon and he was holding a grand opening that Carrie would cater. Until he had a full roster of patients he'd only be open three days a week, supplementing his income by being on call at the Bandon emergency room. Deputy Pritkus, a much more efficient gossip than Mac, kept Ashley up-to-date on local trouble, mostly small stuff, but interesting nonetheless. And Frank, who was taking a couple of college level classes even before his senior year, came by when the diner wasn't busy in the afternoon. He didn't pester her; he brought his books, had a cola and studied in a booth in the back of the diner.

He always left the diner in time to get home for dinner. He never told her anything about Downy and she never asked.

Ashley assumed that the whole Downy family would be going to Corvallis for any playoff games happening there and that at least one or two of them would travel to out of state games if they could. She could ask Frank, but she wouldn't. She did ask him why he'd started coming to the diner to study and he said, "I've been doing this for a couple of years. It's always noisy at my house—TV, music, people making noise, sometimes arguing. It's easier to concentrate here. And it's even better since you started working here." And he grinned.

So when she wasn't busy, she'd grab herself a cola and slide into the booth across from him. "Just tell me if I'm bothering you."

He looked up from his books and smiled. "You're not bothering me, Ash."

"Anything new?"

"As a matter of fact, I got an invitation to meet with an early admissions counselor at MIT."

Her eyebrows shot up. "Was that your plan?"

He shook his head. "Wasn't even on my wish list. I think they want to look at me, talk to me, just to be sure I'm not some hick from a little fishing village before they process my application. I'm trying to decide if I can afford it. I should try since my focus is on math and computer science. You know, I think they actually looked at the computerized study guide I developed for high school students. I recorded it and loaded it on YouTube."

She stared at him in wonder. "You did that? I didn't know about that."

"I just did it for the people who ask me for help all the time. It's almost always the same questions. It was efficient. I put a link in my letter to admissions. I didn't expect anyone to actually look at it."

"How do you come up with these ideas?"

He just shrugged. "There are several online tutoring programs—some of them have millions of hits. There are a few things I'm good at...."

She laughed at him. "A few, huh? Do you know your IQ?"

"No," he said with a laugh. "Do I need to? I promise you, it wouldn't change anything."

"I think you're a genius or something. It must be so much fun."

"To be a geek?" he asked. "To be different from everyone?" He shook his head. "I get bored real easy. My mother calls me high-maintenance. It's hard to make friends that last after they pass the test they needed help for. I think it would be easier to be good at football or baseball."

"You think that? Well, don't. What you have has a longer shelf life." Then she rolled her eyes and laughed at herself. "Spoken like a waitress, huh? One of my jobs is to check dates on the packaged food! And, as for friends, you better not ditch me for a smarter girl because you made very big promises about my visits to the east coast. Very big. If you get a girlfriend, first thing you tell her is that you have a commitment to me for visiting and you're the tour guide. She'll just have to live with it."

"I'm pretty sure we won't run into that problem.

Have you decided where you're going to apply? Still looking at State?"

"Funny you should ask—I'm thinking of taking my first year at community college so I can keep my two part-time jobs. They're good jobs—good tips. And if I ever want to go farther away than State, I'll need money."

He grinned at that. "Oregon State is an excellent school."

"I know. And believe me, I'm not thinking of avoiding it because of you-know-who. I like my jobs. Doing it this way might give me a leg up. You know?"

"I know. Probably a good idea to keep your options open. Listen, do you have any days off? Ever?"

"I can easily get time off, as long as I give Stu and Gram a little notice."

"I can borrow my friend's boat. He might insist on coming along, but maybe not. Doesn't matter, really. We could spend a day sailing."

"I could bring lunch," she said. "I get a great deal at the deli. Like free. What's a good day?"

"I have classes Tuesday and Thursday mornings. Any other day."

"Next Monday?"

"Make it early. Seven in the morning?"

"It's usually kind of foggy...."

"I know—it's very cool to sit in the bay and watch the fog burn off."

By nine on week nights, Ashley was closing out the cash drawer and mopping the floor and she was usually on her way home by nine-thirty.

Ashley always walked home. It was only a couple

of blocks in a safe town. Unlike what she read about big cities, if she screamed for any reason, all the porch lights would pop on and people would stick their heads out to see if anyone needed help. Sometimes she got home to find her mom and Mac on the porch, talking and holding hands.

Tonight Stu locked the diner door behind her and said goodbye. She'd barely taken two steps when she heard, "Ashley?"

She just about jumped out of her skin! She whirled to see that right behind her, Downy was leaning against one of the lampposts on the street, not far from the diner's front door. "Oh, my God, you scared me!"

"Sorry, Ash," he said, stepping toward her. He had his arm in a sling. "I just wanted to see you."

"What happened?" she asked, nodding toward the sling.

"Nothing too much. Dislocated shoulder. I'm resting it for a couple of days, then it'll be fine."

"Does it hurt?"

"Nah, it's okay. Ash, listen, I'm sorry. About everything."

She felt color rising up her neck. Then she realized it was anger and not self-pity and that felt so good. "Is that right? Well, it's over." And she turned to head for home.

"Wait a sec," he said. "Can we talk? For just a minute?"

She turned back to him. "What on earth can we talk about, Downy? You're sorry, it's over, we're done."

"No, look," he said. "I made mistakes, all right?"

"No kidding! Crap, why didn't Frank tell me you were going to be home?"

"I just got here a couple of hours ago. I'm not sure Frank even knew I was coming."

"And you're going right back, right? Because you're staying at school all summer...."

He gave a pathetic shrug. "Plans change. I'm home for the summer."

"Well, the girlfriend must hate that."

"We broke up," he said. "Ash, I made some bad decisions. Really bad. I need you to listen to me."

She shook her head. "I really don't care what bad decisions you made. You didn't care about me, about my feelings, about anything. Do you really think I'm going to worry about you now? Just go home. Your mommy will snuggle you, not me!"

"I got cut from the team. My scholarship's in trouble. I might not have one anymore. I couldn't play and then we lost. Maybe not because of me, but I wasn't there to help. And they're all pissed."

"Cut?" she said, curious in spite of herself. "Pissed? How could they be angry if you got hurt?"

"I didn't get hurt playing. I was mad and went to a batting cage and swung a bat for hours and hours and got unhinged."

It didn't make any sense to her. "Why'd they cut you, then?"

He looked down and shook his head. He tilted his head to the bench. "Will you sit down with me?"

"No," she said. "You can sit there and I'll sit over here. But only for a minute. And only because I'm curious."

He sat down on one side of the diner door while she was on the other. And they just looked at each other.

Finally she said, "Well, what? What do you want to tell me?"

"That girl, Selena. She seriously messed me up."

"Oh, brother," Ashley said, standing up.

"No, really." He stood, as well, wisely keeping his distance. "She gave me pills she said were vitamins, supplement drinks for strength, but there were steroids in them. Low dose, oral steroids. I kept them in my locker because why wouldn't I? Then someone accused me of using performance enhancers. They looked at the pills, tested me for doping and…everything came crashing down. It's all a big misunderstanding. I didn't know I was doing anything wrong. It's not like I injected it."

"Bullshit," she said. Ashley looked at him in astonishment for a second. Then she laughed. She put a hand over her mouth.

"You think that's funny?"

"No," she said. "I think it's a lie. Or maybe an excuse. I know you, Downy. You know steroids—you've used them in the past. They're not illegal—my grandmother takes steroids for her knees. I think you told me the doctor gave one of your little brothers growth hormone because they were behind in growth. Or sometimes you can find small, supposedly safe amounts or protein drinks that are supposed to have nonsteroid enhancers, but they sure act like steroids—they bulk you up and make you cranky and short-tempered. We've argued about it. You like that stuff—you like being really strong. You're addicted to being strong. She didn't slip anything by you."

He shook his head. "She said it was undetectable. She gave it to me in a vitamin pill bottle."

"Right. But you knew."

He looked at her pleadingly. "I knew I shouldn't, but there were rumors about being an early draft pick and I wanted to hit everything, catch everything, run faster.... I felt like it was a chance, a safe chance, that wouldn't hurt anyone and would make me just a little better. I wanted that break so bad, Ash!"

"You're an athlete! You know what the problems with steroids are! Not only does it hurt your body, your personality, but it changes the playing field so it's not athlete against athlete but athlete against superdrugs! And you can't blame this on some girl."

"It was her," he said. "I think she used me and tricked me. I think she wanted me to do whatever it took to go pro. She wanted to hook up with a ballplayer."

"Well, we'd all give you the prize for being stupid, except you and me—we're in a dead heat for that prize."

His brow wrinkled in confusion; he didn't get it. "Ash, give me another chance. I'll make it up to you. I swear to God."

"No."

He took a step toward her; she took a step back. "I need you, Ash. I need help to get through this. I need to feel like someone's on my side. Please."

"No."

"Ashley, I've been wrecked by this. I know I made mistakes, but Jesus, nothing I did is so bad I should have to go through this! I lost everything! Everyone is pissed at me and no one understands the pressure I was under. Everyone was counting on me—my team, my friends, my family...."

She just shook her head. She actually did feel sorry for him. But not that sorry. "What happened to you, Downy? You went to State as this town's shining star.

You had a nice girlfriend who would never cheat on you, a full ride scholarship so you could get an education—something a lot of us little people are working our tails off to try to pay for. You even had agents sniffing around, telling you you'd go pro before you're even dry behind the ears. And how did you respect all that? You decided to break all the rules. You cheated. You hurt everyone and now you want them all to be a little more understanding, to let it go. You know what, Downy? You have your work cut out for you, because you're going to have to earn back the respect you lost."

He was quiet for a moment, then he said, "Tell me what to do, Ash. I'll do whatever you want."

She smiled and shook her head. "Hey, there's nothing for you to do for me—I'm over you. I think when an altered naked picture of me went out to about four hundred cell phones and Facebook friends and you shrugged it off and said, it was just a joke, that put the last nail in the coffin."

"Hey, come on, I was mad about that! We had a fight about that! That was wrong, that she did that!"

"And you couldn't even call me, explain and say you were sorry? I went through all that alone, and did you care? Nothing is ever your fault. Yeah, you have a long way to go. Good luck, Downy."

She turned and walked away. He called to her; she heard him but she didn't turn around. In that moment, with a smile on her face, Ashley knew she was finally well and truly over Crawford Downy. When Ashley was home, she found her mom and Mac sitting on the porch steps, a little votive candle between them. She told them she was tired and went inside.

Ashley went to her room, got into her little boxers

and tank top and sat cross-legged on her bed with her cell phone in her hand. It was ten. Probably too late. But she took a chance and put through the call. When he said hello, she said, "Eric? It's Ashley. It's late, I know—should I try you another time?"

"It's okay," he said. "I was going through some paperwork and I'd love an excuse to stop that. What's up?"

"I would have called earlier, but I worked at the diner until after nine."

"You put in some long days, don't you, Ashley?"

"Sometimes, I do. This is very last-minute, but I don't have to go to work until three on Sunday afternoon and I'm not working at the deli at all that day. Would you like to come to Thunder Point and go paddleboarding? I think you have potential."

He laughed. "I wouldn't miss it. What time?"

"Can you be at my house at about ten?"

"I'll be there."

On Sunday morning they launched off the marina dock and even though the bay was completely calm, Eric went in almost immediately. And getting back on the board wasn't exactly graceful. "I know we've been over this, but you're a good swimmer. Right?" Ashley asked. "I'm not going to have to save your life, am I?"

He spit and sputtered. "I'm a good swimmer."

"Take your time. It's a good day on the bay."

"It's a beautiful day all around," he said.

But after that first big splash, Eric found his footing and kept up with her. They paddled around the bay, skirting the big, protruding rocks. A couple of small sailboats left the marina and headed out to the Pacific.

"Does everyone in this town have some kind of board or boat?" he asked.

"Just about. A lot of people like to dive, but the best diving is up the coast a little bit. There are a few places where the water is deep and clear and there's lots of marine life. A few of us have taken our boards up there, past Coos Bay."

"You don't dive?"

She shrugged. "Diving gear is pretty expensive." At the mouth of the bay, she stopped and sat down on her board, just enjoying the endless expanse of ocean. "You don't want to get too far to either side out here," she cautioned. "There are some sharp rocks and big waves at the tips of the points. It's best to stay in the center and if a boat's on the way in, get out of the way."

Eric sat down. He was quiet for a moment. "This is awesome," he finally said. "What made you decide to call me?"

"You're a pretty nice guy," she said. She turned and looked at him. "I'm glad I didn't know you when you weren't."

"Me, too," he said. "Thanks for giving me a chance."

"I guess it can't hurt to get to know the other half of my DNA." She laid down on the board and looked up at the sky. "I saw my ex-boyfriend last night."

Eric, still sitting, looked down at her. "How'd that happen?"

"He's back in town and was waiting for me outside the diner. He's now sorry and would like a second chance with me. But this is all because he's in big trouble and was cut from the team and might lose his scholarship." She turned to look at him. "Doping. He claims the new girlfriend messed him up, got him doping and then dumped him. Of course, it's not his fault and is all a big misunderstanding."

Eric whistled.

"He was a star in high school," she said. "All-conference football and baseball. He was the Homecoming king. Maybe I didn't see it then, but I thought he wore it pretty well—that kind of popularity. I thought he was a nice guy. He *was* a nice guy, I think. He looked out for his younger brothers and I think he was loyal to me. We talked on the phone and texted many times a day—something he stopped having time for when a new girl came along. But I also remember—he used all kinds of supplements when he was strength training. Nonsteroid, he said. But he didn't think there was anything wrong with steroids, if you weren't competing. Downy's a big guy—very strong. He saw a chance at going pro real young and he didn't want to miss it. He caved. He caved all over the place—gave in to the pretty, snotty college girl, the drugs, probably other things. He wanted it all and he was willing to take a lot of chances and... Well, he lost it all."

"Do you feel a little sorry for him?" Eric asked.

She nodded. And then in a very quiet voice she added, "But he sure didn't feel sorry for me. He was cruel. When I was broken he told me to go away and quit bothering him."

Eric smiled at her. "I don't think you're broken any-more."

"I'm much stronger. But I might never have another boyfriend. I don't ever want to feel that bad again."

He laughed.

"You think that's funny, what I went through?" she asked, an edge to her voice.

"Not at all. I was just thinking, you're young. You'll

get past that and take a chance again. You know why? Because you'll look around and notice that even though you had a very painful experience, no one gets through this life without some major disappointments and hurts. You'll see that a lot of people had it even worse than you and you'll take notice. You'll see that to get through life you have to be strong and smart and patient and humble. What happened to Downy? A classic example of hubris—the deadliest of sins. And I know—I was there. I wasn't lucky enough to go there with a ball and full scholarship—but I thought I was above it all, invincible, more important than anyone else."

"Hubris?"

"Arrogance. Pride before the fall. The feeling that the universe is there to serve up our selfish wants no matter what it does to other people. Downy let down his teammates and his school and his girl. But I stole from people."

She thought about this for a moment. "Well, he should be ashamed. Most of us have to work real hard just for a chance to go to college. He had it all and threw it away by wanting still more."

"Sometimes you learn your best lessons when you add up all your losses."

She lifted an eyebrow at him. "Most of the time you don't sound like a grease monkey."

He grinned. "Is that right?"

"You know who's been just supernice to me for the last three months? Downy's brother. Frank."

"Is he a lot like Downy?"

She sat up. "Nothing like Downy. I've known Frank forever—we've been in school together since kindergarten. He was always the skinny little runt with the thick glasses, but so smart it was scary. The bigger kids used to pick on him and try to beat him up and if not for Downy... Well, Downy was his bodyguard and Frank was the nerd. But Frank has changed a little bit lately—he's grown up, for one thing. He's taller, stronger, got contacts. He's actually good-looking, but you can tell he doesn't know it. He likes to sail and paddleboard, so he built muscle. He's not an athlete like Downy, but he has an appointment at MIT for an early admission scholarship."

"Seriously?" Eric asked, surprised and impressed.

She nodded. "All in one family. Why couldn't I get some of that?"

He chuckled. "You have what you need, Ashley. I promise. Hey, your mom knows I came over to board with you, doesn't she?"

"Of course. She said she hopes I don't end up disappointed."

"She has good reason to worry about that," he admitted. "That'll take time. Hey, you almost ready for some lunch? We can come back out after, if you feel like it."

"Sure. Let's go in."

Eighteen

Sarah had continued to put off talking to Landon about her potential change of assignment. In fact, she had been in some denial. It had been a while since Buzz had dropped the bombshell on her and as the days, and then weeks, passed with no confirmation she found herself taking the irrational position that if she didn't think about it, maybe it wouldn't happen. But she was going to have to deal with this. School had been out for less than a week and Landon was already talking about football practice starting up in August. He was working at Cooper's part-time for the summer and was running and lifting weights, getting ready.

She'd been in her office for thirty minutes when her phone rang. She should have looked at the caller ID. She innocently answered, "Dupre." And then she just listened to the voice on the other end of the line. Orders were being cut, she'd receive them in a few days—and she was going to Miami. She was slated to move in August, but she had two weeks to either accept the transfer or resign her commission. If she planned to accept the new assignment the chances were excellent that she'd be offered a promotion within a few months of her arrival in Florida.

That's what service meant—you go where you're needed, when you're needed. And she was needed in Florida.

Sarah hung up the phone and sat, stunned, for a few minutes. She needed to talk to Buzz. She went to his office, tapped on the door, went inside as he looked up. She closed the door but she didn't sit down. "I just got my orders," she said.

He turned away from his computer screen. "Was it what I heard?"

She nodded. "Miami."

"What are you going to do?"

She shook her head. "I guess I'm going to talk to Landon...."

"What about your guy? Cooper. Have you talked to him?"

And say what? she asked herself. Goodbye? "I haven't told anyone. I wanted to wait until I knew for sure. First, I'm going to talk to Landon. What do you say to a sixteen-year-old kid who is looking at being king of the world in his senior year? You know the story, Buzz. What do I say?"

"I don't know," Buzz said. "I have a sixteen-year-old kid and he thinks I can pick money off the tree out back. So does his mother, for that matter. I've had to do the hard, unpopular things and it has cost me. I don't know what else I could've done, but the price was high."

She looked down. He'd probably paid the ultimate price for the less than stable lifestyle and she knew why he was here, why she was here. He loved the Coast Guard; he believed in their mission just as she did. In every branch of military service there was instability and risk, it took its toll on relationships.

"Need a couple of days off?" Buzz asked her.

She shook her head. "I'm fine. I'll get back to work. I think better when I'm busy."

"If I can do anything..."

"Thanks," she said. "If I think of anything, I'll let you know."

For the next couple of days she tried not to let on that her brain was about to explode, trying to decide how to do what she had to do. Landon didn't really notice—he had his new job on the beach, which he loved, and Eve, who he loved even more. Cooper noticed; he asked if there was another evaluation coming up and she said, "We're facing some transfers and the whole station is going to have to adjust and figure out how to fill some gaps. But I'll figure it out, don't worry."

Just when she was about to sit down and spill her guts to Cooper they learned that Austin and Spencer were coming for another visit. The toy hauler was ready for guests once again and Sarah knew she'd have to put off talking to Landon and Cooper just a few days longer.

The activity around the RV led to every person from the road to the beach asking what was going on.

"Spencer and Austin are coming for a visit, now that they're both on summer vacation," Cooper said. And he said it over and over again. "Kind of last-minute, but it's a good thing. Austin loves being on the water and it saves me a trip to Texas to visit him."

Late Friday afternoon when the deck and bar were full of beachcombers and neighbors and folks from neighboring towns out for a summer evening, the back door burst open and little freckle-faced Austin stood grinning in the doorway. "Hey, Cooper! I'm here!"

Cooper's face lit up and he laughed, coming around the bar. "So you are," he said. "Nothing like an entrance!" He put out his arms and Austin leaped into them.

"Can we go out on the bay for a while?"

"You've been here less than a minute. And I'm a little busy here. Does your dad feel like taking you out?"

"He wants to unload and unpack," Austin said with a pout. "And eat something. But I want to go out on the bay!"

Sarah leaned on the bar. "Hey, Austin," she called. And to Cooper she said, "I can cover this if you want to go ahead. Landon will help me and Rawley is still here."

"You sure?" he asked.

"I'm sure."

Cooper put Austin on his feet. "Fifteen minutes. I'll run you around the bay on the Jet Ski. Get your suit on."

"Yay!" He wiggled out of Cooper's arms and headed for the toy hauler.

Cooper had never longed for children, but he wasn't opposed to the idea. He figured he might have one or two someday, which was one of the reasons the idea of marriage hadn't spooked him. But he had no idea one skinny, goofy, freckled little kid could bring him so much happiness. Five minutes later he had Austin in a life vest and on the back of the Jet Ski. When he'd bought this thing, it was in his head that he'd be loading a variety of beautiful bikini-clad young women behind him, holding on to him, but not one of them could have given him as much pleasure as this kid. *His* kid.

A half hour later he had Austin off the bay, sitting

at a table on the deck, devouring a pizza. Spencer was having a beer, his feet up on the railing.

"*You* didn't want to take him out on the Jet Ski?" Cooper asked, joking.

"I've just spent hours traveling with him. He wiggles worse than a box of worms and he is a talking machine."

After dinner, Cooper had him fishing off the end of the dock, and then they played checkers for a while. Spencer coaxed Austin into the shower and by the time the sun was setting, Spencer had him tucked into bed in the trailer. After Landon and Rawley left, Cooper lit the little candles on the deck tables. He had a half-dozen customers enjoying the last of the sunset over the Pacific. Finally Spencer reappeared, showered and changed.

"I better have another beer," he told Cooper. "Can I help myself?"

"Of course," he said. "In fact, you can bring me one."

Cooper scooted his chair close to Sarah and put an arm around her. The beach began to come alive beneath the deck and a couple of fires appeared.

Spencer was back with the beers and sat down with a heavy, exhausted sigh. He was quiet as he took in the last of the sun's pink rays over the ocean. He took a pull on his beer. "Doesn't get any better than this," he said.

"Is he asleep?" Cooper asked.

"Oh, hell no," Spencer said. "The TV is on and I told him to call me if he needs anything."

"He'll pass out pretty soon. I tired him out the best I could," Cooper said.

"How can something so small wear a person out so thoroughly? Listen, I have to tell you something," Spencer said. "I hope you'll take this as good news.

There's a professional reason for us being here. Your football coach and athletic director is retiring and I applied for the job."

"You did what?" Cooper asked, sitting straighter.

"Not good news?" Spencer asked.

"Hey, I didn't say that, but why didn't you tell me that's why you were coming? Maybe I could've said something to someone. I knew about Coach Rayborough retiring!"

"You haven't been here that long. I didn't think you'd be tight with the coach."

"Well, I'm not and I was pretty surprised to be included in the discussion. But what about your family?"

"My parents are in the same nursing home in Missouri. I have some aunts out there but I'm an only child. The last time we visited, my mom couldn't remember who Austin was. I don't know how long it'll be before they're gone, but probably not long. You're probably thinking of Bridget's family, too. They're grieving and I think they're going to be grieving for a long time." He shook his head sadly. "We've had enough of death and illness. Austin and I need a fresh start. I like your little town. And Austin loves it."

"Do you think you can get that coaching job?"

Spencer smiled. "You don't know that much about me. I had to check you out and make sure Austin was safe with you, but you probably never took a close look at me. I'm not a born-and-bred Texan, you know that, but I've been a Texas high school football coach and athletic director for years. My teams go to state, and it's a big-ass state. Texas is serious about football. There's a lot of competition for a job like this in the Northwest, but not a lot of experienced teachers and coaches who would be willing to take the size of the Thunder Point paycheck if there are bigger schools hiring. This is a good place for Austin for a lot of reasons." He smiled. "Bio-dad is here." Then he grew a little serious. "We do fine, Cooper—me and the little man. But we seriously need to move on. We'll visit Bridget's family, but we're due a new agenda. I'll apply and interview, but in the end it's all up to the school board."

Cooper leaned toward him. "What if this doesn't work out for you, Spencer? What if you don't like it here?"

"I can't answer that," Spencer said. "It could swing either way—it either turns out to be a positive move for me and for Austin. Or if it doesn't live up to my expectations, I could be looking again. And if it's visits instead of living in the same neighborhood, you can count on me to help with that. I didn't do this to pin you down, Cooper. I did this for an opportunity, a positive change. This town and, in fact, the high school, both have very good reputations. Even with a smaller paycheck, it looks good on paper."

"I think you're going to find it feels as good as it looks," Sarah said. "I moved here for Landon. He should be the starting quarterback in the fall, unless something happens, like maybe some hotshot moves here over the summer. I was looking around for a proactive football coach in a place I could afford, in a school that boasted athletic and academic scholarships. A place with opportunity for Landon. And it's worked so far."

"Maybe it'll work for us," Spencer said. "I haven't given my notice in my school district and I haven't looked anywhere else yet. This was a complete coincidence. I visited you, liked your little town, started looking around for Oregon job opportunities. I thought if there was something within a few hours' drive, this piece of coast makes for a nice weekend. But I never imagined something like this would show up."

Spencer turned in, but Sarah and Cooper stayed out on the deck. Once the sky was dark and the million stars came out to play, it was just impossible to leave. All the customers had gone, leaving just the two of them. There were two campfires on the beach and the presence of the Razor made it clear Landon was down there somewhere. They heard a clumping up the stairs and Ham came panting toward them, tongue hanging out and drooling.

"And hello to you," Sarah said, giving him a pat on the head

Then a whistle rent the air and he ran back down the stairs and across the beach to where the kids sat around a fire.

"Landon would probably like us to go inside and leave them alone," Sarah said.

"So what? It's a perfect night." He pulled her chair closer.

She sighed and looked out over the water. "You really do have a perfect life."

"Close," he agreed.

"And now your son is here," she said. "That's everything, Cooper. That's the whole thing for you."

"Maybe. Spencer still has to apply for the job. Sounds like he'll get it, though. I had no idea he was a championship coach. That's pretty cool. I hope Spencer is up to the job of making the most out of Landon, for his sake. For the sake of college opportunities. And for the coach—he really wants an exit strategy after forty years."

"Mmm," she agreed. "How does it feel, really? Being a dad?"

He grinned. "Pretty damn cool. Doesn't hurt that he's an awesome and hilarious little kid, which I owe to Bridget and Spencer." He chuckled and shook his head. "Bio-dad." He laughed.

"Did you ever see yourself in this situation—the father of a ten-year-old?"

"Sort of," he said. "In the back of my mind I thought I'd accidentally get married and have a kid or two, even though I had no idea what responsibilities that really entailed. I figured I'd grow into it. I thought I'd eventually tie myself down to a house, a couple of kids, a steady job that didn't change every two years. I didn't think it would take this long. I've always known I'm a one-woman man," he added, giving her shoulders a squeeze. "But, I wasn't ready at twenty-seven when Bridget was ready. I was still moving fast back then."

"Are you saying you're ready now?"

He turned and looked into her eyes. He smiled. "I'd better be—it's here. And it feels pretty good. I don't know how Spencer will like it here, but I couldn't ask for more than this. I mean, come on—listen to that surf. Look at that sky."

"What if this job hadn't come open?" she asked. "What if Spencer and Austin weren't here? And what if it doesn't work out for them?"

"I guess I'd be on a plane regularly. Single parents do that all the time. It's not the best situation, but it works."

She leaned against him. The sound of lapping water at the shoreline and the laughter of teenagers on the beach was soothing. "You sound really unfucked-up for an ex-helicopter pilot who runs a beach bar."

He laughed at her. "And for the first time in a long time, I feel that way, too." And he kissed her brow.

Nineteen

Ashley walked home after her shift and found her mother sitting on the front porch in the dark alone. "Why are you still up?" she asked.

Gina smiled and sighed. "Mac just left and I stayed out here. Did you have a good shift?"

"I did, but I'm tired now—I'll sleep in a little tomorrow. Are you okay?"

"Oh, I'm okay. I was just thinking how lucky I am. Having Mac in my life—he's such a good, strong man."

"You're acting kind of sad for someone who is planning to get married," Ashley said, sitting down beside her mother on the porch.

"It'll pass. Give me ten minutes. But I will say this— I look forward to not saying goodbye to him at the end of every day. And you know what worries me? I know this is going to sound very strange, coming from your mother—but I've never been a wife. What if I stink at it?"

Ashley giggled. "I bet you'll get the hang of it."

"I hope so. I want so much to be a good wife to him,

and a good stepmom. I have no doubt he'll be an awesome stepfather."

"He practically has been, Mom. He's been my stand-
in dad for four years."

"I guess he has, hasn't he?"

"Well, it sure wasn't Stu at the diner, or Downy's
dad, Ford. If I had any situation that I'd mention to a
dad, or talk to a dad about, it was Mac. In fact, ever
since all that drama with Downy, Mac seems to keep
a real close watch on me." She laughed. "He really is a
busybody, isn't he?"

"He is. In the best possible way. It used to frustrate
me so much that he just thought of me as a good friend,
but now I realize that all those years of friendship before
romance has been a good thing. He's a patient man—he
knows me as well as you do. He's easygoing and gen-
erous, not prickly like some men. I think Lou softened
him up, taught him how to live with a woman."

"I don't know why you two are waiting to get married. You know that Gram and I could put together a
wedding in a week. Two at the most."

"But we haven't really figured out all the sleeping
arrangements.... We have to give it at least till the end
of summer."

"By the end of summer everyone will know their
places, but you don't have to wait that long. Eve and
I have talked it out. For the past four years I've either stayed over at her house or she's stayed here at
least once a week, but it's usually even more often.
When she's had enough of Lou and the younger kids,
she might be here most of the weekend. And when I've
had enough of—" She stopped suddenly and even in the
dark, Gina could see a flush darken her cheeks.

"You can say it. My feelings won't be hurt."

She took a breath. "Our house is quiet. People go to bed early. Eve's house is lively. Lots of kids get together there because the deputy likes to have eyes and ears on them, but our house is a good spot to bring boyfriends after a game or dance because Gram is out like a light with her ear buds in her ears. When Eve gets enough of lively, she's here, where we can just walk to the beach, or to the diner, or to McDonalds and Pizza Hut. When I'm looking for a little more action, I'm there. I might move in there—probably into Eve's room—but Gram will let us come here to spend the night anytime we want to. It'll probably be a lot like it is right now, except you'll be paired up with Mac, just like you should be. And I bet Aunt Lou moves out—I bet she moves in with Joe. She's making those kind of comments, thinking no one is listening. But Eve and I will be the same. We study together, we wear each other's clothes, we carpool and double date. The only thing we don't share are boyfriends."

"Huh," Gina said. She reached out and touched Ashley's hair. "I'm not sure how I feel about my house being the best make-out house. But I caught on to your agenda a long time ago."

"Well, that's not my agenda anymore, but this house is a really good one for marathon *Criminal Minds* shows. Eve's gets a little wild with Ryan and Dee Dee competing on the drums and piano and video games."

"I like those movie and TV nights," Gina said.

"If Mac lets you out, you can join us sometime." Then she grinned at her mother.

"I hate that you had such a hard spring, baby. But you're better than ever. And you were amazing before."

"Thanks, Mama," she said, smiling. "I feel better than ever. I don't like how I had to learn a few things. But I like what I had to learn. And as a bonus, I got Eric." She grinned. "I like him."

"Whew. I'm so glad that worked out."

"It worked out. At least so far. So about you and Mac... We could fix up a quick wedding. Lou can still take all summer to decide what she wants to do. You two can live in the same house for a couple of months if it takes her that long to decide. Maybe she'll want to hang around for Ryan and Dee Dee while school's out. Think about it, Mom—we've been like one family the past few years. We do everything together."

"He keeps suggesting we just elope. And it's tempting, but I think people expect a ceremony, a reception, a party."

"Would you? Elope? Just run off and get married?"

She shrugged. "I haven't given it serious thought. I admit, having four kids between us, a nice dinner out and a night or two away sure sounds nice. But we can wait till August so we don't take anyone by surprise...."

"You could also tell Gram and Lou and the kids that you'll be away next weekend, getting married. Everyone wants you to get married. No one except Dee Dee has a big need to be in a wedding," Ashley said.

"What about you? The maid of honor?" she asked.

"Don't take this the wrong way...you know I love Mac and the whole family but I'm a lot more interested in this idea of Frank's—going out on the bay at night when there's a full moon."

"Seriously?" Gina asked.

"Frank has seen dolphins out there. I'd give anything to see a dolphin up close. Do you know if you shine lights down into the water at night you can see massive marine life?"

"Frank?" she asked, lifting a brow.

"Another gift—I never really knew him before even though I've known him my whole life. We're good friends now. And that's where it's going to stay. Good friends. And it's very nice."

"Well, I'll be darned. Frank. Huh. And you wouldn't be hurt and deprived if I didn't have a wedding and party you could be a part of?"

"Mom, the whole town has expected you and Mac to get married for years. The two of you are so lame, thinking no one could see the way you look at each other. Put your lives together and move on so we don't have to all watch you sneaking kisses. No one cares. Well, except Dee Dee. But we can have a pretend wedding for her and she'd be just as happy—she's ten. We could let her be the bride!" And then she grinned. "Did you know Frank plans to go to college on the east coast? One of the big ones—MIT or Harvard or Boston University. He knows everything out there to see and do! He says if I ever go visit him he'll take me everywhere. To New York City, the D.C. Mall to see all the museums and monuments, to all the planetariums and observatories. I am *so* going to do that! And Eve and I have been talking about Europe. You know, after we finish college. There's a big world out there. It's not all Oregon State University and Thunder Point and some baseball player, you know."

Gina sighed and gave her daughter a loving stroke along her arm. "I know, baby. It's so good to see you have dreams. Big dreams. And you will do it, too. All of it."

* * *

Gina called Mac's cell phone. "Did I wake you?" she asked softly.

"No. Saying good-night again?"

"I have Ashley's permission to elope," she said. "Are you still tempted to do that?"

"I'm more than tempted. Want to leave in an hour?"

She laughed at him. "I think one needs a marriage license to elope...."

"We'll go to Coquille and get one tomorrow. This weekend?"

"Shouldn't you ask your family if they're on board with that idea?" she asked.

"Oh, hell no, I'm not asking. I'll tell them, though. I'll find us a little chapel, we'll do it Friday night and have the weekend away."

"I'll move into your place, if Lou has no objections. Tell her I'm prepared to take orders. For as long as she's there, forever if she chooses that option, I understand it's her domain."

"Ach, she talks tough. I'm sure she'll be glad to have a little help around the house. What made you decide?"

"It was Ash. I told her that it's hard to say goodbye to you at the end of every day and she said, 'What are you waiting for? Just do it!'"

"I love that girl," he said. "I just want you to have what you want, Gina. Big or small, I don't care. I'd even go common law. I just want you to be the last thing I feel against me at night and the first thing I feel in the morning. I love you."

"You're the strangest man," she pointed out to him.

"It takes you years to kiss me and then you're a runaway train. There will be adjustments, you know."

"I know. Extreme contentment. I'm a tough guy, Gina. I'm up to the job."

Cooper was a genius. It wasn't lost on him that something serious had been bothering Sarah for at least a couple of months. She tried to pass it off as just work stuff, but it was obviously much more serious than that. And the past few days the quiet had grown deep and a little scary. He was a very straightforward guy, so of course, he confronted it, told her he'd noticed a change in her behavior lately and wondered what it was about.

"I realize I've been moody," she said. "It'll pass. I'm sorry."

"Spencer was told they hadn't even hoped for a candidate of his caliber for that job at the high school. It's all done but the shouting now. Is it about Austin living here?"

"No, no, of course not. That's wonderful for you. And I enjoy Austin—I think he's adorable and exhausting, just as a ten-year-old boy should be. It's just work stuff. I'll tell you all about it when I get a handle on it."

"Your ex isn't giving you a hard time, is he?"

"No, he's ben completely silent. In fact, rumor has it he's found women up there in Alaska, which means he'll be very busy and will be leaving me alone. Listen, don't take it personally, okay? Now and then work gets a little stressful at the command level. You know. I'm cranky. I just need a couple of days off."

"And you'll get 'em," he said. "You have the weekend off, right?"

"Right. I'm looking forward to spending it on the beach!"

"Well, maybe except for one night. I have had an interesting request from Mac. Apparently Gina and Mac aren't waiting any longer—they're going to get married Friday night in Coos Bay at a little chapel on the water. They'd like us to meet them there, be the witnesses, join them for a nice wedding dinner and then disappear as quickly as possible. It'll be small, just the four of us. There will be someone at the chapel to take a few pictures and they're going to hide away for the weekend. We can come back here. Or, if you're feeling adventurous, I'll take you on a sleepover. I can get us a reservation somewhere that has a vibrating bed and mirrors on the ceiling."

She laughed. He could always make her laugh.

"Let me think about that—Mac'll be out of town, I'll be out of town, Landon and Eve will be in town...."

"I bet Mac's got a shotgun Lou knows how to use...."

Again she laughed. "For right now, let's plan on coming back to Thunder Point on Friday night, but I'll think about the mirrored-ceiling option."

"That's my girl. I'll call you again tonight."

Cooper knew it wasn't the Mac and Gina marriage that bothered Sarah, since she'd just barely found out. He hoped she wasn't worried about the fact that Spencer and Austin would be making Thunder Point their home. But he'd told not only Sarah, but also Spencer, that if his circumstances changed he could be flexible, he would travel to see his son. So it couldn't be those things. He'd asked her about Landon—he was under control. No more scary romance issues with him, at least for the time being. Cooper felt as if he was beginning to make things up—none of it made real sense. Of course, there was the dreaded possibility that Sarah had taken this thing with him as far as she could and was ready to end it all, but even that idea seemed pretty far-fetched.

It would be hard to stay strong through something like that because he loved Sarah. He loved her like he'd never loved before. He wanted her forever and he knew he wasn't just fantasizing—it was real for him. If she dumped him it would put a serious kink in some plans he had to surprise her. Not to mention the idea that she might leave him would kill him.

But things remained the same all week. Sarah was aloof. Preoccupied with some itchy problem, yet not seeming to be terribly unhappy with him.

On Friday he picked her up to go to Coos Bay to meet Mac and Gina. "We're stopping at a florist," she said. "I ordered flowers."

"How did you know to do that?" he asked.

"I asked," she answered with a laugh. "I asked Gina what she'd like me to wear, and if she'd planned for flowers or a wedding cake or anything like that. She said she was keeping it very simple, that her mother wanted to have a party sometime this summer and if she didn't get to make the cake, she'd be crushed, so flowers it is." She gave a sigh. "She said as boring and unromantic as it sounded, they had so much to do with their hard-earned money—educations for one thing— and they didn't want to splurge on a big wedding. She said getting out of town for a weekend was definitely going to be romantic and *not* boring!"

"We should do that sometime," he said while driving.

"We should," she said quietly.

They stopped off for flowers, took two lovely bouquets to a small chapel near the waterfront and found an excited and thrilled bride and groom. Gina was astonished by the gorgeous flowers. Sarah pinned a simple rose on Mac's lapel, and then one for Cooper. And Cooper was so proud of her for her thoughtfulness and generosity. He'd gotten them a gift to give them later, which he hoped they would like.

When the bride and groom stood before the minister, Cooper whispered, "We could do this, you know."

With a heavy sigh that was filled with disappointment, she said, "I wish."

"It would be a game changer."

"I know," she said softly.

Before anything more could be said, the vows began. It was the simple, straightforward pledge—for better or worse, richer or poorer, sickness or health, forever and ever. A very short, balding minister who wore glasses and a robe stood before them at the front of the pretty little chapel; his voice was soft and caressing, but Mac's voice was strong and firm, Gina's voice was tinged with emotional tears. Sarah cried and smiled at the same time, and in seven minutes the vows were pledged, the kissing done, the certificate of marriage signed by everyone and a half-dozen pictures were taken by the minister's oldest son. Cooper and Sarah took photos on their cell phones, then immediately texted them to Lou and Carrie. Ten minutes later they were entering a nice waterfront restaurant where Mac had reserved a table with a view.

Before even sitting down Cooper excused himself for a moment. He saw the maître d' and ordered a bottle of champagne. He hadn't been seated long when it arrived to the surprise of the new husband and wife. When the cork had been popped and the flutes filled, he lifted his glass and said, "Here's to a wedding in which the kiss lasted longer than the vows!"

Mac leaned against Gina and said, "Hear, hear!"

Gina said, "And look at us—at a restaurant that's not Cliffhanger's."

"And if Mac doesn't mind, I'll order for myself tonight," Cooper said. "He's pretty fond of telling people what to eat."

"This is the pot speaking of the kettle," Sarah pointed out.

"So where are Mr. and Mrs. McCain knocking boots tonight?" Cooper asked, getting an elbow in the ribs from Sarah.

"Joe has a lake cabin," Mac told them. "There are plenty of really nice hotels around here, even some bridal suites, but the cabin is just perfect—we've been there before. It's isolated, comfortable, there's a boat to take out on the lake. Gina packed a cooler with some of Carrie's best dishes and sandwiches premade, plus some breakfast groceries. I made the beverage run and confirmed that the cell phones don't work up there. There's a landline for emergencies, but we'll be alone, which is the main thing. It's an hour away, but well worth the drive. We promised to be back by six Sunday night. We'll stop by Carrie's for dinner with Ash and Carrie, then on to my house—Gina's new home."

"We hope," Gina said. "A lot of people are facing

change with this marriage—the kids, my mom, Mac's aunt. They all say they want this, but we're hoping the adjustments won't be too confusing or disruptive."

"Gina will have the biggest adjustment to make," Mac said. "Her house has been like a convent—not a lot of noise or traffic. My house is the bigger house, but it's filled with kids and dogs and… Well, there's Aunt Lou, who is very protective of what little space she gets. She's threatening to get her own place, or move in with Joe, who is staying there with her this weekend. Whatever she does, she won't be far away. My kids are her kids. She's raised Ryan and Dee Dee since before they were potty-trained."

"As far as I'm concerned, my mom and Aunt Lou have made all things possible," Gina said. "I don't know how either of us would have raised our kids without them. You, Sarah, doing it on your own as you have… my hat's off to you."

Cooper put an arm around her, giving her a squeeze. "She doesn't give herself enough credit. She's amazing."

Cooper noticed that she looked down, nodded and murmured something about Landon being a wonderful kid. In spite of the happy occasion there seemed to be a sadness about Sarah and he began to imagine she was hiding even more dire problems Maybe she was sick. Terminal! There was something terrible going on to cause her to withdraw like this.

After dinner, Cooper and Sarah walked the happy couple to Mac's truck, bid them farewell and wished them a great weekend. After they had gone all Sarah said was, "It was so lovely. So lovely."

"Let's go for a little walk," Cooper said, his arm

around her shoulders. "Just around this block to the waterfront. To finish watching the sunset."

"We should get home, Cooper...."

He stopped and turned her toward him. "No, baby. We have to talk about whatever is eating you."

"I should figure out what to do before I dump it on you...."

"Maybe you could use some help with whatever it is."

She took a deep steadying breath. "I've been notified that...I got reassignment orders, Cooper...soon. I haven't had the guts to talk it over with Landon yet. This isn't going to go down well."

Shock widened his eyes. It was the last thing he expected. "I thought you had another year here."

"I should have. That's what I thought when I came here—that's what we had all predicted. But there's a pressing need for someone at my level of command and I'm the most logical person to fill it. And it's for a south Florida Coast Guard station."

"Whoa." He rubbed the back of his neck. "Could they give you a more distant assignment?"

"They don't have Coast Guard stations on the moon yet," she murmured.

"Well," Cooper said, thinking for a moment. "You're right, this is going to go down hard. I was moved right before my senior year and I'm still pissed about it. And I didn't have a shining football career ahead of me. I was just an ordinary high school kid."

"This will devastate Landon," she agreed.

"Is it at least a decent job? In Florida?"

"Depends on your definition of decent. It's a good position and I'm in line for a promotion. It will mean less flying and more administrative time. But I'm good at both, so..."

He thought maybe they should continue walking... and thinking. But for some reason his feet were rooted to the ground. "Maybe it would help if...I could get him down there early, like right away. We could look around, make sure he gets into a good school with a good football team and give him a chance to adjust before school starts. By the time you get there, maybe he'll be human about it...."

Her eyes were round and her mouth actually hung open. She shook her head as if to roll the marbles back into place. "You would do that?"

"Of course I could. Or I could take care of him here. He only has one more year. But it would be so damn far for you to travel to see him. That would be really hard on both of you. I mean, you're a team, you and Landon. But there's another fact you have to face—in one more year he could choose a college on the other side of the country. He's going to leave your care eventually. But if things stay as they are now, I think he'd probably opt for the left coast...."

"Live with you...here?"

He grabbed her arms and looked into her eyes. "Okay, maybe you don't want me to be a part of this. But if that's what it is, you have to tell me, Sarah. I've been bent out of shape worrying that you want to dump me. We've been together nine months. You know I love you—you know I want to spend my life with you. If you don't want that, you have to tell me."

"But you have a business here! A son!"

"I haven't lived with my son for the last ten years. He wouldn't be devastated if I only visited. In fact, there's no guarantee Spencer and Austin will stay in Thunder Point—that all depends on if this job works out to be a good thing for them both. You and Landon, that's a different situation. It's just the two of you and you're real tight."

"And the bar? The beach?"

"Ah...I love the beach and the bar is working out, but I'm not more tied to that than to you, for God's sake. I could sell it. I could even sell it responsibly, so it doesn't hurt the town. Or I could rent it so there's something to come back to. You do understand that if I had to make a choice..."

"You'd be giving up everything you love!"

He just smiled at her and shook his head. "Not everything I love."

"What if I quit?" she said. "What if I didn't take the assignment and just resigned my commission and didn't have an income? What if I turned out to be just a part-time barmaid who couldn't pay her own rent just so Landon could finish school here?"

He laughed. "Don't tease me," he said. "Sarah, don't you know by now? There's no deal breaker here. I'll take any part of you—career Coast Guard pilot or simply my wife. And I'm not asking you to give up anything you love or have worked hard for." He grinned. "I know how controlling you are. And I also think you love me. You love us together. If you don't, you have a good fake going on."

"Cooper..." she whispered, her eyes misting.

"Hey! How long have you been carrying this around? This worry and burden?"

She shrugged helplessly. "I got wind of it a couple

of months ago, when it was just rumor, when there was still hope that—"

"A couple of *months?* Aw, baby! We could've talked it out a long time ago! This has been eating you up! Sarah, honey, you don't have to manage everything alone anymore. You can count on me, don't you know that?"

He looked around uncomfortably. They stood on a sidewalk under a restaurant's neon sign. The surf was audible, but so was passing traffic. He grunted, reaching into his shirt pocket. "This isn't what I planned. Man. I'm no great romantic, but I thought I could do better than this. And I don't know if it will help your decision or just make it harder, but..." He produced a ring. Not a box, just a ring. But he thought it a damned beautiful ring. "I've been carrying this around for a while now, but you were so bitchy. Sorry to say that, but really..." He held it out, in his palm. "Please don't make me get down on my knees," he said. "The ground is wet."

A laugh sputtered out of her through her tears. "You're not kneeling?"

"On a wet, cracked sidewalk, in the mist, on a busy street? Only if it's the difference between yes and no. I'll kneel for you later.... Sarah, I want to marry you. I want to bind you up and take you off the market. I want you to trust me with your problems. I want to be your other half. I want us to share the same life, whatever that means. The only caveat is that I will always visit Austin, wherever he lives. But you? You, I want to be with every day. And I will never ask you to give up anything for me—just say you'll be my wife." He picked up the ring and slid it onto her finger so she could look at it.

"Is it real?" she asked.

"Of course it's real! It's not a custom design or anything, so you can exchange it for something you like better. It's damn hard to pick a ring for a woman who never wears jewelry and who goes to work in combat boots, so I can be flexible here. But you have to say yes first."

She looked up at him. "I'm scared," she whispered.

"I know you are," he said softly. "Plus, you hold a grudge. It takes a lot to piss you off, but man, when you get there... Look, I know you're scared, but I'm not. For the first time in my life, I'm not nervous about commitment like this. And eventually you're going to stop being scared because there's not one thing about us that's suspicious or scary or risky. Everything works with us. We're solid. And you know it. You should take a chance on us. We can be happy, I know we can."

She blinked and a tear escaped. "Then...yes," she said in a whisper.

He lifted her chin with a finger and kissed her, at first lightly, then with hunger. His arms went around her waist while hers went around his back, molding her to him. Their mouths fit perfectly, searching and caressing and devouring, the taste of her tears on his lips.

A horn honked and someone yelled, *"Get a room!"*

They broke apart on a laugh. "Let's get a room," he suggested.

"Let's go home," she said.

He kissed her again. "Home," he repeated. "Sounds good to me."

It was hard for Gina to say goodbye to an idyllic weekend at Joe's little cabin on the lake, but Mac said,

"He promises that any time we can get away and it's not in use, it's ours."

They headed home, as man and wife, all ready for a new adventure in Thunder Point. They would have dinner with Carrie and Ashley, at which time Gina would pack up what was left of her toiletries and a few other personal items and bring them over to Mac's place. School might be out for the summer, but Gina and Mac both had to get back to work on Monday morning.

As they pulled onto Main Street sawhorses had been set up with detour signs hanging from them. "What's this?" Mac said. "I wasn't told about this. I wonder if there's trouble in town."

"Why would they close the street through town?"

He put the truck in Park. "I couldn't tell you. Broken water main? Fire? Maybe they're moving a wide load through town? Let's go have a look, Mrs. McCain."

They walked the rest of the way into town and as they got closer they spotted the Sheriff's Department SUV, lights flashing, blocking the street in front of the diner. There were people everywhere, milling around the closed off street.

"Oh, Mac, this doesn't look good...."

They took a dozen more steps when someone yelled, "It's them! They're here!" And a surge of people moved toward the police vehicle. Behind the crowd a banner was raised between the diner and Carrie's Deli that said, *Congratulations Gina and Mac!* Suddenly they were being embraced into hugs, slapped on the back by laughing, smiling, happy friends and neighbors. Since neither of them could move, they were pulled into the center of town. There were long tables full of food, wide grills steaming, a Sno-Kone machine, an ice cream truck. Wayland had a bar set up outside his bar and Cliff, wearing an apron, waved from behind one of the grills. And music floated toward them—"Here Comes the Bride" rang out on electric piano and guitar. There was a band set up on a platform at the end of the street! And right in front of Carrie's deli, on a special table, was a very large wedding cake. Large enough for a town.

Ashley pushed through the people. She was grinning. "Told you we could throw a wedding together in a week or two."

Gina looked up at Mac and the only thing she could think of to say was, "I'm wearing jeans."

He grinned at her and said, "I like you in jeans." And then to the pleasure of a cheering crowd, he grabbed his wife and kissed her senseless.

Not far away, another car was parked outside the roadblock. It was a ten-year-old Pathfinder with a lot of miles on it. Cee Jay was driving, Maddy was in the passenger seat and their luggage was piled in the back. Cee Jay got out of the car and looked down the road into the town. The banner had been raised, the music played and it appeared there was dancing in the street as the sun made a lazy decline over the rocky Pacific coast. Kids and dogs ran amok, laughter rang out, a couple of fireworks shot into the sky.

A wedding party, Cee Jay thought. An entire town celebrating its favorite couple.

"Wanna go congratulate the happy couple?" Maddy asked with a laugh. "Throw them off balance just a little bit?"

Cee Jay shook her head. No one could see her, but if

they could they would see a very melancholy, remorseful look come into her eyes. "No. I've played my last card here." Then she took a deep breath, shook herself of the sentimental musing and smiled over the top of the car at her girlfriend. "So. What sounds good? Miami? Atlantic City?"

Maddy got back in the car. "You're driving. Just get me outta here. I've had enough of these hicks."

Cee Jay looked for another moment at the hundreds of people, all with what appeared to be happy, untroubled, connected lives. "Yeah," she said softly. "Yeah."

* * * * *

Acknowledgment

I am deeply grateful to Sgt. Joshua Helterbran for the use of his poem "Final Inspection" in this novel.